A dynasty in cri

THE ASHTONS: JILLIAN, ELI & CHARLOTTE

Three of your favourite authors bring you
three sexy and seductive romances following
the scandalous Ashton family

We're proud to present

MILLS & BOON
SPOTLIGHT™

*A chance to buy collections of bestselling
novels by favourite authors every month –
they're back by popular demand!*

April 2010

The Ashtons: Jillian, Eli & Charlotte

Featuring

Just a Taste by Bronwyn Jameson
Awaken the Senses by Nalini Singh
Estate Affair by Sara Orwig

Maitland Maternity:
Triplets, Quads & Quints

Featuring

Triplet Secret Babies by Judy Christenberry
Quadruplets on the Doorstep
by Tina Leonard
Great Expectations by Kasey Michaels
Delivered with a Kiss by Mindy Neff
And Babies Make Seven
by Mary Anne Wilson

THE ASHTONS:
JILLIAN, ELI &
CHARLOTTE

BRONWYN JAMESON

NALINI SINGH

SARA ORWIG

⊙™ MILLS & BOON®

All the characters in this book have no existence outside the imagination of the author, and have no relation whatsoever to anyone bearing the same name or names. They are not even distantly inspired by any individual known or unknown to the author, and all the incidents are pure invention.

THE ASHTONS: JILLIAN, ELI & CHARLOTTE
© Harlequin Books S.A. 2010

First published in Great Britain 2010
Harlequin Mills & Boon Limited,
Eton House, 18-24 Paradise Road, Richmond, Surrey TW9 1SR

The publisher acknowledges the copyright holders of the individual works, which have already been published in the UK in single, separate volumes, as follows:

Just a Taste © Harlequin Books S.A. 2005
Awaken the Senses © Harlequin Books S.A. 2005
Estate Affair © Harlequin Books S.A. 2005

Special thanks and acknowledgement are given to Bronwyn Jameson, Nalini Singh and Sara Orwig for their contributions to the
DYNASTIES: THE ASHTONS series.

ISBN: 978 0 263 88034 2

64-0410

Printed and bound in Spain
by Litografia Rosés S.A., Barcelona

JUST A TASTE

BY
BRONWYN JAMESON

THE ASHTONS

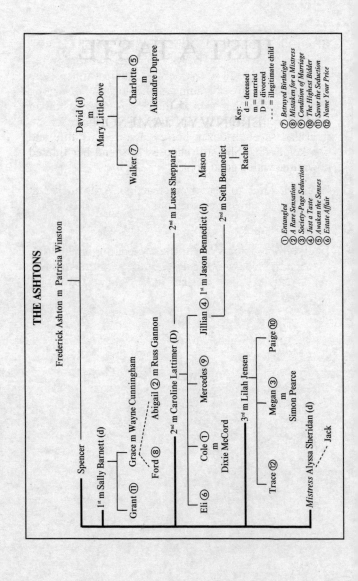

Frederick Ashton m Patricia Winston

Spencer

David (d)
m
Mary LittleDove

Walker ⑦

Charlotte ⑤
m
Alexandre Dupree

1st m Sally Barnett (d)

Grace m Wayne Cunningham

Abigail ② m Russ Gannon

2nd m Caroline Lattimer (D)

2nd m Lucas Sheppard

Mason

Jillian ④ 1st m Jason Bennedict (d)

2nd m Seth Bennedict

Rachel

Grant ⑪

Ford ⑧

Mercedes ⑨

Cole ①
m
Dixie McCord

Eli ⑥

3rd m Lilah Jensen

Paige ⑩

Megan ③
m
Simon Pearce

Trace ⑫

Mistress Alyssa Sheridan (d)

Jack

Key:
d = deceased
m = married
D = divorced
- - - = illegitimate child

① Entangled
② A Rare Sensation
③ Society-Page Seduction
④ Just a Taste
⑤ Awaken the Senses
⑥ Estate Affair
⑦ Betrayed Birthright
⑧ Mistaken for a Mistress
⑨ Condition of Marriage
⑩ The Highest Bidder
⑪ Savor the Seduction
⑫ Name Your Price

Bronwyn Jameson spent much of her childhood with her head buried in a book. As a teenager, she discovered romance novels and it was only a matter of time before she turned her love of reading them into a love of writing them. Bronwyn shares an idyllic piece of the Australian farming heartland with her husband and three sons, a thousand sheep, a dozen horses, assorted wildlife and one kelpie dog. She still chooses to spend her limited downtime with a good book.

Bronwyn loves to hear from readers. Write to her at bronwyn@bronwynjameson.com.

To that pair of fabulous Desire™ authors
Kathie DeNosky and Kristi Gold – thanks for the
inspiration, the guidance and the laughs.
Love your work, girlfriends!

Prologue

As the first strident notes of the bridal march screeched through the Vegas chapel, Spencer Ashton didn't bother hiding his wince. He closed his eyes to shut out the faux-marble columns and the ceiling painted—poorly—as a cloud-scattered sky.

Unfortunately, losing the faculty of sight only intensified his other senses. The recorded music sounded even tinnier. The sweet sickliness of massed flowers and candles clogged his lungs.

He didn't deserve this. He'd earned his cathedral and pipe organ and choir. He wanted to turn and see the pews overflowing with business and society luminaries, to feel their handshakes and back-slapping congratulations as they welcomed him into their elite kinship of power and privilege. And more than any of that, he deserved to see his bride walking down the aisle on her father's arm.

Oh, how he would have relished the moment when John

Lattimer handed over his only child and answered the question of "Who gives this woman?"

That was the only "I do" that mattered to Spencer. The two little words that meant his boss and mentor for the past five years was handing him the final key, not just to his investment-banking megalith, but to the entire Lattimer wealth.

Self-satisfaction hurtled through Spencer's blood, turning his earlier wince around. At his side, Caroline completely misinterpreted that smile. Her biting grip on his elbow fluttered into a soothing caress as she leaned close and whispered, "I know. I feel the same way."

Spencer doubted it, but why not indulge her?

He wasn't getting the ceremony he deserved but he was getting the result. He squeezed her trembling hand and smiled right into her eyes. "You make a beautiful bride, Caroline."

Easy words, when he stood to gain so much. As easy as the romantic words he'd chosen to sweep her off her feet. As easy as the avowal of everlasting love that preceded his let's-get-married-right-away, I-can't-wait-darling proposal.

No, he hadn't wanted this quickie wedding, but he couldn't risk the publicity or the complications of a high-profile wedding preceded by an engagement party and all manner of but-you-must-have-family-to-invite occasions.

He had no family that he cared to acknowledge, but today he would join one of California's finest. Soon he would sit at his father-in-law's right hand in the boardroom of the Lattimer Corporation. In time, it would be the Ashton-Lattimer Corporation.

Oh, yes, that had a near-orgasmic ring to it, as rich and glorious as the cathedral bells that tolled in Spencer's imagination, in the wedding he wasn't having. The rich and glorious sound of his future. All he had to do was pretend he adored the mousy blonde who was about to become his wife.

The minister swept into the chapel, apologetic for his tardiness and obviously pressed for time since he launched into the ceremony without preliminaries. Spencer half listened. His eyes drifted down to the Lattimer pearls at Caroline's throat.

She might not match him in looks or ambition or character, but John Lattimer's daughter was his ideal wife in other ways: demure and agreeable, quiet and giving, rich and ready to inherit.

He smiled and gazed into her moist and tremulous eyes as he repeated the same meaningless vows as last time. In his mind he added an extra vow. He promised to spend enough time in Caroline's bed to breed the babies she wanted, children to keep her occupied and out of his hair, grandchildren to link the Ashton and Lattimer names and bind him more securely to all that would be his.

As the minister said the final words that joined them together as man and wife, euphoria rose again from Spencer's gut, stronger this time, almost choking him with its intensity.

Spencer Ashton had traveled a long way from the farmstench of Crawley, Nebraska, and finally he had arrived. He hadn't gambled and gotten lucky. He'd succeeded because he was smart enough and shrewd enough and focused enough to turn ambition into reality.

Everything he had ever wanted, everything he deserved, everything that mattered would soon be his.

Everything.

One

Napa Valley, California. Thirty-eight years later.

In naive, lust-crazed, love-addled ignorance, Jillian Ashton wagered everything that mattered when she eloped to Vegas with Jason Bennedict. And when the marriage ended in a fiery late-night car wreck, she lost it all.

Her lying, cheating husband, her home, her savings, her job, and the last tattered shreds of her self-respect.

Poof, all gone.

Two years later Jillian had a home and a job in her family's Napa Valley winery. As for that lost esteem…well, today she stood a chance of regaining a sizeable chunk. More literally she stood—in two-inch businesswoman heels—in the Louret Winery meeting room gaping at her brother. As Louret's business manager, Cole controlled the purse strings. He did not, by virtue of his job and his personality, ever make things easy.

And yet…

"Everything?" Jillian asked on a rising note of suspicion. April Fool's Day wasn't until Friday, surely. She waved a hand at the flip chart by her side. "You're agreeing to *all* these changes?"

"Don't get ahead of yourself, Jellie. I'm saying your idea has merit. Get some quotes."

"But you haven't seen the rest of my—"

"Pretty pictures?" Cole rocked back in his chair, looking more amused than impressed by the presentation she'd slaved over. "Save the rest for next Monday's meeting. I've a ten o'clock appointment to get to."

Jillian sucked in a breath and released it slowly. Sure, his casual use of her childhood nickname and the pretty-pictures dig rankled, but she should be used to her brother's—to both her brothers'—patronizing indulgence.

As the youngest of four siblings, she'd endured such head-patting all her life.

In retrospect the flip-chart presentation *had* probably been a tad over the top for a family business meeting—especially since Cole and his dog were the only family members to show for said meeting—but she'd wanted to knock his socks off. For months she'd worked on her proposal to expand and remodel the winery's tasting room.

This was important.

She needed the challenge, creatively and professionally and personally. She needed to prove herself to her family and, most importantly, to herself.

"What's your time line on this project, Jellie?"

Jillian—aka Jillie, aka Jellie, aka Jellie-Belly—felt her shoulders tighten reflexively. Oh, yes, she definitely needed to prove herself more than the little sister. She might have failed at her marriage but she was a graduate in viticulture and enology. For the past eighteen months she'd successfully managed Louret's tasting room.

And she was past thirty, for heaven's sake!

Biting back her annoyance, she carefully packed away the last of her presentation materials before responding to Cole's question. "Ten to fourteen days, depending on the selected contractor's schedule."

"You have a list of contractors?"

Jillian smiled sweetly and tapped her portfolio. "It was on my next pretty page. The one preceding my proposed time line. How many quotes would you like me to get?"

"Your call, as long as Seth Bennedict is one of them." He paused to study her closely. "Will that be a problem?"

Yes. She swallowed a lump of imminent panic and met his eyes. "No."

Cole nodded. "Good. If Seth's your man, I know it'll be done right."

"I'll keep that in mind."

With the portfolio tucked under her arm, she calmly left the meeting room and closed the door at her back. For a brief moment, she indulged the tremor in her limbs by leaning against its solid timber strength.

But only for a brief moment. Irritation skated the edges of her nerves as she stalked to her own office, the smallest of half a dozen built atop the tasting room in Louret's winery building.

If Seth's your man, I know it'll be done right.

So much for her brother's confidence in *her* ability to manage this task. As it happened, she'd done her research. She'd talked to a stack of locals about their dealings with Napa building contractors. And, so okay, her brother was right about whose name kept popping up, but...

"Seth Bennedict is not *my man,*" she muttered as she sank into her chair, inordinately bothered by that wording.

Oh, Seth Bennedict was a man all right. A big, dark, brooding mass of male with a disturbingly intent gaze and an equally disconcerting habit of taking charge.

He was also her brother-in-law and the only living soul who knew the most humiliating details of her disastrous marriage.

Even when she'd not wanted Seth's help—especially when she'd not wanted it—he'd bulldozed over her objections. Sure, he'd untangled the financial mess that was Jason's legacy, which meant he also knew how gullible and witless she had been in allowing their joint affairs to become so knotted.

Jillian's fingers curled into the cushioned arms of her chair. Success with the tasting-room redesign was her chance to drag herself beyond the crippling grip of her past. If that meant working with Seth Bennedict and his indissoluble links to those dark years, then so be it.

It wouldn't be any fun, but she would deal with it.

And she would start dealing today. Right now. Before she chickened out.

She grabbed her purse and car keys from her desk drawer, then shook her head ruefully. The way her life had panned out, she wouldn't recognize fun anyway, even if it came tap-dancing across her desk wearing a Team Fun sweatshirt.

Seth Bennedict recognized fun. A bosom buddy of hard physical labor and on-the-job satisfaction, it screamed through his muscles with each swing of the ten-pound hammer then settled damp with sweat on his skin.

Man, he didn't get to do this often enough.

The downside of success as a building contractor was too much business and planning and consulting, not nearly enough hands-on. He couldn't think of a more gratifying

way to spend his thirty-eighth birthday than pounding
down walls.

Well, okay, so he *could* think of one.

He'd woken that morning thinking about it, with the
remnant shreds of a broken dream hard in his body and hot
in his mind.

But then his phone had rung—Lou, foreman on this job,
calling in sick—and before he could replace the receiver
his daughter had propelled herself onto his bed, bouncing
and gabbing with it's-your-birthday-Daddy excitement.

His phone rang again. Then his housekeeper Rosa appeared, looking for Rachel and breakfast orders. And that
was reality.

A thriving business, a phone that never quit, and a three-
year-old daughter who owned him heart and soul. No time
to indulge his body in anything more than a stray early-
morning fantasy—forget the real deal!—which left the
only other physical release he was getting any time soon.

Seth squinted through the dust of demolition, fixed his
gaze on the target wall and lifted his hammer.

"Boss."

He turned to find one of his younger laborers standing
in what remained of the doorway.

"You have a…uh…visitor." Tony thumbed over his
shoulder and shuffled his feet in a way that invoked ghosts
of birthdays past.

Seth released his breath on a sigh. He was too old for
this—for whatever *this* turned out to be. Reluctantly, he
downed tools, removed his dust mask and goggles, and
schooled his expression to take in good humor whatever
strip-o-gram surprise came sashaying through the door.

Please, just let her keep her hands off of me.

But when he looked up, genuine surprise wiped all expression from his face and a good amount of cognitive

function from his brain. Possibly because every early-morning fantasy of the last year exploded through his blood.

He did notice that Jillian Ashton-Bennedict was overdressed…for both his fantasies and for the reality of a building site. She wore a dress the color of sandstone, a slender column of material that ended just shy of her knees. She wasn't sashaying. Instead she picked her graceful way through the rubble, all long legs and high heels and cool female elegance.

No one did cool elegance like Jillian Ashton-Bennedict.

And nothing turned Seth on quicker or hotter than her particular brand of femininity.

With one hand she smoothed her hair—shorter than last time he'd seen her, curling around the elegant length of her throat in soft ash-brown layers—and he caught the glint of gold on her ring finger. Then she looked up and her eyes met his across the pile of century-old bricks and timber that separated them.

Debris of the past. How appropriate.

It never changed, this first stilted moment born of their shared history. The hurt to her pride because he'd witnessed her lowest point. His forced restraint, hiding the fact that she turned him on just by walking into a room.

And underlying both, the knowledge of what bound them together—the accident that had killed both their spouses.

"Stay there," he said, more sharply than he intended or wanted. Damn. And she *still* wore his dead brother's wedding band. "Tony shouldn't have let you in here without a hard hat."

"I told him I wouldn't be long."

"Which doesn't change a blessed thing. He knows the rules."

"Don't blame Tony," she said quickly. "I sort of lied."

Seth peeled off his gloves as he started toward her. After five years with Jason, he knew how highly she valued honesty. Knew her bending of the truth would barely register on any fib-o-meter. He stopped in front of her. Waited for her explanation.

"I said you were expecting me."

Which, while no whopper, did qualify as extremely untrue. He hadn't seen her since a few days before Christmas, and on that occasion only by chance. She'd brought a present for Rachel and hadn't expected to find him home.

Seth stopped in front of her. "I haven't seen you in over three months. I was starting to think you were avoiding me."

"No." She shook her head in denial, but her eyes didn't quite meet his.

"I'm surprised Tony believed you. Since you're such a lousy liar."

"Oh."

Oh, indeed.

The whisper of a sigh escaped her lips. "You're right, I am, and I suspect Tony thought the same. He said he was only letting me in here because it's your birthday."

"Did he think you might have brought me some sort of birthday surprise?"

She met his gaze then, a momentary connection before she blinked and looked away. Seth didn't blame her, since he imagined his eyes burned with all kinds of erotic birthday surprises.

Most of them included her. Naked and gift-wrapped.

"Sorry." And, dammit, she really did look sorry. "I should have remembered."

Seth tried but he couldn't stop himself asking, "And if you had?"

"I'd have at least brought you a card. Or maybe even a cake."

"With candles?"

"Wouldn't that constitute a fire hazard?"

Only to Seth's imagination.

Somewhere during their birthday-cake banter, he'd started to picture Jillian wearing nothing but teeny tassels and those sexy high heels, bursting from the top of a tacky surprise cake. The kind his buddy Lou might have arranged had he not been out sick. The kind he had no right placing in the same fantasy as Jillian, the sister-in-law he had no right lusting after. But since he'd done so from the first moment he laid eyes on her, and since she'd never shown any sign of being anything other than uncomfortable in his company, he figured he'd keep right on lusting from afar.

Part of the ongoing penance for coveting his brother's wife.

She looked uncomfortable now, no doubt because he couldn't help staring—yeah, and lusting—and because the silence between them had stretched into the realms of long and awkward.

"I called in at your office," she said, bridging that conversational gap while casually widening the gap between them. "Mel told me you were working out here. She didn't say you were destroying Villa Firenze."

To indicate the scene of carnage, she did this little gesture thing with her hands. They were elegant and eloquent, Jillian's hands, and one of the many, many things he'd noticed that first time he met her as Jason's new bride.

One of the many, many things that turned him on.

"The Maldinis are converting the ground floor into a restaurant."

"Ahh." Pivoting on her high heels, she took in the whole scene through thoughtfully narrowed eyes, as if picturing the completed renovation. "It looks like a big job."

"A satisfying one."

And not only because he'd lucked out and gotten the chance to wield tools today. He followed her gaze around the Italian-style villa, solid and structurally sound, yet with the soul of its century-long history alive in the cellars and gardens and kitchens.

"I hope they'll go with Tuscan food," she said.

"They will."

Jillian nodded, satisfied with his assurance. Seth Bennedict had that way about him. He said; you believed. And she grabbed at the perfect segue into her reason for being here. "That's what I want to talk to you about, Seth."

One thick dark brow lifted in surprise. "You're starting a restaurant?"

"No. Oh, no." She loved good food, which meant someone else needed to cook it. "But I am extending and remodeling our tasting room. I'd like you to quote."

There, that hadn't been so difficult. Not once she'd gotten past the unsettling sight of Seth looking so rough and, well, uncivilized. Although she wished she'd known about his birthday. A card, a cake, a gift of wine would not have been inappropriate.

Staring at the tiny snagged tear in his T-shirt, at the teeny sliver of dark skin and darker chest hair…now that *was* inappropriate.

"Is this not a good time?" she said, looking away. Rattled because she'd been staring, and just a bit giddy with a sense of airless heat. "To talk about this?"

"You're here now. We can talk, but let's take it outside."

He wore a hard hat. He'd already mentioned the fact that she didn't. "I guess I'm breaking all kinds of safety regulations."

"Yeah." He met her eyes, his as dark and intense and disquieting as always. "You are."

* * *

"So. How extensive is this job of yours?"

This question she could answer, now that Seth had removed himself from her breathing space. With an extremely disconcerting hand at her back—not quite touching, but hovering thereabouts—he'd shepherded her away from the curious sidelong glances of Tony and his co-workers and into a stand of olive trees beside the villa.

Leaning against the gnarled trunk of one old tree, arms crossed over his chest, he looked relaxed and receptive.

Reassured, Jillian waved a hand toward the villa. "Not very extensive compared with your present job. A lot of the work is remodeling and refitting, but there is a storage room that has to go so I can expand the tasting room space."

"Business is good, then?"

"Busier than ever. Easter weekend was complete madness and we're anticipating even more traffic over the summer, since we're doing a national marketing push."

His brows rose a little. "I thought boutique wineries like yours were all about word of mouth and competition medals."

"Yes, but we're releasing our first chardonnay. Plus with the economy tight the gap between premium wines like ours and the average bottle is narrowing."

"You're losing market share?"

With Cole at the helm? Oh, no, her brother would so not allow any market to get away from him! "Our sales are still growing, but we're not resting on our laurels."

"What's your schedule for the renovation?"

"I really need this to be quick and hassle-free. I don't want to close tastings, so I'll be setting up a temporary area in the cellar." Which Eli was going to hate. "As for starting time—" She drew a breath and looked right at him. "That will depend on you."

He stared back at her for a long minute, those dark eyes even harder to read than usual in the mottled pattern of light and shade. "I haven't said I'll do it, Jillian."

"Are you saying you won't?"

"Not won't. Can't. Not if you want it done in the next month or two."

Jillian's stomach plummeted. "You're that busy?"

"Signed contracts on two new jobs last week, and that's on top of a heavy schedule."

All the emotional energy she'd spent worrying over coming to see him and asking for his help, and he couldn't do it? Why hadn't she considered this outcome? Why hadn't she realized that his reputation would always keep him booked way ahead of time?

Well…blast!

Except right on the heels of that initial sense of anticlimax, came a subtle easing of tension in her shoulders and limbs. It felt almost like relief. She had identified Seth as number one on her best-builder list; she'd driven over here and done the asking; he'd said no.

Now she could carry on as before, not exactly avoiding him but not needing to seek him out. She wouldn't have to deal with his macho intensity or her reaction to it. Truth be told, the man scared her, unsettled her, made her too aware of herself. And she neither liked nor trusted any of those reactions.

With her thumb she touched the back of the wedding band she still wore on her left hand, not to remember, but as a caution against repeating the mistakes of her past.

A caution to proceed slowly and with care, especially when it came to men.

Yet this man—this *builder*—had brought her out here,

encouraged her to talk about her plans. What was that about? "If you weren't interested," she began slowly, frowning, "why didn't you say so before, inside?"

"I didn't say I wasn't interested." Something shifted in his gaze, deep and dark, making her feel as breathlessly off-kilter as when his hand had hovered at her back. "I said I can't fit your time frame."

Semantics. Jillian dismissed the whole conversation with a frustrated little shrug. She didn't have time for this…for this bandying of words or for her body's rogue responses.

Whatever the reason, he wasn't interested in quoting for her tasting room renovation. Discussion closed.

Seth watched her press her lips together and straighten that long, elegant backbone. Gathering her poise and dignity after copping another blow on the chin. He'd seen her go through the same motions many times before, and knew she wouldn't try and change his mind.

And, damn, just once he wished she would beg a favor of him.

Exasperated with himself—for wanting something that would never happen, something so out of character for Jillian—Seth straightened from his slouch against the tree and rubbed a hand against the back of his neck.

"Just a minute." He wasn't going to change his answer, but that didn't mean he couldn't help in a smaller way. "I hear Terry Mancini's finding retirement tough. He might be interested in a job like yours. Or I can call around and see who's—"

"There's no need to do that," she interrupted. "I can manage to find someone else on my own."

Posture straight and her shoulders all stiff with pride, she turned to leave. And wasn't that just like Jillian, going all cool and haughty and knocking back his offer of assistance?

Once she *had* accepted his help, eventually, but not because she had wanted to. She'd had no choice. And oh how she'd resented that lack of choice, his intervention, and the inevitable slam to her dignity when the truth about Jason's affairs unraveled.

Seth felt his own shoulder muscles bunch with tension. "I'm sure you can find any number of builders who'll jump at the work, Jillian. But will they do a good job?"

She had already started to turn, preparing to leave, but she paused to look back across her shoulder. "I don't know, Seth. That's why I came to you first."

"I'm sorry I can't help."

"So am I." She looked right at him then, her gaze clear and direct. "I wanted the best."

Well, damn.

Two

The sun was still sleeping when Jillian rose. She tiptoed from her second-story bedroom and down the winding staircase without missing a step in the near-dark. She'd taken the same path so many times she imagined she could do it blindfolded. This was her family home, where she'd grown up and lived into her twenties, and she'd moved back after Jason's death.

She didn't mind living with her parents. It wasn't as if she had a social life—or, Lord help her, a sex life—to consider. Safe, secure and nonthreatening, her life at The Vines was everything she'd rushed to escape in her early twenties and everything she wanted in her future.

At the foot of the stairs, she swung toward the kitchen… and barreled right into her mother.

The solid impact drove a *whoomph* of breath from Caroline Sheppard's lungs. Surprise startled a squeak from Jillian's. With one hand flattened over her wildly thumping heart, she peered through the wan predawn light into her mother's face.

"Good grief, Mom, you scared a year off my life! What are you doing skulking around at this hour?"

"I might ask the same of you."

"As it happens, I do have a reason." Jillian held the riding boots she carried aloft. "I'm on stable duty this morning and I have to be finished before eight."

"Another builder?"

"Yes." Unfortunately.

The sigh in her answer must have sounded as weary as she felt because her mother's hands came up to gently squeeze her shoulders. "Don't put too much pressure on yourself, Jillie. There's no rush."

"After dealing with the crush over Easter?" She shook her head ruefully. "The remodel needs to be done before summer, Mom, and the sooner the better."

Yesterday seemed about perfect to Jillian.

After a week of calling and chasing and calling again, she had exhausted her A-list of builders. Every morning she woke with nothing more concrete than, "I'll do a quote and get back to you." And today she faced Louret's weekly business meeting with no solid quotes and only one builder of questionable reputation showing any solid interest. Cole might well decide that *he* should be overseeing the job.

"I can do this, Mom," she said, straightening her shoulders. And she would, once she found a builder who wasn't booked solid right through summer. Or who didn't think he knew better than she how her tasting room should look and function.

"I know you can do it, hon." Her mother gave another reassuring squeeze. "So, who is it this morning?"

"Travis Carmody."

Caroline frowned. "I can't say I know him."

"He hasn't been in California long."

"Is he any good?"

"He's available." Which, somehow, had moved way up Jillian's priority list. She bit her bottom lip, worried all over again. "Or at least he says he is."

"You don't trust his word? Isn't that telling you something?"

"That I have deep-seated trust issues?"

Caroline smiled at her wry attempt at humor, but it was a small smile tempered with maternal concern. "Or perhaps he's not the right man to hire. Have you tried Seth Bennedict?"

"He gave me a straight 'can't do it.'"

Her mother's finely shaped brows arched expressively. "Well, I am surprised that Seth wouldn't help you out."

"I didn't want him to help me out, Mom. I wanted him to quote the same as anyone else. A business deal. No special favors."

She met Caroline's eyes, and the circumstances of her previous dealings with Seth Bennedict arced between them. They had never discussed the nitty-gritty of Jillian's marriage, and her mother, God bless her, had never asked for explanations. She'd simply offered her love, the sanctuary of her childhood home and a shoulder to cry on.

Yet Caroline had been in a similar place herself after the crushing demise of her marriage to Spencer Ashton. Jillian saw that empathy in her mother's eyes now, and her throat tightened with emotion.

She flung her arms, boots and all, around her neck and held on tight.

"What's this for?" Caroline managed to gasp around that constrictive hug.

"Just because." Jillian's smile wavered and her vision misted for a second before she blinked the gathering moisture away. "And I haven't had enough sleep to do emotion real well at the moment."

"Oh, honey." Her mother gathered her into an even tighter hug, then saved the moment and both their tears by suddenly pulling clear. "You know what you need?"

Jillian shook her head, her emotional state too rocky to chance words.

"A good bracing gallop to clear your head."

Oh, yes. That sounded perfect. She and Marsanne both needed a rousing blowout.

Instantly enthused, she dropped down on the bottom step and pulled on her boots. Then was struck by an even better idea. "Why don't you come too, Mom? We haven't been out riding together in ages."

They'd galloped, a little more sedately than Jillian's long-legged thoroughbred would have liked, but she'd held Marsanne back in deference to her mother's elderly mount.

Now, with that initial burst of energy spent, both horses were content to walk on a loose rein. Their elevated breathing puffed clouds of steam into the air, adding warmth to the cool ribbons of mist that wisped off the lake.

A perfect spring morning, Jillian decided, breathing the commingled scents of warm horse and fresh growth and the crisp chill of the dawn air. Perfect both from her own perspective and that of the vines that stretched in flawlessly drilled lines to their left and right.

The frost alarms had remained silent last night. Good news for the sensitive new growth that grew apace with the warmer, lengthening days. Good news too for the vineyard staff, including Jillian, who bounded out of bed to turn on overhead sprinklers at the first shrill of those temperature-triggered alarms.

"That smile looks good on you," her mother commented.

"Well, it feels good, too." Jillian's smile turned into a laugh of pure and simple pleasure. "Thank you for suggesting this, Mom. You always have the best ideas."

Something changed in her mother's expression, the tiniest hint that she didn't agree. Jillian felt it as much as she saw it, and her ebullient mood faltered. Caught up in her own troubles, she hadn't considered her mother's state of mind. And an awful lot had happened in the last months—the last week, even—to trouble Caroline's mind.

"You haven't told me," Jillian commenced in a casual, reflective tone that matched their ambling progress through the vineyards, "why you were wandering around the house at the crack of dawn."

"I woke early." Her mother smiled, but the effort didn't quite reach her eyes. "Lord knows I love the man, but Lucas snores loud enough to rattle bottles in the cellar."

"You're stewing over this Spencer ruckus, aren't you?"

"This Spencer ruckus" had blown up in January, when they'd discovered a whole unknown chapter in Spencer Ashton's past. Another family in Nebraska. An earlier wedding that made his vows to Caroline bigamous.

It hadn't only blown up within their family circle, either. Every sordid note had played, loud and embellished, through both the tabloid and mainstream media. Ashton-Lattimer shares had hit an all time low after the latest revelation: an illegitimate child born from an affair with his former secretary.

Was that particular association disturbing her mother's sleep?

"I hope you're not worried about us, Mom. About us thinking we're illegitimate or something." To reinforce the concern she felt tight in her chest, Jillian leaned across and rested a hand atop her mother's. Just for a second. "I mean, it doesn't matter whether you were married to Spencer or not as far as I'm concerned. We all think of Lucas as our father."

"I know, honey. But I can't help wishing he were your father in the eyes of the law. I wish he could have adopted you, that you all could have taken his name." Regret coated Caroline's words, but then she shook her head and clicked her tongue. "Just listen to me, bemoaning what I can't change."

"If wishes were horses…?"

Their gazes connected, mother and daughter, and a whole world of understanding flowed from one to the other and back again. A sharing of present strife and past misgivings, some unspoken but none forgotten.

Then, with uncanny timing, Marsanne snorted and jiggled her head, breaking the gravity of the moment and surprising a bark of laughter from Jillian—perhaps simply to release some of her pent-up tension.

"Was that a laugh?" she asked her horse, leaning forward to stroke the gray silk of her neck. "Or a suggestion that it's past your breakfast time?"

Marsanne didn't answer, although her ears pricked and her stride lengthened as they turned by the lake to head back to the stables.

"I have been thinking a lot," Caroline said, after they'd walked in silence for several minutes. Silent but for the *hwark* of a wood duck they startled from its nest by the water. "And, yes, a lot of it while I should have been sleeping."

Jillian smiled her acknowledgment.

"But not over the legality of my marriage to Spencer. I said my vows before God and I stood by them. In my mind and my heart, it will never be anything but a real marriage since it gave me four of my greatest gifts."

Eli, Cole, Mercedes and Jillian.

They had both reined their horses to a halt, as if tacitly

acknowledging the significance of this conversation. Too important to continue while idling along on horseback.

"I no longer care how it started or why it ended," Caroline continued, her voice as soft as the morning light. "But I am so very glad that it did end. Otherwise I would not have found Lucas. I would not have all this."

And although she waved one hand in a delicately expansive gesture, Jillian knew she referred to more than the rich physical landscape and the boutique winery she had fashioned into one of Napa's finest.

"All this" encompassed the solid strength of love she'd found with Lucas and the happiness she'd forged for herself and her family.

This is what worried her sleep—the threat of further disharmony within her family due to Spencer Ashton. Caroline had lost out badly in the divorce settlement, and finally they'd agreed to seek legal counsel. Since there'd been no marriage, there could be no divorce settlement, right?

"You don't want to pursue legal action, do you?" Jillian asked.

"I'm afraid it will cause more hurt, more bitter words, and for what? What will it achieve? I have everything I want right here." Caroline waved that same hand around, this time with more vigor. "Already this brouhaha has sent Cole and Dixie running off to elope."

Because they hadn't thought it an appropriate time to arrange and celebrate a wedding, with all that was going on. Of course that bothered Caroline. She'd married Spencer quickie-Vegas-style, and Jillian had followed suit.

Not exactly happy precedents.

"Selfish, I know," she said softly, "but I wanted to be there."

Jillian leaned across and took one of her mother's hands in her own. "No, not selfish. A mother's right."

One they all should have recognized earlier, one they'd lost sight of in all the acrimony. Perhaps it wasn't too late to make amends....

"You know what I'm thinking?" she said, a smile brimming as the idea gathered momentum.

"Please, Jillian, if it is anywhere near as wicked as that glint in your eyes, you can stop thinking it right now."

"Wicked? I don't think so." She tipped her head to the side, considering. "Unless we make it a surprise party—and that would serve them right, seeing as they surprised us all by running off to tie the knot."

The smile started in Caroline's eyes, then spread all over her face. Her fingers curled around Jillian's and held on tight.

"A party to celebrate Cole and Dixie's marriage? Oh, yes, Jillie, that is a fine idea!"

They sat a moment, hands still linked, smiling at each other and the possibilities. A family celebration, a reason to laugh and dance and remember what mattered. Oh, yes, it was a very fine idea, even if she did say so herself!

"If Travis comes through—" Jillian mentally crossed both fingers and toes "—if he can do the renovation right away, we could hold it in the tasting room."

"A wedding reception cum launch party," Caroline murmured. "When?"

"Would early May be good?"

"Spring. The season of rebirth." Jillian felt her mother's hand move, felt the touch of her thumb against the wedding band she wore. Never had she commented on that symbol's continued presence, and she didn't now. She simply looked into her daughter's eyes, rubbed her thumb along the gold band again, and said, "It's the perfect time to forget past problems and concentrate on new beginnings, don't you think?"

Jillian felt herself tense. Oh, no, this was not about her, not in any sense.

She started to shake her head, but Caroline blinked and her gaze shifted, as if distracted by something out of Jillian's view. She pulled her hand away and pointed. "That will be your builder, stopping up by the stables."

Now why would he do that? Was he lost, despite her specific directions to meet at the winery?

Jillian frowned as she gathered up her reins and urged Marsanne around.

"He's early. Now that's a change for the—" The rest of the sentence died on her lips as she caught sight of the truck. Her mouth probably hung open for a second. Her pulse definitely jumped.

"Is something the matter?" Caroline asked.

"Absolutely nothing," Jillian answered slowly. Except for the fact that Travis Carmody drove a weather-beaten red truck, and this one was a distinctive shade of blue.

Her hands must have clenched with involuntary tension because beneath her Marsanne started to prance, her muscles bunching as if preparing for flight. Jillian settled deep in the saddle and soothed her in a low voice.

"I think she's keen for a last gallop home," Caroline said. "Why don't you go on ahead?" When Jillian demurred, she shooed her off. "Go on, Jillie. I'll potter back at my own pace. If your builder finds the barn deserted, he might not hang around."

"Sorry, bud, I didn't understand a word of that. I don't speak horse."

Seth didn't feel all that comfortable speaking to a horse either, but this particular horse seemed to expect a reply…although calling the short-legged equine a horse might be stretching things. Whatever, the animal had a real gift of gab. Not your usual horsey neigh or squeal—his pony-mad Rachel had mastered both, along with a credible mane toss—but an eloquent combination of sounds and facial expressions.

A regular modern-day Mr. Ed, only shorter.

Mini Ed's ears pricked up, his attention shifting to the open doors at the end of the barn. Seth heard it then, the thud of hooves striking the ground in a deep rolling rhythm, and his body quickened with expectation.

His companion whinnied and snorted. Seth managed not to, at least out loud.

He strolled over to the doorway in time to see horse and rider loom into sight. He knew Jillian rode, that before marrying Jason she'd competed in three-day events, but he'd never seen her on horseback. And the five minutes he'd spent cooling his heels in the barn hadn't nearly prepared him for the impact.

Sure, he knew those mile-long legs would look spectacular wrapped around pretty much anything, including a huge gray horse. But he'd pictured her straight-backed and ladylike as she approached at a collected pace, not bent over the monster's neck and thundering up the hill at full speed.

Not out of control, he decided, although that didn't stop his whole body tensing for the eight seconds it took her to steady and slow to a walk. Seth let his breath go on a long gust that mixed relief with a strange sense of discovery. This was a Jillian he hadn't seen before, her face flushed with exhilaration, her eyes shimmering as they locked with his.

So, the cool and prissy lady got off on speed. Who would have thought?

"Nice morning for a ride," he said pleasantly.

"Nice?" One corner of her mouth quirked up. "Nice doesn't do this sort of morning justice."

"Point taken," Seth murmured as she reined the horse to a stop.

When she swung her leg over and started to slide down, he moved in to catch her. After all, it was a long way to the ground. And somehow—despite his architect's eye for perspective and measurement—he managed to misjudge the distance. Probably because he was distracted by the curves of her backside, clad in stretchy riding pants that fit like a second skin, coming right for him.

His vision actually glazed over for a second. The next, his hands were on her hips and sliding to her waist as that tight little backside connected with his front side. Quick, accidental, over before the heat burned right through his pants.

Yet the quick hitch of her breath, the instant tension in the lithe body beneath his hands, told him she'd felt something, too.

Yeah, well, she had cause.

Reluctantly he let her go, stepping back enough that she didn't elbow him anywhere delicate when she started doing whatever had to be done with her saddle. It appeared to be quite a bit.

"Need a hand?" he asked after several seconds of watching her tug and fuss with straps.

"I can manage. And I'm actually quite competent at getting off my horse unassisted, too."

He made a note for future reference.

"What are you doing here, Seth?" She glanced over her shoulder, her face prettily flushed. From the ride, Seth reminded himself, not from the impact of that sliding dismount. "I was expecting someone else."

"So I heard."

Her brows pinched together. "You heard that…where?"

"From Eli."

"My brother called you?" she asked on a rising note of disbelief.

"No, I called you this morning to see if you'd found a contractor. Eli answered. He said you were out riding and then he mentioned that Carmody was coming to quote."

He tried, but obviously didn't succeed, in keeping his tone flat and free of condemnation. Her gaze narrowed a fraction as she turned around to face him. "And you don't approve?"

"You said you wanted the best. Carmody doesn't come close."

"The best isn't available. Travis Carmody is." The clear green of her eyes deepened. "Unless that's changed since Monday. Is that why you're here, Seth?"

"I'm here to save you from employing a substandard tradesman. Hell, Jillian, I offered to give recommendations. I would have helped you line up someone dependable."

"No one else is available. Not Terry Mancini or the Maine brothers or O'Hara. I tried them all. Travis is my last alternative." She crossed her arms, sighed and met his eyes. "Exactly how bad is he, Seth?"

"After I got off the phone to Eli, I jumped straight in my truck and drove out here. Before my first cup of coffee. What does that tell you?"

"That bad, huh?"

Her smile was game, but deep in her eyes Seth saw the gathering shadows of disenchantment. He almost caved, almost offered…anything, but then she unfolded her arms and broke eye contact. She studied her hands, and he saw her twist that damn wedding band back and forth.

Rubbing in everything that was wrong about him wanting to offer her anything and everything, this woman who still loved his brother two years after he'd died. Two years after she'd discovered what a lying, cheating bastard he was.

Then she straightened and leveled her eyes right on his. "It's a small job, Seth, but it means a lot to me. Would you reconsider taking a look at my plans?"

"Since I'm here anyway?"

"Yes. Since you're here."

That direct green gaze didn't waver, and she stood tall and still and proud as she waited for his answer. She had asked for his help and he didn't stand a prayer of saying no.

"No promises." Cautioning himself as much as her. "But I'll see what I can work out."

"You'll take a look at my plans? Now?"

"I'm not agreeing to take on the job or even to quote. But I'll take a look and help you work out a solution."

"I understand." She huffed out a rueful-sounding breath. "And I'm not about to look that gift horse in the mouth a second time."

Seth's gaze dipped to *her* mouth, to the relieved smile that itched around its corners, and he couldn't for the life of him think of a suitably light and witty response. Kissing her was out of the question, he supposed, but that was all he could think about doing, just bending forward and tasting the warmth of that smile in the quiet morning air....

"Seth Bennedict?"

Jillian started backward. Seth turned slowly and realized he'd—they'd both—been so engrossed that they hadn't heard Caroline Sheppard's approach. She entered the stable yard on a considerably smaller horse and at a much more sedate pace than her daughter.

And she smiled at Seth with a mixture of surprise and pleasure. "It is you!"

"How are you doing, Mrs. Sheppard?"

"I would be doing much better if you called me Caroline." She started to dismount, waving away Seth's offer to help. "I have all morning to lever myself out of this saddle, and I'd be much happier doing so without an audience, thank you all the same."

Given his recent experience helping with the out-of-saddle procedure, Seth conceded her point. Which prompted him to turn and seek out Jillian.

In the process of dragging the saddle from her monster horse, she met his eyes with a surprising note of humor. "Don't even think about helping me again, Seth. I can handle this myself."

"We know you can," Caroline interceded, her gaze flicking from one to the other with carefully contained curiosity. "But if you two have business to attend to, I'll look after the horses and finish up here."

"That would be great, Mom. Seth's agreed to take a look at my plans after all."

"I'm pleased to hear that. Why don't you join us for breakfast, Seth, once you're done?"

"Thanks for the offer, but I promised I'd be home to take Rachel to day care. I don't have a lot of time."

"Then we'll catch up another day."

"I'd like that." He turned to Jillian. "Ready?"

"Once I get rid of this saddle."

She hurried off into the depths of the barn. So, okay, she didn't want his help toting saddles but he couldn't just stand here and watch, right? Not when watching took in the quick left-right hitch of her backside.

Funny, but he'd always thought those beige riding pants a bit starched and prissy. Not anymore. He followed those fast-moving pants inside—in case there was a door to open. Or something.

Off to his right he heard Mini Ed snicker. Probably at him. Seth Bennedict, unable to say no to the lady, despite his promise to keep a healthy distance and save himself this torture of seeing and wanting and not touching.

He knew he would lament this morning, from his fool-hardy charge out here to save her from the mistake that was Travis Carmody, to his offer to look at her plans and help her find a workable solution. Then he remembered how she'd stood tall and looked into his eyes and all but admitted she needed his help.

And he couldn't for the life of him summon up one scrap of regret.

Three

Three

Two days later, Seth swung his truck into the parking lot beside the Louret Winery building and cast his eyes over the assembled vehicles. Besides the staff cars, he counted one minibus, two rental cars and several out-of-state plates. More than enough, he figured, to keep Jillian busy in the tasting room.

Excellent.

The rushed Monday morning run-through hadn't been nearly enough, not done cold, not with him mindful of getting back for Rachel. He needed to see Jillian at work, to see *how* she worked, before he could be satisfied with her ideas for the remodel. Structurally, the job would be simple enough, but this type of renovation was about more than knocking down a wall or two.

Inside the tasting room he paused while his vision adjusted from strong afternoon sunlight to the muted interior.

Too dark, he decided, despite the number of light fixtures and the one floor-to-ceiling window.

His narrowed gaze swept the room, taking it all in, assessing, seeking…and taking too long to find Jillian. Standing behind one of two tasting bars situated along the side walls, she poured for a group of women who, curiously, all wore red hats. She didn't give any sign of noticing his arrival.

Bad positioning, bad space planning, bad for business.

Jillian's design with one bigger bar running smack down the center improved all of the above. Seth, the architect/builder, needed assurance she'd optimized them. He strolled farther inside, circling around, sensing the instant she saw him.

He waited at the end of the long bar while she excused herself to the tasting group and came to meet him.

"Hello, Seth. I wasn't expecting you." Her smile was warm and welcoming. If his unexpected arrival flustered her, she didn't let it show. "You've caught me in the middle of a tasting."

He tilted his head toward the group at the bar. "Seems like a decent number for midweek."

"Shannon has another half dozen or so looking through the winery so, yes, it is busy enough. It has been since opening, actually."

She did this cute little wince, a token complaint since her face glowed with busy-is-good contentment. Man, he liked that. The hint of warmth he wasn't accustomed to seeing in the cool and restrained lady. The absence of those haunted shadows he was too used to seeing.

And the knowledge that she got off on both galloping her horse *and* her work.

Work. He stopped staring into her eyes and straightened off the bar. "I'm just here to check on a few things. Don't let me interrupt."

"You should have called. I'd have said to come later, after I close at four."

"I wanted to watch you work." Seth met her eyes, saw them cloud with…circumspection?…and decided he hadn't worded that so great. "I need to see how your tasting room operates. I'll just be wandering around. You won't even know I'm here."

She didn't look convinced. "Wandering around, doing what?"

"Some measuring—"

"You don't need to check my measurements," she interrupted with a spark of her trademark pride.

"Yeah, I do. That's my job." To illustrate that that's why he was here—work, his job, nothing personal beyond a favor to his brother's widow—he gestured toward the women in the wine-tasting group. "We'd both better get back to it."

He went to work, starting down at back, taking measurements for the repositioned doorway between the tasting room and the winery, checking out the storage room she wanted gone, then working his way back down the room. Checking against her—detailed and accurate, he conceded—draft plan, making notations, setting up a work schedule in his mind.

And all the while aware of her voice, like the soft, rich melody of background music, as she went about her business. As he worked nearer, the hum of that voice took on the shape of words, then sentences, then the full commentary, and Seth reached three fundamental conclusions.

She knew her wines. She knew her audience. Her job in this tasting room married the two.

Oh, and yeah—if he took on this job, he was a masochist.

Squatting on his haunches to check the cypress flooring—it was making way for slate tiles and although well-worn, it might be salvageable for resale—he felt the passion for her work and for her wines play over him in warm, velvet notes. Not a good position with all that wine-talk flaring through his body.

Shaking his head, he stood. But being a masochist, he decided to observe for a few minutes, out of her line of vision but close enough to listen in as she finished up the current wine and selected another bottle.

She poured a small measure into each glass as one of the red-hatted crew—who were all dressed in various shades of purple—expounded her knowledge of big California reds.

"I think you'll appreciate this cabernet sauvignon," Jillian interjected smoothly when the expert paused to draw breath. "It's our ninety-eight reserve."

"My husband says cabernet is a man's wine," a woman commented. "And we don't have the palate to appreciate it."

"Carol, isn't it?"

The fiftyish-looking woman nodded.

"Well, Carol, your husband might be interested in the Human Genome Project which showed that women, in fact, have finer palates. As a gender—" she paused to smile conspiratorially at the all-female group "—we're better at sensory evaluation."

"No kidding?" Carol grinned back. "I told Jim he was talking horse-spit."

He watched Jillian temper her smile. "The 'man's wine' comment is interesting since cabernet sauvignon is regarded as the king of red grapes. They make into wines that are big and bold and full-bodied. Some might say those are masculine attributes—others might think that's a sexist viewpoint. Or simply horse-spit."

They all laughed, Carol longest and loudest.

"And there are some women who prefer those qualities in their wine," Jillian continued. "What about you ladies?"

"I like my men big and bold and full-bodied. Does that count?"

More laughter, and since the joker looked prim and ladylike and had to be pushing eighty, Seth grinned, too. Amused by the interplay, intrigued by Jillian's easy rapport with the group—another facet he'd never been privy to—he leaned himself against a thick vertical support beam, crossed his arms and settled in to enjoy the show.

"Do you like the big wines, Jillian?" another woman asked.

"When I'm in a certain mood, yes. Other times I'm in the mood for something more elegant and refined. Less ballsy, if you will."

"You must have a preference though," the woman persisted. "What's your favorite of the Louret wines?"

Jillian lifted a glass, tilting the angle until the opulent ruby color of its contents caught the light. "You're about to taste it."

"So, you're feeling ballsy today, are you Jillian?" Carol asked.

No, Seth decided, as the warmth of the group's laughter rolled through him. That didn't describe her current mood. Ballsy was Monday when she'd galloped that monster horse up the hill. Today she was more relaxed and supple and confident.

"Pinot noir," he suggested softly.

In his peripheral vision he saw a dozen red hats swivel in his direction, but his eyes were fixed on Jillian as she carefully placed the glass back on the bar and even more carefully turned his way.

"Why pinot noir?" she asked as her eyes met his. No wariness there, more a watchful stillness, as if she held her breath while she waited for his answer.

"My interpretation of your mood."

Wow. Between the impact of those dark chocolate eyes fixed on hers and the complexities of his answer, Jillian could find no ready response.

Assuming that his pinot noir call wasn't some off-the-cuff pick-a-wine retort.

Later, she would stew on that. Possibly for days. For now she needed to concentrate, since this tricky group was already firing questions at their new quarry.

"Do *you* think cabernet is a man's wine?" Carol wanted to know.

"What's your opinion on that gender research project Jillian mentioned?" another asked.

"Are you a wine drinker?"

"Have you ever done a tasting with Jillian?"

She really did need to concentrate, since she somehow heard that as "tasting *of* Jillian." And the notion of Seth's mouth on hers, on her body, tasting her…

Oh, boy. Instant dizziness and disorientation. Her mouth turned dry. Her hand shook as she reached for water and took a quick mouthful, washing away the taste of full-bodied wine and the forbidden heat of her thoughts.

Better. Except the women of the Golden Elms Red Hat Social Club looked set to drag Seth over and into their tasting circle. Making a time-out *T* with her hands, she raised her voice enough to be heard above the hubbub. "Ladies, let's give Seth a break."

Thankfully—and surprisingly—they quietened. Enough that when Kitty spoke, her cultured little lady's voice chimed as clearly as silver on crystal.

"Is Seth your man, Jillian?"

Please, Lord, let me slip through these floorboards and disappear.

Of course the good Lord wasn't listening. No doubt because of her previous sinful thoughts about tasting. And because she couldn't look anywhere near Seth until her face stopped flaming, she focused on the faces in front of her as their interested observation turned to speculation.

I have to answer here. Let me do so with some coherence and dignity.

"Seth's a builder. An architect and a builder, actually."

Heartened because—hallelujah!—her voice did work, she chanced a glance his way. He didn't look embarrassed. In fact, leaning against that beam with his sleeves rolled up to reveal dark forearms folded across his broad chest, he looked…like the embodiment of Eli's ninety-eight reserve cabernet.

Big and earthy and full-bodied.

Good Lord, she did not mean that! She meant he looked less serious and intense than usual. Not exactly smiling, although there might have been a glint of amusement in his eyes.

"He's helping me," Jillian continued, looking to distract the women and herself, "with my plans to renovate the tasting room."

"You're changing this room? Why on earth would you want to do that?"

"I hope you're going to lighten the decor with some pastels."

"You can't be serious, Linda! I love all the timber. It's part of the ambience."

Much diverted by the notion of a design and decor makeover, the women were off and running. They asked questions, but didn't wait for answers. Suggestions and counter-suggestions swirled in a debate as lively and colorful as their own purple-suited, red-hatted attire.

After several minutes, she tried to bring them back on topic but failed. She shook her head and directed a helpless shrug in Seth's direction. His full mouth crooked into a smile and for a beat of time Jillian just stared.

Completely mesmerized.

And it struck her that she'd never seen Seth Bennedict smile, or at least not right at her. Her heart stuttered and her skin tingled with warmth. Her internal sensors sounded a *danger-danger* warning, but she could not look away until the quietest of the group—Helen—touched her on the arm, breaking the spell.

"If you need to go talk to your man, Jillian, it's fine with us."

This time she let the "your man" assumption slide right by. It wasn't worth explaining all over again. "I do need to have a quick word about the renovation plans."

"Then vamoose. We'll still be here when you're done."

That's what she was afraid of. But she excused herself, they waved her off, she went...although not quickly enough to miss Kitty's whispered comment about big, bold and earthy.

The wine. Of course she meant the wine, since they'd all lifted their glasses and taken a first sip of the ninety-eight reserve she'd poured.

It was a very big wine.

Still, her cheeks bloomed with heat as she slipped out from behind the bar. Who knew if Seth had overheard? He wasn't smiling anymore, just standing there watching her approach in a way that made her nerves and her pulse lollop all over the place.

To compensate, she held herself erect, shoulders straight, and strived to make her smile polite and business-like. "I have a few minutes if you want to talk about my plans, now you've had a decent look at the place. Why don't we go over by the window?"

"Where it's a bit more private?"

She glanced back over her shoulder and, sure enough, they were being watched.

Still, Seth seemed to be taking it in good humor, so she smiled and shook her head as they made their way to the far end of the room. "I'm not used to such a fascinated audience."

"Not your typical tasting group?" he asked.

"Hardly. I don't know if I could handle someone like Kitty several times a day!"

A smile twitched at the corners of his mouth. It wasn't the full disarming dazzler of before, but an attractive near-smile that made him look more relaxed. Not that it completely relaxed Jillian. When she took the chair he offered at the setting by the window, she tried to sit back and enjoy the sensation of resting her feet for the first time since breakfast. But then he leaned his hips against the table, stretched his long legs out in front of him, and goodbye relaxation.

"I don't think there is any 'typical' group," she continued, looking out over the vineyards, a safe alternative to other, closer, scenery. Right at eye level, actually, not that she was noticing. "We get all kinds through here, although I would say less drop-ins and more of those who seek us out."

"People who are serious about their wines?"

"Yes, we get plenty who know exactly what they want. They might ask for a specific flight of wines or a vertical, say, of cabernets." She predicted the next question and explained. "That's a tasting of one wine's various vintages, youngest to oldest, as opposed to a horizontal, which is the same vintage from several wineries.

"Anyway, that's the enophiles but they're balanced by groups like this one." Turning from the window, she gestured toward the group at the bar.

"You mean groups with odd dress sense?"

"I take it you've never encountered Red Hatters before?"

"Not in numbers," he muttered. "Scary."

She couldn't help laughing. "Only if you're scared by women of a certain age who aren't afraid to have fun."

"They're an organization?"

"A *dis*organization, according to these ladies."

And she only hoped that one day she'd have the chutzpah to wear purple and red together. To look toward the future and laugh about the past. Even to indulge the hormones that had hummed to life in her blood.

"They're having fun," he commented, "but they're also keen to learn."

"Yes." She looked back up at him, found him watching her with interest. Not so threatening, that quiet intentness, when it focused on her work and when he got it so absolutely right. That made her confidence hum in perfect tune with her hormones. "That combination makes them my favorite kind of wine tourist."

"The way you run your tasting—" he looked back at the group as a chorus of laughter rattled the window "—it's different to what I envisioned."

"Different how?"

"Your focus isn't taste-and-buy like some other places I've seen. You're giving them a whole lot more."

Insanely pleased that he got it and unable to hold all that satisfaction inside, Jillian smiled. Deep inside she straight-out grinned. "Our philosophy is to provide a wine experience and education, without being too stuffy. I think we're succeeding since we get a lot of traffic through word-of-mouth recommendations."

"I imagine you do," he said slowly, his eyes serious as they held hers. "You're good."

A small compliment should not create such a dizzying effect, but Seth's did. It went to her head as swiftly as a good red straight from the barrel. She should not have felt the schoolgirlish need to push for more, but she did. "Not stuffy?"

The ladies laughed again, more raucously than ever, and Seth simply cocked one dark brow. Answer enough.

"Is that your focus with the refit? Not stuffy?"

"That's one of the reasons I want to open the place up and bring in more light. That, and because to really show the differences in appearance and color of the wines you need natural light."

"I've been thinking about the light problem."

Seth pulled those long legs—which she hadn't been noticing—under him and stood. When he moved along the wall, touching, inspecting, contemplating, she was intrigued enough to get back on her tired feet and follow.

"What would you think about arched windows, both sides of the room?" he asked.

"How big?"

"Floor to ceiling. Modeled on your entrance doors. Same shape, same width."

"Yes. Oh, yes," Jillian breathed, containing the excitement that cannoned around inside—*he's going to do it! He's taking on the job!*—by pacing out that width of window and nodding her satisfaction. "Arches are perfect, Seth. A reflection of the shape of the wine barrel, the bottle, the glass. Will knocking that shape into the walls be a problem?"

"Not for me, but the windows have to be custom-made. They won't come cheap."

"I'll figure out a way to sell them to Cole."

"I could talk to him—"

"No!"

She cut him off too abruptly, given the way his eyes narrowed, but she felt a strong need to keep control of this project. To let him know she wasn't the weak basket case he'd had to rescue from Jason's mess.

"There's no need for that," she added in a more reasonable tone. "Cole should be getting used to my additions and changes."

"Yeah?" The focus of that narrow-eyed interest shifted. "What else have you changed since Monday?"

"Uniforms. These—" she held her arms out a little, showing the claret polo shirt all the tasting-room staff wore "—have to go."

"Too stuffy?"

"And not individual enough. The marketing campaign is based around Louret's individual hands-on approach and attention to detail. So, Mercedes and I decided we needed non-uniform uniforms. We'll have a range of separates—tops and bottoms—in the same palette of colors, but every one different according to our own tastes."

Seth nodded, seemingly impressed. She was impressed that his eyes hadn't glazed over as Cole's and Eli's had when she pitched the idea to them. Not that they weren't interested in the tasting room's vital function at Louret, more that they weren't interested in wardrobe choices.

Plus they'd both been distracted lately by the ongoing legal meetings over Spencer Ashton and the Lattimer estate.

"So, you're after a bright and relaxed atmosphere and a functional, comfortable work space."

"Yes, that's it exactly!" Seth Bennedict didn't only understand her plans but the reasoning behind them, and that set him apart from every other builder she'd spoken to.

That and the fact that he was here, tape measure and notebook in hand.

"So." She drew a slow breath in a bid to steady the nervous let-this-work-out churning in her stomach. "Does this mean you are going to quote?"

"Yes."

Yes! But she contained the urge to punch the air, needing to ask one more question. The biggy. "Is this a serious quote, Seth? Do you really want the job or are you only humoring me because I practically begged?"

He looked at her strangely. "I'm sorry. Did I miss the begging?"

"The other morning, at the stables." She waved a hand in that general direction, but she did not want to go back there. She did not want to remember the desperate edge of panic that had driven her to swallow her pride and ask, straight out, for his help. "You said you'd take a look, no promises. What changed your mind?"

For a second he looked right at her, and something in his eyes made her draw herself back, as if that might deflect the impact of all that dark intensity. Then he hitched a shoulder and answered ever so casually. "Like you said, it's a small job. And I've decided to take the opportunity to get my hands dirty."

Oh, my Lord, it would be Villa Firenze all over again. The dangerous glint in his eyes. The masculine scent of hard work and hot muscles. The glimpse of his skin, glistening with sweat. Her own unaccustomed reaction, part fascination, part run-like-hell terror.

Jillian swallowed. "You're going to do the work yourself?"

"Yeah. I'm looking forward to it."

"But you said you were booked solid right through summer." She scrambled to bring order to her thoughts. "How will you fit this in?"

"By juggling and overtime. Will working at night present any problems?"

Yes, no, probably not. Frowning, she considered the situation. If he worked nights, there'd be less disruption. Less bitching from Eli about builders under his feet. "No, that would work," she said slowly. "But what about Rachel?"

He stared at her a moment. "I thought you wanted me on this job."

"I do. Yes. Absolutely."

"Then stop reminding me why it's not going to be easy."

"Okay," she said, exhaling in a long rush. "But promise me that if there's ever a problem with Rachel and child care, you'll let me know."

"Rachel's not your problem, Jillian."

"I know that." And she had no reason to feel stung, no matter how she felt about his little girl who'd lost her mother due to Jason's recklessness.

Not your fault, she reminded herself. *You had no influence over him. You couldn't slow him down, settle him down, or keep him satisfied. You can't hold yourself responsible for his actions.*

She lifted her chin and looked Seth square in the eye. "And I don't want to create any problems for her, either, Seth. You're doing me a big favor here. Let me do this one small thing in return."

"*If* it's ever an issue."

"You'll call me, let me help you out?"

She didn't think he would relent, and he did so finally with the barest inclination of his head. A small acknowledgment rather than any kind of surrender, but that was enough.

Unlike his brother, Seth Bennedict was a man of his word and Jillian intended to keep him to it.

Four

Eager to get his quote approved and the project underway, Jillian had convened a meeting with her brothers and sister for late Friday afternoon. No problem, Seth assured her, when she called and asked him to attend. His sister was coming up from San Francisco for the weekend. Eve could leave earlier and babysit Rachel.

He didn't count on the trailer rollover and Eve's phone call from the middle of traffic chaos. His housekeeper Rosa had already left for a weekend off. What could he do but get on the phone and reschedule?

"Sorry, but it's too late to arrange another sitter," he explained to Jillian.

"Where is Rachel now?"

"I'm about to pick her up from day care."

"Bring her with you," she said. "We'll shift the meeting to the house. Caroline will love the chance to spoil her."

Seth frowned, not because of the Caroline-spoiling

thing but because his daughter had a shy streak. She hadn't ever met any of Jillian's family. "I don't know if that's a good idea."

There was the tiniest hint of a pause. "You said you'd let me help out with Rachel. Are you going back on your word, Seth?"

Hell.

"We'll see you in half an hour, then."

Twenty-eight minutes later Seth pulled up outside the Vines.

Still dressed in her work uniform, Jillian jogged down from the portico of the big rustic house before he'd even turned off the engine. Like she'd been watching for his arrival. The kick of that notion—Jillian waiting for him—resonated through his body as she approached, a warm and welcoming smile curving her lips.

A warm smile welcoming his back seat passenger.

His gaze flicked to the rearview mirror and found it filled with his daughter's anxious little face. Her thumb went straight into her mouth. Damn. After Karen's death he'd vowed never to let work come before his daughter. He should not have compromised that vow. He should not have brought her here.

By the time his boots hit the ironstone drive, Jillian was unstrapping Rachel from her car seat. But she didn't grab her and swing her into her arms. Nor did she overpower her with meaningless remember-me? prattle. Hunkered down by the open door, she smiled quietly at his daughter and fixed on the perfect opener.

"Is that Pinky Pony?" She leaned back a fraction and inspected the toy Rachel held clutched to her chest. The one Jillian had given her last Christmas. "I'm so glad you brought him back to visit with me and his friends."

Slowly the thumb slid from Rachel's mouth, although her big brown eyes maintained a note of suspicion. "Have you got other ponies?"

"I sure do."

Rachel maintained her wariness for, oh, another three seconds before wriggling out of the seat and tucking her hand in Jillian's. "Are they in your bedwoom?"

"Yup. Should we ask your daddy if it's okay to go and see them?"

"He woan want to come. He doesn't like ponies. He says they got bad additudes."

"Really? I did not know that."

As she straightened from three-year-old level to standing, Jillian's eyes sought and found his, and while her face and voice echoed his daughter's serious-subject tone, those green eyes danced with amusement. "Is that right, Seth? You don't like ponies because of their attitude?"

He shrugged helplessly. "I don't know where she gets these things."

Lips twitching as if to suppress laughter, she tilted her head and fixed him with a challenging look. "So, do you want to come and look at ponies with Rachel, then?"

"In your bedroom? I don't think so."

Which probably wasn't the smart thing to say, not when he'd been enjoying standing close enough to absorb the warmth of her teasing mood. Not pinot noir today, but something as lively and vibrant as that spark in her eyes. A sparkling rosé, perhaps.

And, she didn't shy away as he'd expected. She blinked slowly and something shifted in her expression. A hint of man-woman awareness, a knowledge that to Seth her bedroom was not a place of ponies and girlie tea parties but of feminine scents and lacy garments and every midnight fantasy he could remember.

Of course he had to be imagining things. If she detected any of that on his face, she'd run a mile. Instead she stood eye-locked with him, a touch of pink in her cheeks and a touch of mystery in her green eyes.

Until Rachel tugged at her hand. "Come on, Aunt Jellie. Pinky wantsta see your ponies."

Jillian allowed herself to be towed off toward the house by his purportedly shy daughter, pausing only to call back over her shoulder. "Come on inside. Cole's waiting in the library and Mercedes isn't far away. Eli may or may not make it."

A timely reminder, Seth decided, of his purpose and place here today. Not in her bedroom, breathing the intoxicating mix of wine and woman that clung to her skin, but in the library, talking business. He would do well to keep that in mind.

"The library is just through to your right." Jillian's voice drifted down from high on his left, and he looked up to find her partway up a winding staircase, still hand in hand with his daughter.

"Go on in," she said. "I'll be down in a few minutes."

"Are you all right then, princess?"

"I'm going to see Aunt Jellie's ponies," his princess informed him in an imperious tone. Of course, she was all right. What was he thinking?

"Have fun, then. And don't eat too much hay."

She giggled, the sound muffled by the hand she slapped over her mouth. And as Seth started toward the library, he was smiling all the way into his heart, warmed by that spontaneous giggle at a very lame joke.

"Aunt Jellie?"

On the threshold of the library he turned to see Jillian crouched down and listening intently to whatever Rachel had to say. One small hand rested on Jillian's shoulder as his daughter leaned forward to whisper in her ear, and that tableau with its hints of intimacy and implicit trust hit him mid-chest with paralyzing force.

For a second he felt as if he'd run full pelt into a steel girder. He simply couldn't breathe. But then the pressure eased, leaving in its place a hollow sense that he had erred—in a way he hadn't contemplated—taking on this job and bringing Rachel here today.

He was old enough and tough enough to deal with his infatuation with Jillian, but what about his daughter?

Jillian returned ten minutes later. Rachel did not. And while Seth went through the formalities of winning a job he didn't need and would probably spend the next month regretting, his daughter—he knew—was falling for a second Ashton-Sheppard woman.

Caroline.

"Goodness knows how long they'll be," Jillian said as they walked from the library, the meeting over. "It might be best if you pick her up at the stables."

Where, no doubt, she was falling for the Ashton-Sheppard pony. Mini Ed. Oh, yeah, Rachel would find that talking, snickering wiseass pony irresistible.

"It might be best if you come along, help me pry her off of that pony of yours," he said.

She crinkled her nose apologetically. "I suppose that's the least I can do, seeing as I mentioned Monty in the first place."

"Monty?"

"My pony."

"Ah." Not that he would ever think of the animal as anything other than Mini Ed. The name suited him too well, as did the current easy, teasing mood that accompanied them into the foyer.

He hadn't forgotten his earlier unease, rather he'd shoved it aside in favor of a more rational reaction. In the future, he would keep his business and personal lives apart. For now he knew Rachel was in good hands and he…well, he couldn't resist the temptation to stall and prolong the moment or the mood.

"It all started with that pink pony," he teased.

"By 'it all' do you mean the fact she's a little keen on horses?"

"A little?" Seth shook his head with mock gravity. "You created a monster."

"Obviously you can't be referring to a certain three-year-old who does not have an ounce of monster in her sweet little bones."

"Obviously you haven't spent time with any three-year-old who is tired and crabby and not getting her own way."

"No, I haven't." A trace of emotion flitted across her face, swift and ephemeral, chased away by a rueful smile. "Although I'm assured by my brothers that I was a perfect monster at that age."

"I find that hard to believe."

"If I did indulge in any monster-like behavior—not that I'm admitting culpability, you understand—" She cut him a look from under her lashes, which his body completely misunderstood. "But *if* I did then Eli and Cole would have provoked it. They've always taken great delight in razzing Mercedes and me."

"I noticed." In the meeting there'd been much to notice in the family dynamics and Jillian's responses. Especially those she tried to hide. "You don't much like being called Jellie, do you?"

She all but shuddered. "God, no!"

"Yet you let Rachel get away with it."

"Aunt Jellie from a three-year-old is cute. From my

brothers in a business meeting? Let's just say cute is not a desirable workplace image."

Seth bit his tongue. He figured it wasn't Kosher to mention how desirable he found the contrast between elegant, ladylike Jillian Ashton and this Jellie who got all flushed with restrained aggravation every time one of her brothers needled her.

She released some of that latent frustration on a sigh and folded her arms across her chest. "Dare I ask what else you noticed in the meeting?"

"Eli was preoccupied."

"He has a lot on his mind."

"Cole was in a hurry to get away."

"Newlywed."

"Mercedes likes chocolate-chip cookies."

"Mercedes skipped lunch." She laughed, a soft and husky contrast to their rat-at-at nail gun exchange of lines. Then she shook her head and met his eyes with narrowed consideration. "I didn't know you were so observant."

"You don't know me that well," he said slowly, and in one heartbeat the mood changed shape, gathering a new intimacy in the deep quiet of the unlit foyer.

"No, I don't. And I suspect you have the better of me there."

"You think I know you?" Hell, this week she'd turned everything he thought he knew about cool and prissy Jillian Ashton upside down. Sauvignon blanc. Cabernet sauvignon. Pinot noir. Sparkling rosé. She was a complete cellar full of diverse moods and he couldn't help enjoying every one.

"You know more about me than I would like." Chin lifted, she held his gaze. "More than anyone outside my family, actually."

"You're talking about the past, Jillian, about Jason and the mess he made of his life and his marriage. Not you."

She dismissed that with an adamant shake of her head. "You know I was too gullible and naive to see any hint of reality. You know I believed him when he said that *he'd* been conned, that he had nothing to do with the investment scam. You know I actually believed he would get my money back, that he would stop cheating and lying and playing me for a thousand kinds of fool!"

Yeah, because she loved him. Because she was loyal and faithful and committed, and—dammit—he admired her because she had stood by her husband and partner.

So unlike his own wife.

"You were his wife, Jillian. I've never judged you for that."

Something shifted in her expression, and in the deep evening shadows he couldn't tell if it was acceptance or surprise or disbelief. She hitched her shoulders in a tense little shrug that echoed through him, tight in his chest and his gut and his head.

"I don't know what to say to that except thank you," she said quietly. "Thank you for the lack of judgment and thank you for sorting out that mess of my past."

What could he say but, "You're welcome."

"And especially thank you for helping me now." Her gaze fixed on his, so serious and earnest that his heart fisted in his chest. "This job means so much to me, and you taking it has lifted a weight off my shoulders."

Not just rhetoric, Seth knew. She'd come to him, she'd asked for his help, she'd thanked him already the day she offered to lend a hand with Rachel. And now she felt a need to repeat those thanks.

"Why is this project so important to you?" he asked.

"Work's my life," she answered with simple sincerity. "And my bliss."

Yeah, he understood the first, and the second he'd noticed that day at the tasting room. Except it wasn't that simple, he knew. During the meeting he'd studied her much more closely than any of her siblings.

This wasn't only about work, it was personal and somehow it was driving her.

"What are you trying to prove, Jillian?" he asked, studying her closely now. Seeing the giveaway flicker deep in her eyes and knowing he'd guessed right. Not that he needed any psych degree to figure out her motivation, but he didn't want to put words in her mouth. He knew patience—he had a three-year-old. He waited while the pause spun out between them, silent but for the rhythmic ticktock of the wall clock behind him.

Five ticks and four tocks before she drew an audible breath and made one of those expressive here's-how-it-is gestures with her hands.

"I have a lot of mistakes to make up for, Seth, a lot to prove. The way I walked away from Louret because I didn't think they respected me as a professional—"

"When you took the job over in Sonoma?"

"Yes."

And that's where she'd met Jason, his baby brother, the spoiled, smooth talking sales manager who'd wanted Jillian because of her surname and her connections. An Ashton, Jason had figured, could take him places he didn't work hard enough to make on his own.

"My family didn't want me to leave but I thought I knew better," she said evenly. "I thought I needed to prove I was all grown up and could make my own decisions."

"And now you think you need to—what?—make a big impact on Louret to prove your worth?"

"No, I just need to do something positive. For myself, mostly, and to put the past behind me."

"There's something to be said for knocking down old walls and rebuilding."

A smile ghosted across her lips, as if she appreciated the metaphor, although her eyes remained serious. "Sometimes when the old walls collapse around you, it takes a while to clear the rubble."

"Sometimes that clearing is more than one person can handle."

"And sometimes the only person avail—" She stopped abruptly and pressed her lips together.

No way was she getting away with that! Eyes narrowed, Seth leaned closer. "The only person available…what? Spit it out, Jillian."

"Charges into the rubble and stirs up a whole lot more dust!"

"I don't get your point," he said heavily. "A couple of minutes ago you were thanking me for clearing up Jason's mess."

"Yes, and my thanks weren't insincere. It's just…how your efficiency made me feel. The way you took over and cleared everything so effortlessly when I was still operating in this fog. You made me feel insignificant and useless."

All he'd done was take matters out of her hands so she wouldn't have to deal with the whole nasty truth—so he could protect her from the nastiest of those truths. She'd been operating in a fog. Her words. Yet he'd made her feel—

Seth rubbed a hand over the back of his neck. Hell, he couldn't repeat the words she'd used, they were so much bunk. "Do I still make you feel the same way?"

"No."

He stared at her, probably scowling, still struggling with what she'd revealed. And not believing her quick answer.

After a couple of seconds she sighed and her shoulders slumped a little, relenting. "Okay, you don't make me feel insignificant and whatever else I said. You just make me feel…uncomfortable. Sometimes."

"Because I'm Jason's brother?"

"Yes. That's one thing."

"And the other?" he prompted, thinking about that knowledge in her eyes earlier. Feeling his whole body tighten with expectation.

"You're so serious. And intense." She paused, the frown between her brows drawing tight with concentration as if she were unsure of what to say or how to say it. "You have this way of looking at me and I have no idea what you're thinking."

So much for bedroom awareness.

She did not have a clue, and for one barely constrained moment Seth felt like shocking that frown of concentration right off her face. He ached to tell her all about what he was thinking when the heat seared his veins and the tension burned in every cell of his body.

Except he'd shaken hands with her brothers ten minutes earlier. They had a deal to work together, for better, for worse. And he'd made a deal with himself to keep business and personal apart.

"Is working together on this project going to be a problem?" he asked.

"I thought it would be, that day I came to see you at Villa Firenze. But after this week and especially after today—" She blew out a breath and straightened her shoulders, although her eyes still looked troubled. "Yes, Seth. I can work with you."

"Especially if I lighten up?"

"That would help." Relief chased some of the uncertainty from her expression. "Are we good, then?"

Not that good, Seth thought, but she sounded so hopeful, what could he do but lie? "Yeah, we're good."

His reward was her smile. Big and open and warm, it streamed over him and through him, stirring something rich and deep in his very core. Something he wasn't used

to feeling—and damn sure wasn't comfortable feeling—
from any source other than his daughter.

His daughter. Damn. Frowning he shot back his sleeve
to study his watch. How could he have forgotten about Rachel? "I need to get going, to pick up Rachel, or my sister
will beat us home."

Her eyes widened a trace, as if she too had forgotten.
"If you don't mind waiting a few minutes, I'll change into
my riding gear and come down to the stables with you."

"You're going riding? Now?"

With her hand on the banister and one foot on the bottom step, she paused and cut him a look across her shoulder. "If I have time before dark, but mostly I need to help
you pry your daughter off Monty. I won't take more than
a minute to change into my jodhpurs."

"Only a minute?" he muttered as he watched her ascend
the stairs at full speed. Her skirt fluttered around her legs
and he thought about her stretching those skintight riding
breeches all the way up those long limbs and over her hips.
"I've seen how tight those jodhpurs are."

Five

Surely he hadn't meant her to hear that muttered closing quip…had he?

Jillian kicked aside her work skirt and flopped onto her bed, jodhpurs clutched in her fingers. Heat flared with the vivid and visceral memory of how he'd come to see—and feel—exactly how tight her jodhpurs were. Talk about your over-the-top fireworks response! At the time she'd put it down to her after-gallop high, her euphoric mood, her adrenaline-revved senses.

Now she knew better.

It was time to come clean with herself, something she hadn't done downstairs. Yes, he made her uncomfortable, much more often than she'd admitted to, and only in part because of that serious, intense thing he had down pat.

It didn't matter if he lightened up or not. She was attracted to him. Physically, irrationally, but there it was.

Her hormones had stretched and yawned and fluttered

back to life, reminding her that once upon a time she'd enjoyed the heat of flirtation and the intimacy of man-woman contact. Back when she'd had a sex life. Back when she'd thought her husband loved her and cherished her and wanted to make a life and a family and a home with her.

Back when she'd been a naive, love-struck fool.

And now her poor deprived hormones wanted to play with a complete non-candidate. One, he had just signed on to work for her. Two, he was her brother-in-law and father of her niece. Three, he was serious and intense and intimidating when she craved warm and comfortable and safe.

When she was ready for another relationship, she wanted what Caroline and Lucas shared. That deep bond that had nothing to do with hormones and everything to do with trust and respect.

She groaned and buried her face in her hands for a second. Then she dropped her hands away to stare fixedly at the ceiling. She was not Jellie, the shy and self-conscious teenager. She wasn't Jillie Ashton, rebellious twenty-something striking out for independence, either. Nor was she Jillian Ashton-Bennedict, demoralized wife and disabused widow.

She was Jillian Ashton, grown woman and graduate wine expert. She needed to win back the respect she'd lost during her marriage and its dusty, rubble-filled aftermath. She needed to maintain a working relationship with Seth and hopefully, somewhere along the way, she might also earn his respect. After that day in the tasting room, when he'd complimented her work, she thought she was on the right track. Lying here worrying about the man's view of her backside was not forwarding that cause.

She propelled herself upright and struggled into her skintight jodhpurs. So, she'd put on a few pounds since her competitive days in the saddle. That was ten years ago and she refused to make apologies. Shoulders straight, she marched to the door and pulled it open, balancing on one leg to pull on the first of her riding boots.

Voices drifted up from the foyer and her heartbeat went into instant overdrive, thudding loud and heavy in her ears—most inconvenient for a person trying to eavesdrop. On one socked foot she hopped down the hall closer to the staircase, where she could hear the exchange between Seth and her mother.

Rachel, she surmised from the soft-voiced conversation, had nodded off during the short drive back from the stables.

The chicken in Jillian suggested she hang back a minute longer and they would be gone. She wouldn't have to face Seth with the brand new recognition of sexual attraction still warm in her face and swirling in her belly.

No need to see him cradling his sleeping daughter in his arms. No need to watch them drive away, her chest aching with what she didn't have, with all that her marriage had not provided.

Then courage grabbed her by the scruff of the neck and gave her a big old-fashioned wake-up-to-yourself shake. She tugged on her second boot and headed down the stairs. Just before the curve that would bring the foyer into view, she paused to suck in a deep breath, to stiffen her spine and school her features into cool composure. Her heart still beat fast and hard but that wouldn't show.

She rounded that last spiraling curve as the front door closed, leaving the house empty and silent and Jillian straddling the chasm between intense relief and disappointment.

She'd desperately needed a head-clearing, emotion-leveling, spirit-lifting ride after Seth and Rachel left—it would have been her first since Monday morning—but when she arrived at the stables, the sun was already kissing the Mayacamas Mountains good-night. Tomorrow, she'd promised herself, and as soon as she cleaned up the tasting room after Saturday closing, she rushed back to the Vines with that promise in mind.

Grab a quick snack, change clothes, then straight to the stables.

The old car parked in front of the house gave her a second's pause, but she shrugged her curiosity aside and hit the kitchen at a near run. Luckily it wasn't a full run or she would have collided with Mercedes. Since her sister carried a tray set with Caroline's best crockery, the result would not have been pretty.

"Where's the fire?" Mercedes asked.

"Where's the tea party?" Jillian retorted, before she took a close look at her sister's face. Not smiling, even more serious than usual, the creases between her brows tight with worry. "What's the matter?"

"Mom has a visitor."

"A lawyer?" she asked automatically, thinking of Cole's many meetings these past weeks, then rejecting her ready assumption just as quickly. Lawyers did not drive the kind of beat-up small sedan she'd seen outside.

"Worse." Mercedes grimaced. "Anna Sheridan."

Good thing Jillian wasn't holding the tray. Its contents would now be strewn all over the kitchen floor. "*The* woman? With *the* baby?"

"That's the one. And she has the kid with her."

The kid who happened to be their half brother. One of their many half brothers, all unmet, sired by the man she refused to call 'her father.'

Jillian's stomach churned with anxiety. "Why is she here? What does she want?"

"I have no idea." Mercedes hiked up the tray. "But if you grab yourself a cup, we can go find out together."

* * *

Seth drove out to the Vines with one intention. To find his daughter's precious pink pony, inadvertently left behind the previous night. Apparently she'd been so entranced by the real thing she'd discarded Pinky without a second thought. Imagine that?

Except tonight she had remembered. Tonight she refused to go to bed without her favorite toy. And at the end of a hellish day packed floor to ceiling with work snafus, all he'd wanted to do was kick back and enjoy his sister's company. Dinner, a glass or two of wine, some relaxed conversation that didn't include anything connected with Jillian Ashton.

When Rachel whined and pouted, he didn't bother negotiating. Sometimes it was easier to concede defeat. "Yes, I will go find Pinky." Even if I have to get down on my hands and knees and look under every individual strand of straw.

As he pulled up outside the stables, he noticed the absence of vehicles. The big white barn slumbered in the encroaching darkness, seemingly empty of all but its equine residents. Good. Although help might shorten the needle-in-a-haystack search, he wasn't in the mood for polite chit-chat with Caroline Sheppard or for pretending to lighten up around her daughter.

Not tonight.

"We're not that good," he muttered as he strode into the barn…through doors slung wide open.

No lights, no activity save the rustle of straw beneath hooves and a distinctive pony snicker, yet those doors had to be open for a reason. Seth ignored Ed, his narrowed gaze fixing on the adjacent empty stall. A quick head tally confirmed the absence of the gray she'd been riding on Monday.

It was too late for riding, too dark for safety, too dangerous for the speed she'd favored that morning. He retraced his steps outside and halted, hands on hips and head lifted, all his senses on high alert. First he felt it, the rumbling in the ground under his feet, and then he heard the thunder of hooves.

Déjà vu.

The horse appeared like a gray ghost in the twilight, galloping at breakneck speed. Not controlled this time, no way, and everything inside Seth roiled in a volatile mix of fear and fury.

"You reckless fool," he muttered. "If you don't break your neck, I will wring—"

The threat caught in his throat, choked by pure dread, as he realized why the horse approached at such helter-skelter speed. This time it *was* out of control, the reins dangling uselessly around its forelegs, the saddle on its back empty.

Fear clenched deep in Seth's gut as he raced to his truck and wrenched open the door. Without pausing to close it, he fired the engine and sent the back wheels spinning and spitting up gravel. The door slammed shut when he swung into the driveway at bone-jarring speed, spinning his back end so far out he almost collected a gatepost. His headlights sliced through the dusk and bounced off the white railing fence that bordered the lane, close—too close—to his right-hand fender, warning him to get a grip.

He needed to slow down, to think about where the horse had come from, to search with more method and less foolhardy haste.

Ahead he thought he saw a dark shape beside the road, and an image of Jillian's unmoving body jammed his mind with dread. But it was nothing. A shadow, perhaps, or a darker patch in the roadside vegetation. He sucked in a deep breath, eased his foot off the accelerator and loosened his punishing grip on the wheel. His breath, he realized, was still ratcheting in his lungs from that short, sharp sprint through the stable yard.

Or simply from the adrenaline shock of fear.

On a mental flip of the coin—Left? Right? No, left— he turned and followed the dirt road all the way to the cottage at its end. No lights, no sign of life, but whichever Louret worker lived here could be out or away for the weekend. Vaguely he remembered a time when Saturday night meant something besides fewer work calls. More clearly he remembered this end of Louret from driving by on Route 29. He'd noticed the cottage and beyond it an artificial lake, postcard pretty in the blue-skied daylight, now an eerie hole of darkness as night stole over the land.

And there was no way of knowing if Jillian had taken a tumble into that eerie darkness.

Realistically, she could have been riding anywhere on the acreage, in any of the vineyards or down one of the many tracks cut for machinery access. He needed help. Cursing the frustrated speed of his departure from the stables and the cell phone left back in Napa, he turned his truck in a slow circle, scanning the wide arc of his headlights one last time as he prepared to head back to the Vines.

And there she was, a slender silhouette shading her eyes from the blinding glare of the high beams. Relief surged through Seth, overpowering in its intensity. Then he sucked it up and got moving, switching his lights to low before bursting from the truck and striding forward to meet her.

She was frowning—scowling even—but he didn't give her time for more than, "Seth? What are you—" before his hands skated over her shoulders, down her arms and back again, tipping her face up and into the light.

"What are you do—"

"I'm checking you're all right," he cut in. Abruptly, harshly, but he had cause.

"Doing here?" She finished her question on a lame note, then drew an audible breath as he cradled her face between his hands.

"Are you hurt?" He dipped down closer, scouring her face and her eyes for any sign of injury.

"No." But she must have sensed his lingering doubt because she lifted her hands to his and pried them from her face. "Apart from my bruised pride, I'm fine. See?"

Yeah, he saw. And he let his breath, his fear, his earlier crazed worry go in one solid exhalation. She was fine. She was standing there frowning up at him with a peculiar expression on her face, but since he'd turned his grip around, trapping her hands in his, she was probably trying to work out how to free herself without an undignified arm wrestle.

Right now it'd likely take that.

If he let go of her hands, he might yield to the real temptation of hauling her into his arms and holding her tight against his body. Of kissing her brow and her face and her mouth in a combination of repressed need and thank-you-God relief.

He figured he'd better keep holding her hands.

"What are you doing here, Seth?"

"Performing search and rescue, apparently." Seth tried for levity but failed. Light humor, he decided, is a hard task when your heart's still pounding with a crazy, dark dread.

Jillian shook her head slowly. "I don't understand."

"I was up at the stables when your horse came in."

"Is she all right?" Her fingers clutched at his, suddenly tense and agitated. "Marsanne? My horse? She wasn't lame?"

"Not that I noticed. She came galloping up the hill on all four legs."

That seemed to offer the reassurance she needed. Her

heavy sigh sounded a little shaky, but her posture eased from poker-backed alarm to a relieved slump. When her fingers relaxed their grip on his, Seth couldn't help stroking his thumbs over the back of her hands. He felt her tremble and knew she was shaken up, no doubt more than her bruised pride would allow her to admit.

"I trust you didn't come off at that speed?"

"No, and I shouldn't have come off at all!" With a sound of disgust, she tugged her hands free. It seemed she couldn't continue her explanation without their contribution. "I was lollygagging, not paying attention, and she shied at a quail in the grass. I wouldn't have forgiven myself if my carelessness injured Marsanne."

"What about injuring yourself? Did you spare a thought in that direction?"

"I told you—I only bruised my pride." She dragged her hands over her backside and feigned a wince. "Or mostly only my pride."

Okay. He was not going there. Not thinking about checking out that part of her anatomy for injury. Instead he brushed a thumb along her cheekbone, touching what looked like a smudge of dirt. "Looks more like you landed face first."

"Perhaps I bounced."

"Perhaps," he said, and with a will of its own, his hand continued to stroke her face, down over her cheek, tracing the line of her jaw and the point of her chin. Her acceptance of that simple touch, the warmth of her skin, the subtle rhythm of her pulse in her throat—they all combined to stir a deep response, something beyond the usual lust.

He should stop, get his hands the hell back where they belonged, but he couldn't make himself respond. He didn't want to respond. Not yet.

"Lucky I was wearing a helmet," Jillian managed to say

in a husky whisper of breath, a perfect match for Seth's caress, as tender and tantalizing as the stroke of velvet.

Then her words must have registered, because he gripped her chin firmly between thumb and fingers. His eyes locked on hers. "You're not, you know."

Not...what? Not covered in dirt? Not being stroked by velvet? Not about to be kissed—

"You're not wearing a helmet," he pointed out with indisputable logic. Even more annoyingly, he let her go and it felt as if her whole body sighed with disappointment.

"I was."

"Did you lose it when you fell off?"

So, okay, she had fallen off, but did he have to remind her? Did he have to douse the lovely ripple of pleasure his touch had stirred in her veins? And did he have to stand there, looking as if no explanation but the complete truth would suffice?

"No, the helmet did its job when I became unseated." Which, Jillian decided, was a more dignified description than 'fell off.' "I lost it afterwards."

"While you were walking back here?"

"Does it matter? I'll find it tomorrow. I know exactly where I tossed it."

Hands on hips, he stared down at her until she caved.

Until she threw her hands in the air and admitted, "Yes, okay, I had this minor temper attack. I don't like being dumped at the farthest point of my ride, especially when it's my own fault."

She should not have mentioned the temper fit. In retrospect, her honest admission sounded childish and apparently it had rendered Seth speechless. So much for her efforts to earn his respect!

Feeling a peculiar sense of letdown, she gestured toward his truck. "I wasn't looking forward to the long walk. I'll grab a lift back to the stables, if that's all right."

* * *

As soon as she climbed into the passenger seat and Seth closed the door on the enclosed intimacy of the cab, she knew it wasn't all right. Her emotions teetered all over the place, her skin tingled everywhere he'd touched, and now she was drawing his earthy, masculine scent into her body with every breath.

And they weren't moving, weren't going anywhere.

Frowning, she turned his way and found him watching her, intently yes, but with a strange expression on his face.

"What's the matter?" she asked.

He shook his head and murmured something that sounded like *graciano* but couldn't have been, since that made no sense. Unless she'd landed face first in wine-colored earth.

Self-consciously she lifted a hand and scrubbed at her cheek. "Is my face coated in dirt? Is that what you're staring at?"

"I was trying to picture you throwing a tantrum." He shook his head again, put the truck into gear and swung onto the road. "And not succeeding."

Chastened because—let's face it—a temper tantrum is not a pretty image, Jillian wriggled in her seat. "If it's any consolation, this is a rare occurrence."

He cut her a look. "I hope riding in the dark is also a rare occurrence."

"I intended being out and back a lot earlier, but…" She shrugged, and in that absent little gesture felt the tension of the afternoon return tenfold and then some.

"But…?"

"But I wasn't." She waved a hand dismissively, then sat up straight because he wasn't slowing. "The turn's coming up. To the stables. You'd better slow down."

"I'm taking you home."

"There's no need to do that."

"You've just fallen off your horse."

"I didn't hurt myself, Seth." She reached across and put her hand on his arm, forcing him to look at her, since he'd developed that rigid steel-jawed, I'm-in-charge look she recognized. Her brothers had turned it into an art form. "I have a horse to attend to, and then I will take myself home."

He didn't answer, although he did pull over to the side of the road. Carefully she took her hand away and folded her fingers into her palm, enclosing the delicious warm charge from that contact. Sad, but she couldn't stop herself anymore than she could stop herself continuing on her theme.

"I don't need you or anyone to make decisions for me, Seth. I know I admitted to a minor tantrum before, but I'm not a child."

"I know that, Jillian." He turned to face her, a movement so deliberate and measured it could have been slow-mo. "Believe me, I know."

Suddenly the space in his cab seemed to shrink, or perhaps the air just thickened with a meaning that sucked up all the spare oxygen. He was talking about seeing her as a woman. He was looking at her as a woman, and her body responded with an embarrassing lack of restraint.

Her heartbeat ran amok, heat rioted through her blood, her hormones went completely ape.

It had been a long, long time since she'd experienced anything so involving and exciting and terrifying all at once. The terrifying part came from the notion that *he* wanted *her*, and that changed everything. Her own one-sided crush she could handle, but Seth Bennedict? An unrestrained shiver raced through her blood.

She did not know if she could handle a man like Seth, or even if she had the courage to try.

Nervous and panicky, she straightened her backbone and pushed her chin up, in full defensive mode. "Will you take me to the stables or will I get out and walk?"

"Sure I'll take you to the stables," he said without moving a muscle.

Jillian's pulse thudded in her ears. She knew there was a proviso coming; knew he wouldn't give in so easily.

"After you tell me why you were out riding so late."

That was it? No tricky questions about the simmering tension between them? About whether she still saw him as Jason's scary big brother or as a man?

"I'll tell you why I was out riding," she said, mimicking his even tone. "After you tell me why you were at the stables tonight."

He huffed out a breath. "Search and rescue mission."

"What?"

"Rachel left that pony toy of hers at the stables last night." He rubbed a hand across the back of his neck, his frown turning introspective. "She refused to go to bed tonight without the damn thing."

"Pinky Pony?"

"Yeah. I don't suppose you know where I can put my hands on it?"

"No, but I will help you look after I put Marsanne away. I'm sorry to have held you up with this second search and rescue mission."

"Find that pony and you're forgiven," he said with an unexpected quirk of humor.

Attractive, so deadly attractive, especially on top of all this tenderhearted concern. Not only for her, but for his daughter. Jillian's chest felt tight, dangerously constricted and breathless.

"Worse comes to worst," she said, forcing herself to concentrate on the conversation. On Rachel. "I have a whole collection in my bedroom. If we can't find Pinky I happen to know which would work best as a substitute."

"Substitutes don't cut it with Rachel." His gaze seared into hers, so dark and hot and intense she swore her heart stalled in her chest. "They're never the same as the real thing."

Six

Pinky Pony wasn't at the stables, it turned out. After returning to the Vines for a substitute, Jillian had found Rachel's toy amongst the others in her bedroom. Of course, being Jillian, she'd insisted on sending the surrogate home with Seth, too.

Of course, being Rachel, his daughter insisted that Pinky should visit Aunt Jellie to express his gratitude for the new playmate. She'd been at Seth since breakfast and now, fresh from an after-lunch nap, she climbed onto his knee and started in again. "You said saying thank you is good manners, Daddy. You said I should *always* wemember to say thank you. You said…"

And so it went, wearing into the fabric of his patience with unrelenting and finely tuned precision. His own three-year-old version of the power sander. Finally, to buy some Sunday afternoon peace, he agreed to an over-the-phone thank you. "But Jillian's working today. We can't call until she's finished," he cautioned.

"I call you at work."

"I have a cell phone. Jillian does not."

Rachel's brow puckered. Seth sighed and prepared himself for the next... "Why?"

"Because I have a chatterbox daughter who likes to call me at work." He tweaked one of her pigtails, already askew from her nap. "That's why I have a cell phone."

"Aunt Jellie doesn't."

He thought Rachel was talking about cells, until she fixed him with her big, solemn eyes—the look that did him in every time—and said, "That's why she lets me share her ponies. She hasn't got a daughter of her own."

Okay. He did not need to know if that insight parroted Jillian or came directly from a fertile three-year-old mind. And he did not need *his* fertile imagination fostering notions of Jillian and babies and activities for making babies. Bad enough that it infiltrated his nights without seeping into his days.

He set Rachel off his knee and onto her feet in front of him. He fixed her with his best I-mean-business face. "Let's make a compromise."

"What's that?" she asked suspiciously.

"A deal. If you promise to quit nagging me, I'll call Caroline and find out when Jillian finishes work. Then we'll know what time to call her and say thank you. Deal?"

"Can we call her now?"

"We can call Caroline now."

His daughter shook hands on the deal like a pro, and skipped off to fetch the phone and the pony friends who "might want to listen, Daddy."

While he waited for Rachel's return—and she could take a while, given the audience she was assembling—he recalled his other recent deal with a female. Last night, in return for his lift to the stables, Jillian had promised to tell him why she'd been out riding so late.

No handshake, but a deal just the same, and one she'd welshed on.

In the distraction of finding Pinky Pony, he'd let it slide. Today it nagged at his sense of fair play with a persistency rivaled only by his daughter...and the temptation to give in so *he* could visit Jillian.

Problem was he wanted to see her a little too much. Hell, and that was a straight-out lie. He wanted to see her a *lot* too much. He ached to test the sexual energy he'd felt between them last night. He needed confirmation that the buzz of attraction didn't exist only in his mind and his blood and his too-long-without flesh.

He wanted her, but he knew the ferocity of that want would scare her off as quick as look at her. Send her scurrying back behind that cool, aloof facade that for years he'd assumed was the real Jillian Ashton. Well, now he knew otherwise and he wanted the otherwise.

He wanted the woman who slid from horseback into his hands, hot with the thrill of the ride. He wanted to taste her teasing smile and sink into her warmth while she hummed with passion for her wines. He even wanted her stormy-eyed with pique after she'd kissed the earth and hurled her helmet at some innocent bystanding vine.

Oh, yeah, he could almost taste the pleasure of taking her, right there on the soft spring earth, with only the vines and the moon and his own driving desire as their witness.

Of course that wasn't going to happen. Not yet.

Late last night, long after Eve had left him alone with his turbulent emotions and a second bottle of Australian Shiraz, he'd determined to take it slow. To foster Jillian's trust through their working relationship and not to compromise that trust. The job meant too much to her. And he'd wanted her for too long to blow it—as it were—with his body's impatient need to make up for lost time and for all the substitutes that never proved any substitute.

That's why he hadn't caved to temptation today. The next few weeks in her proximity would test him seriously, he knew. Lucky his wells of willpower and endurance ran deep.

Standing by that arms-length decision sounded all well and good in theory…until Caroline Sheppard's gentle method of persuasion turned it on its ear.

Half an hour later, Seth was still shaking his head with rueful how-did-that-happen bafflement as he took the turn off Route 29 and headed toward Louret for the third time in three days.

"We're only saying a quick thank you," he reminded Rachel, who was already wriggling with impatience in her car seat.

"And saying hullo to Monty."

"A *quick* hello."

This prompted a chorus of hellos, at various speeds, as Rachel attempted to settle on his meaning of "quick." Seth shook his head again, but this time with a slow grin.

How had he gotten so lucky? What had he done right to end up with such a crackerjack kid? And what would his life be without her sudden spurts of insight and humor, or these sudden kicks of chest-squeezing love that reminded him of what really mattered?

"I'll just say hi," Rachel announced finally, "'stead of hullo."

"That should work." Although he didn't know how anything else would work this afternoon.

He drove between the stone gateposts and open iron gates at the entrance to the Vines and saw Caroline and a redheaded stranger bending over a flower bed. They both straightened when they heard his vehicle, Caroline waving and smiling as she pulled off her gardening gloves.

No, despite his quick-hello warnings to Rachel, he didn't know how this visit would pan out. He turned off the engine and scrubbed a hand over the back of his neck as he tracked Caroline Sheppard's smiling approach. He had a strong suspicion that the outcome was about to be neatly charmed out of his hands.

Jillian received ample warning of Seth's and Rachel's Sunday afternoon visit. Her mother had called with the information. "I suggested four-thirty. That will give you enough time to clean up after closing. I'll send Seth down to pick you up and we'll have coffee in the garden."

Enough time, also, to engage in a little self-indulgence, some harmless recollections of his last visit to the tasting room and the whole surreal encounter after her tumble last night. Then she packed away another layer of chardonnay glasses and, with each, she tucked away a layer of sensual memory.

His Tokay voice, deep, thick, intoxicating. The smooth curves of muscle in his folded arms. The bold burn of his gaze and a dozen imprints of his touch on her face.

Then she closed the lid of the packing case and gave it a solid all-done rap. This was her work space, her place of confidence and control, and she intended to maintain her professionalism despite the scary newness of this Seth thing. Today was a test, sooner than she'd expected, but she was prepared—prepared with the kind of nervous, let's-get-this-done butterfly accompaniment she'd always experienced at exam time.

Bring it on, Seth Bennedict. Do your worst. I'm ready for you and your macho sex appeal.

Except five minutes later, when she heard heavy footsteps crossing the tasting-room floor, she realized that while she'd prepared herself mentally, her body hadn't been listening. Did it not understand the meaning of professional behavior? Ignoring the champagne fizz in her blood and the sultry tango of her heartbeat, she turned around just as his footsteps halted at her bar.

So.

That was as much as she could force from her brain in that first electric second of eye contact. Then she blinked the charge from her eyes and gave herself a mental shake. She needed to stop staring and start breathing or smiling or talking.

Or something.

It would help, no doubt, if she stopped staring at his eyes, his mouth, the stretch of a cornflower-blue T-shirt across his broad chest. His *anything*, really.

"How are you?" he asked. "After your fall?"

"I'm fine, thanks. It was only a tumble, barely a fall." She cleared her throat. "Where's Rachel?"

"Up at the stables. I bet she's feeding your pony rice cakes with peanut butter right about now."

"In which case my pony will be her slave for life." Jillian felt his gaze dip to her mouth, to her smile, and her heart warmed in her chest. "It also puts me in my place."

His brows lifted in a silent question.

"I thought her visit this afternoon was to thank me. At least, that's what my mother implied. Do you suppose it was a ruse to visit Monty?"

"I don't doubt it for a second."

Before she could do more than moisten her lips—and feel his gaze follow the sweep of her tongue in another flutter of heat—he said, "Your mother was right."

"About the purpose of your visit or something else?"

"She guessed you'd be packing up." He inclined his

head toward the boxes of glasses stacked on the bar. "She thought I could be useful. Where does this have to go?"

"The cellar."

"Now?"

"Well, I have a builder starting here some time tomorrow," she said, straight-faced. "Everything has to be moved out beforehand."

"You're not intending to do that by yourself?"

"Eli's organized some cellar staff to come in later and clear out all the big stuff. I'm only taking care of the glasses and bottles."

One dark brow lifted. "You don't trust anyone else with the glassware?"

Jillian smiled and prodded one of the boxes down the bar toward him. "I trust you."

A throwaway line in an exchange of banter should not have imbued the room with heavy meaning. And perhaps it didn't. Perhaps it was his response, his still intensity as he locked eyes with her.

"Do you?" he asked slowly.

Yes, she trusted him with her tools of the trade. She had complete faith in his word and his straightforwardness and his honesty. And, she realized with a pang of surprise, she *would* turn to Seth Bennedict again. She trusted him as a builder, as a friend of sorts, and as a person she could depend upon and borrow strength from in a crisis.

But as a man, as a potential lover?

Her heart danced a couple of hot, heavy steps. No, it wasn't Seth she feared. It was herself, her own lack of judgment, her own inability to tell lust from love. And she certainly didn't trust this sensual soul he'd awakened from its long, deep slumber.

"Do you trust me, Jillian?"

"Yes," she admitted. "I do."

He nodded, just once. Then he stacked three boxes together and picked them up. "Good. While we're taking these down to your cellar, you can tell me what was going on with you yesterday evening."

Jillian blinked at the rapid change in mood, in pace, in topic. "What do you mean?"

"You promised to tell me why you were out riding so late. And why you were so distracted that you fell off."

"Was unseated," she muttered. Then, when he looked askance, she waved her nit-picking comment aside and slipped out from behind the bar. "I imagine you've heard the latest about Spencer Ashton?"

"There's talk your family's taking him to court."

She picked up one box of bottles from the bar and headed toward the winery. "I'm hoping it doesn't come to that. For Mom's sake."

"From what I've heard, the Ashton estate should have been hers." Seth nudged the swinging door open with his hip and elbow and motioned for her to go first. "Seems like she has cause to sue."

"That's what Eli says, and I know it's not right that she lost all the Lattimer assets, but she hates what could happen in the backlash. To our family and to his other family. *Families,*" she amended on a note of disgust. "Lord knows how many more of those he has hidden away!"

They kept moving, down the narrow hallway, through another door and into the winery. Just talking and thinking about Anna Sheridan's story—and Grant Ashton's beforehand—tied her stomach in knots.

She bore Spencer Ashton's genes. This unprincipled, unfaithful, cheating bastard was her birth father. In the mirror every morning and every night she saw his eyes, his nose, his height and his long, lean bones. And at least once every day she thanked the Lord for her mother's steady, loving influence that had balanced the brew.

Her mother, who now had so much to deal with, all over again.

"When I got home from work yesterday afternoon, we had a visitor," she said. "At least, Mom had a visitor."

"Anna Sheridan?"

Jillian stopped dead in her tracks, eyes widening as she rounded on him. "You *know* Anna?"

"I met her back at the house just now."

Well, of course he had. If her brain weren't so addled she would have worked that out herself. "Did you happen to meet Jack?"

"Yeah. Cute kid." Steady, perceptive eyes fixed on hers. "I'm guessing this is one of those hidden families you mentioned."

"Nice guess." She exhaled heavily. "The cute kid's mother was Spencer's secretary. She died not long after having the baby."

"Anna's not his mother?"

"His aunt. She's had custody ever since her sister died. She was doing just fine without Spencer's help until the news about Jack's paternity hit the tabloids. Then she had the pleasure of a raft of photographers staking out her doorstep."

"Oh, and some nutso is sending her threatening letters."

With a box of glassware occupying her hands, Jillian couldn't throw them in the air to illustrate her frustrated impotence. So she growled instead. Growled and swung away, stalking off toward the cellar entrance.

Seth caught up in three long-legged strides.

"And she came to *Caroline* for help? Why not the police?"

His puzzlement echoed her own reaction the previous day, when Mercedes dropped the clanger on her. "Apparently the police investigated and came up with zip. She thought Spencer might be able to use his influence, to get the police to take the threats more seriously or something, except she couldn't get to see him and she had to get out of San Francisco."

"Did she try his estate?"

"Yes and his wife all but ran her off. I gather she either didn't believe Anna or didn't want to believe her, and Megan—one of her daughters—overheard and suggested she come and see Mom."

"This was yesterday afternoon and she's still here?" he asked slowly. "That's some visit."

"And it's going to get a whole lot longer!"

Jillian stopped. It was either that, slam into the cellar door, or turn and stride back from where she'd come. She exhaled harshly, and discovered she'd spent enough aggravation to continue in a more reasonable tone. "When Mom heard that Anna and Jack were living in a sleazy motel room, she insisted they move into a guest room at the Vines."

"And you have a problem with this stranger moving in?"

"No, that's not it. You met Anna. She's gutsy, she's genuine, and she dotes on little Jack. She only agreed to stay after Mom played the guilt card over what's best for him."

Jillian's brows drew together in concentration as she tried to settle on what, exactly, disturbed her most. There was so much to choose from.

"I'm worried about how this whole situation will affect Mom," she decided finally.

"She didn't look worried or upset today."

Trust him—a man—to sound so reasonable. "I know, but she stews over things. At night, when she's not sleeping. How could she not be affected by this? Spencer's current wife was his secretary, too, you know. When Mom was married to the bastard."

"History repeats," Seth said evenly.

"In Spencer's case, over and over again."

She felt his gaze on her face, lingering on the tired circles beneath her eyes, touching her with that same velvet-edged tenderness as last night. "Sounds like *you* need to do something more positive and less dangerous than stewing and losing sleep."

Her reflexes kicked in before her brain, stiffening her shoulders, framing the automatic objection. What about the family celebration she and Mercedes were planning for the new tasting room? That was positive, wasn't it?

Or was it only a cosmetic fix? Like a fancy label plastered on a bottle of poor wine—nice effect, but unlikely to fool anyone once the cork came out.

Jillian inhaled deeply through her nose, and the familiar layers of fruit and oak that pervaded the winery air steadied her churning emotions. The man at her elbow might unsteady her senses but talking to him was no hardship, she realized. Not even when the topic itself was.

"You're right," she admitted softly.

"I usually am."

That response startled a snort of laughter from Jillian, and with it an easing of the tension in her shoulders and neck and head. Seth was more right than he knew, she decided in a moment of absolute clarity. This renovation project was only step one in building her future. Steps two through ten involved clearing away the rubble of her past, starting with Spencer Ashton and working her way up.

And once you clear away that rubble, will you be ready for a man like Seth Bennedict?

A wild little rhythm beat in her chest as she cast a sideways glance at her companion and found him watching her, all serious and intense for three rapid heartbeats before he jerked his head toward the door and eased the mood with a dry comment.

"I don't know about you, but if I don't dump these boxes my arms are gonna be permanently curled."

Jillian breathed a sigh of relief and cut him a look through her lashes. "Your fault for going all macho and taking three boxes."

"I can handle 'em."

And to illustrate, he shifted the entire load into one arm—Jillian's breath hitched with shattered-glass fear and, yes, because of how his biceps flexed as it took the extra weight. Vaguely she registered him reaching out to open the cellar door. Mostly she registered the heat and scent of his body as she ducked under his arm and started down the stairs.

"Steady," he cautioned from behind.

"I know these stairs like the back of my hand." She glanced over her shoulder, all cool and haughty until she realized that Seth lagged two stairs behind. Which meant she copped a nice eyeful of strong thighs gloved in faded denim. Big and bold and full-bodied.

"I could take them with my eyes closed," she finished, turning smartly to face front. *"Them" meaning stairs, not his jeans.*

"Well, don't," he said dryly. "I'm not up for dusting off your backside again."

Jillian scooted down the rest of the stairs without a word. She did not think about his hands on her backside or about taking his jeans with her eyes closed. Much.

She deposited her box on the long table she'd coaxed Eli into setting up that morning and watched Seth follow suit. A new tension seeped into her body, as sultry and musty as the cellar atmosphere with its rich scents of aging wine and earth and timber.

Empty hands, alone with this man, in the place where her senses sang with the spirit of wine.

Not good, Jillian, not good.

Leaning her hips against the edge of the table, she forced herself to relax. She would not run away. She would face temptation with mature, rational calm. "This," she said, patting the table with one hand, "is where we'll be doing the tastings while you're working upstairs."

Apparently he took that table pat as an invitation, since he parked his denims right beside her, not touching but close enough for her hormones to rattle and hum with near-Seth stimulation. To flex muscles of their own as they sucked in deep drafts of his body heat.

She should move. She didn't.

Seth was looking around through narrowed eyes, a long, slow sweep of their high-ceilinged subterranean world, and Jillian followed his gaze. Attempted to experience it with fresh senses, as he was doing now and as her tasting-room visitors would over the next few weeks.

"The controlled temperature and the low light are ideal for the wine. For aging and storage," she said.

"But not so good for your tastings?"

"I'm looking forward to the change, actually, and I've always loved the atmosphere down here. My brothers locked me in once, when I was eight or nine, and they hated that I didn't dissolve with terror." A soft smile curved her lips as she remembered. "I asked Lucas that night if I could move in down here."

"Did he let you?"

"He convinced me my ponies would hate it."

One dark brow arched. "You had a collection back then?"

"Lucas gave me my first the year we moved here. I wasn't much older than Rachel," she said softly. "My stepfather is responsible for my two grand passions. Horses and wine."

"Your only two passions?"

She turned then, found him studying her. Dark, silent,

still. A tiny ripple of excitement raced over her skin. Did she want to answer that question? Did she even know the answer?

Two things she did know.

He was going to kiss her. And she was going to let him.

Seven

"Just a taste," Seth murmured as their eyes met and held and his body resounded with the knowledge that she wasn't going to stiffen or turn away, that she wasn't going to reject his kiss.

One sip, he promised himself, as his lips slanted over hers and stilled in surprise. Unexpectedly cool, those lips, when her reminiscent smile had warmed him right through. Cool and exquisitely soft, like the first sip of a delicate white.

"Another," she whispered against his lips and when Seth hesitated, her breath hitched and caught at his willpower.

No, he cautioned himself. *Bad idea.*

But then her hand crept up his arm, her fingers curled around his biceps, and her mouth moved against his. "One more taste," she pleaded, a low, husky appeal that curled through his blood like liquid temptation.

What harm could one small sample do? One sip of the passion he felt simmering beneath his mouth and his hands?

When his lips moved over hers, changing the angle and deepening the contact, she made a tiny yielding sound. Barely a sigh, it echoed through his body, bouncing off every tense, hard surface—and there were plenty—until it thundered in time with his pulse. It didn't help that her other hand had fastened around his neck, holding him tight, urging him to forget every take-it-slow vow he'd ever made to himself.

Then her mouth opened under his and he was a goner.

Their tongues met and the essence of the kiss changed in one stroke of heat. Like one of her big California reds, she exploded in his mouth. Hot, intense, packed with complex flavors he knew would linger long after this kiss had ended.

End it now, he told himself. *While you can.*

Ah, but he couldn't, not when this had been so many years coming, this chance to get his hands and his mouth on Jillian Ashton. He nipped at her bottom lip and dived back into her mouth. He eased back to taste her lips with his tongue, to press kisses to the corner of her mouth, to her chin, to her lips again. He kissed her throat because he couldn't stop himself, and she tasted as he'd imagined, as addictively sweet and supple as the flesh under his fingertips. The flesh that curved in wicked torment—

He stopped cold.

He had his hands inside her jeans?

What had happened to take it slow, earn her trust, give her time? How far did he think he could stretch his willpower before it snapped? Before he lay her down on this table and ripped away her clothes and tasted the wine and woman on her body, in places he'd dreamed about, in ways he'd only fantasized about, for so many years.

Not the kind of horizontal tasting this table was intended for.

Carefully he slid his hands from the curves of her backside and up to her waist. He put her away from him and watched her faraway green gaze struggle to refocus as her grip loosened and slipped away from his neck.

And there they sat in an awkward afterward vacuum, their breathing ragged, her face flushed with sensual heat and his feeling about the same. Seth figured he should keep his mouth zipped until his brain started being helpful. Anything would be better than his current mental blame game. It didn't matter who started the kiss or who goaded whom for more, only that he'd extinguished the hot connection before it burned out of control.

He should apologize—she probably expected at least a *sorry, won't happen again*—but, dammit, he wasn't sorry.

"I'd forgotten about kissing."

Huh? Seth stared back at her for a second, completely thrown by her comment. "You'd forgotten what?" he asked, since she clearly hadn't forgotten the how-to part. Maybe, like him, she was having trouble with cognitive function.

"The things that stir my juices," she murmured absently. "Like a good wine or a hot gallop."

He hadn't known what to expect from Jillian, what reaction, which first words. Fair to say he hadn't expected that comparison. "Are you saying that kissing should be on your short list of passions?"

"Possibly." She pressed her fingertips to her lips, then—*holy Moses*—she reached up and touched him the exact same way. "And it should be on your list of skills."

"Yeah?"

"Oh, yeah."

God, she was turning him inside out. The candor of her words, the heat in her eyes, the gliding touch of her fingertips across his cheek. Seth covered her hand with his, trapping it against his cheek and savoring its smooth warmth for the time it took him to feel something else.

The smooth warmth of her wedding band.

It lay flush against his skin, a real and visceral reminder of why he shouldn't have been kissing her. Why he shouldn't have been dreaming up some go-slow, win-her-over fantasy, either. His brother's widow still wore the symbol of her love, of her enduring connection to a man who'd scorned the sanctity of marriage.

Right up until the night he died.

Seth's gut twisted as he peeled her fingers from his face. "I shouldn't have kissed you," he said shortly, and he stood up. "I'll go get the rest of your glasses."

Confusion clouded her eyes as she stared up at him. "There's no need to do that."

Oh, yeah, there was a need. To get the hell out of here before the bitter churning in his gut had him saying things that didn't need saying. He folded his arms and narrowed his eyes. "You don't trust me with your glassware anymore?"

"I trust you, Seth. You've always been straightforward and honest with me, so please don't walk away now. Not without explaining what just happened here."

No, he hadn't always been straightforward and honest. He'd kept things from her, painful truths that he'd buried deep beneath the rubble of the past. There was no reason to share them, then or now or ever. No need to share the truth burning hot in his blood, either, but she was watching him with a steady, direct gaze, quietly pleading for the same from him.

"I haven't always been honest with you," he admitted tightly. "Not about you and me."

A stillness came over her body, her expression. "Do you mean about this…attraction?"

"Yeah. That's exactly what I mean."

"Oh, okay. Because I've felt something, too, this past week. I know—"

"Not just this week, Jillian. You had reason to feel uncomfortable around me. That kiss has been a long time coming."

Yeah, she had reason to look shocked, too. A right to stare at him with those big green eyes while the thick cellar air enclosed them in recollections of that kiss.

"And now it's been—the kiss, that is—" She swallowed and moistened her lips. "What now?"

Seth straightened, preparing to leave and get those glasses, whether she wanted them or not. Preparing to get the hell away from honest-eyed temptation.

"While you're still wearing that ring? Nothing, Jillian. Not one blessed thing."

Seth might have rocked Jillian's world on that sultry Sunday afternoon, but one breathtaking kiss and one ground-shaking revelation didn't change much in the big scheme of things.

Afterward, back at the Vines, Caroline had insisted on serving coffee and cake in her garden. Rachel snuggled onto Jillian's lap and made her chest ache with a hollow tenderness. Nobody seemed to notice the studied lack of eye contact between Seth and Jillian.

And the next day, life went on. The renovations started with Seth using the winery's two visitor-free days to attack the heavy work. Better that no walls fall on tourists, she supposed, and she'd left him alone to do his thing. He knew where to find her if needed.

Obviously he hadn't needed.

A good thing, Jillian reminded herself for the umpteenth time on Tuesday afternoon. Not seeing him meant she didn't have to worry about forgetting herself and staring at, say, his mouth in a moment of unprofessional weakness. She had enough to keep busy anyway, what with setting up the tasting stations in the cellar and priming her staff on the new layout and procedure. On top of this, she'd initiated her let's-stop-stewing-and-start-acting strategy regarding the Anna and Spencer situation.

If one could label a tentative first step with no planned future steps a strategy.

On Tuesday afternoon, with Mercedes for company and moral support, she'd visited the Ashton estate and met her half sisters Paige and Megan and their cousin Charlotte for the first time. Tea was taken, pleasantries exchanged, concerns expressed. Although nothing concrete had been accomplished, they had opened the lines of communication between the two families. And not a lawyer in sight!

A promising start, Mercedes and Jillian concluded on the drive home.

Jillian turned her car into the winery parking lot, and her heart did its usual upbeat jive when she saw the blue truck parked alongside the tasting room. Even though she was only dropping off Mercedes.

"How's the work coming along?" her sister asked from the passenger seat.

"Apart from Eli bitching about the dust? Pretty good, I'd say."

"Glad to hear it, since it looks like a nasty big mess to me."

"You think?" Jillian peered more closely and felt a quiver of excitement deep where it mattered. "Oh, look, he's done the windows!"

Mercedes stared, too. "Hate to break it to you, but those are holes in the wall."

"No, they're windows. Great big, rounded arches that reflect the shape and size of our wines."

"You've obviously been working too hard, since you're sounding scarily like me." Mercedes shook her head as she reached for her door. "Go ride your horse and clear your head of that marketing-speak."

Jillian grinned. "I intend to."

But first she needed to change clothes and report to Anna, a thought that turned her smile upside down as she drove back to the Vines. While their half sisters had seemed friendly enough, she'd seen the exchange of looks when she'd broached the topic of Anna and Jack. The cooling from friendly to wary to let's-not-push-this-too-far. It would not be easy, winning acceptance and a fair deal for this latest addition to the Ashton clan.

She parked her car and hurried upstairs, pausing at the open door of the guest room. Anna looked up from where she sat cross-legged on the floor, surrounded by piles of clothes and baby gear, and her eyes widened in surprise. "You're back."

"And still in one piece." Jillian sidestepped a stack of cuddly toys and perched on the end of the bed. "Where's Jack?"

"Being thoroughly spoiled by your parents." Anna picked up a onesie, and smoothed her hands over the garment before she looked up at Jillian again. "It didn't go well, did it?"

"Well, we met Megan and Paige and Charlotte. They were all open to what we had to say—especially Megan."

"Except?"

"Except the news about Jack has come as a shock to them. I suspect they just need a little time to adjust."

Anna released a harsh snort of breath. "I can't say I'm surprised but thanks for trying, Jillian."

"Hey, that's only step one. You're not giving up. *We're* not giving up."

"*I* won't give up." Anna clutched the onesie tight in her fingers, then pressed it to her chest. To her heart. "I'll do whatever it takes to protect him and keep him safe, you know."

Yes, Jillian did know. She saw the determined set of Anna's jaw and the fierce light in her eyes, like a tigress set to defend her cub, and it echoed in the hollow of her own maternal soul. "I'm sure I'd feel the same way if he were mine."

Anna nodded, a little stiffly, then returned her attention to the clothes. For the first time Jillian focused on that folding and stacking. "Are you packing?"

The other woman's hands stilled for a second. "I've imposed on your family's hospitality enough."

"Oh, no, you haven't even begun to impose. You haven't let me babysit once, and you know I'm dying to have Jack all to myself."

"You say that because you've never changed his diaper."

"I muck out six stables every day. One little baby is nothing."

Anna smiled at her attempted humor, but the effort looked forced. She picked up a stack of baby clothes, so small and innocent, and carefully placed them in a duffel bag. "I have to go, Jillian. I can't take your charity indefinitely and I don't want to leave owing your family any more than I do now."

Pride held her shoulders straight, and that posture and the quiet determination in her voice chimed a loud note of recognition in Jillian. She understood Anna's need for independence, to not feel beholden as she had done to Seth. Seth who had stepped in and insisted on helping, as her mother had done with Anna. Seth who wouldn't take no for an answer.

Seth, whose kiss had been a long time coming.

Jillian straightened her own shoulders, to ward off the stray stroke of desire. "Are you going back to your apartment in San Francisco?"

Anna shook her head. "I can't risk that. Between the threats and the photographers."

"Then where?"

"I'll find somewhere."

She had nowhere to go, nowhere except another cheap room like the one she'd fled to before. With nowhere for Jack to play, no company for Anna, and no security against whoever had threatened Jack's safety. Jillian leaned forward and put her hand on the other woman's shoulder.

"Stay a few more days, until you find somewhere clean and comfortable and safe for Jack. I'll help—we all will. If we put our heads together I'm sure we can come up with a decent rental. An apartment or a cottage or even a room in a boarding house." She could feel the tension in Anna's shoulder, knew pride wouldn't allow her to give in easily. "Promise you won't go right now. Give us a few days."

"Until the weekend," Anna relented finally.

Jillian smiled. "We'll find you somewhere before then. I promise."

Jillian hadn't expected to find an answer to her promise so close at hand or so soon. Half an hour later, it loomed out of her afternoon ride so unexpectedly that she reined Marsanne to a halt and just stared in why-didn't-I-think-of-that bemusement.

"Caroline's enchanted cottage," she murmured. "How utterly perfect."

She urged Marsanne into a canter and by the time they halted beside the pretty rail fence, her mind was humming with certainty. The cottage had been empty since their vineyard foreman fell for Abby Ashton and moved to Nebraska a month or two back. They could set a nominal rent, enough to satisfy Anna's pride but not too much that she couldn't afford to pay. How could she object?

Because she wanted to keep Jack safe.

Jillian's excitement dimmed as she studied the pretty but

not very childproof fence and the lake beyond. She clicked Marsanne into her long, loping stride and circled the perimeter, studying the fence with an objective eye. "It wouldn't be too big a job, would it?"

Marsanne shook her head.

"Well, yes, you're right. For me it would."

But what about for—say—a builder? A builder who had survived the toddler years as a single parent, keeping his child safe and protected and loved.

Her heart quickened and tightened in her chest.

A builder she'd avoided these past two days because she lacked the courage to deal with his answer to her "what now?" question.

It had been so much easier to bury herself in work and the busy-ness of life than to face the consequences of that kiss and Seth's admission. *That kiss has been a long time coming.*

"Not good enough, Jillian," she muttered, stiffening her spine despite the clutch of nerves in her stomach.

Today, by driving up to the Ashton estate and meeting her half sisters, she had conquered one fear of the unknown. Perhaps, she decided as she touched thumb to ring finger and turned her horse back toward the winery, it was time to face another.

Seth had left before Jillian rode up to the winery on Tuesday afternoon, but she caught him on his cell phone the next day. He was working on another job, but he promised to take a look at the problematic fence before the weekend. Sometime. Thursday he found himself driving by Louret on his way home from a site inspection, and he decided he might as well swing by the cottage.

Three minutes, give or take, and he'd worked out a fix for the fence. He'd also worked up a decent level of irritation. Any half-handy vineyard or winery worker—or brother or stepfather—could have repaired this fence. She hadn't needed to call in a builder any more than he'd needed to say, "Sure, no problem, I'll take a look."

Hell, and weren't those the words that got him into trouble in the first place? Agreeing to take a look at her tasting room when every instinct had screamed "no" and "are you a masochist?"

Seth stalked to his truck and slapped on a tool belt. Since he was here, he might as well fix the loose screen he'd seen on one of the windows round back. While he was at it, he'd check all the latches. According to Jillian, Anna Sheridan was nervous about security.

He heard a vehicle but paid no attention until it pulled up out front. Then every disgruntled cell in his body stood up and took notice. Damn. He didn't even know who was out there. It could be Anna or Caroline or some half-handy worker come to fix the blessed fence.

Except it wasn't.

Instinctively he knew that before he saw her coming through the gate, her arms loaded up to her chin with God knows what. With his truck parked in clear sight, his presence here was pretty much a given. Yet Jillian pulled up short when she saw him round the corner of the veranda. Her mouth softened in a soft "oh" of surprise, and all Seth could think about was that kiss.

Four days and he could still taste her on his lips and in his blood. Four nights of shouldn't-have-done-it recriminations and all he wanted now was to kiss her again. To simply walk right up and take that open mouth with his.

Except he didn't.

Instead he leaned his shoulder against a veranda post, crossed his arms, and concentrated on anything but her mouth's wet heat.

The stuff in her arms. That would do for starters.

"Moving in?" he asked, inclining his head toward her heavily laden arms.

She blinked, then glanced down. "Oh, this. No. It's just some things for Anna, to make the place more comfortable. For Jack's room, mostly."

"She's agreed to take the place?"

"She took some convincing, but yes." With a small grimace, she readjusted her load. "This isn't heavy, but it's awkward. Maybe you could get the door for me…?"

The door. Right. He straightened and started to turn. Then remembered it was locked. "Keys?"

"In my hand." She jiggled the keys in said hand, somewhere beneath the voluminous folds of what looked like a duvet. Then, with a sharp yelp of alarm, she clutched at her slipping cargo.

Seth leaped in to help—what else could he do?—and ended up with his arms full of soft duvet and his veins filled with the heat of body contact. Carefully, with a minimum of self-indulgence, he redistributed the weight.

"It's okay, I've got it," she said, her voice low and husky. They were standing close, and when he looked down into her face their eyes met and held, and the connection, her nearness, the four-day-old kiss pulsed through him with the slow, steady beat of desire.

"The door," she said quickly. "Can you please get the door because this is starting to slip again?"

Yeah, and so was his willpower. One kiss, one taste, one fleeting contact arm-against-breast and he wanted so much more. He wanted—

With a snort of disgust, Seth swung away and strode to the door. *He wanted a good hard kick to his senses. He wanted his head examined. He wanted to build a wall of aggravation to keep this insidious desire at bay.*

"Any more in your car?"

"No." She shook her head. "Mom had Lucas bring down the cot and some other bits and pieces earlier."

"You didn't think Lucas could have checked the fence, too? Seeing as he was here?"

She'd started fussing with the duvet and a baby blanket, folding them, smoothing them, but his snippy tone brought her head up slowly. "Yes, but I thought you'd do a better job, since you've probably faced the same toddler-proofing problems with Rachel."

"It's not rocket science."

"If you didn't want to help me," she said, her tone frostier with each carefully delivered word, "you should have said so."

She was right, but why waste her snooty mood? Why not slap a few more bricks on the wall?

"I'm not doing this to help you, Jillian." He crossed to the living-room window and checked the catch. "I'm helping Anna. Seems like she can use all the help she can get."

As he moved to the kitchen, he felt her gaze shadowing him every step of the way. Felt it in every tense muscle of his body, every wired nerve. In every brain cell that urged him to stop acting like a jerk and admit what he wanted, straight-up and honest.

Except what would be the point? He wanted her, but how could he have her?

"I'm glad you see it that way," she said finally. "Anna can use a friend or two."

"Yeah, well, I wouldn't have felt the same way about her sister."

"Why is that?"

Slowly he turned from the window and met her puzzled gaze. "She had an affair with a married man."

He brushed by her on his way out of the kitchen, left

BRONWYN JAMESON

her standing there in stunned silence, while he moved from room to room, systematically noting the locks that needed changing, the latches he could shore up. Work, system, routine: the props that had kept him functioning through his short and troubled marriage, and through his discovery of Karen's infidelity.

Jason hadn't cared that she wore a wedding band or that she was married to his own brother, but he wasn't like his brother. He would never sleep with another man's wife…or widow while she still wore that ring.

Why the hell did she still wear it?

Why the hell don't you ask her?

Seth huffed out a breath. Yeah, it was time to talk. It was past time.

He walked to the last room and saw that she'd spread the brightly patterned duvet over a single bed and draped the baby's blanket over the side of a cot. Jillian herself stood with her back to the door, holding a framed picture to the wall, and the sight of her there, amidst all the trappings of family, hit him hard.

Same as the day at the Vines when she'd taken Rachel to check out her pony collection. Same as Sunday evening, in Caroline's garden, with Rachel's pigtails mushed trustingly against her shoulder.

Damn, but this was supposed to be physical. The sweet ache of lust, the slow throb of sexual need. That's all he wanted. No emotion, no happy families. None of that phony fantasy.

"You want that picture hung?" he asked, his voice as surly as his mood.

"Yes, but I can manage." Cool, so very cool. And she didn't even turn around. "Have you finished out there?"

"Checking the locks, yes." He stalked over and took the picture out of her hands. "Center of this wall?"

For a second he thought she would argue—for a second he hoped she would—but then she nodded stiffly. "Where you have it is fine."

Not a picture, he noticed after he'd positioned the small whitewood frame, but a message done in some kind of fancy stitching.

You're braver than you believe, stronger than you seem, smarter than you think.

"Yours?" he asked.

"My mother made it for me." Then she said, "It's from *Winnie-the Pooh*."

"Huh." He straightened the frame and stepped back from the wall, his ragged mood soothed by the simple task of hammering a nail. And by her softly voiced explanation. "I didn't know the bear was such a philosopher."

"Christopher Robin said it to Pooh."

"Not sage advice from mother to daughter?" he asked as he moved forward and thumbed the frame up a tenth on the left. He edged back and surveyed it through narrowed eyes. Gave a small grunt of satisfaction. Waited for Jillian's response.

She couldn't answer right away. She'd been so ready to show him the door, to slam it on his moody brooding back, but that quiet question turned her around all over again. The affirming message, stitched by her mother's hand so many years ago, resounded through her with an escalating rhythm, reminding her of the decision she'd made two days before.

A decision made and put on hold.

Well, Christopher Robin, let's see how brave and strong and smart I am.

Drawing a deep give-me-courage breath, she turned to face Seth. The hand she extended trembled like a newborn colt, but she still managed to hold her shoulders straight as she splayed the naked fingers of her left hand.

"It feels very strange after wearing it for so long." She wriggled her fingers. Yes, it felt strange in several ways. Strange unfamiliar, strange scary, and strangely liberating now she'd finally taken this positive step forward, out of the shadows of the past.

"Why did you keep wearing it?" he asked after one long beat of intense silence.

"Not because I still felt married or bound to Jason." And since her hand wouldn't stop shaking, she tucked it in the pocket of her jeans. Then she lifted her chin and looked right at him. "I wore it as a reminder of all that marriage cost me. I'm ready to put that behind me, now. To move on."

"What are you telling me?"

"I'm not telling, Seth, I'm asking." Jillian paused to moisten her suddenly dry mouth. "What now, Seth? Now that I'm not wearing the ring?"

Eight

Still and silent, he stared back at her, but today that intensity didn't make Jillian uncomfortable. The fact she'd obviously read him wrong did. She'd thought that Seth wanted her, but then she'd believed the same of Jason.

Could she be any worse a judge of men and their motives?

"I'm sorry," she said briskly, avoiding Seth's eyes in case she detected any—Lord help her—pity. That would be the last straw. "I've overstepped and put you in an awkward situation. Forget I said anything."

She swung away and would have kept on walking, except his harsh expulsion of breath brought her gaze back around. And what she saw there halted her in her tracks. Her limbs, her thoughts, her heart all seized in that one second of sizzling heat.

"Why would you think I could forget it?" he asked.

"You didn't say anything. You didn't respond. You just stood there looking so…stunned."

"Yeah, well, you got that right." He shook his head slowly. "Hell, Jillian, you could have given me some kind of warning."

"I'm sorry, but I don't know the warning system. Is it lights or hand signals or semaphore flags?"

His response fell somewhere between a snort and a laugh, which would have gotten Jillian's back up again if not for the heat in his eyes. They remained steady and unwavering on hers, igniting a lick of hunger in her veins and a surge of courage in her gut.

"So." She lifted her chin a fraction. "You said the kiss was a long time coming."

"I did."

"And was it worth the wait? Was it something you might want to repeat or was once enough?"

"One kiss wasn't close to enough," he said, his voice as deep and dark and hot as his eyes. "I want to do much more than kiss your mouth."

"Oh." Heat suffused her skin, a small part of her shocked and a much larger part aroused. Intensely aroused. "More…in what way?"

"Don't push me, Jillian. My willpower is hanging by a loose nail here."

Okay, but she had to know where she stood, in case the nail gave way while she was standing in the danger zone. In case all that dark and dangerous intensity came toppling down on top of her. "I just need you to tell me straight, so there's no misunderstanding. Is that all right?"

His expression screamed no, it's far from all right.

"Please?"

His nostrils flared slightly and he jutted his chin in a gesture that was pure male aggression. Jillian's heart did an *uh-oh* kind of lurch, but then it was too late to back down. He'd started talking. Telling her exactly what he wanted to do with her in short, blatant terms that blew her mind and tempted her secret, hidden core.

He wanted sex—all those ways—with her, the good girl, the ice princess, the wife who couldn't keep her husband satisfied. Oh, wow.

Jillian closed her mouth and swallowed audibly. Their eyes clashed with enough heat to set the timber cottage ablaze. She didn't blink, didn't flinch, just held his gaze with wide-eyed, I'm-shocked-but-in-the-nicest-way interest, and stunned them both by saying, "Okay."

Okay?

Seth stared back, unable to muster enough blood to jump-start his brain for several long drawn-out seconds. Enough blood had mustered in other places to jump-start all kinds of motors, to send them revving and roaring and rocketing into overdrive.

"Okay?" he asked finally, on a rising note of disbelief. "All you have to say is 'okay'?"

"Actually, no." A whisper of a smile crossed her lips. "But I'm having some trouble with words. With finding a path from here—" she tapped her head "—to here." She touched those same fingers to her mouth. "I suspect your straight talk just melted a few synapses."

Yeah, well, same here, he thought. He'd thought he'd shock her right out the door with his hard-core honesty, by laying his every erotic midnight fantasy on the line, but all he'd done—apparently—was incite her sloe-eyed interest.

She couldn't want to do all that with him.

His head spun with the improbability. And then he remembered the look on her face when she'd galloped up that hill. He recalled her passion in the tasting room and the cab sav headiness of her kiss.

Yeah, she could.

"Have you found those words yet?" he asked, needing

to know for sure. To hear more than "okay" from her lips. He didn't know whether it was dread or hope that thudded hard in his blood and his head and his ears, whether he wanted her to tell him to go to hell or to see her start unbuttoning the prissy pink shirt she wore.

"Sex," he said, just to make sure she had the picture. "Once, not as any kind of a relationship."

"I'm not looking for a relationship, Seth. I don't have a great record with those. But I've never had a one-night stand or an affair or whatever this is we're talking about. How do we, um, go about this?"

With creditable control Seth rocked back on his heels. "You sure you don't want to think it over?"

"Good Lord, no! After all those things you said…" She huffed out a breath and straightened her backbone decisively. "I don't want to think about it, Seth. I want to do it."

She was killing him. Slowly. Inch by painful inch.

"The logistics are going to be awkward," she continued in a rush, "since I can't ask you over to my place and vice versa. Do we book a room somewhere?"

Hell, no. The tacky hotel room was Jason's modus operandi. Get a woman, get a room. Seth's jaw locked hard. He couldn't do this, not this way. "We're not getting a room."

"Well, there is here," she suggested after a moment's hesitation. Her hands waved around to indicate the cottage. "It's empty until Anna moves in. And sort of isolated."

Which made it sound as if they'd be sneaking around behind her parents' back like a pair of horny teenagers. Didn't that just beat everything? She lived with her parents. He lived with his daughter. And this wasn't going to happen.

He rubbed the back of his neck, tried to find the words, discovered that the one word he needed to say—no—kept sticking in his throat.

"How would Saturday night be?" she asked, hesitant,

hopeful. "I'm babysitting Jack tomorrow night while Mom and Mercedes take Anna out to dinner. Maybe I could fix a pic—"

"I've got something on Saturday night."

Her mouth formed a silent "oh." Disappointment and something else flickered in her eyes, then she looked away. Moistened her lips. "Like…a date?"

"You think I'm dating someone? And spending every night thinking about sex with you?"

A flush pinkened her cheeks but she lifted her chin. "Of course not. That just slipped out. I suppose it's something to do with work?"

Yeah, right, because that was the only social life he had. It irked him that she was right, irked him that she was watching him and waiting for an explanation. "It's a dinner up near Oakville. Robert and Sophia Neumann asked—"

"You're going to the Casinelli dinner? Wow. I am speechless!" But only for a second, because then she was shaking her head and saying in an awed tone, "I heard Sophia's pouring her 2001 pinot noir and you can't get a ticket for love or money. How did you come to get one?"

"They're friends."

"I adore their wines. Are you good friends? Old friends?"

Irritated with her enthusiasm, and more with the whole situation of wanting a woman and not being able to say *right, let's just do it,* he leveled a piercing gaze at her shiny-eyed face. "What is it you want, Jillian? An introduction? A job reference?"

He might as well have slapped her, she recoiled so sharply. "Of course I don't want anything like that."

Cool tone, haughty expression, hurt eyes. And Seth realized what he'd accused her of and how that would sit. Jason had used her that way. He'd pursued her and married her for a shot at the Ashton name and money and connections with the wine industry.

And that's exactly why Seth had never broadcast his close friendship with the couple behind the world-famous Casinelli label. Jason would have used that, too. Jillian wouldn't—she had too much class, too much pride, too much self-respect.

"I'm sorry," he said. "I was way out of line."

"You don't have to apologize."

"Yeah, I do." And he also needed to do something to repair the damage of his thoughtless words, to wipe away the cool detachment that he knew was her defense. To bring back the sass and the heat of the cab sav woman. He bent down and touched her shoulder. "Hey. I really am sorry."

"I shouldn't have pried. I just got carried away by the notion of the Casinelli dinner." A wry smile quirked her lips. "I guess I poured the enthusiasm with a heavy hand."

Don't do it, Seth. You don't want a date; you don't even know if you want to risk the complications of uncomplicated sex with this woman. "You'd like to go?"

She went very still. "Don't mess with me, Seth."

"Is that a yes or a no?"

"Sophia Neumann is a goddess. I worship the grapes she walks upon."

"But?"

Slowly she shook her head. "But I feel as if I've finagled this invitation and that's—"

"Do you want to go or not?" He looked into her face and saw the suppressed gleam of longing. "I'll pick you up at seven."

She opened her mouth, probably to object, then closed it again. Smart girl. He'd made up his mind—she was going. And right now he had to be going. He'd stayed far longer than intended and Rachel would be testing Rosa's considerable patience with her heavy-duty where's Daddy nagging.

Later he would deal with Jillian's *okay, I want to do it* bolt from the blue. Because for all his big talk about how many ways he wanted to make her come, the notion of booking a room for a sexual tryst didn't sit right. She was his sister-in-law, his daughter's Aunt Jellie, his seven-year fantasy, his—

"Wait."

Scowling, Seth stopped in the doorway and turned back.

"What will I wear on Saturday night? I mean, what's the dress code?"

"Black tie," he said, amused by her very female reaction despite himself. "There'll be plenty of serious money on show, so don't be afraid to knock yourself out."

Knock yourself out? Man, she knocked *him* out when she came down the winding staircase at The Vines, looking like his idea of a goddess in a dress that draped around her body and flowed with her long legs. It was red, as in the cherry-rich hue of a young cabernet. Red, as in the color of passion. Red, as in, the blood hurtling through his veins and the haze that clouded his vision.

When he whistled through his teeth, she stopped a couple of stairs from the bottom, her brows pinched together. "Is it too much? Too 'look-at-me?'"

"Take off the wrap and turn around."

After only a beat of hesitation she did. And, yeah, with the one shoulder strap and a low-cut back that bared about an acre of silky skin and with whatever the hell she'd done with her hair to draw attention to the elegant length of her neck—

How could she look so cool and classy and so damn hot at the same time?

"Well?" she asked, still frowning.

"Yeah, it's 'look-at-me,'" he said slowly. "But not too much."

That seemed to please her, or at least to reassure her. She relaxed enough to almost smile—and to give him a covert once-over through her lashes—as she came down those last steps.

"Do I pass muster?" he asked.

A delicate flush climbed her cheeks. "I haven't ever seen you in a tux. It's…well, it's a change from the jeans and toolbelt I last saw you wearing."

At the cottage.

Reference to that place and time weighted the mood as he took the wrap from her hands and moved around her, draping it over her shoulders as he went.

"I like your hair." Better, he liked the way it curled around her ears and exposed that sexy bite-me neck. He traced its silky length with the knuckles of one hand and leaned closer to breathe the warm scent of her skin. "And the way you smell."

"I'm not wearing any perfume. I never do. It interferes with the tasting."

"I know." He stepped back. "Ready?"

A pulse fluttered at the base of her throat, but she lifted her chin and met his eyes. "Ready as I'm ever going to be."

Yeah, but was he?

Seth rarely enjoyed this kind of function, no matter how lauded the chef or the wines. He'd accepted the invitation because it was a charity fundraiser and because Robert had caught him at a weak moment. He didn't expect to enjoy himself, yet that's exactly what he was doing.

How could he not get a kick out of watching Jillian?

Surrounded by winemakers and wine lovers and, yeah, the wine snobs these events attracted like ants to a picnic, she was in her element. Seth sat back and watched as the tension from their taxi drive up to Oakville unraveled in a shimmering ribbon of wine talk.

Sure, it helped knowing he was responsible for bringing her here and for the animated pleasure in her eyes and the glow of heat in her skin. Because while she seemed riveted to the conversation that flowed across the table and back, she was also very aware of Seth at her side. Without words, without more than a fleeting touch and a momentary sizzle of eye contact, he knew she was as finely attuned to his presence as he was to hers. And, in a warped kind of way, he was enjoying the torture of a body already turned on by anticipation.

She was, after all, going home with him.

A waiter appeared at her elbow to clear away the second course, disrupting her discussion with an intense-looking vintner on her right.

"Enjoying yourself?" he asked.

Her response, a guttural *mmmm* of pleasure, played nasty games with his state of semi-arousal. "Only one bad moment so far."

Seth lifted a brow.

"That French winemaker we met earlier? He works for my—" Her brows came together in a half frown. "For Spencer. For Ashton Estates."

"And?"

"I had a moment, a tiny panic, thinking this is exactly the sort of function Spencer might be at." She huffed out a soft sound of derision. "Ridiculous, since even if he were here, I wouldn't need worry my cheeks about it."

"He avoids you?"

"Oh, I wouldn't say 'avoids.' That would denote action when he just doesn't notice we exist. Anyway—" she waved a dismissive hand and her tone turned upbeat "—I am enjoying myself, immensely, so let's forget I mentioned it."

Seth wouldn't forget, not when the vulnerability behind her remark caught hard in his chest, but he could pretend. The last thing he wanted was for the mood to turn serious and intense. The second-last thing he wanted was the shadow of Spencer Ashton—the man she took such pains not to describe as "my father"—darkening her enjoyment.

"Forgotten," he lied, and she rewarded him with a wide smile.

"Thank you for inviting me, Seth."

"My pleasure."

He met her eyes and didn't bother hiding that pleasure was, indeed, front and center in his mind. Heat sparked in that knowledge and smoldered between them until a waiter risked third-degree burns by leaning in to pour the next wine. Jillian thanked him and the waiter departed, his job done.

Seth touched the back of her hand with his knuckles and inclined his head toward the newly poured wine, left to breathe as they awaited the next course of food. "Well, there it is. Your reason for coming tonight."

"Not the only reason." She moved her hand against his— just a brush of contact but it sizzled through his knuckles like hot solder. "Not the only reason, but a nice incentive."

A smile whispered over her lips as she touched her wine glass, fingertips to stem in a delicate gliding contact. Probably innocent. Probably not meant to provoke, but that's what it did. Already he was one sorry case of aroused red corpuscles, and with three courses still to go. He swallowed hard. Better than groaning out loud, he figured.

"I'm like a child at Christmas," she said softly, "waiting to open my Santa present."

Yeah, he agreed silently. Same. He inclined his head toward the wine. "What is so special about this Santa present?"

"Everything."

"You want to expand on that?"

"Oh, I could expand on that for hours," she said through a smile, "but I don't want to put you to sleep."

Not that that was a remote possibility, but Seth played along. "Give me the abridged version and I'll take my chances."

"Okay." She tilted her head, eyes narrowed thoughtfully. "Everyone's trying to make a pinot noir these days. It's like the wine of the moment, the new chardonnay, but pinot's an unforgiving little beggar. It's not only a matter of vinifying the grapes—which Sophia does better than anyone on this side of the world—but in growing them right, since it's a terroir wine."

"Meaning?"

"It expresses the vineyard conditions more than other varieties. If you can find the right soil and microclimate, and you can plant your vines thick enough, and if you can get into that pocket of hell-dirt to tend and pick the grapes, *then* you stand a chance of making a pinot like this."

She picked up her glass by the stem, tilted it so the color stood out in stark contrast to the white tablecloth. *Like the cherry-red silk of her dress against porcelain pale skin.*

"Look at that," she said in raw reverence. "Beautiful."

Yeah. Beautiful.

"This is the wine I want to make one day." Gently she swirled her glass, and the set of her mouth turned rueful. "Well, not this wine, precisely, since Sophia has already made it. But my own thing of divine beauty."

"Louret makes a decent pinot."

"*Eli* does," she corrected, "and he'd thank you not to refer to it as merely decent."

So, she wanted to make her own wine, and not just any

wine, but a great wine. From what sounded like the fussi-
est grapes. "Your own label?" he asked, "Or for Louret?"

"I'd love to make for Louret, but Eli's got that covered.
Then there's Mason waiting in the wings."

Matter-of-fact, no bitterness, but just a hint of yearning
in her eyes. Not for the first time, Seth considered the family dynamics and what it must be like to work in such an
environment. Yeah, there was a lot of love and support, but
tough for the youngest to prove herself with such dominant
forces as Eli and Cole Ashton running the show.

"You have the resources to hand-make a small batch
under your own name."

"Yes and no." A small frown creased her brow as she
swirled the contents of her glass. "I would need to source
the grapes."

"Is that a problem?"

"Getting the right grapes is. They're low yielding, high
cost. Difficult, temperamental, risky. And, Lord knows,
I've had enough of those things to last the rest of my life!"

"Some risks are worth taking."

"And some definitely aren't." Her gaze swung up from
her glass, serious, intense, troubled. "How does a person
distinguish which is which?"

Was she talking about wine making? Her low-yielding,
high-cost, difficult, temperamental ex-husband? Or about
the risk involved in, say, a knee-jerk "okay"? The risk that
it wouldn't be about sex, that once wouldn't be enough, that
there'd be no delineation between fantasy and reality…

"You trust your instincts. Go with your gut or with
storybook philosophy—whatever works." What else could
he say? What advice could he give from his own sorry state
of flux? "Sometimes they're all screaming 'too risky' and
you've got to do it anyway. The passion's got your throat
in a choke hold and won't let go."

"Maybe I'm not passionate enough."

"Maybe you just need a gentle shove to remember the passion."

"Good response," she said softly after a contemplative pause. Her gaze drifted down to his mouth and then back to his eyes. "You are good with those gentle shoves, aren't you?"

"They have their uses."

He placed his hands palms down on the table, and after a moment's hesitation, she—God help him—spread one of her hands over his. Her left hand, bare of jewelry, and despite those long, elegant bones it looked tiny in contrast.

Pale, tiny and incredibly erotic.

"Big hands," she said, low and husky, "have their uses."

Seth picked up her hand and brought it to his lips. More civilized, he decided, than putting it where he wanted it. Then someone—probably Robert, although Seth didn't bother checking—chimed silver against crystal until the cacophony of conversations and the loud, hammering pulse in his head and between his legs dimmed to a low hum. Amazing. All these other people in the restaurant—at the same table, even—and his focus had narrowed to one. For how long they'd been immersed in their own sensual vacuum, he had no clue.

He turned now, pretended to listen as his friend formally launched Casinelli's 2001 pinot noir. Robert kept it short and sweet, ending with "let the wine speak for itself." Much applause then a hundred-odd enophiles reached for their glasses.

Seth watched Jillian go through the motions. Nose in glass, the long inhalation, the longer moment of reflection before she lifted the glass to her mouth. She took her first taste and her eyes drifted shut as she held it in her mouth. The heat of her rapt expression, the subtle movement of her throat as she swallowed, the ruby sheen on her lips: they all combined to create a moment of near-violent longing in Seth.

To generate such passion, to watch those lips part so softly, to see that same rapture when his mouth was on her, tasting her, driving her wild with pleasure.

"As good as anticipated?" he asked, and his voice sounded about how his body felt. Hot, gruff, hard.

"Mmm, better, although that may be partly due to anticipation." She sipped again, contemplated, her eyes focused somewhere deep within herself. "Silkier than last year. Big hit of fruit. Rich cherries, some raspberry. And there's a floral note that reminds me of the ninety-seven."

Seth picked up his own glass, sniffed. "You can tell the vintages apart?"

"I've scored a hundred percent on blind horizontals and verticals." She frowned. "Does that sound conceited?"

"It sounds…interesting." And erotic. Jillian, blindfolded and horizontal.

"Interesting in what way?"

He smiled slowly as the idea took form. "Interesting, as in, would you like to prove it?"

She looked up from her glass, a stillness in her eyes, her face, her body. "How?"

"I have a pretty decent collection."

"Of pinots? Of *Sophia's* pinots? How?"

Seth shrugged. "I told you the Neumanns were friends."

"And, what, they just send over a bottle each Christmas?" Her gaze swung toward their hosts and back at him. She coughed out a strangled laugh. "They do, don't they? They actually send you bottles as gifts."

What could he say? She was right.

Slowly, disbelievingly, she shook her head. "And you made out as if you were a complete philistine. You encouraged me to rabbit on about pinot noirs and about Sophia's wine."

"I have the wines. Doesn't mean I know a blessed thing about them."

She didn't look convinced.

"It's a cliché, but I know what I like to drink and that's my only interest in wine."

Apart from this fantasy of licking the stuff from your body.

"So." He turned the glass through his fingers. "Are you up for the challenge?"

"A blind tasting of Casinelli pinots? You're kidding, aren't you?"

"You told me not to mess with you over these wines."

She moistened her lips. "When?"

"Tonight."

Seth savored the spun-out moment as he waited for her answer, the anticipation, the expectation, the certainty of what she would say.

"Okay."

Nine

"Oh, no, Seth. No, no, no!" Jillian held up both hands in combination denial and horror. "You are not going to open all those bottles."

"Backing down?"

After growing up with brothers, Jillian could pick a taunt a country mile away. Even when delivered in a deceptively soft and silky tone. She lifted her chin. "I'm trying to stop you doing something completely crazy."

Seth gathered up the half dozen bottles he'd selected from the mind-blowing collection in his cellar and tilted his head toward the stairs. "After you…Chicken little."

Jillian only moved to narrow her eyes. "I won't let you waste thousands of dollars on testing my palate."

"This—" he lifted the bottles of red gold in his hands "—didn't cost me a dime."

"Be that as it may, they're worth big money. I won't let you open them."

Amusement flickered over his face. "How do you plan to stop me? Are you going to confiscate my corkscrew?"

She threw her hands in the air and marched to the stairs. "Your wine. Your money. Your loss."

"No," he said softly as she brushed past him. "Not my loss."

A stinging retort in the making, Jillian paused on the bottom step and looked over her shoulder and into his eyes. Not a glimmer of laughter remained in their deep, dark depths. Only heat and a stunning predatory intent. The breath caught in her lungs, caught and hitched and shifted her mood from foot-stomping aggravation to heart-thumping awareness in one stalled second.

"And on the crazy front—" He leaned in close and shocked her with an open-mouthed kiss to the back of her neck. "Too late."

By using very specific instructions—left, right, up, up again—she managed to coax her legs into carrying her up the steep staircase.

Too late? Oh, yes, much too late to stop the slide into complete sensual thrall with this man.

Crazy? Oh, yes, crazy to know without a backward glance that he watched her, all the way up those stairs and into his huge open-plan living area, every step of the way. That knowledge emanated from the base of her back and shivered up the length of her spine. Then, like the spill of wine from an upset glass, it spread through her body in red ripples of heat.

Crazy, too, that his watchful intensity no longer made her uncomfortable. All through that wonderful dinner she'd felt his attention with a mixture of quiet nerves and deep self-awareness and secret delight. It had been so long since she'd been on a first date that she'd forgotten the thrill of anticipation.

The not knowing how the night might end.

Well, she still didn't know. She had come home with him, but this was a family home, shared with a daughter and a housekeeper. She had no reason to believe there'd be anything beyond the wine-tasting test, no grounds for the weird sense of their aloneness as she watched Seth deposit bottles and corkscrew and glasses on a low glass table.

No reason, either, for the leap of her pulse as he reached up to slide his loosened bow tie from his neck. In the taxi they'd shared on the drive back to Napa, he'd shed his jacket and untied the tie. "Feels like I'm trussed and bound," he'd said.

But now—

"What are you doing?" she asked, her stomach jumping with nerves as he stretched the length of fabric between his hands and started toward her.

"You did say a blind tasting?"

"Yes, but—"

"This is your blindfold." He stopped in front of her. "If you still want to do this."

"Yes, I just—" Her gaze skittered toward the staircase and back. "What if someone comes downstairs?"

"Rachel is sleeping over at Rosa's. We're all alone."

Jillian's pulse raced. Was she ready for this? For being alone with this man and doing all the things he'd told her he wanted to do with her? She sucked in a slow breath. One step at a time, she told herself, starting with the tasting test. This she could do. Blindfolded, she would be better able to concentrate on the wine and not on Seth with his crisp white shirtsleeves and dark male aura.

With an accepting shrug, she turned around. Her belly swam with nerves and anticipation as he moved close behind her and covered her eyes with the slice of black silk.

Oh, how wrong could one girl be?

Instead of blocking him out, the darkness intensified Seth's nearness. The tie carried his scent—nothing artificial, just earthy, sexy man. And he stood so close that their bodies brushed with charges of electric friction as he worked to fasten the tie.

The task seemed to be taking an extraordinarily long time, between the slippery fabric with its undulating widths and his big hands trying not to catch her flyaway curls in the knot. Her chest constricted, tight with the knowledge that he would take the same care of her, with her, in his bed.

Oh, yes, she could do this. In the dark, with her senses filled with Seth, anything was possible. Anything, except standing here passively while he fiddled and diddled....

"To get the wide part over my eyes, you need to tie it here—" she found his fingers and moved them to her temple "—instead of at the back."

"Right."

The word was low and thick; his breath fanned the side of her face; her body gravitated toward the source of heat. Could he be any slower? Any more of a tease?

"Stand still," he growled. "I'm nearly done."

Yes, and so am I, she almost growled back. But then his big hands were on her bare shoulders, turning her to face him. "Can you see me?"

I can feel you, smell you, all but taste you in my blood, but...

She shook her head. "No."

His grip on her shoulders tightened for one long, dizzy moment when she thought he might bend down and kiss her—please, yes!—but then his hands dropped away. "Do you want to sit down?"

"Standing's fine." *I think.*

A low grunt of acknowledgment and he moved away. To the table, she imagined, to the expensive bottles of pinot that waited. A dozen thick, thudding heartbeats later she heard the distinctive suctioning sound of decorking, and that jarred her out of her sensual stupor.

"Please, just start with the one." She pressed her hands together in entreaty. "I can't stand to see you waste those."

No answer, except a clunk—metal corkscrew against glass?—and the liquid slush of pouring. Then the sense of movement, the whisper of fabric, the shift of air, the scent of man in her nostrils.

The sweet tremble of desire deep in her belly.

He pressed a glass into her hand. Wine, Jillian thought, as her fingers folded around the stem, grounding her in a familiar world.

"We'll start with one," he said. "Seeing as you asked so nicely."

Jillian smiled her thanks, for that consideration and for the several steps he took back out of her space. Now she could at least try to concentrate on the wine. Normally she would have let it breathe, but this wasn't normal. She swirled the wine in her glass, wished she could—

"You need help getting the glass to your mouth?"

"I'm sure I can find my mouth, even in the dark," she said, surprising herself with her prim tone. She swirled some more. "Since this beauty hasn't breathed sufficiently, I'm helping release the aroma." She lifted the glass, surprising herself again, this time with the steadiness of her hand. "And holding it to the light to check the color."

His low smoky laughter slid through her. "Would you like me to do the honors, seeing as you're at a disadvantage?"

"Please."

He didn't touch her, but she felt his nearness, the nudge to the base of her glass, lifting and tilting it for his inspection.

"Well?" she prompted. "What color do you see?"

"Red."

Laughter exploded from her throat, laughter and backed-up breath and tension. A whole big barrel full of tension. "You don't want to try for a more specific description? Like, which shade of red?"

"Like your dress." Fingertips brushed over the one shoulder strap. "Pinot noir."

The soft touch shivered through her skin, and the weight of his words echoed through her memory chords. Frowning, she searched for the time he'd said those words in that exact tone. In the tasting room. Yes. "That afternoon with the Red Hat ladies, you described my mood as pinot noir. What did you mean?"

"If you were a wine, that would've been my pick. That day, pinot noir."

"And other days?"

"A cool white, a summer sparkly, a bold red. But as I said, I don't know wines. Only what I like."

Jillian pictured the hitch of his shoulders, felt a similar hitch in the region of her heart. He'd really seen that many facets of her personality?

"You're a bit like a blind tasting." He fingered the blindfold at her temple. "I never know what's in store."

Oh, my.

"So, we've established you're holding a pinot noir," he said, steering her attention back to the glass that remained steady in her hand. Amazing given the fine tremor in her blood and her flesh. "What else?"

She swirled that glass, the familiar, the anchor, but her senses were jarred, her perception askew. Amazing that he hadn't completely floored her with those seemingly casual comments. Amazing that she hadn't seen this coming, given how often he'd slayed her in these past few weeks.

This…wow, she did not know what to call it, did not want

to put a name to it. Deeper than infatuation, richer than lust, scarier than sexual fascination. And, blast it, she liked him.

Momentarily rattled, she stuck her nose in the glass and sniffed deeply. Again, until the aromas filled her senses and drove out the disturbing sense that she'd strapped herself into a roller coaster. She sipped and tasted until her world rocked back on its axis. Safe and steady again, she felt the texture in her mouth, chewed on the flavors, and her confidence skyrocketed as the complex layers revealed themselves.

Too easy. This wine she would pick through a head cold. In the middle of a roller coaster ride.

"This is the ninety-nine," she declared with a satisfied smile. "The nose is knock-your-socks-off intense—a distinctive personality you can't mistake. Earthy and brooding. Robust. There's a bigger structure, more complex than the ninety-eight, but still the Casinelli mouthfeel."

No confirmation needed, she knew she was right. That knowledge danced through her like a cocky Travolta two-step.

"If you were a wine—" she lifted the glass in a smiling salute "—then this one is you."

"An expensive pinot?" he asked after a thick beat of pause. "Are you sure about that?"

Was she? That day in the tasting room, he'd struck her as a big, bold, full-bodied cabernet. Other days he seemed so centered and together and confident, like a perfectly balanced Shiraz. Tonight at that dinner, the smoky chocolate notes of a merlot.

She moistened her lips as the possibilities shivered through her body. Too tempting, this chance to compare and contrast, with her senses primed by black silk and one of the valley's finest wines. "Perhaps my call was premature. Perhaps I do need to reassess."

Silence, when she'd expected a teasing comeback. Silence that ached in her breasts and tightened in her nipples as she felt him move closer, felt him take the glass from her hand. *Oh, no.* Her humming senses, her aroused body, her soaring confidence all took immediate umbrage.

If she was doing this, *she* was doing it.

Before he could react, she ducked under his arm and around behind him, using his big, solid body to anchor herself in the darkness. Her hands were on his sides, just below his waist and spanning the fine sleek fabrics of his shirt and pants.

Through both, his body heat scorched.

Jillian inhaled deeply, for strength and to control a sudden attack of lightheadedness. Then she commenced her analysis. "Appearance is tough to call, given I can't see a thing, but I'm guessing this is a big red." She slid both hands higher and spread them against his back. "Surprisingly fine texture, although…"

It was only his shirt, and she wanted to feel skin.

Emboldened by the dark, by the guise of the "wine-tasting" experiment, and by the way he stood still and compliant beneath her hands, she fisted her fingers in the fabric and tugged it clear of his trousers. Using her hands on his body for guidance, she worked her way around to the front and started unfastening.

"What are you doing?" he asked, low and throaty.

"The first step is opening the bottle. Letting it breathe." With a side of his open shirt in each hand, she leaned in until her nose all but touched his throat. "Aroma is the most important part."

"Why is that?" Deep, close, his voice seemed to rumble from his chest. Fortuitous that she didn't need to think to answer because Jillian had ceased thinking. Now she operated on senses, on a purely visceral level.

"A good wine has its own distinct aroma. Very recognizable." Like Seth, she decided. She would recognize him anywhere, purely by her body's reaction to his scent. She breathed deeply, her senses so heightened by his nearness that they quivered. "The nose picks up so much more than the palate, so while the aromas are still in your nose, you take your first sip."

She thought about tasting the hot skin of his neck, right there where she had sniffed, but at the last second suffered an attack of temerity. Instead, she stretched up on her toes and tasted his mouth. A slow sip from his lips that stirred her blood like the first juice from the presses.

"White pepper, a little heat," she whispered. "Rich, velvety mouthfeel."

"Mouthfeel. Is that what it sounds like?"

"Mmm." She rubbed her lips against his, purred somewhere deep inside, then ducked back for another slow taste. "It's all about how the…wine…feels in your mouth. As opposed to body, which is the weight on your tongue."

She stroked his bottom lip with her tongue, and that was it. No more games, no more teasing, no more lessons in the art of wine. Strong, bold, assertive, he took her face in his hands and her mouth with his tongue. Just a meeting of mouths and bodies and a desire that shuddered through them both. She couldn't get enough of his kiss, of his hands on her face, in her hair, and—thank you, finally!—on her body.

Even when that first swell of fever abated and the mating of their mouths turned less frantic, less carnal, she could not stop kissing him. She nibbled at his lips, along the whiskery harshness of his jaw and dipped down to the vulnerable spot at the base of his throat where life beat hard and fast.

No shyness now, when she nuzzled the hair-rough texture of his chest and licked one hardened nipple. His hands fisted in her hair and he muttered a caution about slowing down, something that urged her to, yes, slow it down and savor every moment before it slipped away. She slid her hands up and inside the sleeves of his shirt, peeling away each side until she could curl her fingers around the smooth, hot skin of his biceps.

A work of art, those muscles, to be explored and appreciated by hands and mouth and tongue.

Vaguely, his gravelly sound of frustration registered and she knew that his fastened cuffs had caught on his hands, holding him captive to his own shirt and her exploring mouth. Empowered, she smiled against his skin and carried on…until a loud bump and a low curse and the clink of glass against glass brought her head up.

Blinking, she realized the blindfold was gone—when had that happened?—and that he'd backed into the table. In another time, another mood, the situation might have struck a funny note, but now the only chords twanging were off-tune and awkward and terrifyingly serious.

Terrifying enough to rock her back on her new two-inch ruby-red heels as she broke an intense moment of eye contact. She waved a hand at his predicament. "Here, let me help."

Surprisingly, he accepted, and she managed to fumble the cuffs undone and his hands free and it struck her hard—fist in chest, hard—exactly what she'd been doing.

Tasting him, undressing him, seducing him.

And now what?

They faced each other, hotly aware that the next step had to be taken, honestly, without the camouflage of darkness and the teasing game of tasting. Jillian's heart pounded. Her tongue, she feared, had fused to the roof of her mouth and her knees started to wobble. She sank down onto the leather sofa and picked up the glass that had rolled to the floor—

the empty one, thankfully—and sat it back on the table. Next to the open bottle of ninety-nine Casinelli pinot noir.

That she picked up, too, a solid prop for her nervous hands and a topic to get her tongue unstuck and working again. "So, I did get the ninety-nine right."

"Was there any doubt?"

"No."

Her heart bounded when his black pants moved into her line of vision. Right in front on her. He reached down, took the bottle from her hand and carefully placed it on the table. "Now it's my turn."

She looked up and her eyes snagged first on his thighs. Because they were so close and broad and imposing. Because she didn't want to stare higher, where those pants jutted with his arousal.

Okay, so she had looked. She had noticed. How could she not?

Heat flushed her cheeks, her breasts, between her thighs. "Your turn?" she managed to ask.

"To taste you."

Her gaze rose all the way to his face, and she knew that he knew exactly where she'd been looking. Even before he added, "Unless you hadn't finished."

Was he inviting her to continue tasting him? As she'd done with his chest and his mouth?

Hazed with heat, her gaze dropped back to his pants. Her hands itched and her whole body surged with illicit excitement, but Lord, no, she couldn't. Not now that the blindfold was gone. And she knew this was her moment of truth, honesty time. He wanted to taste her, like he'd told her that day at the cottage.

"It was easy in the dark, but now I'm trembling inside." She pressed a hand to her churning belly. "All those things you said you wanted to do…"

"I didn't mean to scare—"

"No, that's not why I'm trembling."

"Then, what?"

She inhaled, slow and deep. "I'm afraid that I won't be what you're expecting. I'm afraid that I'll disappoint you."

That I'll be caught short again, inadequate, not brave enough, strong enough or smart enough.

For a long drawn-out time he just stared at her. Then, with a low sound—frustration? denial? disgust?—he reached down and pulled her to her feet. "That's not about to happen, sweetheart."

"How can you know that?"

"I know," he said, straight and direct. "You just had a straight view of your effect on me. You should know, too."

Oh, yes. She'd seen. And now she looked into his eyes and saw the honesty, the rawness, the restraint, and the nervous fluttering of her belly steadied. A little. "Yes, I know."

"And?"

"Okay," she said on a long breath. "Are we going upstairs? To your bedroom?"

"You're sure?"

No. Her heart pounded. She moistened her lips. "Yes."

Fire sparked in his eyes, caught in her blood. Towing her by the hand, he started toward the stairs. Then, with a low sound of impatience, turned and doubled back.

"What?" she asked, her head spinning with the enormity of what was about to happen and with the speed of his turnabout.

He picked up the bottle of wine. The opened ninety-nine. "This," he said in answer to her question. "You said you couldn't stand waste."

Ten

In that moment of uncertainty, she'd handed Seth the perfect out. The opportunity to put a clamp on his body's demands, to listen instead to his instincts, to his gut, to every cautionary inner voice that urged him to take a giant step back. To say, *I don't believe you are sure, so let's rethink this whole sex thing and the risks involved.*

He thought about it for a split second, but he couldn't do it.

The passion had him by the throat long before she turned him hard and wanting with her tasting game. And then she went and looked at him with all that insecurity quavering in her big green eyes. Damn her for blindsiding him with the power of his need—not for physical release, not to fulfill his fantasies, but to obliterate that vulnerability from her face and her soul.

And damn himself for not having the strength to say no.

As he shouldered open the door to his bedroom, his grip

on the bottle tightened. The wine, his reminder that this was about the sensual experience. About driving her as wild as she had driven him downstairs. Only more so.

Because she thought she might disappoint him.

Yeah, right, and tomorrow hell might freeze over.

Seth led her right over by his bed before he let go of her hand. He deposited the wine on his bedside table, turned on the lamp, and kicked himself for ignoring an earlier compulsion to buy candles. He hadn't because…well, it had felt too cocky, too contrived, too much like a planned seduction scene.

"You didn't bring glasses," she pointed out.

He turned around and the visual of her in his bedroom slammed through his body. Forget the candles. She might find the darkness easier, but he wanted to see every shift in her expression, to watch every shudder of her body when he proved she was no letdown.

Forget the candles, and forget the glasses—

"We don't need them."

"Oh? Then, how…what …?" She stopped, swallowed, flapped a hand toward the wine. "You said you weren't going to waste it."

"I'm not going to waste it. I'm going to taste it. On your body."

Oh, yeah, that's why he wanted light. To see those big eyes widen and that mouth soften and the sweep of her tongue as she wet her lips. To watch her nipples press hard against the silky red fabric, as if her imagination had been let loose in a very erotic playground.

"I told you it was my turn," he said softly, as he moved toward her. "My turn to tease you and to taste you."

"Payback?" she asked.

"Yeah."

A pulse beat in her throat, like the nervous flutter of wings.

"Downstairs you said it was easier in the dark. Would you like the blindfold again?"

Her nostrils flared as she drew a breath. "I…no. I want to see you."

Deep in her eyes Seth saw the knowledge of all she wanted to see, the heat, the excitement, the directness. His body bucked in reaction as he thought about her watching him, watching his hands on her naked skin, his mouth on her body as it arched beneath him. Him burying himself deep in her body.

"Good." Low and gruff, almost a bark. He touched her hair, threaded a silken curl behind her ear, needing the softness to soothe the savage edge to his need. "I want you to know it's me."

"I would know you, Seth, even in the dark."

Too intense, too much, too soon. He needed to remember that this could only be about satisfaction, about pleasure—that's all it could be, this one time, this one night. Not the tightness in his chest, the urge to bury his face in her throat and hold her close against his pounding heart.

Hell, but he needed to lighten the mood, to get back to that teasing of downstairs. He stroked his thumb across her cheek, touched her bottom lip. "Ahh, but then you're the master taster who picks any wine blind."

"Not any," she whispered, her breath warm against his hand. "Only distinctive ones."

"You never did get back to me on whether I'm a distinctive pinot or a rough red."

She almost smiled. "Maybe you're one of a kind."

"Seth Bennedict. Vintage sixty-seven." He tapped a couple of fingertips to his bare chest and that was a bad move, teasing-wise. The smile fled as her gaze dropped and touched his bare chest with the same velvet stroke as her tongue.

Hot, wet, arousing all over again.

And then she was looking into his eyes and everything she'd done, every way she'd touched him, ached in his groin. So much for light, so much for teasing. Raw primal desire gripped him so hard he could barely breathe.

"Please, can you kiss me?" she asked, and his mouth was on hers before she stopped asking. He struggled to contain the kiss, especially when she parted her lips and welcomed his mouth with a throaty moan that fed the fierceness in his blood.

Quick and desperate, her hands slid around his neck and tangled in his hair. His hands slid down the warmth of her bare back to cup her buttocks and pull her in close. Soft against hard, need against need, she moved against him in the same rhythm as the kiss.

Lust billowed as he gathered the silky folds of her dress in one hand, dragging it higher at the back, all the way up until his hands were on bare flesh. Curved around warm, tight bare buttocks. That ended the hungry kiss and drove the gathering tension from his lungs in a gust of stunned surprise.

Either she'd elected to go commando—unlikely—or the lady wore a thong.

"Who would have thought?" His voice thickened with arousal as he traced the midline of her underwear with his thumb. "Do you wear these under those riding pants? The ones you spray paint on?"

She laughed low in her throat, the sound of silky skin and sexy underwear and pure, raw, howling stimulation. "When I'm out riding I'm not worried about visible panty lines," she told him. "Usually."

Okay, she was killing him.

Seth eased away, let the dress flow back over her bare skin, indulged himself by touching her back, her shoulders, the elegant arc of her collarbone. He needed to slow down, get a grip. He'd promised no disappointment; he'd promised payback; he intended to deliver on both counts.

Which meant that he had to intercept her hands when they reached for him. He held them trapped in his, squeezed them a little when she struggled to free herself. "Oh, no. This is where I get my revenge."

"There's no need for—"

"Yeah, there is. You have no idea how much pain you caused me downstairs." He put her hands away, arranged them primly by her sides. "Turnabout is fair."

"For it to be fair—" her voice hitched as he unfastened the first of two buttons at her shoulder "—you would need to be blindfolded."

"Not going to happen." The second button slid free and she grabbed for the dress and held it to her breasts. "I want to see you." His eyes held hers as he coaxed her fingers from the dress, as he slowly enticed her arms away and the dress slithered to the floor and pooled around her feet like a silken spill of pinot noir. "I want to see all of you, Jillian."

He waited. He didn't look—much—not until acquiescence glimmered in her eyes. Pink traced her cheekbones with shyness but she lifted her chin and when he asked her to turn around—his voice nothing but a husky, parched rasp—she did.

And, God, she was even more magnificent than he'd imagined. A proud, slender, straight-spined goddess, standing there in her pool of ruby satin wearing nothing but a thong and a blush. He stood statue still, needing to fill his eyes and his mind with the image, but she started to tremble—he saw it in the arms she still held extended at her sides—and that earlier note of vulnerability, of uncertainty, sucker punched his memory.

"Hey." He moved in close and folded her in his arms,

her back against his front, and held her until the trembling
eased. He wanted to tell her how beautiful she was, to tell
her anything more meaningful than "hey," but voice and
words were lost in the sensations rushing through him, too
many and too swift to pin down and name.

Too many and too swift and too troubling to name.

So he kissed her temple, her brow, the bridge of her
nose, but when he nuzzled her cheek and the side of her
neck, she made a low, achy sound in her throat and moved
against him, restlessly, reflexively.

Maybe he'd read that deep shudder all wrong. Maybe
he'd read that flush of pink in her cheeks wrong, too.
Maybe they weren't signs of nervousness but of intense,
female arousal.

Again, she made that throaty purring noise and it shot
straight to his sex. The weird, tender sensation in his chest
hardened too, releasing him, relieving him, reassuring him
that this would be all right.

Gently he nipped at her earlobe and she stretched her
neck and rolled her head to the side, giving him better access to that sexy bite-me neck. What could he do when she
asked, silently, but ever so nicely? He sucked her skin
against his teeth, marking her with primitive possessiveness and not caring. Not when she arched her back and
pressed the swell of her naked breasts against his arms. Not
when she rolled her hips and stirred him to steel-hard pain.

Who was supposed to be torturing whom, here?

Slowly, deliberately, he unfolded his arms. Ran his hands
all the way down her arms as he set them at her sides again.

"What are you doing?" she asked, her voice as husky-
edged as his mood.

"Kissing you." And he did, starting at the back of her
neck and moving all the way down her spine, dropping to
his knees when he had to, kissing all the way over the firm

curve of her bottom and down the backs of her thighs. "Kissing you and tasting you."

With hands wrapped around her thighs, he held her steady when she trembled and threatened to buckle, shushed her when she tried to object.

"I've wanted to do this for so long." To run his hands the length of those mile-long legs, to press his mouth to the backs of her knees, to ease her legs apart and nuzzle the soft yielding flesh of her inner thighs. "And this."

The sound of his breathing, of his need, raged in his ears as he turned her in his hands and peeled away the skimpy panties. Naked. He had her naked as the day she was born and he couldn't stop looking. Even when her hand shifted in an attempt to cover herself.

Those long, elegant fingers hovered over the core of her femininity, and that was about the most erotic thing he'd ever seen. That and his hand, his fingers, touching hers, and —with the gentlest pressure—easing their conjoined touch lower, deeper, dipping between her legs.

It was unbelievably erotic, the doing, the watching, the soft hiss of breath dragged between her teeth. It was too little, too much, not enough.

"I want to taste you," he rasped, and she started to tremble, so deep, so strongly, her legs gave way. His bed caught her fall, his hands eased the drop, and she was there laid out before him, open and vulnerable and beautiful.

"Please," she breathed, and that was enough for Seth. Her fingers clutched at his sheets as he touched her, stroking the soft skin of her thighs, the slick swollen flesh between, while the blood roared through his veins and hunger took hold.

He touched her with the tip of his tongue, heard the reactionary grab in her breathing, then he tasted her, long and slow and deep, until her whole body trembled and her back arched to press herself against him, seeking, questing, driving him to increase the pressure, the speed, the intensity until she exploded against his mouth in the hot rush of her release.

He wanted to keep touching her, prolonging her pleasure, but her taste exploded in his blood, headier than any wine, more intoxicating, more addictive, and he had to roll away, to slam his eyes shut and grit his teeth to control this maelstrom of sensations that clamored at his restraint.

"That was…" she said after a second, a minute, who knew? Her voice trailed off and he felt the flutter of her fingers against his arm. A weak, whispery contrast to the hard pulse of need in his body.

"Too long coming."

"Yes. That and…" Her hand shifted restlessly again, as if grasping for description. "I haven't— I've never…"

Again she couldn't finish, but her part-answer caught at Seth's consciousness. He rolled onto his side and the look on her face, the almost puzzled look of wonder, caused his heartbeat to stall.

"Haven't, what?"

Her gaze skittered. The flush in her cheeks deepened. Seth came up onto one elbow, took her face in his hand. "You've never what, Jillian?"

"Orgasmed like that. With—" she paused, moistened her lips "—with oral sex."

"You were married—" He stopped himself short. God, what was he doing? Inviting Jason into bed with them?

"For five years? Yes, I remember." Silence strung out between them, taut and awkward, until she made an impatient sound and wrenched away from his slackened hold. "That surprises you? That your brother was as selfish in bed as out of it?"

No, it didn't. That's not what had hit him with staggering force. It was the notion of first, the primal masculine force, the knowledge that he'd given this woman something no other man had.

She turned her head, slowly rolled it against the sheets until she faced him again. Her gaze was direct, but not steady enough to hide the anxious flicker in their rock pool depths. "I've pretty much wrecked the mood, haven't I? Mentioning another man while I'm in your bed."

"No."

Their eyes met and held and whatever she saw in him caused her to still, to steady. To swallow. "You're not touching me."

"I'm thinking about it."

"Can I," she said, wetting her lips, "touch you?"

His hardness ached with the thought. And strained toward her hand as she stroked his belly, as she dipped her fingertips inside his waistband.

"Let me," she whispered as she turned onto her side. He kissed her with her taste on his tongue and lips and she stretched her long body against his and touched him through his pants. Tortured him with those long, elegant fingers.

Seth sucked air through his teeth and swore softly. "Take them off," he said tightly. "Undress me."

But when her fingers dawdled at his waist buttons, when she unzipped his fly and sat back on her heels and stared at him with glazed eyes and flushed cheeks and moist lips, he was caught in a strange ambivalence.

He wanted that mouth on him. The wet stroke of her tongue, the curl of those fingers, the caress of her hair against his belly and thighs. But, God, he wouldn't last a minute. Too long coming, he told himself, too long for the first time not to be where he most craved.

Deep in her body, eye to eye, her legs tight around his waist.

"Later," he ground out when she reached for him, when he enclosed that hand in his and held it tight against him for one on-the-brink second. "You can have me later, sweetheart, for as long as you want. Now I just got to get inside you."

Shoes, socks, pants, he shucked them all with an efficiency he didn't feel, with a haste he felt in every drum tight cell of his body. He found and donned protection, rolled back onto the bed and kissed her, promised himself that later it would be slow, worshipful, memory-feeding. Promised her that later he'd taste the wine on her breasts, lick it from her nipples, drink it from the sweet dip of her belly.

Later.

Now they rolled together in a tangle of limbs and skin and edgy greed. He fed on her mouth, her throat, her breasts, and she arched and whimpered and fisted her hands wherever they could grab hold. His sheets, his hair, his body, it didn't matter. And then his hand touched her slick heat and whatever she moaned into his mouth he heard as *I'm ready, take me now.*

"Too long," he told her as he moved between her legs, as she lifted them and—God help him—wrapped them all the way around his waist. "Too long coming," he finished as his one long, controlled thrust filled her.

The sensation stunned him, held him still, buried in her tight, wet heat, while his pulse thundered and slowed in his ears. The pleasure was so intense, so white-hot, so razor-edge, he didn't want to move, to risk shattering it, but she stretched beneath him and somehow changed the angle of their meeting.

Their mating.

Her legs wrapped higher, drawing him deeper—unbelievably deeper—and he couldn't hold back. He moved slowly, the friction unbearably intense, the sight, the feel, the scent of her wrapped him in spiraling coils of sensuality. Her skin shone golden in the lamplight, mysterious in shadows, as she moved with his rhythm, as she flowed with the dance, as pleasure gripped her and stretched her tight beneath him.

This was the risk he'd taken. This risk of it never being enough, of never having enough to give this woman who'd captivated him for seven long years. This woman who looked right into his eyes and hid nothing as she took her pleasure, a long, shattering climax that drew him with her. He arched his back and surrendered to the hammering need, the screaming pressure, to pour himself deep into the heart of her welcoming body. To empty himself into her soul.

Dawn was leaking through the slatted blinds when Jillian woke, painting pale stripes of light over the gray carpet and charcoal sheets. And the man, spread-eagled in sleep, at her side. For a moment she lay perfectly still, waiting for her sluggish mind to come awake along with her body. Her heart, she noticed, was very much ahead of the game, beating too fast, as if she'd woken with a start.

Except she hadn't. Perhaps it had simply never slowed down. Perhaps it never would.

Carefully, she turned on her side, wincing with the pull and tweak of body parts unused to such activity. Oh. Dear. Lord. *Such activity.* She squeezed her eyes shut and stretched the sheet higher over her naked body, all the way up to her chin. And then she shook her head at the ridiculous attempt to hide from all she had done during the night.

Not the exciting things, not the first-time things, not even the shockingly illicit, but the complete trust, the no-holds-barred giving, the raw emotional intensity of the lovemaking.

Her eyes jarred open. Lovemaking? Panic sent her racing pulse into overdrive.

No, no, no. Not lovemaking, Jillian, sex. That's all he wanted, that's all you wanted. She'd been there before, allowed the lines between lust and love to blur. Not again, not ever again.

Instinctively she reached for her ring finger, found it as naked as the rest of her body. Naked, unprotected, vulnerable. And still her heart thudded, too fast, too loud.

She had to get out of here, to put some space and perspective and sanity between her and this man and her unsettling thoughts of love. She abandoned the sheet, and slipped silently from the bed…until her foot tripped on a shoe and tipped her against the bedside table.

The lamp rattled and rolled on its base. The half-full bottle of wine rocked, and with a soft curse she lunged to rescue it before it spilled. Saved. Exhaling her relief, she collapsed onto the edge of the bed and pressed a hand against her racing heartbeat. She stared at the wine, her flesh shivering hot and cold with the memory of how he'd licked it from her skin.

Oh. Dear. Lord.

Behind her she heard the rustle of sheets, felt the motion of the mattress shifting underneath her.

Oh, no. She so did not want to do this. She so did not know how to handle a morning after.

Breath held, she glanced across her shoulder. He still slept. On his belly now, arms holding a pillow tight, disturbed by whatever etched frown lines deep in his forehead, but asleep nonetheless.

She did not want to smooth them away. She did not want to slip into his arms to replace that pillow. She did not want to kiss the tight line of his mouth until it relaxed and softened and opened under hers.

No, Jillian. You do not!

More careful with her feet, she slipped from his bed

again, stooped to gather her clothes and shoes, and hustled her bare backside out the door and to a downstairs bathroom to wash and dress. Quickly. She didn't stop to call Mercedes until she was outside, hurrying away down the quiet cul-de-sac to wait for her ride.

Eleven

Jillian didn't know much about these things, but if the night meant anything, then surely he would call? At the very least she'd expected an angry call because she'd left while he slept. She didn't think that would sit well with Seth.

Well, apparently she knew diddly-squat.

The only phone call came Monday morning while she was out riding. Eli scribbled the message on a scrap of paper, and she read it as: *S.B. away today. See Lou (surname indecipherable). Will need yr OK on floor.*

Message received, loud and clear. They were back to a business relationship. He was possibly even avoiding her, sending Lou to this job in his stead.

Loud and clear yet difficult to accept, apparently, because when she drove up to the winery on Tuesday morning, the sight of his truck drove all the air from her lungs and left her chest feeling tight and achy and empty.

Not even *him*, just the sight of his blasted truck! And it

wasn't as if they'd even be alone, she realized as her perception widened to take in three other tradesmen's vehicles lined up side by side in the parking lot.

"You are pathetic, Jillian."

She slammed her car door and stood there, drawing deep breaths and remembering a time when she'd found it easy to hide her emotions behind a cool, calm facade. Now she didn't even have the crutch of her wedding band to twist on her finger, to remind her she didn't need these crazy, heart-lurching sensations stealing her sleep and her sanity and the very air from her lungs.

Remember what matters, Jillian, what you can depend upon. Your career, the wine, your family.

"Precisely." She straightened the cuffs and turned-up collar on her crisp, business-first shirt and started for the door. Late yesterday a subcontractor had laid the floor. With the wrong colored slate. And, despite Seth's message, she hadn't come by to check until after they'd all gone home.

She pushed through the door and into...chaos.

Power tools roared, the floor was halfway uprooted, and Jillian could still hear the thunder of her pulse as her eyes zeroed in on one figure. Yes, she could pick him in the dark. Dressed or undressed. Her face heated at the thought, the memory, the image of his strong, broad-shouldered nakedness.

Flapping a hand in front of her over-warm face, she considered coming back later. Yes, she was pathetic *and* a coward. Then Seth sensed her presence, she knew. A stillness came over his body even before he turned and their eyes collided across all the disorder and debris.

Déjà vu, intense and dizzying, washed through her. *Villa Firenze*. Only two weeks ago? It seemed much longer. So much had happened, so much had changed.

Or had it?

As he approached, she caught the guarded expression on his face, the tightness in his jaw and mouth, and she wondered if anything had changed at all. If, in fact, their past would always clutter the space between them.

And then he was there, right before her, and she couldn't think of a thing to say. No, that was a lie. She thought of—and rejected—several attempts. A polite *How are you?* A blithe *I didn't kill you, then?* A catty *Glad you could make it today.*

She settled for a hand-waving gesture toward the mess before them. "You're redoing the floor?"

"It wasn't what you wanted or what I ordered," he said curtly.

He's talking about the floor, Jillian. Slate. Tiles. Not what anyone ordered or delivered on Saturday night.

Annoyed with how she'd over-read his comment—and with his snippy tone—she glared back at him. At the side of his face, actually, and the muscle that twitched below his cheekbone. "Perhaps if you'd been here yesterday instead of sending Lou, you would have caught the gaffe in time."

That brought his head around. "I can't be in two places. That's why I asked you to double-check. Was that too much to ask?"

Stung, by his tone and by the truth, Jillian pressed her lips together. "No, and I apologize. Perhaps you should have spoken to me directly, if you anticipated a problem."

"I didn't anticipate anything. I was covering my back, I thought." He jerked his head toward the boarded-up gaps where the windows were to go. The windows still in production. "I had to go to the city to deal with another problem."

And she'd thought he'd sent Lou as a means of avoiding her. How unprofessional and unfair. He'd been working, looking after business, and she'd do well to take a lesson.

"How are the windows coming along?" she asked briskly.

"Fine, now. They've promised I'll have them in a week."

Jillian frowned. "That's cutting it close."

"Close to what?"

"May first. The party we're planning. Will the room be ready?"

Hands on hips, he stared at her for a strung-out second. "Don't you think you should have asked that question *before* you started sending out invitations?"

"You said two weeks."

"I estimated two weeks. If everything went right." He shook his head with patent disgust. "Does this look like a site where things are under control?"

No, and he looked close to losing control. Seth Benedict, the man she'd always considered so calm and on top of things…except on Saturday night in his bedroom. Then he'd been raw and edgy in a different way.

The two thoughts came together in Jillian's mind with a thunderclap of understanding.

"What, exactly, are you so ticked off about, Seth?" she asked slowly. "The subcontractor not doing his job? Me not checking the slate for Lou? Or is there something else on your mind?"

For a moment he went completely still—except for that muscle kicking up a storm in the plane of his cheek—and then he scrubbed a hand at the back of his neck. Expelled a breath. And when his eyes swung around to hers, they simmered with temper. "You didn't have to sneak off in the middle of the night. I took you out—I expected to take you home."

Wow. Okay. So, she'd known he wouldn't like that. And she'd deduced that his bad mood might be personal as much as work related. But she hadn't expected such an explosion of frustrated emotion. It put her at a momentary loss.

"I'm sorry," she said finally. What else could she do but apologize? "I didn't realize it would be such an issue."

"It's not an issue. It's how I do things."

He was curt enough, his stance confrontational enough, to tickle the edges of Jillian's temper. She stiffened her backbone. "And I have no idea how these things are done. I've never had casual sex before. And since I'm being honest, I might as well add that I knew it would be awkward like this afterwards. That's why I left."

Seth stared at her, incredulous. "Casual sex. Is that what you think we had?"

"That's what you said you wanted. Sex, once, not a relationship." Their eyes met and held, hers clouded with confusion and… Hell, he didn't want to know what else. "Are you saying that's changed?"

He didn't know what the hell he was saying, or why, but he did know that everything *had* changed except the one fundamental truth. "I can't have a relationship with you, Jillian, any more than I can have 'just sex' with you. There's too much between us. Too much past, too many complications."

"Because of Jason and Karen?"

She knew?

For a second his heart seized, but then he realized what she was asking. Them dying together, not sleeping together. The twined ropes of their marriages and relationships. He huffed out a breath. "They'll always be there, between us. The third and fourth in our bed. That's why I can't have a relationship with you."

"Yet you slept with me."

"I didn't say I didn't want you. That has never changed." He wondered if it ever would, if there'd ever come a time when he could look at her without this fierce desire eating at his gut.

He couldn't do this.

Couldn't stand here and watch the confusion, the questions, the need for explanation, flitting across her open face. Too shocked for her usual poise, he took it. He jutted his chin toward the work site. "I need to get back to work."

"Can we talk later, then?" she asked.

"There's nothing to talk about, Jillian."

She blinked, as if taken aback all over again by his abruptness, and he wanted to knock himself down for being such a jerk. Hell, he ached to touch her, hold her, just breathe the warmth of her skin and the softness of her spirit.

But she straightened her shoulders and nodded. "Okay, but you've been straightforward and honest with me—I owe you the same. I didn't find anything casual about Saturday night. It was intense, incredible, amazing." She met his eyes, full on, no flinching. "So intense and involving, there was no space for anyone else in that bed, Seth. No one but you and me."

Proud and self-possessed, she turned and walked away.

You've always been straightforward and honest with me.

Seth felt like taking that honest word and slamming it against the wall, grinding it to pulp under his boot heel, hammering it into dust. He wouldn't need any tools, either. He could pulverize it with his mood.

Straightforward and honest. What a load of BS. He hadn't been honest with himself and, worse, he hadn't been straightforward with Jillian. And it was too damn late to change that. Two years too late.

By the time she'd closed up on Thursday and driven into Napa on several party-planning errands, Jillian had convinced herself that Seth was right. All along she'd known that their shared history complicated things between them. Whether she'd stayed or not on Sunday morning did not alter that.

She hadn't seen him since Tuesday, and she didn't know if this was a good thing or bad. Seeing him, not seeing him, expecting to see him, yearning to see him—she hated every stressful minute. This tasting-room project was supposed to win back her respect and confidence, not turn her into an angsty, sleep-deprived, lovesick basket case.

Lovesick. Oh, dear.

She'd used the term unconsciously without batting an eye. It didn't mean she was in love. She didn't know how to differentiate between the intense, white-hot cravings of lust—she definitely suffered from those!—and the deeper, lasting bond of love.

So, okay, she enjoyed Seth's company, she trusted him, she admired him as a father and as a man, and she loved how strong and desired and womanly he'd made her feel on Saturday night. But she did not want a relationship, either. Not yet. She simply wasn't ready.

She parked her car and, yes, she couldn't help scoping the street for blue trucks since his office was on the next block. Her heart, she realized, had lodged in her throat and it only subsided after she'd double-checked and established that his truck was nowhere in sight. Not that she would have sought him out.

There's nothing to talk about, Jillian.

"Precisely."

She locked her car and while she walked, dug for her list in the depths of her bag. Distracted, she almost collided with a woman as she rounded the corner.

Her apologetic smile faltered then widened with recognition. "Charlotte? It is you! Hello."

The day she'd visited with her half sisters, she'd felt an immediate affinity with their cousin Charlotte. *Her* cousin Charlotte. As the younger woman returned her greeting now, with shy but genuine warmth, she felt it again. An

I-like-you response deep inside. She also experienced a jab of guilt. She'd been so focused on Seth and the renovations, she hadn't done anything to further the bond of connection she'd established that day at the estate.

"I don't suppose you have time for a coffee?" she asked. Then she gestured toward several heavy-looking shopping bags in Charlotte's hands. "If you've finished shopping."

"I have. And, yes, I'd love a coffee."

"Enzio's?"

They agreed on the coffee shop and while they walked, Jillian searched for a conversation starter. "I'm shopping, too. For a florist, of all things."

"Maybe I can help you," Charlotte offered. Then, "I do the flowers for The Estate."

"You're a florist?" Jillian laughed softly at the fortuitousness. "Yes, I would love to pick your brain. But that means I'm buying the coffee."

Over the first coffee, they talked flowers and Charlotte recommended two home-based florists as the most creative. Jillian thought about asking Charlotte if she would like the job, but decided not to press the friendship yet. Not with all the family problems unresolved.

Over their second coffee, they talked about family and Jillian learned that Spencer and Lilah had taken Charlotte and her brother Walker in after their parents had been killed in an accident.

Except I'm not convinced my mother is dead.

Walking back to her car, Jillian frowned over Charlotte's staggering revelation. Intuition, she'd said, was all she had to go on. Plus a bone-deep distrust of her father's brother. "Spencer has lied and deceived to suit himself so many times, who knows what else he has hidden from us?"

"Indeed," Jillian muttered.

Lies and deceit had been Jason's weapons of choice, too. Her father—her *birth* father—and her ex-husband were two of a kind and so very different from Lucas and Seth.

Seth. Her heartbeat skipped and restarted low in her belly. It was so obvious why she'd fallen so easily into this…this…*non*-relationship with him.

He fed her confidence, as a professional, as a person, as a woman. Those big hands had gently shoved her into action when she'd shilly-shallied over Spencer and Anna and what to do. He understood her goals with the tasting room and appreciated how she elected to run it.

More importantly, she trusted him.

She trusted his straight talk—he didn't fill her with false hopes. She trusted his strong protective streak—he would not hurt her. She trusted his honesty—he would not lie to her.

And, where, exactly did that leave her?

If only she knew. If only she had the strength and courage to trust her instincts, to take a risk. If only there was no past, no Jason and Karen, between them.

If only, if only, if only.

Seth couldn't avoid seeing her over the next week. Every day there was something to work out as the remodeled tasting room came together. He hated these exchanges. She polite, he stiff, both of them pretending to ignore the sexual energy that charged the air around them.

That need ached in his body, night and day, unrelenting. Worse in his bed at night, better when he could pound out his physical frustration at work. But then he'd catch her watching him, and the intensity on her face, in her eyes— *the wanting*—would damn near bring him to his knees.

In those seconds, he knew, he'd only have to ask. Or not. Just grab her by the arm and take her mouth and they would both be lost.

Somehow he made it through to Saturday afternoon, when he had to go seek her out. He found her at work in the cellar, told her he was finished for the time being, until the windows arrived. Then they just stood there, not touching, eyes not quite connecting, but unable to walk away.

And he had to explain, to do a better job than on Tuesday morning, because he couldn't stand this stilted, uncomfortable formality between them. "About the other morning…what I said about us and a relationship."

"It's okay," she said quickly. "It's not a good time for either of us. I'm just starting to find my feet again. This—" she did that hand-waving thing, her trademark "—my job, the new tasting room, what I want to accomplish here. And I am going to make that wine. My wine."

This was all good. He should be happy for her. Would be, he knew. "You better send me a bottle."

"The first one has your name on it."

He nodded, accepting all that his mind resisted. He didn't want a bottle sent in the mail. He wanted it hand-delivered. No, he wanted to share the creation, her passion and excitement, to see her—

"So, we agree then. Neither of us wants a relationship." Except she said it slowly, hesitantly, almost like a question, and he knew that she, too, was battling the same internal war. Need versus want. "The past makes it all too…complicated."

"It's not just the past. It's now and it's the future—it's Rachel. If we were to continue *this*—" Their eyes met and held, with everything *this* entailed steeping the air between them. Sweet and aching with suppressed passion. "What happens when it ends? Things are awkward enough after one night. Rachel adores you, Jillian."

"The feeling's mutual."

"I know, and I don't want that jeopardized. I don't

want her to suffer again because I can't keep a relationship together."

She stared at him an unnervingly long time. Enough time for Seth to realize that he'd said more than he had intended, more than he'd ever wanted to say about his marriage. But she either didn't pick that up, or she ignored it, focusing instead on what really mattered. Rachel.

"That is such a cop-out. You know I was seeing Rachel every other week for two years and hardly ever bumping into you." Her eyes sparked with heat, but her voice chilled with every word. "I would never let whatever is between us affect my relationship with your daughter, Seth. She means too much to me."

She was right, but he let her walk away. What else could he say? What else could he do?

Theoretically, with no tours or tastings, Monday and Tuesday constituted Jillian's weekend. But Seth knew she rarely took days off. So when he didn't catch a glimpse of her all day Monday, he figured she was avoiding him. He didn't blame her. He'd avoid himself, too, if he had the choice.

But he did need to tell her that the windows turned up a day under the promised week. He'd installed the first—yeah, to check they'd gotten the specs right, but also to see the end product of his design. Satisfaction sparked in his gut as he stood, hands on hips, surveying the effect. He almost smiled.

Oh, yeah, she'd definitely want to see this.

He tried the offices first, just in case, but Mercedes confirmed that her sister had taken the day off. "She and Mom went shopping in the city, but try the house. They may be back."

They were…at least, Caroline was. "I'm sorry, Seth. Jillian couldn't get up to the stables quickly enough when we got back," she told him. "Would you like her to call you later?"

"No, it's not important. I'll see her tomorrow."

Halfway to the highway, he almost turned back. Almost gave in to a reckless whim to go find her and take her to see the window in person. But he didn't trust himself in his current mood.

Too dangerous, too edgy, too needy.

He gripped the wheel hard in his hands, locked his jaw and headed for home. Later, with five miles and a phone connection between them, would be safer to talk to her. Barely.

Of course, it turned into one of those nights. A clingy three-year-old wanting *one more story, Daddy, just one more.* Guilt because he hadn't been there for enough bedtime stories lately. And after he tucked in her tiny sleeping body, the phone didn't let up. It was well after ten before he caught a minute. Too late to call. Probably. Still, he was tempted, so sorely tempted. He dialed once, then, swearing softly, hung up. An early riser, Jillian was probably early to bed, too. He would call first thing in the morning. And try not to spend the whole night imagining her in bed.

"I woke you."

"No. No, I'm wide awake," Jillian said quickly.

No one could sleep with their heart pounding a thousand beats a second. And that was only partly due to the strident wake-up buzz of her bedside phone. The other part was from hearing his voice. First thing on waking. In her bedroom. In her bed.

"You're a lousy liar."

Smiling in this dreamy, besotted fashion was okay, she figured, since he couldn't see her. "Usually I would be up and gone by now, but I didn't sleep well last night."

"Me neither."

His gruff, early-morning voice curled through her body and all the way to her toes. Jillian pushed her sleep-messed hair aside and pressed the receiver closer to her ear. She wanted to feed that bedroom voice right into her senses.

"Are you there?"

"I'm here."

"I thought you'd gone back to sleep."

Hardly. "Caroline said you called yesterday. I did wonder why…?"

"Is that what kept you awake?"

"No." She stretched a little, and her nightgown scraped against sensitive, turned-on nipples. "I was remembering last weekend," she admitted after another breath of pause. "And wishing things could be different."

If only, if only, if only.

Silence. She'd managed to shock him. Well, good. She liked the idea that she could.

"Are you there?" she asked, mimicking his earlier question. "You haven't gone back to sleep?"

He laughed and said, "Not possible," in a way that made her wonder about his state of morning arousal. She wished she had the courage to straight out ask, to *really* shock him.

Are you still in bed, Seth? Are you naked under those charcoal sheets? Are you turned on like I am? Are you sleek and hard and—

"It's not working, Jillian."

His tight, almost reluctant-sounding admission stopped Jillian stretching under her sheets and, well, touching herself. A little. As he'd done that night in his bedroom. "What's not working? Is there a problem with the windows?"

He laughed again, short and harsh. "No, the windows are just fine. Better than fine, in fact."

She jackknifed upright. "They're here? They're in? Why didn't you say?"

"That's why I called."

Well, of course it was. Jillian gave herself a mental slap to focus as she shucked her sheets. "I have to go and look. Are they as wonderful as I'm picturing?"

"Better."

She laughed, then paused in her excitement. "Thank you for understanding that I'd want to know first thing."

"I didn't want to miss you."

She knew what he meant. He'd called early to catch her before she left for the stables. But her heart read another meaning and responded in kind.

Oh, Seth, I didn't want to miss you, either. "But I do."

Silence. Jillian stood statue still beside her bed. She'd actually said that. Only a whisper, but definitely out loud. Into the phone still clutched to her face. Heart thudding, she sank down onto the edge of the bed.

Perhaps he didn't hear. Perhaps he didn't understand. Perhaps—

"It's not working for you either, is it?"

Jillian closed her eyes and gripped the phone harder. Her hand had started to shake. No, not just her hand, her whole body was shaking with reaction or nervous tension or just plain need. "No," she whispered. "It's not."

She heard him exhale, a long soft sound of relief or relenting, that left her oddly breathless.

"Are you coming out this morning?" she asked.

"I can't." He swore softly. "I have another job."

"Damn."

"Yeah." His laugh was a soft, rough catch of sound. "God, I want to see you."

"Me, too." To see him, to touch him, to hold him. She closed her eyes and drew a ragged, needy breath. "What time will you be finished with this job?"

"Late morning. But I've got an in-office meeting."

"Can I come to your office after your meeting?" *Please?* She didn't care if she sounded desperate. She was.

"I should be finished by one-thirty."

"I'll bring lunch."

"No, just bring you."

Jillian's heart rolled over in her chest. "Okay. I'll see you then. One-thirty."

He said, "See you later," and disconnected, and Jillian was still sitting there on her bed staring at the phone and wondering what she'd just done—and why—when it rang again.

"Not the office," he said without preliminary. "My house."

"What about Rosa?"

"It's her day off."

Twelve

Jillian pulled up outside his house five and a half minutes early. It didn't matter. His truck was already parked in the driveway.

By the time she'd cut the engine and unfastened her seat belt, her hands were shaking so badly she couldn't get the key out of the ignition. That didn't matter, either. For driving in this condition she deserved to have it stolen. Driving Under the Influence of Lust. There should be a law against such a downright dangerous practice.

The front door swung open before she lifted her hand to knock, and for a long moment or a short second—she had no concept of time—she stood there gazing into his eyes and all she could think was, *It's only been a week. Why does it seem like forever?*

"You'd better come inside," he said, like the perfect and polite host inviting her in for a visit. Except his eyes held no hint of politeness, only a hunger with the same dark edge that jangled through her nerves.

"Or?" she asked, liking the idea of skating that edge.

"Or I'm liable to shock the neighbors."

"Are you going to shock me, though?" she asked, ducking under his arm and into the foyer. The door closed behind her with a sharp click, and before she could draw half a breath, he'd swung her around and hard up against its solid surface.

"Probably," he muttered as his mouth came down on hers.

She met him halfway, already on her toes, as frantic for that first meeting of mouths as he. But after those first few greedy seconds, the kiss slowed and stretched into a sultry feast of lips and mouths and tongues.

Her hands relearned his body, tugging at his T-shirt and hauling it over his head, then touching as many smooth planes and hard muscles as she could find. He laughed and asked, "Who's shocking who, here?" and she told him she hadn't gotten started yet.

Eyes met and held, he reached for the hem of her very proper knee-length dress, and started to slide it up her thighs. She didn't blink, didn't break eye contact, just watched and waited until he swore softly.

"Hell, Jillian. You could have warned me."

"I thought about it." She leaned into him and nipped at his ear. "I thought about calling you at your office and warning you."

"That would have shocked me."

"Especially if you were on speakerphone."

His laugh turned into a growl as he stroked her panty-free behind and between her legs, as he lifted her against the hard ridge of his fly. And whatever teasing remark she'd been working up next was driven from her mind by the powerful wave of longing that racked her body.

She saw the same in his eyes, the connection, the recognition of equal and matching desires, and knew this was the only man she had ever—could ever—feel this liberated with, this trusting of, this intensely for.

"You're already wet."

"Since this morning in bed."

He groaned, low and rough, and touched her again.

"You make me wet, Seth," she whispered. "I want you inside me. Now."

"Here?"

"Here. Now."

"I have a bed upstairs."

She undid his pants, cupped the tight fullness between his legs. "I have all I want right—"

He cut her off with a feral growl. "Wrap your legs around me."

Vaguely she registered the pause, the package he fished from his pocket, but then he gripped her hips and thrust inside her. He rasped out a curse, a blessing, a promise, and held himself still, all the way inside her, filling her body while her heart overflowed with sweet, blind want.

"Take my dress off," she whispered, desperate for skin against skin, for his hands and his mouth. "Quickly."

The dress was gone in a flash of heat and he licked her breasts and took her mouth and started to move inside her with a strong, pulsing rhythm that stole her breath.

How could she have missed what she'd had for only one night? How could she have missed it so intensely? He bit on her earlobe and spoke low and hoarse at her ear. "Last time I marked you here." He thumbed the soft skin of her throat. "And every day I wanted to shift your hair and see. To know it was real. That you'd been mine."

The elemental, possessive message blazed through her body, as hot as the skin beneath her hands, as intense as the expression on his face, as savage as the edges of her control.

"I'm real." She bit at his skin, then lathed it with her tongue. "And I'm yours."

The burning intensity in his eyes consumed her. The sound of their ragged breathing wrapped them in a sultry cloak of need. And their joining grew teeth, barely contained, barely civilized, until he thrust fierce and deep and they shattered together.

"I *am* on the pill."

Jillian's quiet words came some time later, when they lay naked and replete in his bed. Seth had thought she was asleep—God knows, they both needed to catch up!—she felt so relaxed and boneless against his side, her head and one arm draped across his chest.

Relaxed and so damn right it hurt.

"For reasons other than birth control," she added, possibly an afterthought, probably a prompt.

So, she wanted to talk. Seth had expected as much, but what he hadn't counted on was his own response. Or lack thereof. No instant tension. No urge to run, hide, avoid. A wry smile might have curled his lips if he had the energy to spare, but he was so done in he could barely lift a hand to settle her damp curls that tickled his chest and throat.

Her shower-damp curls.

Yeah, she deserved an explanation for his extreme response in the shower. Not the sexual one—she'd seemed pleased enough with that—but his biting retort on the question of protection. Round one downstairs should have taken the edge off, but they'd ended up just as wild in the thick steam and streaming water.

No clothes, no pockets, no condom on tap. And she'd urged him to just do it. *I'm safe, I'm protected.*

And he'd been so damn tempted, so close to succumbing—

"It's not that I didn't trust your word," he told her now. He stroked the smooth length of her naked spine. "I take that responsibility seriously these days."

Under the idle caress of his hand, he felt her body tense up. Knew she'd ask about the reckless encounter that had shaped his future. "You and Karen?"

"At the time I thought I'd made the biggest blunder of my life."

"But now you have Rachel."

Her simple statement said it all. *He had Rachel.* And that chimed a chord in Seth's memory. Rachel, that day after she'd lost her toy pony, had pointed out how Aunt Jellie didn't have a daughter of her own. "Did you ever consider...?"

"Having a baby?" she finished for him, when the words lodged in his throat. Surprise brought her up on her elbow, her expression rueful. "Not many men in your position would dare ask that question."

The naked-in-bed-with-a-woman position? She had a point. "Yeah, well, you may have noticed how I didn't get the whole question out."

She acknowledged that with a smile.

"So, are you gonna answer?"

"Yes," she said after a beat of pause, "I considered babies. Back when I thought my marriage would last forever."

He'd never heard her use such a cynical tone before. Never. And his surprise must have shown, because she fixed him with a wry look. "I wasn't a complete fool, Seth. At least not for the whole five years."

He didn't want to ask but he had to know. "Did you love him?"

Something intensified in her eyes, a depth of emotion

that grabbed and banded his chest like a vice. He didn't think she would answer, not when she settled her head back on his shoulder. But then she spoke, so low he had to strain to hear the words. "I thought I did, but I didn't even know him. How could I have loved a man who was so dishonest and immoral and selfish? *How could I?*"

"Why did you stay with him?"

"Pride. Stubbornness. Fear of everything I'd lose by leaving. Fear of admitting I'd been wrong, that I'd failed." She exhaled on a humorless laugh. "Gee, if I think hard enough I'll have an excuse for every year of the marriage."

"Maybe you believed you could make it work."

Her hand shifted fretfully against his chest. "You know what I felt when I first heard he was dead?"

Seth stilled, waited, hating the direction of the conversation and all the crippling memories it churned in his gut but knowing it had to be said. It was long overdue.

"Relief," she said thickly, as if she'd dragged the word from some deeply hidden place. He didn't know what to say—if there was anything to say—so he stroked her back, pulled her closer to his side, touched his lips to her forehead.

"I'm not proud to admit it, but all I could think was, I'm free." Against his heart, her fingers clenched and unclenched. "Then I heard that Karen was with him, and I thought about you and Rachel and I loathed myself for that selfishness. I hated Jason for what he'd done but I loathed myself more."

Self-loathing. Oh, baby, he knew all about that yawning black chasm. And listening while she opened up her heart, while she confessed things he knew she'd never shared with another soul, stirred a deep longing in Seth to share the pain and guilt that had festered in him too long.

He just didn't know where to start.

She shifted then, turning her body in a fidgety little move that lifted her out of his loose hold. "I'm sorry, Seth. I didn't mean to get this heavy."

"There's a lot of heavy between us."

"A lot of past, I know." She made a rueful sound. "And there's Jason and Karen, just like you said."

The third and fourth in their bed.

"I think we need to talk," she said slowly, "not about the past, but about now. About what we're doing here."

"I think we're taking it one step at a time."

"One *step* at a time? Nice euphemism."

He grinned. Shrugged. And she surprised him by stretching up to kiss him. "Are you hungry?"

"I could be."

"You should be." A spark of all they'd expended earlier flickered between them. "Is it okay if I go and throw something together? In your kitchen? We can talk about our non-relationship while we eat."

"You're asking permission to feed me?"

"I'm asking permission to raid your fridge."

He spread his hands. "Knock yourself out."

"Don't get too excited," she said over her shoulder as she rose from his bed. "I'm not known for my cooking."

"I'll keep that in mind. When I'm looking for a cook."

In the doorway she paused, and Seth crossed his arms over his chest and waited for her sassy comeback. But she pressed her lips together and ducked away, leaving him with a big sense of letdown. He shook his head and huffed out a breath.

"You are something else, Jillian Ashton."

In the space of a minute she'd turned the tight angst in his chest into something bearable. She wanted to talk? Fine, he could listen. If she put some clothes on first.

He pulled on jeans and padded downstairs in bare feet,

stopping at several points to gather up stray pieces of clothing. A smile curled his lips as he noted how none belonged to Jillian. She'd driven here without a stitch between that prim ladylike dress and her bare silky skin.

At the foot of the stairs he whistled a hot breath through his teeth, remembering, then his attention caught—not on the clatter of plates from the kitchen but the sound of a lock turning. A second later the front door swung open.

Rosa?

Yes, and carrying Rachel. He was there, taking his daughter from the petite housekeeper's arms, before the door closed behind them. "What's up, princess?"

"Her lunch, mostly." Rosa had a way of cutting to the chase. "There's some kinda stomach flu going through the day care place. Looks like the chicken caught it."

Rachel lifted her head long enough to whine, "I'm not a chicken," and Seth reassured her that she smelled more like a pony, just as Jillian came out of the kitchen, concern etched all over her face.

Of course Rachel wanted Aunt Jellie, and the pathetic look on her pale little face would have slayed a much harder heart. Seth let her go. For the minute. He turned to Rosa and asked the burning question. "Why didn't they call me?"

"They tried." Knowing eyes flicked from him—in his jeans and nothing else—to Jillian and back again. "Maybe you turned your phone off."

Yeah, and maybe he'd been in such an all-fire rush, he'd left the blessed cell phone in his truck. Day care wouldn't have tried the house, not on a Tuesday.

"It's okay, boss. They found me."

"On your day off," he said tightly. Damn.

"You want me to stay now, look after her?"

"Thanks, Rosa, but I'll manage."

"You sure you don't need me?" She directed the question right past Seth, and Jillian reassured her. "I can stay and help, Rosa."

Seemingly satisfied, the housekeeper departed, and Seth turned to his daughter. "C'mon, princess."

"I wan' Aunt Jellie."

She met his eyes over Rachel's head and mouthed, "It's okay."

No, it was far from okay. This afternoon was the perfect illustration of all he'd feared and all he'd vowed to avoid. The perfect illustration of what he'd tried to explain to Jillian that day in the cellar. How do you explain to a sick three-year-old that the woman cradling you in her arms isn't staying? That she and Daddy are having some sort of sexual non-relationship that neither wants but neither is strong enough to say no to?

Hell, he couldn't even explain that to himself.

"Don't beat yourself up about this, Seth." Her quiet words brought his head up, stilled the hand rubbing at his neck. "Rosa was there for her. It's all right."

"No." His jaw locked tight. "None of this is right. You. Me. Rachel."

She stiffened a little at his tone, but her eyes shifted to Rachel and back to him. "Not now, Seth."

He acknowledged her point with a tight nod. "But we will talk later."

"Yes, but for now can we concentrate on a bucket and towel? I do believe we're about to be sick again."

Later was *much* later, after an exhausted Rachel finally succumbed to sleep and her bed. The aroma of coffee lured Seth downstairs to the kitchen, where he found Jillian mumbling to herself while she fussed with the makings of…food of some sort. He was too rocked by the picture of domesticity to notice or care what.

Too rocked by the thickness in his chest and the intensity of his desire to keep her there. In his house. To stay.

The notion took root quickly, spreading tentacles that wound insidiously into his logic. She'd wanted a baby before her marriage collapsed. She was a natural mother, a nurturer at heart. And Rachel needed—she *craved*—a mother's nurturing touch. Rachel loved her; she reciprocated.

Only one solution made any sense of his tumultuous feelings…except for one small point.

"You said you didn't want a relationship."

Obviously she'd sensed his presence in the doorway, his silent observation, since she didn't start at his voice. However, her shoulders bunched, as if with tension, and she put down a knife and wiped her hands on the sides of her dress. She didn't turn around.

"But we need to work something out," Seth continued, starting across the room. "I don't want a repeat of this afternoon."

"What do you propose?"

Seth swore he could feel his heart knocking against his ribs, in perfect timing with each step until he stopped right behind her. And gave the only possible answer.

"Marriage."

Disbelief, desire, trepidation beat a wild tattoo in Jillian's chest. Had she misheard? Had she conjured that answer out of a silly, heart-struck moment of comedic wordplay?

What do you propose? Marriage. Boom boom.

"We're good together," he said, close behind her. "And we're good together for Rachel. Marry me, Jillian."

She had to turn around then, although her legs trembled so fiercely she needed the countertop for support. "You can't be serious."

"I am."

God. He was. His eyes, grim and resolute, held hers…and instantly quelled that initial moment of *yes, yes, yes* exuberance.

"Well?" he asked.

"I think… I don't…" Exasperated with her inability to put together a coherent phrase, she flung her hands in the air. "Surely you don't expect an answer right now?"

His beat of pause was telling. So was the flash of impatience she read in his eyes. Brief, momentary and curbed as carefully as his answer. "An indication would help."

Yes, it would. An indication that *he* wanted her—not for Rachel, but for *him*—would make a big difference. She didn't expect an outpouring of emotion, just a little sign.

Give me something, Seth, she quietly pleaded. *Something to work with here.*

All she got was that same stony-faced expression, and a strong impression that he held his patience carefully checked. Her stomach churned with the panicky sense of being rushed, pushed, forced, and that was completely without logic. Perhaps if she tried to explain….

"I'm not opposed to the concept of marrying again," she said. "I would like children, a family, a partner to share my life with, but it has to be safe and solid and comfortable."

"And I'm not?"

"Not to me, no. You're white heat and decisions I can't control. Things I've never said before or felt before or done before. Lord, Seth, I keep shocking myself with you and that scares the pants off me." Unintentional, that reference, but oh, what a fine illustration of what she was talking about. "That's not me, Seth, that woman without underwear."

"Maybe it is you," he said, eyes narrowing, dark and intense. "Maybe you don't want safe and secure. Maybe you want to gallop horses and make risky wines and—"

"Oh, no." She held up her hands. "That's something else entirely. We're talking about marriage here. Last time I acted rashly, on passion and instinct, and I made a very bad decision. This time, I know what's at stake."

"Last time, this time—" In the space of a breath, Jillian knew what she'd implied. Saw it in the flare of his nostrils, heard it in the deceptively cool tone of his voice. "Are you comparing me to my brother? Do you think I'm using you? That I'll cast you aside after the honeymoon?"

"You know that's not what I meant. You know I was only trying to explain why I can't rush into marriage again."

He shook his head slowly, huffed out a breath. "You're not the only one with a bad marriage behind you, Jillian. The world's full of us."

His admission hung in the sharp silence, knocking all the breath from Jillian's lungs. He'd never said; she'd never asked; and now she saw regret flash swift and harsh across his expression.

"Look, I shouldn't have said that."

"But you did." Heart beating fast, she tracked the shift of his gaze, waited for it to settle back on her. "Tell me, Seth. Please."

"You know why I married Karen and it turned out to be a bad reason. I used her, she trapped me. We tried but we couldn't make each other happy." He shifted his feet, so uncomfortable talking about this that Jillian's heart contracted with a fierce burst of emotion. *Oh, Seth, you can talk to me. I understand.* "We wouldn't have lasted."

"Despite Rachel?"

"Yeah." He exhaled harshly. "I couldn't have stayed with a woman who cheated."

"Karen was having an affair?"

"Is that so hard to believe?"

It shouldn't be, not for your world-champion cheated-upon wife, but *Karen?* She had a baby. She was married to Seth. "Why would she want another man?"

He laughed, low and harsh, and shook his head. "Apparently I didn't give her the attention she deserved."

"Apparently?"

"I didn't get a chance to ask her straight out." Low, bitter, harsh, the words sounded as if they'd been wrung from his soul.

"What do you mean? Didn't you know until after…?"

After she died. Jillian's heart thudded, high in her throat, as the implication hit. She'd been with her lover the night she died.

"With Jason?" she asked on a note of disbelieving horror, even as her mind rejected the notion. She shook her head and backed up a step, found herself hard against the kitchen counter, unable to retreat any farther from the confirmation in his eyes. "You said he was giving her a lift home from the city. Her car had trouble. She needed a ride."

That's what he'd told her, afterward.

And she'd held him tight and unyielding in her arms and whispered that she was sorry, so sorry, while her heart and her stomach and her soul twisted with the guilty knowledge that her husband's recklessness had killed an innocent wife and mother. Crippling guilt because when the policeman told her he hadn't been alone, she'd known it would be a woman, his lover, beside Jason that night.

And she'd felt glad, relieved, avenged.

Hurt welled in her chest and throat, a thick, choking haze of anger and betrayal. Not because of Jason and Karen, but because the man she had always upheld as honest, true, straightforward—the man she trusted, the man she thought she loved—had lied to her.

He hadn't only concealed the truth, he'd straight out deceived her.

"You lied to me."

"Hold on a minute. That's not—"

"No! I don't want to hear justification and excuses. I heard enough of those from your brother. You knew for two years. You knew and you didn't say a word."

"I did it to protect you, Jillian. I'm not Jason."

"You might as well be."

His eyes narrowed to piercing dark intensity. A muscle jumped in his jaw. "You don't mean that."

"No." She shook her head, appalled at what she'd said but unable to apologize. Not while disenchantment gnawed at her with sharp, unrelenting teeth. "But I can't marry a man who isn't one hundred percent honest with me. I can't even consider that."

Thirteen

Determined not to fall into a heap of self-pity or remorse, Jillian carried on through the rest of the week. Doing her job, supervising as the painters and the cabinet maker and the electrician put their finishing touches on the tasting room, conducting furtive meetings with Caroline and Mercedes over the surprise aspect of Sunday night's party. Fingers crossed, Cole and Dixie hadn't sussed out the truth. They believed they were attending an unofficial opening party for family and close friends and Louret staff.

The pace was frantic and involving until, finally, late on Friday afternoon, the last tradesman left. Apart from a few cosmetic touches, it was done. Finished. Complete. And Jillian walked through the big arched entrance doors and just stood, taking it all in—exactly as she's envisaged, but more so—and she wondered when the joy of completion, of accomplishment, would hit.

She felt strangely hollow. Too tired, too brain-dead, too

emotionally numb, she decided. The party would do it. When wine flowed as it should and the room sparkled with conversation, when music and laughter rose to resonate from the exposed-beam ceilings—then she would feel the satisfaction of a job well done.

In the corner sat several boxes she'd sent up from storage, and she decided to get that job out of the way. It wouldn't take more than an hour to unpack the various wines and souvenir items they offered for sale and display them in the boxed shelves created for that purpose.

Caroline walked in ten minutes later, her mouth dropping in wonder as she turned in a slow circle. "Oh, Jillie, it looks better every time I come through the door!"

Jillian smiled because it was expected. Then she noticed the large flat package under her mother's arm. "What have you got there?"

Gaze narrowed consideringly, Caroline continued her slow perusal of the room, wall by wall. Then she nodded decisively and walked over to a prime spot behind the tasting bar. She held up the picture. A portrait of herself, painted by Dixie for the marketing launch of the Caroline Chardonnay.

"Here?" she asked.

"Perfect."

"Isn't it?" Caroline propped the picture against the wall, then rubbed her hands together with satisfaction. "Lucas can hang it later."

Her gaze lit on Jillian, paused in her task, and she came over to help. They worked together in companionable silence for several minutes before Caroline asked, "Is something troubling you, Jillie?"

"Why do you think that?"

"Mother's intuition."

Jillian sat back on her heels, looked into her mother's

caring eyes, and without any conscious thought or effort, spilled the thing uppermost in her heart. "Seth asked me to marry him."

To her credit, Caroline didn't drop the crystal decanter she'd just taken from its box. However, she did place it on its shelf with very deliberate care before she spoke. "Was that as much of a surprise to you as it is to me?"

Jillian tried to smile, but the effort felt strained and unconvincing so she gave up. "We've been seeing each other."

"And?"

"Oh, Mom, I don't know!"

Instantly her mother's hand was there, on her shoulder, a familiar comforting touch that she leaned into and rubbed her cheek against. She hadn't realized how much emotion she had bottled up, how much she needed to talk, until this minute.

"Do you love him?" Caroline asked.

"I thought so. I really did, Mom, but how do you know? How do you know it's the real thing with a man? I know what it feels like loving you and Lucas and Mercedes and, Lord knows why, my brothers. It's this warm blanket around my heart when everything else is cold and bleak. But, Seth—" She heaved a sigh packed with frustration and anguish. "Half the time it's this stomach-churning angst, this tightness in my temples and my chest and my throat."

"And the other half?"

"The other part is pretty, well, wonderful." She shifted uneasily, not sure she could share all the white-hot wonderful details with her mother. "But I want the kind of warm, strong, companionable love that endures. Like you and Lucas have."

"That's how a good love ages." Caroline took a forgotten bottle of merlot from Jillian's lax hands. "Like a good wine it starts out simple in character and style, but it just keeps growing stronger and more rounded, revealing more and more layers and complex flavors as the years go by."

"Most wines don't age that well."

"They do if they're made right, honey. You know that."

Jillian shook her head and returned to unpacking the display wines. How did she know if she and Seth were right? If their relationship had the right ingredients? If together they would make the perfect blend?

"Lucas waited for me," Caroline said quietly. "He knew I needed time, and he waited."

She wanted to say *but Seth isn't Lucas,* except the words wouldn't come. Perhaps because she knew Seth was a man who would wait, a man who had waited, a man she could rely on and—

"He lied to me, Mom."

Caroline's head came up sharply. "Well, that does surprise me. Did he have good reason?"

"It was something he thought would hurt me, but he didn't only keep the truth from me. He straight out deceived me when he knew how I valued honesty."

"I suspect Seth has a very strong protective instinct," her mother said carefully.

"Well, I'd rather be hurt by the truth than be protected by a bald-faced lie."

Caroline pursed her lips, but said nothing. Not for several, long, fraught seconds. Then she said, "Only you can make up your mind about this, Jillie, but consider one thing. How much do you suppose it hurt Seth to do something so out of character? And how much is it hurting him now?"

With the party to organize and the uncertainty over whether the renovations and redecoration would be finished, Jillian had lined up staff to cover for her in the tasting room over the weekend. Now she wished she had more to do. More than worrying over whether she'd made the biggest mistake of her life in Seth's kitchen on Tuesday night.

When the florist's husband called Sunday morning to say his wife had gone into premature labor before finishing the arrangements for the party, Jillian actually thanked him. This was exactly what she needed right now. A problem she could act upon and solve. A problem with a real and tangible solution.

Charlotte.

Her cousin didn't hesitate before offering to take over, even though she was preparing for a big event in the Ashton estate reception hall that afternoon. "If you can arrange to have the materials delivered from Regina's to the estate, that would be a big help," she said.

Jillian could have arranged delivery, but she relished the chance to escape from the nothing-left-to-do-but-stress atmosphere at the tasting room. Instead she borrowed the winery van, picked up the semi-completed arrangements and extra flowers from Regina's, and headed for the Ashton estate on the other side of Napa.

The housekeeper answered her call from the security gates and let her into the huge walled compound. And although this was Jillian's second visit, she shook her head with the same mix of anxiety and stupefaction as she circled the reflecting pool and pulled up in front of the imposing mansion. Before Spencer pilfered it all in the divorce settlement, the estate had belonged to Caroline. It had been in the Lattimer family for generations. Yet Jillian simply could not imagine her mother in such a formal and ostentatious environment.

Nor could she imagine Charlotte fitting in here, which probably explained why she'd moved into a cottage on another part of the estate. But at the moment she was working somewhere inside, and Jillian wished she'd asked for precise directions when she had called from the gates.

Was the reception hall in the west wing or east? Was there a delivery entrance around the back she should use? And why was she standing by her car dithering when she could walk up to the door and ask the housekeeper or whichever staff member answered?

It had definitely been easier the first visit, with Mercedes for moral support. Together they'd marched up those steps, sisters-in-arms, joking about breaching the enemy fortress. Today Jillian took a deep breath and marched up there alone.

She was half a knuckle away from knocking when the door swung open. She sucked in a breath and took a quick step backward. If she hadn't, the man coming through the door would have ploughed right over her.

Instead she faced Spencer Ashton.

She saw a tiny glint of recognition in eyes the same green as hers, but that was all. No greeting, no acknowledgment, nothing. He glanced back over his shoulder and called for the housekeeper.

I see you, I recognize you, I call the staff.

The perfect snub, Jillian thought, as he made to continue on his way. He would have done so and she would have let him, except for the wave of hot indignation that rose from deep in her mettle. Not on her own behalf, but for a redheaded cherub with those same green eyes. An innocent without the protection he needed, without the recognition he deserved, without the financial support this man should have provided.

"Wait," she called at his retreating back.

Impatience tightened Spencer's features as he glanced back over his shoulder. "You wanted to see me? I'm on my way out."

"Don't worry. I won't keep you."

"You already are."

Jillian came down to the second-from-bottom step, from where she enjoyed the slightest height advantage. "I don't *want* to see you, at least not on my own behalf. But there's a little boy who does need your help. His name's Jack Sheridan and he's your son, although I'm sure you're aware of that."

His response? He pushed back one tailored cuff and checked his watch, as if timing the minute or thirty seconds or whatever he deemed this topic's worth. Probably not even that long.

"His aunt—his guardian—has been receiving threats. She's concerned about his safety. She's tried to see—"

"This sounds like a matter for the police. Is that all?"

Is that all? The cold, heartless, selfish bastard.

"Will you see her?" she persisted. "Will you at least talk to Anna?"

"I don't see that it's any of your concern, Jocelyn."

Was he for real? Did he not even remember her name? Or was that a deliberate ploy, a means to deflect her attention while he turned and walked away.

Jillian released her breath in an incredulous sigh. "You are some piece of work, Spencer Ashton."

For all the sordid press about bigamy and multiple affairs, despite the damage inflicted on Ashton-Lattimer stock, despite her getting in his face about his youngest unacknowledged son, the man looked totally unaffected. Oblivious, or in denial, just like Jason when anything had gone awry in his world.

And what about all the people you've hurt, she wanted to yell after him. *Are they not my concern, either? Have you no conscience?*

She shook her head slowly, sadly, knowing the answer.

The only person he cared about was Spencer Ashton and the knowledge left her oddly…untouched. His callous attitude toward Jack and Anna infuriated her, but his snub hadn't hurt because he simply didn't matter.

Only someone she loved could hurt her—not Spencer, not Jason—but someone she loved deeply.

Someone like Seth.

The party was wonderful. Jillian knew this because everyone kept telling her so. The new tasting room, those amazing arched windows, the marble tasting bar, Dixie's portrait of Caroline, Charlotte's flowers. The surprise on Dixie and Cole's faces when Mercedes wheeled out the wedding cake.

It was all wonderful and her face ached from smiling as she graciously accepted all the acclaim. Her face ached and, as she watched Cole and Dixie dance by, so entranced with each other and in each other, her heart ached and her soul ached.

She'd really thought Seth would come, not to celebrate the completion and accomplishment because to him this was just another job. But because Caroline had made a point of phoning and extracting an acceptance from him. She'd sounded so serenely confident that Jillian had bitten back her own need to call him when she had returned from the Ashton estate.

Foolishly, she'd felt this sense of destiny about tonight being the place and the time to set things right between them.

Despite the lateness, she couldn't stop watching the door, scanning the room—she was doing it again now, dammit. But before she could stop that reflexive crowd scrutiny, her eyes connected with Caroline's across the room and she read the sympathy, the concern, and it was too much to bear.

She couldn't do this anymore. Stand here smiling and acting like the party girl, when her heart was shattering like crystal under a hammer. She couldn't run; she wouldn't run. She had her pride and this was her night. But she needed some air, some space, and a little time to gather her composure.

Them she would return with her smile intact.

Seth found her in the vines, a shimmer of champagne against the leafy darkness. She'd watched him, he knew, from the second he stepped out of the tasting room door. He felt it in every tense, uptight, what-am-I-doing-here cell of his body.

"I didn't think you were coming," she said when he finally stopped at her side. "It's so late that I'd given up on you."

She turned her head then, and when their eyes met he knew exactly why he was here. Despite everything they'd said and wished unsaid, despite every reservation and every fear, he couldn't not be here.

Even if she had given up on him.

She looked away again, back toward the tasting room and Seth closed his eyes for a brief moment, to say a silent prayer that that wasn't so. That he hadn't misread the quiet yearning in her eyes a moment before. That he could find the right words to explain himself and the emotions that had clawed holes in his heart ever since she'd walked out of his kitchen.

"I never wanted to deceive you, Jillian. You'd been through so much." He tipped back his head, released a harsh breath. "I used to look at you and wonder how much more you could take of Jason's crap before you snapped. I thought you loved him. I didn't want to hurt you any more."

"I know." Husky-edged, her voice trembled a little as she turned to look at him. "I know the truth isn't something you take lightly. I know that's not the man you are."

"I'm not Jason. I would never—"

"Hush." She stretched up and put her hand to his mouth to shut him up. "No more past. No more."

It took a minute for the words, the message, the concentrated emotion in her eyes to take hold. Slowly her hand slid from his mouth and across his cheek in a promise-filled caress. Seth swallowed hard. "Are you saying you forgive me?"

"Only if you forgive yourself…and me for what I said the other day."

"You were hurting."

"Badly," she whispered. "The only people who have the power to hurt, to really hurt where it matters—" she touched her hand to her heart "—are the people you love."

Her words, and the way she was looking at him with that glimmer of tears in her eyes, just about brought Seth to his knees. "Are you saying what I think you're saying?"

"Lord, I hope so. I love you, Seth, and I do want to marry you if you'll still have me."

"If I'll still have you? Are you crazy?"

"Yes," she admitted. "Will you still have me if I admit that I'm completely, certifiably loopy about you?"

Seth laughed softly, joyously. "Oh, yes. I'll have you."

"Then why are you standing over there?"

"Good question."

He closed the space between them, and for several long heartbeats he just stood there looking at her, this woman he had loved for so long, scarcely believing, hardly daring to believe. "So, you're going to marry me."

"Yes, I do believe I am."

He closed his eyes again, said a silent thank you, and then he opened them again so he could look right into her eyes while he kissed her, gently, tenderly, stroking the corners of her mouth and still smiling. "I've missed you, baby."

"I know." She closed her eyes. "I am so, so glad you came tonight."

"And if I hadn't?"

"I was coming to see you tomorrow. I had to apologize. But this is right—you, me, here in the vines and look—" She lifted her hand to gesture at the bright arches of light that spun out from the tall winery wall. "You *had* to see how perfect it looks from out here at night. Your design, your execution. You knew exactly what I wanted."

"Yeah, well, I'd much rather see how perfect you look, out here, in the night." He leaned back, enough that she could see all that he felt for her in his eyes. "I love you, Jillian, with all my heart. Thank you for taking a risk on me."

"A wise person once told me that some risks are worth taking."

"He must be very wise."

"It's one of the many things I love about him." Her smile curled with pure happiness as she moved into his arms. "You want to hear some of the others?"

Seth did but not now, not while he was busy kissing her. He figured he had plenty of years ahead for hearing them, all the way to forever.

* * * * *

AWAKEN THE SENSES

BY
NALINI SINGH

Nalini Singh has always wanted to be a writer. Along the way to her dream, she obtained degrees in both the arts and law (because being a starving writer didn't appeal). After a short stint as a lawyer, she sold her first book and from that point there was no going back. Now an escapee from the corporate world, she is looking forward to a lifetime of writing, interspersed with as much travel as possible. Currently residing in Japan, Nalini loves to hear from readers. You can contact her via the following e-mail address: nalini@nalinisingh.com.

This one's for all my buddies in RWNZ.
I'd be lost without your support, humour
and encouragement.

I'd also like to acknowledge the assistance provided by
the following people during my research for this book:
Cheryl Heermann, Gordon Lindsay, Melissa Moraven,
Tom O'Sullivan and Sarah Stephenson. Any mistakes
are courtesy of this author and her artistic licence.

Prologue

Thirty-One Years Ago

"**W**e need to talk."

Spencer looked up from the papers on his desk as Lilah walked into his office. Irritated by the interruption, he frowned. Normally, that would've shut her up.

She continued to speak. "If you don't divorce Caroline, I'm going to leave you." Her voice shook, but in her eyes he glimpsed determination that felt dangerously close to a threat.

Anger blazed inside him, dark and far more violent than anything Lilah could summon. It took no effort to rise and move around the desk until his body was almost touching the reed-thin redhead who'd had the audacity to give him an ultimatum.

Her blue eyes widened. Tall as she was, Lilah had no trouble meeting his gaze. He wondered what she saw there that gave her the courage to straighten her spine. If she'd understood the depth of his fury, the silly chit would've been cowering in fear.

"You're beautiful, Lilah." He saw her pride awaken and almost laughed at how easy it was to manipulate her. "But the second you walk out that door—" he thrust in the verbal knife and twisted "—ten nubile young things will be standing there begging for my attention."

He enjoyed Lilah, enjoyed her body and her face, enjoyed the way she gave in to all of his wishes. Completely under his spell, she would do anything he asked. Now, he watched her swallow and savored the sight of her already shaky confidence seeping out of her.

"I mean it, I want you to leave Caroline." Though that husky, little-girl voice shook, her blue eyes sparked with possessiveness. "You've been with her for six years—it's my turn now."

The sexual attraction he felt for her flared at this display of just how much she wanted him, but coldly, clinically, he squelched it. "And if I don't?" His voice had gone quiet. A warning.

Her slender shoulders squared. "Then I'm going to find another man. You can hire yourself a new…secretary." The last word was a taunt.

Nobody walked away from Spencer Ashton. *Nobody.* Certainly not a female whom he'd bedded and had yet to tire of. Reaching out with one hand, he grasped her hair and pulled her body hard against his, not caring if he hurt her. When he tugged her head back, her eyes met his, fear dawning in the blue.

Tightening his grasp, he leaned in very close and whispered, "What did you say?"

She whimpered as he pulled her head even further back. "I'm s-sorry, Spencer. I d-didn't mean it."

The panic in her eyes acted as an aphrodisiac. He was suddenly very sure that he was going to have Lilah Jensen spread out under him within a few minutes. "Good." He ran his finger down her throat. "What was that about leaving me if I didn't leave Caroline?" Her skin was soft under his spreading hand, her neck fragile.

"I—I'm s-sorry," she said again. "I'll make it up to you." Tentatively, her hands touched his chest, beginning to undo buttons. "It's just that I want you s-so much."

He smiled, aware that she really did want him that much. She *was* a beautiful thing, he acknowledged. And very accommodating in bed. He might end up marrying her after he got rid of Caroline, but that was for him to decide. Lilah had to learn her place here and now, before he gave her anything, much less the right to bear his name.

"I'll do anything you want, Spencer." Lilah's blue gaze was a little less afraid, a little more sexually enticing.

He found the combination seductive, but despite her charms, he wanted her to be very, very aware that this had been her last chance. Keeping one hand clenched in her hair, while the other moved to rest over her breast, he whispered, "A lot of people have tried to threaten me over the years." He kept his voice casual, thrillingly aware of the power he held over this woman.

Her lips parted as she tried to speak. He squeezed her throat slightly. She shut up.

"Not a single one has succeeded in turning threat into reality. *Not a single one.*" He smiled gently and leaned down to kiss her parted lips. "Do we understand each other?"

Lilah nodded, not attempting to speak. He liked her total consent to his will, liked that she'd finally acknowledged and accepted the place she occupied in his life. To him, she was property. He owned her like he owned his car and his home.

Lust awakened inside him, fed by the fuel of her fear and perhaps even by the way she wanted him. Pressing her closer, he said, "Now…why don't you show me how sorry you are."

One

Alexandre wondered if he'd made a mistake in accepting Trace Ashton's invitation to stay at the estate. It had seemed like the convenient option, given that he'd be spending large amounts of time at the Ashton Estate Winery in the coming weeks.

His arrival last night had been unremarkable. The elegant Lilah Jensen Ashton had welcomed him to her showcase of a home and ensured that he was comfortable. Spencer Ashton hadn't made an appearance, but having met the man previously, Alexandre hadn't been the least disappointed. The Ashton patriarch was an arrogant bastard who Alexandre didn't particularly care for. Of course, he thought with cynical amusement, some would apply the same label to him.

He stalked through rows of vines bathed in the early morning sunshine, still dewed with the light rain that had fallen earlier. The soil was a rich brown, the entire vineyard full of life. Fresh green leaves covered the ropey vines and flowering was well in progress. He paused for a second to examine some of the flowers, judging that fruit set would begin soon. But the thought didn't distract him for long, his mind still on his living arrangements.

Though he was an early riser, this morning his slumber had been interrupted by loud voices in the second floor hallway. Soon after he'd come fully awake, a door had slammed and shut out the altercation, but what he'd heard had been enough to tell him that Lilah and Spencer's marriage wasn't exactly on solid ground.

The fact that just before he'd left for this walk he'd seen Spencer drive off at a furious speed, had only cemented his conclusion. That realization didn't particularly throw him off his stride. He'd seen far worse society marriages. But, if this morning had been any indication, it was highly likely that the atmosphere in the house was going to be uncomfortable during his stay.

His other concern was that he might inadvertently become privy to family matters when he had no desire to get caught up in the turmoil surrounding the Ashtons. He was here to advise Trace on the estate's winemaking processes—nothing more. Frowning, he knelt down between the vines, testing the soil with his fingertips. The gesture was instinctive, barely impinging on his thoughts.

As a stranger, he didn't understand all the emotional undercurrents running through the house, but he could make an educated guess given the scandal that had erupted last month relating to Spencer's first marriage.

Alexandre was a winemaker, not a socialite, but it had proved impossible to avoid hearing that bit of news. His *maman* thought it her business to keep him informed of his business rivals' and friends' weaknesses. He smiled at the thought of the woman who'd been the only constant in his life, such as she was, flaws and all.

A strange sound, followed by sudden movement to his left, caught his attention, shifting his thoughts away from his troubled hosts. Irritated at the prospect of having his solitude disturbed, he paused in the act of rising to his feet, wondering who else was awake at this hour. Seeking privacy, he'd deliberately walked away from the main house and the likelihood of company.

"Why are you making that funny noise?" a soft female voice asked. "I gave you a full checkup yesterday!"

Eyebrows raised, Alexandre stood and stepped out of the vines into a narrow abutting lane that he hadn't noticed earlier. The cause of the disturbance was immediately visible. Delight replaced his earlier irritation. Now, this wake-up call was far more to his liking.

She was petite, he thought—her body small but with no lack of curves. One of those lush curves was currently outlined beautifully by well-worn denim as she knelt on the ground and peered at the front wheel of her bicycle. Long, arrow-straight black hair shifted like thick silk as she moved, brushing her bottom again and again.

Interest sparked low and deep in his gut, a sharp hunger that was at odds with the jaded boredom that had crept up on him over the past year. "Do you need assistance, *mon amie?*"

Charlotte spun around so fast, she almost toppled her bike. Not having expected anyone else to be up and about, she was startled to find herself looking up into the most gorgeous male face she'd ever seen.

An amused light in his dark eyes, the stranger held out a long-fingered hand. "My apologies. I didn't mean to startle you."

Swallowing, she let him help her to her feet. His hand was strong, his fingers curling around her own until she felt engulfed…owned. Heat sizzled up her spine and burned through her cheeks. She tugged her hand away the moment she was up, unable to cope with the explosive fire shooting through her body.

"We haven't been introduced," he said, his voice accented in a way that was so very deliciously French, her knees threatened to give out. "I'm Alexandre Dupree."

Alexandre. It suited him. A strong, masculine name for a man who was just that.

"Char—Charlotte," she managed to say around the lump of fascination stuck in her throat.

"Charlotte," he repeated, and on his lips, her ordinary name was suddenly exotic. "And what are you doing here so very early, *petite* Charlotte? You work on the estate, *oui?*"

Perhaps she should've been insulted that he thought her a worker, rather than a member of the privileged Ashton family, but then she'd never wanted to be a member of that family. "No." She hadn't ever met a man like him, one who exuded sexuality like other men breathed. It made rational thought difficult.

"No?" His full lips curved into a coaxing smile that was just this side of sinful. "You wish to be a mystery?"

"What about you?" she blurted out, the compulsion to know more about him overcoming her nervous shyness.

Who was this man who'd smiled at her and in a single moment succeeded in shaking all her beliefs about her own ability to experience passion and desire? She could feel her body sparking with life, embers of something hot and sensual glowing deep inside her. It was as if she'd been waiting for this man since the day she'd become a woman. Was it any wonder no one else had ever measured up?

His eyes, dark as the bitterest chocolate, lingered on her lips and she wanted to ask him to stop, but the words wouldn't come. It felt like he was kissing her with nothing more than a look, making her feel things that should be illegal this early in the morning.

"I am working with Trace Ashton."

A winemaker, she thought, well aware of Trace's ambition to produce award-winning Ashton Estate vintages. Yet, Alexandre didn't appear to be anyone's idea of an employee. Though he was dressed casually in black slacks and an open-necked white shirt with the sleeves rolled up, she could tell that the clothing was of the finest quality, as was the steel watch strapped to his wrist.

"Where do you go, *ma chérie?*" He looked down the pathway, where it curved through the vines. "Would you like some company on your journey?"

Her eyes widened. "N-no," she stuttered, flustered by the charm of his smile, the sinful beauty of his eyes. "I— I have to go. I'm late." Straddling her bike, she pushed off the kickstand and began to pedal away.

Crackle, clunk, crackle.

Her face flushed as the noise sounded, a reminder of why she'd stopped in the first place. Halting, she was about to get off when she became aware that Alexandre had moved in close.

"Stay, Charlotte. I can see the problem." Leaning down, he twisted the back reflector, his strong fingers making quick work of the task. "It had shifted so it rubbed against the spokes of the wheel," he explained when he saw her peering over her shoulder.

Another blush heated her cheeks. She knew that even her darker skin tone wouldn't have hidden that appallingly vivid indication of her complete inability to deal with him. "Thank you."

"You are welcome. *Bon voyage.*" The teasing smile accompanying his words made her want to bite her lip. Or maybe she wanted to bite his…

Taking a ragged breath, she started pedaling, aware of his gaze on her back until she turned the corner. Only then did she exhale and allow herself to think back over the knee-trembling encounter.

Had he been flirting with her?

A second later, she shook her head at that silly idea. Men as deliciously sexy as Alexandre Dupree didn't flirt with shy gardeners like her. But for the first time in forever, Charlotte found herself wishing that a charming, sophisticated and way-out-of-her-league male had indeed been flirting with her.

Alexandre couldn't stop thinking about his early-morning encounter as he went through the day. A bit of subtle investigation on his part had revealed two surprising bits of information. His shy beauty was an Ashton—Charlotte Ashton to be precise.

Her connection to the troubled Ashtons should've made him wary, but he was intrigued instead. The woman he'd met had been easily flustered and uneasy in his presence, yet she was a member of this privileged family.

Not only that, she operated the successful greenhouse located on the Ashton Estate. It was Trace who inadvertently gave him that information while showing him a map of the estate.

"This is Charlotte's greenhouse." Trace tapped at the outline of a building located about two miles east of the estate house. "That's the cottage and her design studio's here."

"A greenhouse?" Alexandre tried to keep his tone casual. "What is it for?"

"Charlotte does all the floral arrangements for events held on the estate. That greenhouse is her baby." The usually reserved Trace smiled. "You should go have a look—I'm sure she wouldn't mind giving you a tour."

"How do I get to Charlotte's greenhouse?" he asked, savoring the taste of her name on his lips.

"Take one of the golf carts—the path's easy to navigate."

Charlotte obviously preferred to ride her misbehaving bicycle. Alexandre smiled inwardly at the idea of tracking her to her territory. Perhaps surrounded by her flowers, she'd be more relaxed with him…more willing to entertain the ideas uncurling in the most male part of his psyche.

Work commitments meant that he didn't get a chance to seek out Charlotte until well after lunch. Around three o'clock, he commandeered a golf cart and headed east. Once he got closer, the greenhouse was easy to find, rising clearly above the vines.

He parked in front of the first building, a stone cottage surrounded by gardens full of wildflowers. Reminiscent of something out of a fairy tale, it perfectly fit the woman whom he'd surprised this morning. Small, a little fey and ultimately enchanting.

Just behind the cottage sat the greenhouse, with another building set close up against its right side. The sign on the smaller building proclaimed it to be Ashton Estate Botanicals, clearly the design studio Trace had pointed out.

Expecting Charlotte to be working in the greenhouse, he walked that way. His whole body sighed as he entered and saw her. Dressed in faded jeans that faithfully caressed every feminine curve and a short-sleeved pink shirt, she looked as fresh as the flowers blooming around her. The silky waterfall of her hair was plaited in one long rope, the end brushing across her bottom as she moved back and forth.

Her back was to him as she worked at the heavy wooden workbench set up in the middle of the greenhouse. It looked like she was repotting. She liked working surrounded by the flowers she nurtured, he thought to himself.

Suddenly, though he hadn't made a sound, she whirled around, a small trowel held aggressively in her gloved hand. Her big eyes appeared to get even bigger as she saw him. "What are you doing here?"

"I came to find my mysterious little *fleur.*" He eyed the trowel she still held pointed to his heart.

Blushing, she put it on the bench behind her. "Why?"

"Are you always so direct?" He prowled closer, liking the look of her even more than he had earlier today. She was certainly small, but she was most perfectly a woman. In the past, he'd tended to go for long-limbed beauties. Looking at Charlotte, he couldn't understand why. "It's very warm in here. You do not mind?"

"It's to help the flowers grow out of season." She watched him as he approached, as wary as a wild deer. "I like the heat."

His eye fell on a small blue notebook on her bench. "What do you write in there?" he asked curiously.

He could've sworn panic turned her eyes black. "It's my g-gardening journal."

Obviously, he'd misread her reaction. "It smells like sunshine and growth in here," he murmured, slowing his pace but not changing direction.

"What do you want?" she repeated, pressing back against the bench as if she wanted to blend into it.

"You don't like me, *ma petite?*" He wondered if for once, his sense about women had let him down. He'd never been one to push where he wasn't wanted, and certainly not with women. They were to be indulged, cosseted and coaxed, not forced. To his shock, he realized that if this woman didn't want him, he'd have a very hard time walking away.

Her gold-dust skin suffused with pink. "I didn't say that."

Scenting victory, he prowled closer, lifting a finger to touch one warm cheek. *"Non?"*

"I…" She stepped sideways, breaking contact. "Please, this is my space."

"And you wish me to leave." Though not a man who gave up easily, he had no wish to cause her any hurt.

Perhaps, he acknowledged, she'd seen the truth he'd been avoiding since the first moment she'd stared at him with those big brown eyes—at thirty-four he was far too old and jaded for her. This woman was as fresh and beautiful as the blooms she tended, and he'd lost his innocence a long, long time ago.

Fighting the urge to touch her again, he sketched a half-bow. "Then I'll go. I apologize for disturbing you." He turned and took the first steps to the door, feeling an unaccountable sense of loss.

"Wait!"

Pausing, he looked over his shoulder. Charlotte closed the gap between them and without meeting his gaze, held out a fragile white blossom. "Put this in your room. It'll make it smell like sunshine and…growth."

Startled at the gift and her recall of his words, he took the flower. "*Merci,* Charlotte. I don't believe anyone has ever given me flowers before." Lifting the bloom to his nose, he breathed in the fragrance.

Her lips curved in a tentative smile. "You're welcome."

And suddenly, he knew he was. All his confidence returned twofold. So, little Charlotte Ashton wasn't averse to him. She just wasn't comfortable in his presence. Alexandre couldn't understand why. She was a lovely, beautiful flower, as exotic as the orchids she grew in this glass garden. Beautiful women had always liked Alexandre, for they knew he was a man who appreciated them.

In truth, *most* women liked him because he genuinely liked them, respecting the steel spines beneath many of their fragile fronts. Charlotte, he thought, probably had a spine steelier than any of them. It took determination and hard work to nurture life and her greenhouse was bursting at the seams with it. Even more, it must've taken strength to follow a different path in this family dedicated to wine and business. His *maman* would like her.

"Tell me about your greenhouse," he coaxed.

Her cheeks bloomed with color but on that topic at least, she was willing to talk. "I grow lots of things in here, from daisies to ferns."

"I can see gardens behind your bench," he said, truly intrigued. "How can you grow things in the ground inside a greenhouse?"

Her eyes brightened. "The earth in that part is exposed. Small pebbles on the floor facilitate drainage."

"Show me," he said softly, seduced by the confidence in her eyes.

After the tiniest hesitation, she turned and walked back through the rows of high tables set with trays overflowing with blooms. He followed, keeping enough distance that she didn't feel crowded. As they walked, he had to duck a few times to avoid the greenery growing downward from the considerable number of hanging baskets.

After they circled her workbench, Charlotte pointed to the lush green garden on the left. "These are my ferns." The ferns were overflowing onto a small wooden bench placed next to the garden.

"And over here—" she moved to the opposite side "—are my tropical blooms. Smell this." Shyness lingered in her eyes but her lips were curved.

Undone, he leaned forward and inhaled the heady fragrance from a creamy white flower, its heart shaded with strokes of sunny yellow. "It makes me want to be on a South Sea beach."

Her smile of delight tumbled his heart. "It's *Plumeria*—frangipani. One whiff and I'm lost in dreams."

Something fell into place. "That's the scent you wear." It had been haunting him since this morning.

Big eyes widened in surprise. "Yes. I order it from the Pacific."

A sense of intimacy invaded the air. Before it could get heavy and alarm her, he asked, "What else grows here?"

She looked relieved. "Next to the frangipani is a hibiscus I've been babying for a year. It's being stubborn about blooming."

He chuckled. "Perhaps it is like you, wishing to be mysterious."

Her lashes drifted down. "I'm just me. Nothing mysterious at all."

"I disagree." Encouraged by the light in her eyes, he took a chance. "Today, I must return to my work, but will you have dinner with me tomorrow?"

All her sweet confidence disappeared under a veil of reserve. "I…I've got plans. Th—thank you for asking." She busied herself with pulling off her gloves.

He wanted to reach over and kiss her, melt her resistance with a gentle seduction. "Ah, *ma chérie,* you break my heart. Perhaps you will reconsider, *non?* If you change your mind, I'm staying at the estate house." With those lighthearted words, he headed out of the greenhouse, her gift held gently in his hand.

Now that he knew she didn't abhor his presence, he had no intention of giving up on his shy blossom. He just wished he knew what to do to win her trust. Given the jaded nature of his own heart, he'd made it a point to stay away from innocents. But, for some reason, he couldn't stay away from this one with her big brown eyes and blushing cheeks.

He knew she was too soft and young for him, but he also knew that he wasn't going to walk away. Instead, he was going to break every single one of his rules and seduce her, seduce her so completely that those brown eyes wouldn't even look at another man ever again.

A frown creased his brow at the commitment implied in that sudden thought. He had no intention of marrying, not when he knew the frailties of the institution so very well, and Charlotte was the marrying kind. A woman made for a lifetime of loving.

His scowl intensified. Why were his thoughts heading in such directions? Seduction and sensory pleasure were all he ever promised a woman. Charlotte's wariness around him told him that she understood that instinctively. He'd never lie to her about his intentions, but he *would* have her.

What most women failed to detect beneath his charming front was a determination that made a thunderstorm look weak by comparison. Once set on a course, Alexandre Dupree would not deviate from it unless it suited his purpose. And right now, he was set on sweet little Charlotte Ashton.

Two

Safe inside her greenhouse, Charlotte watched Alexandre get into the stylish golf cart and drive away.

"Oh, my," she whispered, when he was finally out of sight. The man was lethal. Those dark eyes, that charming smile and especially that way he had of looking at her like he'd like to devour her—they all added up to a combination that spelled danger. Charlotte wasn't the kind of woman with whom dangerous men played.

Rubbing her hands on her jeans, she swallowed at the thought of actually accepting Alexandre's dinner invitation. A second later, she discarded the idea. Except for when discussing her beloved plants, the one topic about which she had complete confidence, she could barely speak in his presence. The pressure of a date would undoubtedly leave her tongue-tied.

Pain shot through her at the reminder of her shortcomings. She was probably the only Ashton on the estate who couldn't hold her own in the kind of sophisticated environment they inhabited. That was why she'd retreated to her flowers. They didn't expect anything from her but kindness.

She knew she was partly at fault for her social inability. If she'd stayed in the big house, she could've learned the necessary skills from Lilah.

Her lips thinned.

Sure, Lilah would've loved teaching the niceties of mingling in society to the half-breed brat who'd been foisted on her. The elegant redhead had always quietly hated the fact that she'd been saddled with the responsibility of raising two children of mixed parentage. Being so enamored of Spencer, Charlotte's brother Walker hadn't much noticed her subtle antipathy. But Charlotte had needed a woman in her life and Lilah had made sure Charlotte knew she could never expect that woman to be Spencer's wife.

Shaking her head, she returned to the seedlings she'd been repotting. Perhaps she could ask Jillian for advice, she thought, sinking one gloved hand into a bag of soil. There was a grace about her older cousin that would've normally intimidated Charlotte, but Jillian also had such warmth that she'd found herself wanting to tell the slender brunette things she rarely told anyone.

Like her belief that her mother was still alive.

For the past few months, that belief had grown stronger and stronger, until she was almost bursting with the need to share it. Since the secret of Spencer's first marriage had come out, her belief had turned into a certainty. If the man could lie once, why not twice?

Though she wanted to share her thoughts, she'd barely been able to broach the topic even with Jillian. Confiding the details would require a level of trust that Charlotte couldn't bring herself to give to anyone.

She shook her head at her own wandering thoughts.

"You have to finish the repotting." Despite the order, her mind kept returning to the topic and she knew why. It was because she'd stalled in her search. Not because she didn't know how to go forward but because she was afraid.

What she found could change her life forever. Going alone and unsupported into the unknown frightened her. After years of hard work, she'd managed to create a haven on this estate where she'd never felt at home. The thought of losing this feeling of safety to the cruel truth terrified her.

Alexandre Dupree had surely never been afraid, never been a coward like her, she thought, unable to keep her mind from drifting to the charming Frenchman who'd walked into her life and far too quickly begun to fascinate her.

He reminded her of all the things she could never be. The man exuded charisma with every breath, as dangerously beautiful as a stalking leopard. His sensuality alone was powerful enough, but once you added the razor sharp mind hidden behind the charm, he became the most fascinating creature she'd ever met.

She guessed his lazy charm fooled many people into thinking him a playboy. She knew better. After meeting him that morning, she'd logged onto the Internet and done some research. Alexandre Dupree was no playboy. He was one of the most respected winemakers in the world. The only reason she hadn't heard his name before now was that her plants interested her far more than the vineyards and their produce. That was Trace's passion.

Not only was he a respected winemaker, Alexandre was a rich one. Filthy rich. The most public of his successful commercial interests was the small winery he owned in France, but she'd also found his name mentioned in relation to several exclusive restaurants. It made sense that a man famed for producing "wines of stunning complexity" should choose to align himself with places that served food fit for his wines.

What made him extraordinary was that instead of hoarding it, he didn't begrudge others his expertise. Witness his presence here, helping Trace find just the right texture, the right taste, to tempt the most fussy of palates.

If Alexandre's wealth and skill hadn't been enough to intimidate her, she'd found several photos of him at high profile events. He'd been photographed at the Cannes Film Festival several times, always accompanied by a leggy, sharply elegant creature in a killer dress. Not only did his women have several inches in height on Charlotte, they had "breeding" stamped on their perfect profiles, elegance oozing out of their perfect pores and grace flowing from their every perfect movement.

Shaking her head at her inability to banish the Frenchman to a corner of her mind, she finished off the final pot and quickly tidied up. When she walked into her cottage to take a shower, the first thing she saw was the picture of Alexandre she'd printed out that morning. Frustrated with her susceptibility to the man, she strode into the shower, hoping the water would wash away her inexplicable fascination.

Fifteen minutes later, she stepped out of the humid glass cube and shrugged into a fluffy white robe. As she stood in front of her bedroom mirror, combing her towel-dried hair, her eyes didn't see the woman she'd become but the painfully shy girl she'd been.

Unable to adapt fully to life with the Ashtons, she'd withdrawn into herself when Walker had begun to spend more and more time with Spencer. To the girl she'd been, it had felt like her uncle had stolen her brother from her…just like he'd stolen her mother.

The phone rang, startling her into dropping the brush. "Charlotte," she said, her voice a little husky.

"Ma chérie, what is wrong?"

Every nerve ending in her body went on high alert at that deep male voice. "Nothing."

A pause. "Have you changed your mind about dinner with me tomorrow?" His words were practical but his tone turned them into a caress…a question from one lover to another.

She knew she should reprimand him for the way he continued to speak to her so familiarly, but she couldn't find the words. "I…" The temptation to say yes was almost overwhelming, but fear held her back—she didn't know how to deal with a man like him. Only in her dreams could she be witty and sophisticated enough for him. "No."

He sighed, as if she'd broken his heart. "Then perhaps I could persuade you into a walk?"

The hunger in her bucked at the reins. "A walk?"

As if sensing victory, his sinful voice became even more hauntingly seductive. "I'll come to your cottage tomorrow around six and we can take a walk through the vineyard. Say yes, Charlotte."

Sweat dampened her palms. "I'll be ready." She couldn't believe her own temerity.

"Until tomorrow then. Good night—sleep well."

As she hung up the phone, Charlotte wondered about the number of women who'd heard the same from him in far more intimate settings. Surely, a man as sensual as Alexandre had no lack of bed partners. Wrenching the brush through her hair, she told herself to stop obsessing.

Unfortunately, she couldn't control her dreams.

Alexandre spent the night alone, as he'd chosen to do for a considerable period of time. Though he had a healthy sexual appetite, simple physical pleasure had ceased to satisfy his needs.

He wanted something more, though if pressed, he wouldn't have been able to say exactly what it was that was missing from his life. He just knew that despite his sexual frustration, no woman had tempted him to break his self-imposed celibacy.

Until now.

Charlotte Ashton had reawakened the craving, a craving sharper than ever before. He might've put the strength of his need down to his long period of abstinence, except that compared to the sensual shimmer between him and Charlotte, all his previous relationships had been mere shadows.

She was…unique, he thought, clasping his hands behind his head as he lay in the guest bedroom allocated to him by his hostess. Apparently, it had once been Walker Ashton's room. All traces of the other man were now gone. A pity, Alexandre mused. Perhaps he might've divined something about Charlotte from her brother.

Both his fascination and frustration with her had been mounting since this morning. For the first time in over a year, he'd seen a woman whom he couldn't get out of his head and she was as wary as a butterfly, as wide-eyed and innocent as a teenager. He wondered if she were truly as innocent as she appeared. Something low in him tightened in expectation and…possession.

Surprise had him sucking in a sharp breath.

Alexandre had never been a possessive man, had never wanted to be, not after the lessons of his childhood. He knew just how changeable women were, knew that a man couldn't rely on them, beautiful and lovely though they might be. While he'd appreciated and enjoyed their seductive femininity, he'd always kept a safe emotional distance between himself and his lovers.

Even the single time he'd forgotten that vow in the headlong rush of youthful emotion, part of him had remained separate. His fiancée, Celeste's defection had hurt him but he'd been far from devastated.

But now, a deeply slumbering part of him was waking and it felt like truth. This possessive tyrant was a part of his psyche that he'd forcibly restrained for a lifetime but it refused to be silenced any longer. The tyrant had sensed Charlotte's compelling scent and decided she belonged to him. Without compromise.

Smiling into the darkness, Alexandre accepted the possessiveness rushing through him, reveling in the powerful emotion after months of jaded weariness. This unabating hunger was uncharted territory, but he welcomed the dangers which lay ahead.

"Charlotte, *ma petite*," he whispered into the heavy darkness. "I shall enjoy our dance."

He spent most of the following day in discussions with James, the head winemaker. To Alexandre's relief, the other man was in no way threatened by his presence. James knew he was good at what he was employed to do—create popular Ashton wines. Alexandre's purpose at the estate was entirely different.

They began with an intensive tour of the winery, including the basement cellars. Alexandre was particularly interested in the nature and size of the barrels used to age Ashton vintages, given their affect on the amount of oxygen that reached the maturing wine.

The rest of the time was taken up with an investigation of the fermentation tanks and discussions on technical matters such as sulphurification and cooling. This was necessary background—before he could advise Trace about the future, he had to understand how the winery operated now.

When he finally called it a day, he had barely enough time for a quick shower before heading to Charlotte's. To his pleasure, she was waiting outside for him, checking things in the outdoor gardens that surrounded her enchanted cottage.

He walked over, taking in the exquisite sight of her in well-worn blue jeans and a short-sleeved white shirt. Detailed with lace and skimming close to her body, the shirt was enticingly feminine. *"Bonjour,* Charlotte.*"*

Having seen him arrive, she wasn't startled, but wariness shadowed her eyes. "Hi."

"Shall we?" With another woman, he would've touched her lower back, or perhaps taken her arm, but with Charlotte, he had a feeling that even such a small advance would be moving too fast.

After a minute hesitation, she began to walk beside him along the lane she used to cycle up to the estate house. There was more than enough daylight left for him to watch his intriguing, mysterious companion.

"You must know much about the vines, having grown up on the estate." He forced himself to keep his tone conversational and light despite the sensual tension that shivered between them.

Beside him, Charlotte moved her shoulders in a shrug that tried to be careless but was just a little too tense. At the same time, something flickered in her expression and he got the impression that she didn't like talking about the world she inhabited.

"I don't know that much." She looked up to meet his gaze. "It doesn't really interest me. I've picked up bits and pieces over the years."

"You're interested only in flowers?" He paused and she did the same, turning to face him.

"Not only. But mostly." A smile spread across her face. "I will admit that I love the vineyard at this time of year."

"Why?" He spoke softly, unwilling to trigger her previous wariness when she appeared to be relaxing.

"It's the fact that they're coming to life." Her fingers caressed the edges of a new leaf. Desire spiked—would she stroke her man as sweetly? "Everything's just beginning and there are so many possibilities in the air."

He was captivated by the fleeting glimpse of the woman hidden behind the self-contained quietness. "Yes, the possibilities are endless."

Her cheeks bloomed a soft pink and he knew she understood that they were no longer talking about the vines. Instead of shying away, she said, "The choices we make now have to be the right ones, though—otherwise the damage to the harvest could be substantial."

"Perhaps that's true," he said, delighted by her willingness to at least consider the idea of taking their relationship further. "But there are also times when chances must be taken."

"It's safer to follow the known path."

His lips quirked at the challenge. "Safe approaches produce palatability, nothing more. I prefer my wine to be far more full-bodied, a symphony of aroma and taste to delight the senses. Do you not, *chérie?*"

"Yes, I do." There was a dreamy sensuality to her voice that he knew had come about because of his words, and he reveled in it. "I don't know much about winemaking."

"I can teach you everything. Ask me any question you wish."

She parted her lips, as if to speak. And that was all it took. Awareness flashed to life between them, sudden and blinding. Her eyes widened but she didn't back away as he'd half expected. Instead, invitation trembled in the lushness of her mouth.

He'd told himself to be patient—to coax, not push—but at that moment he couldn't remember any of his own warnings. Desire washed over him in a powerful wave, obliterating caution. Reaching out, he cupped her cheek with one hand and bent his head. Without any prompting, her lips parted even further, disintegrating his control.

She was soft and tasted like his darkest dreams. The decadent flavor of her was at odds with her innocent eyes and it intoxicated him. He'd intended only a sip but found himself delving deeper, asking for more. For a stunning moment of sensory pleasure, she responded with desire as open and wild as his.

But the moment was far too short. Making a tiny sound, she jerked away. "What…?" Confusion muddled her gaze as she touched her kiss-wet lips with one trembling hand, the other flat on his chest.

He could see that she wasn't ready to deal with the implications arising from the stunning sensuality of their first kiss. The rapid entanglement of their senses had shaken him and he was by far the more experienced party. He couldn't blame her for looking like the world had just crumbled from under their feet.

"It was only a kiss." He kept his hands to his sides, though he wanted nothing more than to hold her. "It was of no moment." He'd meant to reassure her, but knew he'd said the wrong thing when she stumbled back a step, bruised hurt in her eyes.

"I'm afraid you have the wrong idea about me, Mr. Dupree." Tears glittered but her soft tone was suddenly without compromise. "Find another woman for your kisses of no moment. I'm not interested in relieving your boredom while you're here."

"*Charlotte.*" He wondered if she'd react any better to the truth—that though they'd barely met, he hungered for her like he'd never hungered for another woman.

From the instant he'd seen her, his body had recognized hers and ached for completion. What they'd felt in that kiss had been a sign of the sensual surrender to come, something his innocent lover was in no way prepared to accept.

"Don't." She began to back away toward her home. "I shouldn't have come with you."

The words cut him. "I would never harm you."

"It's what men like you do," she whispered and then she was gone.

He could've caught up in seconds but knew that any chase would be futile. She was in no mood to listen. In an attempt to protect her, he'd wounded her pride and made her feel less of a woman. And he was still smarting from her final words.

What did she know about men like him? Did she place him in the same category as Spencer Ashton? Anger flared. Shoving his hands in the pockets of his tan slacks, he began to stride back toward the estate house. He'd ask someone to come down tomorrow and retrieve the golf cart. Right now, he needed to work off both his anger and a fair dose of sexual tension.

It's what men like you do.

Maybe she was right. He had no intention of offering her forever, and she was the kind of woman for whom forever had been created.

But, as he'd decided last night, he wasn't going to let her push him away, either. Not when this thing between them blazed with life on both sides. Charlotte Ashton belonged to Alexandre Dupree—no matter what she'd tried to convince herself of after being singed by the heat of that kiss.

Three

Charlotte wasn't known for her temper, but she was good and mad as she entered the cottage and slammed the door. How dare he kiss her in a way that melted her bones and then say it was of no moment? How could he not have felt what she had? His reaction had humiliated her, made her feel like that gawky, lonely teenager all over again. And it had made her angry.

She might not be as sophisticated as him, but she had her pride and it wasn't something that she'd let any man disparage. As far as she was concerned, Alexandre Dupree could find himself a new toy. It no longer mattered that before their kiss, she'd found herself becoming more and more comfortable in his presence.

Oh, he'd still made her stomach flutter with nerves and her femininity sit up and take notice, but she'd begun to lose her shyness. Each time he'd turned those dark French eyes on her, she felt herself coming to life as a woman.

It was just as well that this had ended before it began. She'd said her final words to him in anger, but they were true. He was a powerful, experienced male used to beautiful women and discreet affairs. He'd break her heart if she let him near her.

After giving them both a night to calm down, Alexandre had intended to seek out Charlotte first thing that morning. However, the minute he appeared at breakfast, Trace informed him that an in-depth tour of the vineyard had been organized for him, to be followed later that afternoon by a tasting of Ashton wines.

Unwilling to reveal his interest in Charlotte and further complicate an already complicated situation, he accepted the plans with good grace. The tour of the vineyard calmed his soul. However, the tasting was a disaster—the sweet aroma of Charlotte filled his senses, allowing nothing else to filter through.

No woman had ever affected him like this. He wasn't sure he liked being fascinated so completely, but he *was* sure that he wanted the object of his fascination in his arms.

Finally free of all his obligations, he drove to the cottage as evening was falling. To his surprise, Charlotte wasn't home tucked up safe and warm. Frowning, he walked over to the greenhouse, wondering if she was babying her hothouse flowers.

However, only a single light burned in the greenhouse—it was unlikely she was there. He quickly walked around to make sure. Because of the layout, it was impossible to see from one end of the greenhouse to the other, especially toward the back where her gardens took over.

He was turning to leave the garden area when something shiny caught his eye. Curious, he retraced his steps. It took him a few moments to spot the blue notebook half hidden beneath a trailing sweep of lush greenery. It lay on the small wooden bench beside the fern garden—the steel spine had reflected the light and captured his attention.

Thinking that Charlotte wouldn't like it if her notes got wet when the garden's sprinkler system activated, he picked up the slender volume and slipped it into the inner pocket of his lightweight jacket. He'd dressed semi-formally, intending to take Charlotte to dinner. He had every confidence in his ability to charm her out of her temper.

When he strode out, he was startled to see a light being turned on in the cottage. Scowling, he crossed the distance between the two buildings and knocked.

It swung open after a small pause. "What are you doing here?" she asked, eyes dark and unwelcoming.

He was hit by the utterly unsophisticated urge to haul her to his chest and teach her to never again ask him such a silly question. If she believed him to be a man who gave up easily, then she was in for a surprise.

But used to keeping his emotions under control, he only leaned lazily against the doorjamb, crowding her back into the house. "I came to see you, *ma petite*. You left me in such anger yesterday—I didn't wish to cause you pain."

"You didn't. I'm fine."

Reaching up, he captured her chin between his fingertips. "Where have you been? Why didn't I see you on the way here?"

She pulled her face away. "None of your business."

He immediately knew that demands would get him nowhere. Anger had given Charlotte the confidence she'd previously lacked around him. Yet this stubborn woman enticed him even more. "I worried for you."

Her eyes softened, exposing the gentle heart of her. "You shouldn't have. I went downtown to do some shopping. You probably didn't see me coming home because I walked through the vineyard instead of using the lane."

"In the dark? You walked, what is the distance—" he frowned in thought "—more than two miles in the dark?"

"I know this land like the back of my hand and it's barely two miles, not over two miles."

He wasn't appeased. "Charlotte, if I were not a patient man, I would be inclined to be very harsh with you for taking such a chance. You know nothing about the temporary workers who may be about." He fought the surge of protectiveness that he had no right to display. Gritting his teeth, he told himself that that would soon be rectified. Then he could look after her as she was meant to be looked after.

"Who said you're a patient man?" Charlotte muttered.

Her feminine temper seemed to have thawed under his concern and when he laced the fingers of one hand through hers, she didn't immediately move to tug them away. He imagined he could feel the quickening beat of her heart through their linked hands.

"I have the patience of a saint," he said, tongue in cheek. "Else I would give up trying to coax you and just kidnap you to my chalet deep in the Swiss mountains."

Fascination glimmered in her eyes.

Leaning over until their lips almost touched, he whispered, "Once I had you all to myself, I would do things to you that would make your toes curl." When her breath caught, he continued, "That kiss was of very great moment—you know that and so do I. Forgive me for trying to lessen it. Come, *chérie,* don't be angry with me."

Alexandre's silkily seductive voice rubbed along Charlotte's nerve endings, setting them afire. It was a potent weapon of seduction, designed to reduce a woman to nothing more than a sensate being, greedy and needy. For a moment, her body swayed toward him.

She believed him about the value of the single kiss they'd shared. She understood why he'd come looking for her when they'd barely met. She understood why he felt he had the right to demand her business, why his maleness sought to brand her with his mark.

That kiss had been far more than anything so simple as a kiss. It had been a claiming and the shocking thing was, it had been in no way one-sided. Barely a breath from his lips, she made the mistake of looking into those dark, enigmatic eyes. There was such hunger there, such possession, such *need*.

Fear spiked.

With a painful start she realized that she could never be enough for this magnificent man. Alexandre needed a woman supremely confident of her own sexuality, her own feminine appeal, a woman ready to accept the invitation in his eyes and partner him in the most intimate of dances. Charlotte wasn't even close.

Her body froze. "Please," she whispered, unable to hide the ache inside her. "Please go."

Stay, her heart whispered. *Stay,* her body moaned. *Stay.* But of course, she couldn't say that. Only in her dreams could she captivate a man like Alexandre and fulfill the sensual demands he would make of her as his woman.

"Charlotte." His fingers refused to release hers. "Do you really believe that I'm a man who hurts women?"

It was the moment's vulnerability in his tone that got to her. "No. You…you tempt women."

"Let me tempt you." His voice alone was temptation enough, the heat in his eyes pure sorcery.

Fighting the sensual pull between them with everything she had, she tugged away her hand and tried to close the door. "I'm sorry but this can't happen." With every word she spoke, she felt more and more the coward. The urge to tell him that what she already felt for him scared her, was almost overwhelming.

"Why not?" He blocked the doorway, big and proud.

Swallowing, she said, "You can't give me what I need. You can't be the man I need." What she needed from a man was a kind of surrender that strong, dominant Alexandre Dupree would never agree to. And even if he did, she'd still be left with her inadequacies.

His darkly beautiful face was suddenly a mask. "You've made yourself very clear. I'm sorry I bothered you." He stepped back, that lithely muscled body held fiercely in check. "Lock the door."

This time, she didn't argue. Maybe she was a coward, but was it cowardice to want to avoid humiliation of the kind which would result when Alexandre realized she wasn't woman enough for him?

Alexandre pulled out of the Ashton Estate in his rental car, a low-slung black Ferrari, a sleek and powerful machine. Instead of letting frustration take him on an aimless drive, he headed toward San Pablo Bay.

Charlotte had asked him to leave. Had told him that he "couldn't be the man" she needed. A woman couldn't find a much clearer way to reject a man—it felt like she'd reached into his body and clawed his heart, an emotional mauling he could barely comprehend.

For the first time in his life, his shield of emotional distance had not only cracked, it had broken into pieces. *And he hadn't even been aware of it happening.*

How had one small woman come to mean so much to him in so short a time? Even after her blunt rebuff, he craved her. Until now, he'd sincerely believed that the attraction he felt wasn't one-sided. Obviously, he'd been fooling himself, something he despised.

Ever since he'd been a child, truth had been the most important thing in his life because he'd been asked to tell lies from too early an age. They may have been lies of omission, but they'd marked him. He'd never allowed himself the comfort of falseness.

Shifting gears, he rose up an incline. How could she not feel the fire that burned him every time he thought of her, of those big brown eyes so full of passion and so unawakened? He hated the thought that some other man would be the one to awaken the slumbering sensuality he sensed in her, hated it in a way that made a mockery of anything he'd ever before felt for a woman.

His eye landed on the speedometer as he turned a corner. He swore sharply and reduced his dangerous speed. It was tempting to keep pushing the machine to the limit, but he knew he'd never forgive himself if he caused someone else an injury because he was in a temper. Ruling out a long drive, he searched for a place to stop and calm down.

A few minutes later, he noticed a small hill. Cruising up, he parked but left the engine running. Unclipping his safety belt, he opened the door and walked out to stand in the cool night air. When he went to put his hands in his pants pockets, he frowned. Something was weighing down one side of his jacket. Reaching into a pocket, he pulled out a slim volume.

The scent of Charlotte rose from the book—frangipani and moonlight. Gut clenching, he moved into the light thrown by the car's headlights and flipped open the book, curious as to what Charlotte wrote about her plants. In all honesty, he felt compelled to learn everything he could about this woman who haunted him.

All these years, women had come easily to him but he'd never taken them for granted, well aware of their fickle nature. Not letting one of them become too important to him had been a simple matter. Yet, somehow, Charlotte was making him break those rules. And the irony was, she didn't want him at all.

The first page was filled with writing characterized by curves and roundness, displaying the writer's inherently giving nature. He found himself tracing the words with his fingers, as if he could feel Charlotte. Unable to read what they said in the low-slung lights, he moved into the car and flicked on the overhead switch.

Lover Mine,

The words slammed into him like a two arm punch. If he'd still been standing, he might've doubled over. His sweet, innocent Charlotte had a lover? A lover she wrote letters to? Was this her copy of those letters?

He knew he should stop reading, but couldn't—not when the possessive beast inside him was growling in outrage. In less than two days, she'd become *his* and he didn't share.

Lover Mine,
Will you be gentle with me the first time we make love? Will you be tender? Will you understand that for me, this act is more than bodies meeting, more than simple pleasure, more than just the physical?

I'd never lie with you if I didn't adore you.

Do I love you? I've seen so much pain and betrayal in this family—I'm not even sure I know what love is. But, I do know that for me to lie with you means that I care…deeply.

Fists clenched, Alexandre checked the date of the entry. Almost six months ago. Surely Charlotte and her lover had consummated their relationship by now. He turned the page.

Lover Mine,
I've always been a good girl.

Except in my fantasies. Of course you know that.
How could you not? You know that in those fantasies, I'm another person, another Charlotte, one
who's wild and wicked and just a little bit dangerous. In my fantasies, I do things that I can't speak of
in the daylight or even in the moonlight.

In my fantasies, I'm a woman of bone-deep sensuality, as alluring and enticing as the Sirens of old,
a woman who draws men not to their doom…but to
their absolute pleasure.

There was nothing overtly sexual about her words, but
his arousal pounded low and deep. The last words lingered
on his retinas, as if burned on them.

Once more, he accepted that he was invading her privacy in a way he could never justify, that he should stop. But
the need to brand the unpalatable truth into his soul compelled him to continue.

The truth that Charlotte belonged to another man.

Jealousy shot through his nerve endings—who the hell
had dared touch her? Touch the only woman who'd succeeded in reaching Alexandre's long jaded soul, succeeded in waking him up to passion again. Reaching out a
tanned hand, he flipped the page.

Sometimes, I wonder what it would be like to give
you such complete trust that I'd do anything you
asked, without question…without hesitation. I can
almost see you, lover mine—see your strength, your
searing sexuality, your dominant tendencies.

In my fantasies, you're strong enough to treat my
submission as the gift it is, to give me commands

laced with rough tenderness, to openly adore my body without seeing it as a weakness. And, you're strong enough to understand and accept that by doing what I ask, you have surrendered to me and my desires.

I've never met a man capable of fulfilling this most sinful fantasy. Will you be the only lover I ever know?

Alexandre felt understanding start to awaken, but it remained tantalizingly out of reach, buried under jealousy such as he'd never thought himself capable of. Unable to bear reading more about Charlotte's sexual awakening with another man, he almost shut the book, but some inexplicable need made him flip through to the last entry.

He had to know—had he made any impact on her? Or had he been nothing to her, adoring as she was of this lover of hers. He opened the page to an entry dated two days ago, the day they'd met.

Lover mine,
Until today, you've never had a face…

Alexandre's eyes widened.

…never had a name. You've just been the lover I needed in every way. You were my creation so I could shape you, mold you, delete the parts of you that I didn't like. You were my ultimate fantasy, a man created for me alone, a man for whom my pleasure was his only goal and my cries as I shattered under his loving reward enough.

"Of course it would be, *ma chérie,*" Alexandre murmured, "why would you think otherwise?"

But today, you suddenly have a face and a voice. You could seduce me with that slow, seductive accent alone. I can imagine you whispering to me as we lie tangled in the most intimate of embraces, that voice of yours rippling along my spine, turning my insides to hot honey.

Alexandre felt excitement begin to flicker through his nerves. Surely he couldn't be mistaken as to whose voice gave Charlotte such erotic pleasure? That would be far too cruel. Taking a deep breath, he read on.

And then I look up into your eyes and I'm lost, utterly yours. You're so tempting, so seductive, so masculinely beautiful that you take my breath away. I know I can't be the woman you need but I ache to try.

When you look at me with heat in your eyes, I can almost believe that I'm the woman you think me to be. I can almost be the woman I fantasize about being, a woman who embraces passion without fear.

Tenderness gripped him, tight and powerful. It shocked him that Charlotte was unsure of her lovely sensuality when she had no reason to be.

Even now, I hesitate to write your name for fear that I'll tempt the Fates and they'll take even the fleeting pleasure of your presence from me. I long to see you, touch you, listen to you.

And yet when you come near, I can't help but run,

for part of me recognizes the hunter in you. I'm not sure I'm ready to be your prey…Alexandre.

His breath punched out of him as adrenaline rushed through every pore. Sweat trickled down his spine. Who would've guessed that his prim and proper Charlotte had such heated fantasies?

Even more shocking was the urgent desire he had to fulfill each and every one of them, in any way she chose. Control came easily to him. It would be no hardship to play her games in bed, even to give her the surrender she needed. The gift of her trust would be compensation enough. But would she give him that gift?

In her fantasies, he was the lover she ached for. But, as she'd written, when he came near her in reality, she ran. Tonight, she'd backed away from him so completely that had he not read this journal, he would've believed that she felt nothing for him.

Why such a difference between reality and fantasy? Frowning, he decided he'd have to read the whole journal. Perhaps a gentleman might've returned it without perusing the rest of its contents, but when it came to Charlotte, Alexandre found he was no gentleman.

The autocratic tyrant in him had finally woken up after years of silence, and he was intent on claiming and branding sweet Charlotte Ashton as his very own. Any worries Alexandre might've harbored about the chains of commitment and desire, crumbled under the force of the hunger and possessiveness raging through him.

Four

Charlotte was frantic. She couldn't find her journal. She'd turned the cottage upside down without success. Panic had her almost hyperventilating. What if someone read what she'd written?

Suddenly, like a ray of light on a cloudy day, she remembered scribbling in it madly the night after Alexandre's first visit to the greenhouse. Breath whooshing out of her, she ran to the greenhouse…only to come to a skidding halt. Her gaze fell on the long, muscular form of the male who'd spent the night tormenting her in her dreams, lounging against a glass wall.

"You are in a hurry, Charlotte."

Her eyes couldn't look away from the inherent sensuality of his mouth. She swallowed. Hard. "I need to check something in my, um, gardening journal."

His eyes glinted for a moment, but then those sinful lips

curved into a smile. "Of course." Reaching out, he pushed open the door.

Unable to avoid it, she ducked under his arm and walked inside. She found her journal exactly where she remembered leaving it. Alexandre prowled in behind her. She thanked God he hadn't come in earlier. What if he'd read the things she'd written? Her face flushed. He'd probably have laughed his head off at her fantasies, at the things she believed herself capable of when it was only dreams and not reality.

"Did you want something?" She turned, aware her voice had become husky and soft.

As always, his presence shattered the calm she'd worked so hard to achieve, the peace she'd tried to create in this world where she didn't quite fit in. Despite that, her eyes drank in the sight of him, her traitorous body sighing with relief.

He hadn't walked away as she'd asked him to do, something she'd spent the night dreading. Her inability to stick to her decision to keep him at a distance unsettled her, but what terrified her was that no man had ever compared to her fantasy lover. No man but Alexandre Dupree.

"Yes, I have a commission for you." Dressed in sand-colored slacks teamed with a simple white shirt, he looked very elegant, very worldly. And yet, he didn't seem the least out of place in her haven of jungle-wild plants and delicate rosebuds, as if he were some wild, elemental creature himself.

It took a moment for his words to penetrate. "A commission? Are you throwing a party?" Even as she spoke, she was reaching for the pad in the back pocket of her jeans, her hand pulling out the pen clipped to the spine. She placed her journal on the workbench.

"Why don't you write in your gardening notebook?" Alexandre's eyes were suspiciously blank, his tone as smooth as melted caramel.

For a moment, she froze, wondering if he'd read her fantasies after all. Then he blinked and the impression was gone, leaving her feeling paranoid. "It's…um, for the notations about the plants, not commissions. So, what did you want and when?" Well aware of the possible double entrende in her last sentence, she waited for him to tease her with a little sensual byplay, as he'd done in the vineyard.

"I need a single arrangement, for a private gift." There was nothing but business in his tone. "By tonight. I'm prepared to pay double your usual fee for the short notice." He had his checkbook in his hands.

She looked up, a sinking feeling in the pit of her stomach. "I don't do private arrangements."

"For a friend of the family, surely you can make an exception?"

Charlotte was shocked by the calm question. Not an ounce of the charm he'd been dosing her with so liberally for the past two days was visible. It was apparent that he'd taken her back-off signal very seriously. There would be no more sensual overtures from this wild wolf of a man who'd been stalking her.

"Tonight?" she asked, trying to fight her overwhelming sense of loss. How could he have become so important to her in mere days? "I have so much work."

"Please? It's very important." His voice was rich chocolate, sinful and tempting.

Her resistance to him was nil. "All right. Is it for a business associate, a friend…?"

"A lover," he said softly.

Her back stiffened, but she could hardly refuse the request now that she'd accepted. It would betray too much. "You want roses?" A bouquet of roses would be easy enough to prepare, she thought, trying to submerge her sudden hurt in a flood of practicality.

"*Non,* roses are too common for one such as she. I want

something unique, beautiful, elegant and utterly lovely, just like her."

A surge of jealousy almost overwhelmed Charlotte. She wanted to slap his handsome face. All this time he'd been flirting with her, charming her, when he'd had a lover tucked away, a lover who was everything she wasn't.

"The arrangement must be alluring, but not overpowering." Alexandre's dark eyes gentled. "She is a bud of perfect beauty and my gift must show that I understand her need to go slow, to take pleasure in every moment of her awakening. It must convey my apology for pushing her too fast, rushing her in my desire for her."

Charlotte was clutching her pen so hard, she thought she might break it. There was no need to write down a single word. Every syllable was emblazoned into her brain. "Come back at seven." The words were clipped.

There was just so much she could take. Right now, she wanted to throw something at him. She'd give him his arrangement all right—she'd give him something so perfectly awful that his lover would never even speak to him again.

But when she finally forced herself to work on the creation, she made it delicate and beautiful, fragrant but not too lush—colored for freshness in creamy white and golden yellow, with the merest hints of red for passion. For Alexandre's lover would have passion. Otherwise, he wouldn't have spoken of her with such intense hunger.

Because his lover was unique, she used rare hothouse orchids in shades of gold, offsetting their sophistication with white pansies so delicate they'd bruise if stroked too hard, for Alexandre's lover required gentle handling. To add the touch of red, the touch of passion, she used leaves; tiny, perfectly shaped leaves of such vibrant beauty that they were almost flowers in themselves.

The centerpiece was, of course, a pure white rosebud of

perfect beauty, carefully hidden amongst the confident orchids, shy but compelling the eye to look its way.

And then it was finished.

She felt a moment of complete joy. This was her art and she was good at what she did. A second later, her happiness crumbled as she realized that this arrangement was one she would've died to receive herself. All those instructions that Alexandre had given her, they were too much like the woman she wanted to be.

Looking at her watch, she saw that it was close to seven. She'd spent hours longer on this piece than she should have. But at least she had the satisfaction of knowing that Alexandre had paid through the nose. It was too little to compensate her for her pain, but she focused on it in an effort to control her emotions.

A soft footfall sounded behind her. Without turning, she said, "It's done."

Coming to stand just behind her, Alexandre reached out to touch a pansy with exquisite care. "You're truly talented, *ma petite.*"

"Don't call me that," she snapped. The way he said it, it was an endearment, a lover's caress, and she knew she was no lover of his.

"As you wish." There was a smile in his voice.

But when she turned, his eyes were solemn. "I'm sure she'll treasure it. Thank you, Charlotte."

And just that quickly, he was gone, taking her creation. For another woman.

As had happened the night before, the phone rang just as she was stepping out of the shower. Dressed only in a big towel tucked haphazardly around her, her hair piled up on her head out of the way, she grabbed the receiver. "Charlotte speaking."

"You sound breathless. What have you been doing?" Amusement lingered in the seduction of Alexandre's voice.

She almost answered him, caught by the undertone of command. "Is something wrong with the arrangement?" she forced herself to ask.

"*Non.* It's perfect. I called to say that I left you something of a thank-you gift."

"There was no need," she began, painfully aware that nothing would make up for the hollow feeling in her stomach. With her own words, she'd destroyed whatever might've grown between them. The quickness with which he'd moved on to another woman should've had her thanking her lucky stars. Then why did she want to cry?

"There was every need," he said, his voice that low purr that always made her want to curl into his lap and rub herself against his body. "It's on the doorstep. I hope you like it." He hung up.

Charlotte stood for a second, debating whether to go and see what he'd left her. More than likely, it was a bottle of wine or chocolates, she thought, indulging her need to sulk.

He'd probably put no more thought into her gift than he would for any other employee. After all, she wasn't a lover whose flowers had to be perfect, had to show that he thought her *unique, beautiful, elegant and utterly lovely.*

In the end, her curiosity got the better of her. She headed toward the door, uncaring of her state of undress. After all, who was going to see her way out here? Pulling open the door, she looked down. Her eyes widened. Tremors shivered through her entire body, starting from her heart and traveling through every nerve she possessed.

Disbelieving, she went to her knees. Hardly daring to touch what she'd handled so easily earlier, she reached out and stroked the silky soft petal of a tiny white blossom so beautifully perfect, it was almost impossibly real.

What had he said?

She is a bud of perfect beauty...

A single tear rolled down her face.

...my gift must show that I understand her need to go slow, to take pleasure in every moment of her awakening. It must convey my apology for pushing her too fast, rushing her in my desire for her.

"Ah, Charlotte, this was to make you smile, not cry." Sounding like he couldn't bear to see her tears, Alexandre was suddenly crouching on the other side of the flowers, wiping them away.

She should've been startled at his appearance, but she wasn't. Not when her body had known all along that he was nearby. She tried to speak but couldn't, shaking her head instead and reproaching him with her eyes. In the space of a single day, he'd shattered her heart and rebuilt it with a fatal flaw. And that flaw was him.

"I'm sorry, *chérie*. I thought you'd like them." He sounded so genuinely distressed that she began to smile. She'd never thought to see cool, elegant Alexandre Dupree out of his element.

"They're perfect," she repeated his judgment. "But you're an impossible man."

"So does this mean you are *ma petite* again?" That charming smile blazed back to life.

She didn't point out that she'd never agreed to be any such thing. The light in his eyes was too entrancing to dim. She had the feeling that despite his easy charm, Alexandre rarely smiled with such simple delight.

At that moment, he touched her cheek. "Will you not return inside? You must be cold."

Startled, she looked down at herself—to her intense relief the towel had stayed put. Holding the bouquet protectively in her arms, she rose and backed into the house. "You can come in."

Every nerve in her body went wild with warning. If she let this wild wolf into her house, he'd corner her until she was completely at his mercy. The thing of it was, she didn't want to resist.

To her surprise, he shook his head. "You make me forget my vows when you stand there looking so very lovely. I meant what I said. I won't rush you. But, I'm man enough to ask you for a kiss—I'm not quite sure you've forgiven me."

She realized he didn't intend to come to her and claim his kiss. He truly was *asking*. Swallowing, she put his gift on the nearby coffee table. Then, heart thudding, she took two steps toward him.

His smile died. "Am I so distasteful to you, *chérie,* that you must screw up your courage to kiss me? If that is so, I withdraw my request. Hurting you is the last thing I wish to do."

Charlotte found herself almost running to him. "How can you think that?" she asked, pained at the bleakness in his eyes. "I…I'm just not…good at this," she admitted. "Help me." It was the first time in a long, long time that she'd asked anyone for help.

Alexandre felt his sophistication shatter under her whispered words. Tenderness that was almost savage in its intensity took hold of him, the passion in him merging with protectiveness such as he'd never before felt. Reaching out, he touched one golden cheek, stunned that a woman with her sensual nature would be so unaware of the sway she held over him.

"Charlotte," he whispered, sliding his hand slowly around her nape. He tugged gently, until she was standing on the edge of the doorway, while he remained outside.

"You smell delicious—can I have you for dessert?"

She responded as he'd hoped, her nervousness buried under amusement. "Stop misbehaving."

He felt a smile light his eyes at her mock-stern expression. "Your wish is my command." On her nape, he moved his thumb, stroking the softness of her skin, the sheer temptation of her. *"Tu es très belle."* Bending his head, he touched petal-soft lips as alluring as any one of her fragrant blooms.

At first, she was still. When he continued to barely brush their lips together in the most gentle of seductions, her body softened and her lips parted on a breath. Moving the hand curved around her nape to the golden skin bared above the towel, he rubbed his thumb along the dip of her collarbone. She gasped, her mouth opening fully under his. Then she finally touched him, pressing those fine, competent hands against his chest.

The urge to crush her sweetly welcoming body against his was almost inescapable—he fought it because he did indeed intend to savor and relish every moment of her awakening. However, he accepted the invitation of her lips, the well-hidden primitive in him starving for a taste of her lush sensuality.

Her soft moan caught him unawares. His hand tightened on her shoulder for the barest fraction of a second before he forced himself to release her, breaking the kiss before he broke his promise. The newly awakened possessiveness flaring through him wanted nothing more than to rip that towel from her body and indulge.

Her lashes lifted and liquid dark eyes met his, half-shocked, half-delighted. "I never knew a kiss could be like that."

"Neither did I." It was no lie. He'd never been so affected by a simple kiss, so hungry that he was hard and ready, more than willing to take any invitation she offered. It disturbed him, the power she had over his body, but not enough to make him stop his pursuit.

"Go to sleep, *ma petite*. Dream of me." Meant to be a tease, it came out an order. He decided he liked giving her that order, particularly when her eyes widened even further.

"Alexandre, you…" She just shook her head and stepped back into her fairy-tale cottage, the princess retreating from the marauder at her door. Just when he thought she'd close it, she smiled just the tiniest bit and said, "Unique, beautiful, elegant and utterly lovely?"

Leaning forward, he picked up her hand and brought it to his lips, placing the softest of kisses on the tender skin of her inner wrist. "I forgot to add something."

"What?" It was a breathy question, her pulse jumping under his touch.

He released her before she seduced him absolutely. Stepping back into the shadows, he allowed himself a smile at having finally breached her defenses. "Luscious."

Five

Long after Alexandre had prowled off into the darkness, Charlotte sat wide-awake. She kept touching the flowers, smiling for no reason and then shivering. Not in cold. Not in fear. In desire.

Luscious.

That divinely sexy man thought she was luscious. She knew she shouldn't believe him, not when he had that dangerous charm. He probably said things like that all the time to get women into his bed. Of course he probably didn't have to try very hard. A man that tempting could seduce with nothing more than a glance.

Did she want to be seduced into his bed?

Charlotte gulped and stroked a glossy red leaf, accepting the truth. Since the moment she'd seen him, *want* had become her constant companion. Her hands fluttered to lips still throbbing from the barely restrained passion of Alexandre's kiss. Hunger had thrummed through that lithely muscular frame, but he'd kept it under rigid control, giving her the tenderness she needed. She wondered if he'd be just as tender in every other step of their dance.

Could she take a chance on him?

Her wariness of rich, sophisticated men rose from her knowledge that sometimes, the core of them was rotten. Witnessing Spencer manipulate Lilah all these years had left her with a healthy disrespect for the type. Yet, something defied her to think of Alexandre in the same breath as Spencer.

Her hands clenched and frown lines marred her brow. She wanted Alexandre but to her, the sharing of bodies was special, a gift to be cherished. It wasn't something she'd ever take lightly. Then again, what she felt for Alexandre was in no way light or easy.

He made her feel fiercely female, a sensual being who hungered to learn of passion and heat. More than that, he made her feel proud of herself, of her worth as a woman. When he looked at her, he saw beauty.

Luscious.

Blushing, Charlotte finally made her way to bed, sliding in between the cool sheets dressed only in her skin. It was one of her secret indulgences, a concession to the sensual core of her, a core that most people would never see. As the sheets whispered over her heated skin, she couldn't help remembering Alexandre's command.

Dream of me.

He needn't have given the order. She'd been doing that since the moment she'd laid eyes on him.

The next day, Charlotte rose before dawn to put the finishing touches on several completed arrangements, her mind on a man with dark chocolate eyes. A shiver ran through her at the memory of those eyes full of barely controlled hunger. What would it be like to have all that hunger focused on her? Could she cope?

Shaking her head, she sprayed some flowers with water and fiddled with the placement of a spray of baby's breath. The arrangements were for the reception that would follow a wedding taking place on the grounds today. The only thing she had to prepare for the wedding itself was a floral arbor, leafy vines and delicate white roses twisting around a metal frame. She planned to do that on the spot, before she organized the arrangements in the reception hall.

The sound of a golf cart arriving interrupted her fussing. Smiling, she walked out and supervised the loading of her precious flowers onto the three carts that had turned up, driven by staff Megan had hired to help with the wedding. She caught a ride up with the flowers, having the men drop her off at the winery with her roses and vines.

The arbor's frame was already in place to the side of the winery, where the actual wedding would be taking place. After sending the drivers to the estate house with strict instructions to place her arrangements gently on a couple of the tables, she spent the next hour and a half on the arbor. Once complete, it nicely complemented the crushed lengths of white silk that marked out the aisle in lieu of ropes.

Megan walked over from where she'd been overseeing the placement of chairs. "Didn't want to interrupt you while you looked so serious," she teased.

Charlotte smiled. Megan had definitely mellowed since her marriage to Simon—she seemed far more at ease with herself these days. "What do you think?"

"Gorgeous as always. I wish I had your artistic ability."

"I'll leave you to it. I have to set up the flowers for the reception."

"At least with you, I know the work will be superb. It's the other idiots I have to worry about."

Laughing, Charlotte hitched a ride on one of the carts going back and forth from the estate house to the winery grounds. As she ran up the four steps into a house which had always intimidated her, she kept an eye out for Alexandre. However, he didn't make an appearance.

Feeling oddly deflated when she finished at around 10:00 a.m., she hopped on her bike, having had it brought up on one of the carts. A sleek black Ferrari purred down the estate drive as she was about to take off.

Curious about the occupant, she took her time pushing off her kickstand and arranging her small backpack. Though she wasn't a woman impressed by material possessions, she was human enough to appreciate the sleek lines of a car that looked like a crouching hunting cat.

To her surprise, the car changed direction and circled around the reflecting pool to head straight for her, stopping inches from her bike. Scowling, she wondered if she'd have to fend off the advances of some playboy guest who'd arrived early.

Then the door opened and a man who looked even more like a predator than his car, stepped out. "*Ma chérie,* do not tell me you have been here all morning?"

"Yes, setting up for the Harrington wedding." She wanted to ask him where he'd been but her throat closed up as he neared her, his big hands going to her own. Startled, she let him pick them up, balancing herself using her feet.

"You're scratched," he accused.

She laughed. "Happens all the time. Flowers are pretty but they do occasionally have thorns."

"Take better care of yourself." It was a command.

"Alexandre," she began, intending on telling him to stop with the orders. After the way he'd kissed her so tenderly last night, after the precious words he'd given her, she was no longer tongue-tied in his presence. This man wanted to hear what she had to say.

Lifting her hand to his lips, he kissed one long, angry scratch. "I like that." He began to nibble teasingly on her knuckles.

She wanted to moan. "What?"

"My name on your lips." The way he was staring at those lips made her want to go up in flames.

"I have to go." She didn't know why she'd said that, when she'd planned this day off weeks in advance. Maybe she wasn't completely over being tongue-tied in his presence.

"Do you have time for dinner with me, Charlotte?" He was all sexy male appeal, deep masculine dimples creasing his cheeks.

Her heart melted. "You're too charming for your own good."

He didn't laugh as she expected. Instead, that coaxing smile faded. "Charm is not all I am."

The fleeting darkness in his eyes took her mind back to their other meetings. Alexandre, she realized, always kept a distance between himself and the rest of the world. He was so charming, she didn't think most people ever noticed that he never revealed his emotions.

But she'd noticed because she was the same. She didn't trust easily. Walker was the only person who was close to her. She adored her elder brother despite her concern about his loyalty to a man like Spencer, but even he didn't know her innermost thoughts and feelings.

Knowing how alone it could feel to hurt inside where no one could see, she ached to soothe the scars hidden beneath Alexandre's sophisticated elegance. Would he ever trust her enough to share his secrets?

Would she one day trust him enough to share her own?

"Dinner? Yes, I'm free," she found herself saying, taking a chance on this man who'd so suddenly, so quickly, touched her in the most well-guarded part of herself.

"I'll come by for you at nine." He released her hands, which he'd been gently stroking the whole time they'd been talking, creating havoc with her senses.

Her eyes widened. "Isn't that a bit late?"

He grimaced. "I'll be closeted with your winemaking staff and then with Trace. Can you wait?"

That he wanted her company that much was something she couldn't resist. "I'll ride up here to meet you."

"It will be dark." His brows gathered.

"It's safe." Watching Lilah had taught Charlotte that women who let men have all the say in a relationship ended up doormats. No matter how beautiful and pampered a life she lived, Lilah was Spencer's puppet. When he jerked, she moved. "I'll meet you by your car at nine."

Still scowling, he muttered something dark in French. "Yes, I think my *maman* would like you very much, *ma petite*."

She wondered what he meant by that. "You're very busy."

"Never too busy for you." A small smile flirting with his lips, he laid a final kiss on the pulse of her wrist. "Until tonight, my lovely, luscious Charlotte." He grinned at her uncontrollable blush. "Definitely luscious."

Alexandre watched Charlotte ride off, his eyes on her sweet body but his mind on her dreams.

Lover Mine,

Do you know what I'd like tonight?

I'd like to be taken on a picnic in the moonlight, under the spreading branches of some majestic tree. I'd like to be treated like a treasure—adored with your eyes, seduced by your flattery, kissed by the touch of your fingers on mine.

I want you to take my hand and dance with me to the music of the leaves in the swaying trees, not a word said between us that isn't a murmur of desire, a temptation of the senses.

But, nothing more.

I want you to give me this moment of romance without asking for anything physical in return. Just my company. And my smile.

Alexandre smiled throughout the day, accompanied by thoughts of Charlotte. She believed that her longing for romance would be a hardship for a man. In truth, charming her in the moonlight would be his distinct pleasure.

Some men didn't understand the value of loveplay, the delight that came from romancing the woman you adored. Alexandre had never been that kind of man. Not even as a youth had he rushed.

He'd always known that seducing a woman's body wasn't enough. A good lover gave just as much attention to his woman's mind, her heart and her soul. He'd always known that but never before had he paid it such heed.

This time, he meant to charm absolutely, to adore without reservation. With her secrets hidden behind midnight eyes and that deep core of sensuality, Charlotte appealed to the carefully controlled savage inside of him. And that part of him wanted everything from her when they took the final steps of this intimate dance. Passion and heat, lust and surrender, trust and desire.

Such trust in bed was the most precious of gifts. Even more so when the woman giving it didn't do so lightly. If Charlotte chose to share her body with him, it would mean far more than a moment's fleeting pleasure, far more than anything he'd ever before experienced.

That night when he met Charlotte by the car, he satisfied himself with a kiss on her cheek and then opened the door. Dressed in a long denim skirt with ruffles of white lace at the bottom, and a silky white blouse that looked as soft as moonlight, she took his breath away.

As they drove out of the estate, he glanced at the shimmering beauty of her. "You look like an exotic temptation."

Her laugh was intimate in the darkness inside the car. "Have you kidnapped me?"

He turned carefully onto the road, mindful of the treasure he carried this night. "*Oui,* of course. I'm taking you to my secret hideout where I shall ravish you." The words were playful, but the images in his mind went far beyond mere play.

"Where *are* you taking me?" There was a smile in her question.

"That's a surprise."

"You've got me turned around already." She looked out at the narrow side road he'd pulled into.

"Good." He wanted to kiss that curious little nose.

"Are you sure you know where you're going?"

"I'm very sure." But, was he?

In the past, carrying on a discreet affair had never been a problem. He'd chosen his partners for the same reason they'd sought him out—neither side wanted the demands of commitment. When it was time to let go, they did so with grace and a smile. Several of his old lovers counted him as a close friend.

With Charlotte, the rules were different—*he* was different. He wanted to cage her in his arms and keep her for himself, to enjoy and adore whenever he wished. His feelings for her already bordered on dangerous possessiveness.

His mind sensed the threat—for the first time in his life, a woman might just seduce him to addiction. It was something he'd fought against for a lifetime, schooled by his childhood to expect nothing from women but their fleeting company.

Never loyalty. Never forever.

And yet, he couldn't walk away from this dance.

"Alexandre." Charlotte's voice whispered over his body like a sweet caress.

His arousal was swift and almost painful. *"Oui, ma petite?"*

"You just went so quiet," she said, gentle in her question. "Is everything all right?"

Her care touched a part of him that nothing had touched for a long time, somehow managing to soothe the raging beast of passion into something more controllable. "Everything is as it should be."

She made a sound of frustration. "You're very good at answering questions without giving anything away."

He admired her spirit. "Perhaps you're not asking the right questions." He'd never given a woman that entrée, that chance to find the right question to ask.

"Will you answer me if I ask the right one?"

"It depends on my mood," he teased. "If you've seduced me into submission, then I shall be at your mercy. I suggest you question me in bed."

"Alexandre!"

He chuckled at her scandalized response, the painful knot inside him unraveling in the light of her presence. At the same time, a startling thought shimmered into being. Could this tiny woman help him find a way out of the darkness of his past? A past shaped by deception and shame—he loved his *maman,* but the lessons he'd learned at her knee were not something he'd wish on any child.

They'd scarred him and he was intelligent enough to know that he was the man he was because of those invisible wounds. A man who cherished women but never enough to place his faith in them, never enough to chance his heart. Even as a child, he'd been comfortable relying only on himself, but this aloneness was of the soul.

Until Charlotte, no woman had ever come close to breaching that wall of scar tissue. But what right did he have to taint her with the dishonor of his past? She was as dew-fresh as a morning flower—what good would it do to sully her dreams of love and loyalty?

Seeing a landmark up ahead, he took a deep breath and forced the unexpected tumble of questions aside. Tonight was for her. And, he realized with surprise, for him. That savage primitive in him was intrigued by the idea of romance under the moonlight with this lovely woman. "Look ahead, my innocent little Charlotte."

"Stop it, you… oh. It looks like a—meadow. How did you find this?" Her eyes roved over the rolling patch of spring green grass silvered by the moonlight.

"I'm a sorcerer, *chérie*. I know many things."

Charlotte couldn't believe the beauty outside the window. Dotted with spring flowers that nodded sleepily in the night, the area appeared enchanted. Several large trees curved around the grassy field, and in the distance she could see fairy mist rising, lending a soft intimacy to the night. It was like something out of a dream. Her dream. As soon as the car stopped, she unclipped her belt, intent on getting out.

"Wait, let me care for you."

Startled, she watched him get out and walk over to open the door. Delighted at the unexpected chivalry, she stepped out. "Nobody does that anymore."

Closing her door, he took one of her hands in his. "You deserve it, Charlotte."

She loved the way he said her name, as if it were something exotic when it was so very ordinary. "I always wanted a Lakota Sioux name," she said, surprising herself with the confidence. "My mother's name was Mary Little Dove—isn't that the most beautiful name you ever heard?"

He tipped his head to the side. "Is that your heritage? The Sioux?"

"My mother was Oglala Lakota Sioux." Walker had told her that when she'd asked him why they looked so different from the other Ashtons. He'd already been pulling away from her by then, distancing himself from the tragedy of their past, but had loved her enough to try and soothe her confusion.

"I'm afraid I don't know much about them."

Her smile was weak. "Neither do I. I was raised with my cousins. I suppose nobody thought it was important to teach me about my mother's people."

"But you miss not knowing half of yourself."

There was a depth of knowledge in his answer that made her heart flood with tenderness. Then and there, her resolve to breach his reserve and discover what haunted him, firmed into a vow.

She knew instinctively that he was a man used to looking after his women. He'd already given her so much—made her feel precious and wanted. Well, she decided, this woman was going to return the favor. But, she let it go for now, aware it would take time. "Yes."

He curved his arms around her waist, as if to shelter her from the night. "Perhaps you should seek out your heritage?"

Trusting the wrong man could lead to shattering pain, but she was tired of the aloneness of her search. And there was a seductive core of honor about Alexandre that made her want to place her faith in him. "I've heard that they're very protective of themselves, that it's hard to gain their trust. What if...what if they don't want to talk to me?"

Alexandre frowned. "How can they deny you when you are one of them?

"But that's just it. I don't belong with the Sioux, just like I don't belong on the estate. I'm an in-between person, someone who fits nowhere." She stopped, dismayed at the depth of hurt she'd betrayed. "I'm sorry..."

"Never be sorry for trusting me." Alexandre cupped her face with one hand and brushed her lips with his undeniably male mouth. It was a gesture of tenderness and it shook her. "Perhaps instead of feeling as if you don't belong in either world, you should think instead that you're lucky to have two worlds?"

Touched, she returned the simple but powerful caress. "I'll think about it. But not tonight. Tonight is for us."

His dark eyes gleamed but he acquiesced to her request. "Let me retrieve the picnic basket and blanket."

As they walked across the field to the moon-shadow of a large tree, Alexandre pondered over Charlotte's revelation. She and her flowers were so much a part of the Ashton Estate, he'd never considered that she might not feel as if she fit in. And yet, once he thought about it, he could see how she was different. Unique.

It wasn't only her looks, though they were stunning enough to send him reeling. That long, waterfall of blue-black hair, those dark eyes, that honey-toned skin—they all marked her as different among the patrician Ashtons. But, even more, it was her personality, the way she *was,* that made her different.

She preferred flowers to people, a bicycle to a flashy car and had an innocence that was completely at odds with the world she'd grown up in. There was something about Charlotte that was pure and untouched, a beauty of the heart that tugged at him more and more with every moment he spent with her.

Putting the basket by the tree, he spread the picnic blanket and then inclined his head. "Sit, *ma belle*. Tonight, your knight waits upon his lovely princess."

Though she was illumed only by the moonlight, he saw the flush that heated her golden skin. "You say the most wonderful things." Her eyes shimmered, large and dark.

That she trusted him enough to confess that made his rusty heart beat with newfound spirit. A twinge of guilt infiltrated the joy spreading through his blood, but he ignored it, certain that he'd done the right thing in reading her journal. How could it have been wrong, when it had brought him to this moment of pure happiness?

"What have you got in here?" Charlotte peeked into the basket, her hair falling over her breast.

"Delights to tempt and seduce you so I can have my wicked way," he drawled, teasing her when all he wanted to do was lay her down and satisfy the savage in him. He had a feeling she could make even that dangerously possessive part of him purr in satisfaction.

Looking up, she made a face at him, startling him with the playful curve of her mouth. "You shouldn't be let out to wreak havoc on the female of the species. You're positively lethal."

He was delighted that she saw him that way. "Where would you put me? In a cage?"

She shook her head, the dark silk of her hair shifting with the motion. Unable to resist, he moved closer and fingered the strands whispering over her shoulders, his eyes on her face.

"That would be a terrible waste." Though she was blushing, there was a look in her eyes that told him she was going to tease him right back. "You should be kept in a bedroom…where you can satisfy a woman's wickedest fantasies."

Six

His temperature skyrocketed. Swearing softly under his breath, he cupped her cheek and kissed the sassiness right off her lips. It tasted far too good for his peace of mind. "You mustn't say such things. I can't be expected to romance you if my body is straining with the urge to bury itself in your sweet body."

She gasped, her eyes huge and dark. "I say the boldest things around you. You're a bad influence."

He grinned. "I'd say I'm a very good influence." Reaching out with his right hand, he pulled out a pre-chilled bottle of champagne from the picnic basket. "Not the perfect temperature, but it'll do."

Charlotte held out the two champagne flutes she'd plucked. After pouring, he accepted one flute bubbling silver-gold in the darkness, his fingers running along the back of her hand. She shivered.

"I love the way you want me, kitten." His voice was low,

dark, husky, that of a lover talking to his woman. He couldn't change that, couldn't make it playful and merely flirtatious, not when the woman was Charlotte.

"You said not to talk that way," she accused, but her dark eyes held a look that told him if he did reach out and touch her intimately, she might just let him. They'd come a long way from that first kiss.

Sighing at the restraints he'd put on himself tonight, he raised his glass. "To my Charlotte. Utterly lovely. Utterly unique. And supremely luscious."

Her responding smile was unknowingly sensuous. "To Alexandre, who should be locked up for the good of the female population."

After a sip, he put aside his champagne and started pulling delicacy after delicacy from the basket. "Do you like caviar?"

She shook her head. "Awfully plebeian of me."

"I don't like it, either," he confessed. "I fail to see why people pay ridiculous sums for tiny fish eggs." Charlotte's quick giggle was unexpected. He looked up into her amused eyes. "What?"

"You drive a car that many people would consider um…an ego on wheels and you can't see the temptation to indulge in caviar?" Charlotte had no idea where her impertinence was coming from. She guessed it had something to do with the way he looked at her, like he'd just like to eat her alive, *after* savoring her with exquisite slowness. Never had she imagined that a man as powerfully masculine as Alexandre would find her that fascinating. The thought intoxicated her far more than the bubbles of champagne fizzing against her lips.

He scowled. "Don't think I didn't notice that hesitation. I can forgive the use of the word ego but anything else and I might've had to get nasty."

"Oooh, I'm scared." She wanted to kiss him. Not just because of desire, but because he'd given her this. This moment of moonlight and magic, a moment when she felt wild and beautiful and desirable, things that she'd only dreamed about being.

As if he'd read her mind, those dark chocolate eyes flared with heat. Without a word, he leaned over and kissed her like he had every right to touch her as he pleased. Her stomach went into freefall. Her toes curled. "Mmmm." Tiny pleasure sounds escaped her.

Alexandre's body tensed and his hand fisted in her thick hair. A little trace of disappointment tinged her joy at that indication of accelerating passion. No matter what he did, she'd enjoy Alexandre's touch but tonight…tonight she wanted romance. Slow kisses and gentle strokes.

"You make me forget all my vows." Then he said something steamy and dark in his native tongue. The unfamiliar word sounded mysterious and sensual, things she'd never considered herself.

Alexandre's lips descended to hers again and she felt the embers in her body ignite into flame. Ready for thunder, she was delighted to discover that he was dedicated to going slow tonight. Very slow.

His lips coaxed, tempted, teased. His tongue stroked across her lower lip, but barely ventured into her welcoming mouth. When his teeth grazed her lips, his tongue was there to soothe the sensual hurt.

"Alexandre," she murmured, reaching for him, her hand fisting in his shirt. He felt so good. So hard and hot and rawly masculine.

Below the sophisticated surface, Alexandre Dupree was very much a man. There wasn't a line of his body that was soft or relaxed. His steely control was apparent in the tautness of the muscles of his waist where her other hand landed. "You don't like this slow kissing," she said, when he let her breathe.

A smile curved his sensual lips. "On the contrary, *ma petite*. Slowly driving you crazy intrigues me." His thumb rubbed over her lower lip. Somehow, the touch tugged at something much lower in her. Much more intimate. "I could spend hours kissing you."

As if to prove that, he closed the gap between their lips once more, his hand slipping from her hair to curve around her nape, his other hand cupping her cheek. She was becoming accustomed to both gestures, but they still made her come undone. The possessiveness of the one hold, compared with the tenderness of the other, completely destroyed her capacity for rational thought. How could he do that to her without even trying?

Thinking became too hard when he ran his hand along her jaw. Charlotte sighed into the exquisitely romantic kiss and gave herself up to Alexandre Dupree's magic. Her surrender was rewarded over and over, his kisses designed to bring her the most extreme pleasure.

Alexandre used every bit of experience he had to kiss Charlotte as she deserved to be kissed. He hadn't lied to her. He could spend hours simply kissing her, drowning in the pleasure that emanated from her, feeling more male than he'd ever before felt in his life. She was such a spirited woman, quiet yet full of strength that would last a lifetime, but her bones felt so fragile under his touch, her body so very small compared to his.

He would never trust any man but himself to handle her with the care she deserved.

The fleeting thought brought a growl to the back of his throat and for a second, the kiss veered from romantic to outright marauding, but he caught himself. Romance, he forced himself to think. His kitten needed romance and moonlight tonight, not heat and raw eroticism. That would come later.

Taking a nibbling bite from the lower lip that he knew had swelled from their kisses, he parted from her. The sight of passion-drenched eyes looking up at him through a veil of blue-black lashes almost broke him.

He bit back his groan and rubbed his thumb over her moist lips. "I want to dance with you in the moonlight. I want to feel you in my arms."

"How did you know?" she whispered, those eyes completely unguarded, completely honest.

"That's a secret," he said, unwilling to spoil the moment by admitting that he'd read her journal. Rising, he held out his hand.

Without hesitation, her fingers slipped into his, slender and fine-boned, but very capable. She stood, a graceful woman with a body that had all the right curves and hollows to drive him insane. It was as if she'd been created for him alone, his most inescapable temptation, so alluring that he couldn't find the strength to break the chains slowly binding him to her.

Slipping one arm around her slender waist, he tangled his other hand with hers. Her free hand came to rest on his shoulder. "We fit perfectly." He wanted to purr in satisfaction, his mind awash with erotic images of how well they'd fit in a far more intimate sense.

"I'm not too *petite?*" She smiled at him with that lush mouth and gave him all sorts of ideas.

"*Non.* You are perfect." And she was. In his arms, she felt so right that he didn't ever want to let her go. Instead of pressing her close as his body demanded, he allowed her freedom. The position let him see her face when she glanced up at him.

"Why...?" she began and then fell silent.

He frowned, disliking the tone of her voice. "What is it?"

When she raised her head, those dark eyes were liquid midnight. "Why are you attracted to me?"

The question shook him with its directness. "You're lovely, beautiful and intelligent. Even more, you're intriguing with those secrets in your eyes, an artist with your work *and* you have a body that tempts me to thoughts that would make you blush. Is that enough?"

He saw her swallow. "I didn't expect you to say that."

"Why?"

"I suppose I thought you'd fudge—try and skim over it."

"I never tell lies when truth will serve." Guilt knocked again, but empowered by the feel of sweet Charlotte in his arms, he pushed it aside. "Come closer." It was an invitation, sweet seduction under moonlight.

She smiled and permitted him to tug her just a tiny bit nearer. It wasn't enough to turn romance to passion but it was enough to offer his taut body some relief. The distinctive scent of her skin enchanted him, part pleasure and part the sweetest pain he'd even known.

"Alexandre, this night is magic," she whispered.

And even though he'd planned it down to the last detail, Alexandre found himself agreeing with her. There had been nothing in his plans about the peace he'd found in her arms, nor about the pleasure he'd derive from such a simple joy as dancing with his lady under the moonlight.

Charlotte spent the next morning in something of a daze. She kept smiling for no reason, and once she found herself dancing around her greenhouse pretending she was still in Alexandre's arms. Laughing at her own giddy delight in the man, she forced herself to work.

Lured by the bright day, she rearranged her schedule so that she could potter around in her outdoor garden instead of working in the greenhouse. The smell of sunshine and growth brought Alexandre to mind once again.

Last night, he'd given her romance, such beautiful wonderful romance that she was still breathless from it. Despite his desire, he hadn't pushed for anything more.

It was a heady feeling to know that she could arouse such passion in a man like Alexandre, but what scared her was that they weren't just about passion. Not any longer. Not after that dance in the moonlight. And perhaps not since their very first meeting.

He was beginning to mean more and more to her. Part of her was afraid of the pain she'd have to bear when he left, but that part was overridden by her hunger to experience all she could with him. She knew herself well enough to know that this was no casual fling—no man had ever reached her as Alexandre did.

"Stop mooning and start working," she ordered herself, realizing she'd been sitting stock-still.

As she began clearing weeds, she was overcome by the feeling that she'd forgotten something. Something important. Frustratingly, no matter how hard she tried, nothing came to her.

Finally giving up, she concentrated on her wildflowers. They were a hardy breed, designed to take the vagaries of the weather from extreme heat to frosty cold. She checked on the seedlings she'd planted to make up for the older plants she'd lost the previous year.

Today was Alexandre's birthday.

Blinking at the sudden answer to the problem that had so frustrated her earlier, she sat down on the ground. Why did she know that? Was it true?

Determined to find out, she walked into the house and to her computer. In her first burst of hungry curiosity about the dark Frenchman who'd left her speechless with his sheer male presence, she'd read several articles on the acclaimed winemaker. One of them had been in a news magazine dealing with his vineyard in France, with a sidebar on him personally.

She found it after a single search-engine query. There it was in black and white. Today was Alexandre's birthday and he hadn't so much as made a reference to it last night. Then again, he was hardly the type of man who needed gifts.

But, she thought, it wasn't the gift that mattered, it was the fact that someone cared enough to give it. Smiling at having found him out, she walked to the greenhouse and began putting together a bouquet. It made her laugh to think of giving her strong, masculine wolf of a man flowers, but she wanted to give him something simple, something joyful.

From what little he'd let slip, she could tell that he was jaded by the things he'd seen in his life, but nobody could ever be jaded by the bouquet she made him. Instead of cultured roses for her wolf in sheep's clothing, she used wild roses in a vibrant yellow that would've made Scrooge himself smile.

She added several gerberas in vivid red and wildflowers in every color she could find, both from the blooms in her outdoor garden and those within her greenhouse. For a hint of mischief, she added some soft pink dahlias, velvety and lovely. Alexandre didn't have a touch of pink in him.

Her cell phone rang as she was debating how to deliver her bouquet. Grabbing it from the workbench, she said, "Charlotte speaking."

"Has anyone ever told you that you have a voice that could bring a man to his knees, *ma petite?*"

Look who's talking, she thought. "Alexandre." She grinned. "What are you doing?"

"I'm in the winery, considering the effect of the estate's

use of cultured yeast strains on the distinctiveness of its wine." He made it sound intensely interesting. The man was clearly crazy about wine.

"Sounds like fun. Are you busy for lunch?"

There was a long pause. "*Non.* Is that an invitation?"

It was the pause that made her realize it was the first invitation she'd ever extended to him. "*Oui,*" she responded, wanting to make him smile.

It seemed to have become very important to her to make Alexandre smile. There was darkness in him, darkness that hurt him. While she didn't yet know the details of what haunted him, she sensed enough to know he needed smiles and laughter, teasing and play.

He chuckled. "Then I shall be there in an hour. Do you wish me to bring anything?"

"No. I'm all set. Don't tell anyone but we'll be drinking Louret wine." Spencer would've had a fit if he'd found a bottle of the "enemy" wine on his property. But, she liked Louret's signature chardonnay and if she couldn't afford to escape the estate in reality, at least she could do so when she indulged her senses.

"Your secret is safe with me."

After hanging up, Charlotte rushed back into the house and began preparing a quick lunch. Throwing some mini pizzas into the oven, she tossed together a salad, created a cheese board and found some fruit to add to it.

She frowned and decided that it wasn't enough. He was a bit larger than her, her wolf. Pursing her lips, she rummaged in the freezer and found some corn dogs. Grinning, she put them into the oven. She wondered what he'd think of those unsophisticated items of food. The final touch was to add a loaf of crusty warmed bread.

She'd just put everything on two large trays that they

could carry outside when she heard a golf cart arrive. Alexandre's voice called out a moment later. "Charlotte?"

"In here."

He prowled into her kitchen, enticing her with nothing more than his walk, his eyes, his sheer male sensuality. Before she could say a word, he kissed her. Slow and deep, it said he had all the time in the world to love her.

"Bonjour." It was a husky rasp against her lips.

"Hello." She smiled, fascinated by the way he looked at her. No man had ever seen such sensuality in quiet, shy Charlotte Ashton.

"Shall I carry these out for you?" He nodded toward the trays she'd put on the kitchen counter.

"Thanks. I put the blanket down there." She pointed out the sturdy old tree behind the cottage.

Nodding, he picked up both trays. "Corn dogs?" His grin was unexpected and startlingly beautiful. "I haven't eaten one for years." Apparently happy, he headed out.

Following him with the wine that Louret had named Caroline in honor of their matriarch, she felt pleasure suffuse her. They'd had kisses and dances in the moonlight, passion and romance, but what shimmered between them this time was something just as rare—friendship.

Alexandre was in a good mood and their picnic was full of teasing and laughter. Charlotte found herself completely at ease with him, her shyness undone by his open enjoyment of her presence. She was, she thought, very close to adoring sexy Alexandre Dupree.

That awareness dawned as she was taking the remains of their lunch inside, having refused his offer of help. It didn't startle her—her feelings for this man had run shockingly deep since the moment they'd first met. If they hadn't, she could've brushed aside that first kiss instead of being so hurt by what she'd seen as Alexandre's game-playing.

Shaking off the melancholy that threatened to darken her mood at the thought of how soon he'd be leaving the estate—and her—she sneaked out to her greenhouse from the front door. After retrieving the bouquet, she walked around the house to surprise Alexandre.

He was sprawled against the tree, his shirt sleeves rolled to the elbows and his sand-colored jacket discarded carelessly to the side of the blanket. Eyes closed in relaxation, he looked very much like a large predator sunning himself after a good hunt. It wasn't until she knelt beside him that he opened his eyes.

"What's this?" He looked at the bouquet.

"Happy birthday, Alexandre." She placed the flowers in his arms and kissed him softly on the cheek.

He couldn't have looked more shocked if he'd tried. *"Ma chérie,"* he began and then seemed lost for words. When he met her gaze, she saw a vulnerability in him that tore her apart. "No one but you has ever given me flowers. I feel as if I'm holding sunshine in my arms."

She fell another step closer to adoration at the way he cradled the flowers, careful not to bruise a single bloom. "I wanted to give you a smile. You don't do it enough. Why is there such sadness in your eyes?"

"Ah, Charlotte," he murmured instead of giving her an answer. Placing the flowers aside, he held out his arms.

She went into them without hesitation, sitting herself on his lap when he tugged her up. Arms around his neck, she looked into a face softened by tenderness. "You should've told Lilah it was your birthday. She would've loved giving you a party."

He shuddered. *"Non,* thank you. I prefer not to spend my time with people who know nothing of me."

The implied statement had her heart thudding. "You're a hard man to know."

"We all have our secrets. Even you. Sometimes, I glimpse such sadness in your eyes that it's almost a physical wound. What hurts you so?"

That penetrating gaze looked at her and there was more than command in them, more than the certainty of a strong man used to getting his way. Those things, she could've resisted. But how could she resist the unhidden care, the open need to protect?

"I was three years old when I came to live here," she said quietly. "Walker was eight. We were orphans."

"Does the memory of your parents haunt you still?" His arms tightened around her.

"In a way." The pause was a chance to take a step back from this relationship. "We were told that both our parents died in a car accident, but…"

"But?"

"Even Walker doesn't believe me. He thinks I can't handle the truth—he doesn't say so because he loves me, but I know that's what he thinks."

Raising one hand, Alexandre cupped her cheek. "I don't know what it is that you believe, but you don't strike me as a woman who chases after fool's gold."

Her heart tumbled. "I have no proof…but I don't think my mother was dead when Spencer took us."

Seven

"I see." Alexandre was silent for a while. Charlotte wondered if he thought she was crazy. Sometimes, even she thought she was delusional. "Have you ever tried to find out the truth?" he asked at last.

"I've done some research on my roots." Self-consciously, she touched her raven black hair, as straight as an arrow and as glossy as polished jet. "I mean, my mother's roots."

"Then, of course, they are yours. No one can steal that from you, no matter where you were raised."

That he'd read her anxiety so easily brought a lump to her throat. "You know my mother was Lakota Sioux," she said. "I didn't remember that, but Walker did."

When Alexandre didn't interrupt, she continued, "I decided to ask Spencer about it when I was about fifteen. He said my mother came from a reservation in South Dakota." His exact words had been "some two-bit reservation in

South Dakota"—scathing, but for once, not malicious. He'd been distracted by business papers when she'd asked him the question and his answer had been instinctive.

"Were you able to trace the reservation?" There was no disbelief in Alexandre's tone.

Reassured, she decided to share what she knew. Though she'd found herself mentioning her belief to Jillian last month, she hadn't discussed it with anyone in depth. Now, held in the arms of a man she trusted and who was willing to listen, she found herself tripping over her words in an effort to convince him that she wasn't grasping at straws.

"There's a really big one called Pine Ridge—it's in South Dakota, but borders Nebraska. The people there are part of the Oglala Lakota Nation." She paused to take a jerky breath.

"I think my mother was from Pine Ridge. Spencer was born and raised in Nebraska, so it makes sense to think that my father, too, would've been in Nebraska in his youth— close enough to meet my mother."

When she looked at him, he nodded. "*Oui,* it's logical to assume this from what you know. Do you know where your parents lived after marriage?"

She shook her head. "No. Walker said that at the time of the accident we had a farm, but he couldn't remember the name of the town. All Spencer would say was that it was a dot somewhere in the middle of Nebraska—he hadn't bothered to remember the name."

She was certain that Spencer knew exactly where her parents' farm had been. Maybe he was afraid that if she learned too much, she'd expose his lies and alienate her brother from him. Walker was closer to his Uncle Spencer than their cousins were to their father, and it would destroy their relationship if she was able to prove her suspicions.

"You have a right to know where you came from."

Something in Alexandre's voice told her that he understood her emotional hunger far better than she could've imagined. "I'd like to help you in your search if you'll let me."

Charlotte's huge eyes focused on him, full of heart-breaking joy. "No one's ever believed me before," she whispered. "No one's ever listened." Wrapping her arms around his neck, she buried her face against him.

Clenching his arms tight, he held her close, suddenly aware of the vulnerability hidden behind her cool, dark gaze. "Ah, Charlotte," he murmured, rubbing her back. Distressed at her pain, he whispered soft words to her in his native language, gentling and coaxing.

After a long while, she relaxed, resting her head on his shoulder. "I thought," she began, "I might be able to trace it through her…death certificate."

"Of course." He was impressed by how far she'd come on her own. "Have you applied for a copy?"

"No," she said, shame in her tone. "I couldn't bear to be wrong. Walker is right in one sense—I don't want to admit that we lost everything. I want someone I can call Mama and have her call me daughter." Her eyes glistened with withheld pain. "I don't want her to be d-dead."

He was undone by her sorrow. Keeping Charlotte happy had become of vital importance to him. Unlike other women he knew, her emotions were never false illusions, her desperately fought tears as honest as her laughter. In mere days, he'd found himself unable to live without one and shattered by the other.

He cuddled her against him, dropping kisses on her lips, her cheeks, her stubborn little chin. When he moved his hands, her unbound hair flowed like cool water over his arm. "But," he spoke against her lips. "I think the not knowing hurts you more than the truth ever could." He believed that, though the truths he'd learned as a child had hurt him unbearably.

"I...you're right." The determination in her gaze awed him.

"I'll be with you if you need me." Though he wanted to do everything for her, find out the truth before it could hurt her, he understood her need to finish this on her own.

It was late that night when Charlotte realized Alexandre had never answered her question about what made him so sad. Caught up in her own emotional upheaval, she hadn't pressed. But, she decided, next time she would.

He was an extraordinary man, and she wanted to know all of him. It was wonderful to have someone who believed in her, but what touched her heart was that Alexandre had urged her to go after the truth. *Whatever that might be.*

Instead of dismissing her claims or giving her false hope, he'd just offered her a shoulder to lean on. It was startling to realize how much that meant. Taking a deep breath, she booted up her computer despite the late hour and logged on to the Internet.

It took only a minute to find the Web site for Nebraska's vital records office. Births, marriages...and deaths. She decided to request the death certificates of both her parents, printing out the forms to post. Though it would've been faster to order them online, she needed something tangible in her hands, proof that she was no longer cowering in fear, but moving forward.

According to the Web site, it would take a few days for the certificates to be sent to her. But what were a couple more days compared to the lifetime she'd waited to learn the truth?

It was only when her handwriting blurred in front of her that she realized she was crying. Without warning, the wrenching, never-forgotten pain of losing her parents shattered her composure, leaving her lost and broken.

Too young to have strong memories, she still remembered emotions and fragments of time. Her father's deep laughter, the sunshine on her face as she ran outside, her mother's gentle hand on her head. *And love.* Deep, warm love that had made her feel safe.

She'd never forgotten that feeling, never been able to, because after their "adoption" by Spencer, there'd been no more parental love. Walker had done his best, but she'd missed her mother so much. That feeling had only intensified as she'd grown into a young woman. And by then, she hadn't even had Walker to talk to—her beloved brother had already belonged to Spencer.

Sobbing, she felt loneliness settle over her like a heavy cloak. Only days ago, she would've borne the burden in silence, but tonight her heart rebelled. Hands trembling, she picked up the phone.

"Alexandre?" she said, when he answered sounding half-asleep.

"*Ma petite?* What is wrong?" His voice was suddenly wide-awake, colored by concern.

"I just ordered copies of my parents' death certificates." She wiped away her tears.

"Would you like me to come to your cottage?"

"I woke you up." She shoved a hand through her hair, wondering what she was doing. "I'm sorry."

"Never be sorry for contacting me if you need me." Before she could bristle, he added, "It's very nice to be needed by a woman fully capable of relying on herself."

"Charmer." Her tears had abated but she still hurt deep inside.

"I'll be there soon. Don't cry in my absence—I won't be pleased."

Half-smiling at that last order, she hung up and headed into the kitchen to make coffee. Alexandre arrived just as it finished perking. He took one look at her face and enfolded her into his strong arms, kicking the door shut behind him. His chin settled on the top of her head as she buried her face against his chest, wrapping her arms around him.

"You've been crying," he accused, as if she'd done something unforgivable.

"I do that sometimes," she said, trying to tease him.

"I don't like it when you cry. You will promise not to do it."

She smiled at the roughly uttered command. "Are you one of those men who crumbles at the first sign of tears?"

"*Non*. It is only your tears that make me so weak. So you must take pity on me."

"I made coffee," she whispered.

"I'm going to hold you first."

She made no protest. Until this man, she hadn't understood the joy of a simple embrace. Something in her melted and she knew the sensation was only going to continue the longer she stayed in Alexandre's arms.

It was a feeling she didn't want to fight. Her fears against becoming intimately involved with him faded to nothing, as she realized that time wouldn't change what she felt for him. The longer she waited, the less time she'd have with him…and she ached for every moment.

She couldn't have said how long he held her, stroking her hair and murmuring in her ear. But, when they finally separated, she felt at peace with herself. Not only had he soothed her hurt, his tenderness had given her the courage to make the decision she'd been fighting against since the first moment she'd seen him.

"You're an extraordinary man," she said, reaching up to stroke the hard line of his jaw.

Caught by the shine in her dark eyes, Alexandre shook

his head. "I'm no knight in shining armor. I wish I could be for you."

Her smile was soft. "I know a knight when I see one. Even if he thinks his armor is rusty."

He began to play with a strand of her midnight hair. "What if I told you my birth makes me a bastard, not a knight?" The deep need to know whether she'd accept the man he was overcame his long held habit of not allowing anyone too close. *Especially* not a woman.

"Alexandre Dupree, how can you be primitive enough to think that a man's birth determines who he is?" She scowled. "If you're a bastard, then I'm a half-breed."

Anger flared. He caught her chin in strong fingers. "Don't *ever* use those words to describe yourself again."

Her eyes widened but there was no fear in them, only trust so powerful, it shook him. "If you promise to do the same."

"You are a tough negotiator." He sealed their bargain with a kiss that edged on being blatantly territorial. "You're also a beautiful, unique woman—the product of a union between two people who loved each other enough to not care about difference. You should be proud."

"I wouldn't dare to be otherwise now." Her smile was luminous. "Will you tell me about your parents?"

"I think we should talk about yours today. Mine can wait." He thought she'd berate him for backing away from the personal subject, but she just shook her head at him.

"I'd like to keep my ordering of the certificates between us…until we know for sure."

"You can trust me, *chérie*. I've had a lifetime of keeping secrets."

Charlotte looked up, caught by the cynicism in that last sentence. Though Alexandre was a man of the world, sophisticated as they came, he'd never before struck her as cynical. "Are you going to tell me what you mean by that?"

His lips curved in a small smile, but there was a bruised kind of pain in those bitter-chocolate eyes. "Perhaps one day."

Instead of annoyance at his reserve, she felt a strange stab of tenderness for this man who seemed so far beyond those things. "Come here." She smiled an invitation, though she was already in his arms.

Surprise chased the pain from his beautiful eyes. "I'm at your service."

When he firmed his embrace, she raised her arms and put them around his neck. Her heart was thudding like a mad thing and she was sure her cheeks were bright red.

Before Alexandre, she'd never let men close enough to make any moves, unable to let her guard down. With this man, she'd been letting him make all the moves, but right now, she had the feeling he needed her to take the lead.

She'd called him because she'd ached to be held, but now that her need had been fulfilled, she wanted to fulfill his. This beautiful, sensual man needed tender care just as much as she did. How she knew, she couldn't say. She just did.

A delighted smile curved over his lips and spread to his eyes. "What is this, *ma petite?*" Leaning down, he met her halfway when she rose on tiptoe.

"I'd like to kiss you," she whispered, voice lost to the passion racing through her bloodstream.

"I'll never say *non* to your kiss." His arms firmed around her, tensile steel under skin gilded by the sun.

Holding herself up by her arms around his neck, she reached up and bridged the breath separating them. His lips were a brush against hers, warm and welcoming. Heart beating so hard she was afraid it would pop out of her chest, she pressed just a tiny bit harder and slanted hers at the angle she liked.

He shuddered.

Something hotly feminine in her stretched awake. Taking another chance, another step, she flicked her tongue along his lower lip. His arms locked tight, and he crushed her against him, making no effort to hide his arousal. This time, it was Charlotte who shuddered, shocked at the heat that sparked to life inside of her, as if her desire were feeding on his.

Opening her mouth, she swept her tongue along his lower lip before suckling it into her mouth. She felt a groan rumble in his chest. Then his lips pressed hard against hers, a silent order for her to stop teasing him and fully open her mouth. She almost smiled at his inability to give up control. Almost. But she was burning up inside and the only thing she wanted was to do exactly as he asked.

Her sigh as she surrendered was a final temptation, a testing of her newfound power. His reaction sent sizzling heat rocketing through her. His body seemed to go impossibly steely, so taut and hard that she felt deliciously female next to his inescapable masculinity.

As she'd come to expect, to delight in, his hand rose up her back to clench in her hair, tilting her head. In response, she pressed herself against him and wrapped her arms around him even more tightly.

Her reward was a kiss so scorching, her knees crumpled. Only Alexandre's uncompromising embrace kept her upright, the arm around her waist solid with muscle, his palm curled around the curve of her waist. With a moan, she buried her fingers in his hair and abandoned her senses to him.

Alexandre was drowning in the feel of Charlotte. It was the first time she'd ever initiated a kiss and that would've been enough for him. But she'd given him so much more, a surrender of the senses that betrayed how much she trusted him to lead this dance.

It was clear she was relying on him to stop despite their

bodies' demands for completion, because Charlotte wasn't a woman who took lovemaking lightly. And he wasn't a man who'd be satisfied with anything less than her total involvement in any intimacy. Taking a final taste of her, he ended the kiss.

Long, dark lashes lifted. Passion-clouded eyes met his. "Alexandre." It was a husky invitation. "Why did you stop?" Reaching with her body, she claimed his lips again.

He shuddered under the caress and firmed his muscles, allowing her to steal yet another kiss before pulling away, though it was the hardest thing he'd ever done. "You tempt a man past all reason."

She nuzzled his neck and planted a row of kisses along his jaw. "I love the way your jaw feels." Running her teeth along it, she nipped gently.

Alexandre felt sweat bead on his forehead. No woman had ever driven him this insane with passion. The desire to simply lay her down and teach her all sorts of ways a man could tease his woman was almost overwhelming, but he knew the importance of this moment. His shy *fleur* was awakening in his arms—her faith in him as a man had never been more apparent.

She was now kissing her way down his neck, her beautiful body sliding oh, so slowly down his, a symphony of delight that tortured at the same time. He knew he should loosen his embrace but he wanted to feel every inch of her as it rubbed over him. She didn't stop her kisses when she reached the open neck of his shirt.

The first kiss fell on the dip where his collarbones met. Alexandre felt his entire body go taut. *"Charlotte."*

Smiling against him, she kissed down to the first button of his shirt. "Can I open this button?" Her eyes were big in that exotically beautiful face.

"Non," he growled. "Definitely not. You will kill me."

"Please," she whispered, in the husky tones of a woman who has just discovered her feminine power.

It was a shock to the system in more ways than one. He'd never thought he'd be encouraging a woman's sexual strength, but faced with Charlotte's blossoming sensuality, he knew that he'd deny her nothing. "One button," he said, moving the hand still clenched in her hair to the warm curve of her nape.

Sliding her hands down from his neck, she undid the first button. Her fingers spread over the exposed triangle of skin, sending his nerve endings into overdrive. "Your hair here feels different—crisper." It was an intimate whisper from a woman to her lover.

He leaned his head closer to hers. "Do you like it?"

Her nod sent the cool water of her hair sliding over his hands. "How good is your control?" Heavily lashed eyes looked up at him, desire alive in their depths.

He had no control where she was concerned. "What is it you wish of me, *chérie?*"

Color stained her cheeks but she didn't back away. "I want to keep going."

He swallowed and tried to breathe. "All right." He knew he should stop her but he didn't have it in him. If she wanted to do this, he'd find a way to rein in the ravenous hunger awakening in his body. A hunger that wanted a long, hot taste of Charlotte.

At least twice over.

Eight

Charlotte undid another button on Alexandre's shirt and wanted to whimper. The man's body was beautiful beyond all reason. Unable to resist the temptation, she pressed her lips to the skin she'd bared, tasting him.

His groan was a rumble against her lips, his heart thunder under the fingertips she had pressed against his shirt. Glorying in her ability to make him feel such pleasure, she undid two more buttons and found herself at the waistband of his pants.

Swallowing, she pulled out the tails of his shirt and slipped the last button out of its hole. The feel of his bare skin under her hands had her gasping for breath. His abdomen was ridged with muscle that tensed under her touch and she indulged herself by running her fingers over him.

"Charlotte."

Biting her lower lip, she looked up into his face. Alexandre's eyes were closed and his jaw clenched tight, as he un-

doubtedly fought his desire to take the reins. It was the final thing she needed to tell her that she'd made the right
decision. "Alexandre?"

His lashes lifted. *Ma petite.*

Gazing into that unapologetically masculine face, she
whispered, "Make love to me."

Alexandre felt his heart kick violently in his chest.
"Charlotte—you're emotional—don't make a decision that
will cause you hurt in the morning." He couldn't bear it if
she regretted being with him.

Her smile was soft and so bright, he felt blinded by its
beauty. "I'll never regret being loved by you."

"Are you truly sure?" he forced himself to ask, battling
the possessive marauder who just wanted to take.

"Yes."

He shuddered and held her tight. "I'm afraid I can't
protect you." Her becoming pregnant didn't scare him. For
the first time in his life, such a thing seemed a gift rather
than a worry. And that worried him. How far had Charlotte
Ashton burrowed into his heart?

She placed a gentle kiss over his heart. "Remember that
day I went to town and you got so angry because I'd walked home in the dark?"

Of course he remembered. Once again, his conscience
told him that he should confess but he couldn't bring himself to shatter her faith in him. "Yes."

"Well…I made myself buy…you know." He could feel
her blushing. "I was so embarrassed—I've never done that
before. I was sure everyone was looking at me."

He bit back his smile. "Why did you buy…you know?"
His words were gently teasing, even as relief whispered
through him. It would've been torture to walk away tonight
when in her eyes, he'd seen a welcome he'd barely allowed himself to imagine he'd ever see.

"Because," she said, "while I might not be experienced, I know myself." She finally met his gaze. "No matter what I tried to convince myself and you, I knew that sooner or later, I'd be in your arms."

It was the first time she'd admitted her inexperience, but he would've guessed, even if he hadn't read her journal. There was an innocence about her that said she'd never known a lover. "Are you happy to be here?" His heart almost stopped beating as he waited for her answer.

Her smile began in her eyes and lit her face from within. "There's no place I'd rather be."

Lover Mine,
I guess every woman dreams of the first time she'll love a man, imagines what it'll feel like, fantasizes about how he'll touch her…how he'll taste her. I'm no different.

Do you want to know what I'd like for that very first time? I suppose you expect me to tell you I want roses and moonlight, a bubble bath and scented oils. Well, I wouldn't say no to that one day.

But for that very first time, that very first touch of skin on skin, all I want is tenderness. Absolute tenderness. I want to be touched as if I am precious, as if my body fulfills your every fantasy, as if you can't bear to let me go.

Charlotte's secret longings whispered through his mind as he took her hand and followed her gentle tug toward the bedroom. His shirt was hanging open and he noted how her gaze kept straying to his chest. He couldn't fight his grin. Giving his Charlotte tenderness would require no effort at all, not when she made him feel so protective of the shine in her eyes.

"What?" she asked, when she saw his smile.

They were in her bedroom now, standing by the double bed. He reached out and ran his fingers through her unbound hair. "I like the way you want me, kitten."

Her cheeks reddened, but when she spoke, her eyes met his. "I look at you and I want to touch."

He shouldn't have been surprised by her courage in this arena, not when he'd witnessed her strength in so many other ways. "It's not something I'll ever deny you." He cupped her cheek. "Not when I can't keep my hands off you."

When she lifted her face to his, he took the hint and kissed her. It started out gentle and slowly became wilder, his hunger for her voracious. Even as he kissed her like he'd dreamed of doing, his hands roved over her body and slipped under the bottom of her thin sweater. The feel of her warm skin was pure pleasure.

She whimpered into his mouth as his hands stroked the skin of her waist and back, but made no move to retreat. He paused long enough to ask, *"Oui?"*

Eyes big, she nodded. And then she raised her arms so he could pull the sweater off. He took his time. He'd never seen skin as beautiful as hers, tawny gold and heated with life. His eyes dropped to her stomach. She sucked in a breath.

He wanted to caress that skin but before he could, he had to bare her. He had to give the hunger in him something to feast on. With one tug, he pulled the sweater off and threw it to the floor. She stood before him dressed in jeans and a lacy white bra.

For a moment, he lost any skill he might've had, any finesse. All he wanted to do was indulge his senses in her. Shuddering, he wrapped one arm around her waist, tugged her to him and buried his face in her neck. The heady scent of her shot through his system like a drug.

"Alexandre?" Her fingers whispered through his hair as she held him to her.

Sliding his free hand up her side, he nibbled at the skin pressed so temptingly against his mouth. A shiver shook her body and in his hair, her hand clenched. It was that reaction which gave him back his control.

Tonight was about Charlotte. He could indulge himself later, once he'd plied her with pleasure. He'd make this night perfect for her. She deserved nothing less.

He murmured a question to her about the protection. Her response was breathed against his cheek. "In the bedside drawer."

Then he stopped thinking about anything aside from making Charlotte feel adored, cherished, beautiful. Moving his lips from her neck, he kissed his way along her jaw and captured her mouth once more. She kissed him back with passion and heat, the sensuality in her nature rising to the surface.

His arousal pushed at the softness of her belly as she arched against him and he had to clench his fists tight to restrain the urge to plunder. Taking a shuddering breath, he relaxed one hand and ran the fingers along her back at the point where bare skin ended and her waistband began.

She pressed closer, a silent invitation for him to take what he wanted. What he wanted most of all was to have his Charlotte naked so he could worship her luscious body from head to toe. Suckling her lower lip into his mouth, he flicked open the button on her jeans.

Their mouths parted as she made a little noise and pulled away. He halted, but realized in seconds that she wasn't saying no. She just wanted to watch. He should've guessed that a woman so intrinsically sensual would want to savor every moment.

Her eyes lowered to where his hand slowly slid down

her zipper. He'd intended to pull her jeans off but with her sultry gaze locked on his hand, he decided to tease her a little—show her that between them, this act would always include tenderness, affection and joy.

At that moment, it didn't occur to Alexandre why it was so very important to him that Charlotte was in no way hurt by this intimate dance, physically or emotionally. Heart thundering, he slipped his hand through her parted zipper and cupped her through her panties.

Jerking, she clutched at his upper arms. He tightened the hand he had around her waist and moved the hand between her legs just enough to tantalize. Gasping for breath, she looked up at him and made a silent request for more.

"What do I get if I give you more?" he asked aloud, teasing, tempting, playing.

Eyes going wide, she licked her lower lip…and then moved against him.

Once.

Twice.

"I think, *ma petite,*" he said, his voice gone rough, "you're going to drive me crazy." He withdrew his hand before the feeling of her damp and hot against him succeeded in destroying his teeth-gritting control.

She pouted a little. "Alexandre."

He pushed her jeans off her hips and to the floor. "Lift your foot for me, kitten." When she complied, putting her hands on his shoulders for balance, he completed the removal of the denim barrier.

Then he glanced up. A dark-eyed siren looked down at him, all sun-kissed skin and midnight hair. Dressed in a white lace bra and matching panties, she looked sexier than a woman had any right to look.

At his continued silence, her hands tugged at his shoulders. As he rose, he ran his fingers up the backs of her legs, luxuriating his senses in the feel of her. She shivered under his touch, especially when he passed over the curve of her bottom.

He kissed her again, tempted by the lushness of her lips, slightly swollen from his earlier caresses. Her arms slipped under his shirt and clutched at his waist, her grip firm and just a tad possessive. He liked the way she was beginning to touch him, liked the fact that she considered him hers.

Accommodating the request she communicated to him by tugging at the material of his shirt, he shrugged it off. She sighed into the kiss and rubbed herself against his skin. He thought he'd lose his mind at the feel of her breasts teasing him through satin and lace.

Aware that his restraint was dangerously close to shattering, he guided her to the bed. "Will you lie down for me?"

Clearly reluctant to stop touching him, she climbed onto the sheets. The beautiful view of her heart-shaped bottom had his erection pounding. Thankfully, she lay down on her back seconds later, giving him a moment's relief. Until she raised a hand and reached for him.

With a rumbled groan, he kicked off his shoes and shucked his pants. Unwilling to shock her with the blatant evidence of just how much he wanted her, he kept on his briefs as he followed her onto the bed.

Then, taking a deep breath, he ran his hand down her sweetly curved body. His throat locked as the marauder in him roared with need. She was perfection. Absolute perfection. He had no need to pretend she fulfilled his every fantasy—it was true. He'd never been with a woman who was so much everything he desired.

Tenderness, he thought, recalling the words he'd read in her journal. Of course he'd give her tenderness this first night—that was not something she should've been worried about receiving from her first lover. *From him.*

"Why are you so quiet?" Charlotte's big eyes were looking into his, a touch of worry in them.

He wanted to erase even that smidgen of discomfort. "I'm simply indulging myself with the sight and feel of you," he said honestly. "You're so lovely, I could gaze at you for hours, though I admit I'd want to touch far too much to resist." So saying, he ran his hand to the curve of her hip and spread his fingers.

She was blushing, the worry gone. "I should've guessed you'd say something outrageous." Her lips tilted up.

Learning down, he nibbled on her for a while, teasing her with almost kisses. He didn't rush despite the tightness in his groin. Tonight, the woman in his arms needed slow seduction, not dark heat.

"You taste better every time I kiss you," he murmured. "I'm addicted to you, *chérie*."

She ran her hands up his chest to his shoulders. "Your voice—you could seduce me over the phone."

He grinned, delighted. "I shall do my best whenever you're away from me." Leaning closer, he urged her to wrap her arms around his neck as he pressed his chest lightly against her breasts.

She shivered. "You feel so good."

"Why do you sound surprised?" He chuckled and kissed the side of her neck, slipping his hand under her body to undo the clasp of her bra.

Her hands slid from his neck into his hair, playing with the sensitive skin of his nape. This time, *he* shivered. He felt her smile against him as he continued to taste the skin above her pulse.

"I never thought it would be this wonderful to just have a man's weight on me."

He lifted his head to glare at her. "*My* weight, not any other man's."

Eyes locked with his, she slid the bra down her arms and threw it off the bed. "I didn't know you existed before," she said, a teasing light in her eyes.

It was an effort to not immediately caress her lush breasts, pressed so temptingly against him. "So who did you imagine would hold you so?"

Her smile turned into something far more sultry. "I think I always dreamed of you without knowing it."

Mollified, he kissed her until she gasped for breath and then resumed his languid stroking of her body, from breast to thigh, indulging himself even as he stoked her desire to fever pitch. Her skin was so damn beautiful, he wanted to kiss every inch of it. Did he have the patience tonight? Could he survive the passionate torture?

Shuddering, he kissed her cheekbones, then the line of her jaw, before moving to her shoulders and her collarbones. When she clenched her fingers in his hair and sighed, he knew he'd find the patience he needed to give her this tenderness.

And then he began caressing every sweet inch of her skin that he hadn't yet savored. Erotic ecstasy laced his blood at the taste on the curve of her breasts, and he had to take her into his mouth. She arched as he tugged at a nipple, her desire open and sensually beautiful. When he finally had his fill—for the moment—her breasts were sheened by the touch of his lips, her chest heaving with her attempts to suck in air.

As he moved his hands over her, intent on this slow loving, his fingers touched the lace of her panties. Frustrated at being unable to touch her without hindrance, he tugged them off and threw them aside. Then he continued on his quest to taste every secret hollow and curve.

It was an intoxication of the senses, an initiation into the arts of pleasure by a master. Charlotte felt her body arch as Alexander's long-fingered hand lingered over the planes of her stomach, the strength of him compelling.

He kissed the edge of her mouth. "You're tense, *ma petite*. Is this not to your liking?"

How could he ask that question when she was burning from the inside out? Swallowing, she turned to face him, as always, stunned by the sheer beauty of him. "I've never felt this much."

His hand slid down her hip to rest on the sensitive skin of her upper thigh, his fingers so close to the heated place between her legs that she felt like begging him to take the next step. "I'm rushing you, Charlotte." The way he said her name was a temptation, an invitation by a fallen angel to join him in sin.

"If you go any slower, I'll melt at your feet."

His smile was wicked. "Ah, but it's not your feet that I want to melt, kitten." That seducing hand curved, the fingers brushing over the delicate skin of her inner thigh. A moan escaped her.

"You're so very sensitive." His husky murmur was a purr against her ear. "The idea of spiriting you away to my chalet, for my eyes only, is looking more and more attractive."

Turning her head, she met that dark gaze. "I'm no trophy," she found herself saying, barely aware why it was so important to her that he understood that.

Intensity flared in his expression. "*Oui*—you're far more prized than a mere trophy."

She ran her fingers across his lips and he kissed the tips before bending his head and capturing her mouth again. Against her body, the hard heat of him pulsed, making her want to rub against him as he kissed her with passion and heat…and heartbreaking tenderness.

The last vestiges of shyness and uncertainty disintegrated under Alexandre's exquisite gentleness. Wrapping her arms around his neck, she kissed him back with every ounce of passion in her. She'd been saving it for a lifetime. For her dream lover—her Alexandre.

He shuddered in her arms and she felt him reach blindly into the drawer beside the bed. Frustration in his groan, he broke the kiss only long enough to find what he needed and then his lips were taking her again, hot and sensuous and unashamedly possessive.

No matter what happened afterward, tonight she belonged to Alexandre Dupree. And he belonged to her.

He whispered something French in her ear, as if he'd forgotten she couldn't speak it and shifted off her. Moments later, he returned to the kiss, pressing the length of his body against hers. She jerked at the shock of sensual heat that sizzled between them as their naked bodies came in full contact.

There was nothing separating them now, nothing but their own searching hands and hungry mouths. When his hand stroked the inner skin of her thigh, she trembled and spread her legs for him.

Gently, so gently, he guided one over his back. She followed with the other, enclosing him in a prison of desire. He trailed a rain of kisses from her mouth down her neck to her breasts, as his hand slipped between their bodies to touch her with stark intimacy.

She gasped. But there was no self-consciousness in her, only pleasure. How could it be anything else when the man parting her slick folds looked at her as if her hunger for him was purest temptation?

As she grabbed at his shoulders, he began to make love to her with his fingers, rubbing and fondling, teasing and caressing. When she moaned, he lavished attention on her breasts, too, doubling the firestorm of erotic heat. She was aware of his fingers asking for entrance into her body and she responded by pushing toward him, drunk on the scent of desire, more than ready to have him inside her.

Those elegant fingers were very strong…and very careful. He caressed her deep inside, seeming to relish her every broken moan, occasionally leaving her sensitized breasts to sip at her mouth.

Unable to speak, she kissed and touched in turn, feeding her sensual need by tracing and holding onto the muscled planes of his back. He nipped at her neck when her fingers trailed over his buttocks, shocking a tiny quiver deep inside her body, where his fingers continued to do their magic. She almost panicked at the aching depth of sensation.

A hoarse male chuckle sounded in her ear as his lips trailed along the shell. "Don't fight it, kitten. I'll hold you safe. I give you my promise." And then he kissed her again and his tongue did something to her mouth that shattered her.

She stopped breathing as pleasure splintered her thoughts into a million pieces, as the most intimate of her muscles clenched around him again and again. Her body arched under his as the darkness of pleasure engulfed her but he kept his promise—he held her safe.

Sucking in a breath after she could think again, she said, "I wanted you with me."

Her declaration made all that beautiful male muscle turn to steel around her. "I'll be with you this time." Removing his fingers from her pleasure-weakened body, he rose over her.

When he pushed for entrance into her, her sensitive flesh shuddered with aftershocks. Wrapping her arms and legs around him, she welcomed him. And when he tore through the finest of barriers inside her, she barely noticed it, the pain lost under the delight.

This time, his kiss was carnal but his body remained

still, letting her get used to the feel of him inside her, stretching her so completely that she ached. But the ache promised such absolute ecstasy that she whimpered for him to give her more.

Kissing the sound off her lips, he pushed again and lodged fully in her. Her breath fractured on a groan as he began to move and their lips finally parted. Inside her, he was a living brand, hot and powerful. Slow and deep, his loving stoked the embers of her desire and she felt another firestorm approaching. Looking into his eyes, she saw the storm mirrored in eyes gone black with passion restrained.

For *her.*

She wanted to tell him that it was okay, that he could let go now, but before she could find the words, stars began to explode in front of her eyes, the weight of his body and his scent overwhelming her senses. But, as if he'd heard her silent permission, his body arched and she knew he'd thrown the reins of control aside.

This time, he came with her.

Nine

Charlotte felt completely boneless. She lay on top of Alexandre, her face buried in his neck, breathing in his maleness and feeling the woman in her sigh. This was her mate and she reveled in him.

A big hand stroked down her back and came to rest on her bottom, possessive and certain of his right to touch her so intimately. "Are you awake?"

Velvet and danger, she thought, that's what his voice sounded like. Velvet to sensuously wrap around her and danger to tempt. "A little." Smiling against his skin, she made a valiant effort and raised her head. "I'm not sure I'm capable of rational thought though."

His eyes glinted with amusement. "You flatter me."

She laughed. "Credit where credit's due." An unexpected thought intruded on her happiness, stealing away a little of the sunshine.

"What is it? Are you hurting?" Concern, sharp and in-

tent, layered his question. The hand that had been stroking her with languid ease was suddenly a band of steel
locking her to him.

"No. I'm fine." Leaning down, she pressed a kiss to his
jaw. "I'm being silly…will you be offended if I ask you
something very personal?"

His arm relaxed. "We've just shared something very
personal, *ma chérie*. We've claimed certain rights over
each other—so ask."

"You're very good at this," she whispered. "I suppose
I'm jealous of the women who came before me."

She expected him to say something sophisticated and
French, something charming and teasing. Despite what
he'd said about claiming, he was a man used to lovers, not
at all like her, for whom a sharing of the body could only
come with a sharing of the heart.

Long fingers stroked down her face. "I always respected the women I was intimate with, so I won't say that they
meant nothing. But what we shared this night—it has little to do with experience and skill and everything to do with
us. Nothing has ever been this powerful, this beautiful."

She adored him all the more for his honesty. This man
would never treat her as lesser because she was a woman.
Even more, by accepting that what they'd shared was special,
he'd given her a glimpse into his heart. She could do no less.

"I've never been with another man," she said, looking
down into his face, "but I know I'll never regret this. You're
the only lover I could imagine spending this first night with."

His jaw tightened. "Perhaps you shouldn't imply having other lovers around me, Charlotte."

Though the words were light, the tone was anything but.
Not having expected possessiveness from her sophisticated Frenchman, she couldn't help but feel joy at this sign
of deeper feeling on his part.

Smiling, she folded her arms flat across his muscular chest and put her chin on her hands. "Have you ever been in love?" she asked, encouraged by his openness.

His cheeks creased with male amusement and that stroking hand began to wander over her body again. "When I was a pup of twenty, I believed myself madly in love."

"And?"

"Celeste was rather lovely, flashing blue eyes, long blond hair. I thought she was the epitome of grace."

Jealousy sunk her fangs into Charlotte once again. "I see." She fingered her own ebony mane.

Alexandre's chuckle rubbed along her skin. "You should be careful. Otherwise, I might begin to believe that you care."

"You already know I care." She made a face at him. "Why didn't you marry Celeste?"

"I decided it would be imprudent to marry a woman who was gracing all of my friends' beds."

Charlotte blinked. "What?"

"She didn't want to—how do you say—put all her eggs in one basket. The only thing she cared about was hooking a rich man. One of my former friends wasn't as fortunate as me. He's now her husband."

"I'm sorry."

"I'm not. At the time, of course I was devastated. It passed. And I was able to see the fate I'd escaped. Raoul never knows where his wife is—I would've never tolerated such a marriage."

She chewed over what he'd revealed. "Is that why you keep your attachments so short and simple? Because you don't trust women with commitment?"

His eyes darkened. "What do you know of my attachments?"

"Only what I've read in the magazine articles I could

find on the Internet," she admitted. "You don't seem to have long relationships."

"I see that you've taken my advice and are questioning me after we've made love."

It took her a moment to recall his teasing words. "I'm sorry, I didn't mean to. I wasn't trying to be manipulative." She was genuinely afraid that he'd suspect her of such base motives.

He tugged at a strand of her hair. "How can I believe such a thing when your big brown eyes are so honest?" Sighing, he shifted their positions so that they were lying side by side, face-to-face.

She put her hands on his chest and cuddled closer. "I'm glad you know that. I wouldn't want anything to spoil this night."

He smiled and wrapped his arms around her. "That would be impossible. There is magic in the air tonight."

Seduced by the warmth in his eyes, she playfully scraped her teeth along his shoulder. He jerked in surprise and then narrowed his eyes at her. "So, kitten, you want to play?"

Delighted by the passionate look in his eyes, the husky timbre of his voice, she tugged one of his hands to her mouth and delicately nibbled on his fingers. He let her have her way for perhaps a minute before a rumble sounded deep in his chest and he switched positions again, placing her atop his body.

"Come, let us play." Then he grinned and ran the nails of his hands very gently up the outside of her thighs.

Shivering, she sat up on his body, a little shy but not enough to forego the experience being held out to her by her sexy lover. "Yes," she whispered. "Let's."

An hour later, Charlotte was lying on her back, smiling dreamily and getting dozy, when Alexandre spoke. "Celeste didn't really change the core of the man I am. I'd learned my lessons long before then."

The realization that he was answering her earlier question had her drowsiness replaced by alert concentration. "Who taught you?" she dared to ask, wonder blooming in her. Alexandre wasn't a man who trusted lightly.

His answer was oblique. "My *maman* is very French, very sophisticated."

That sensually accented voice slid over her body like a physical caress. She couldn't help the tiniest of shivers.

"You're cold." Sitting up, he pulled a spread over them. The sight of his gloriously muscled back had her gulping. She could barely believe she now had the right to touch this magnificent male.

He lay down beside her, slipping his arm under her head and pulling her close. Wanting to see his face, she shimmied up until her chin was resting on his sculpted chest once again. That gorgeous face looked down at her with a distinctly proprietary glint in his eyes.

"What do you mean, sophisticated? Is she one of those elegant Parisian women they always show on the fashion shows?"

He smiled, his cheeks creasing. "*Oui,* she is most certainly elegant, *Maman.* But, I think you'd like her. She is a strong woman."

"What about your father?"

"My *papa* is a very rich man, well-respected and highly sought after in society. His wife is a British blue blood."

She didn't know how to understand what he was telling her. "Your mother was his mistress?"

"Not was, *is.* She has been with him for the longest time. As I said, *Maman* is very sophisticated and so is he. So am I."

Despite the silky charm, the world-weary tone, she

heard the pain. "Did you always know?" She wanted to hold him, soothe his hurts, but knew that a man as strong as Alexander Dupree would never accept anything that blatant.

"*Oui, ma petite.* As a child, I knew *Papa* had to leave us to go to another family. I also knew never to call him *Papa* if we should meet in public." He slid his hand down her body and she moved to accommodate him, aware that the touch was no longer sexual.

"Of course his wife knows of me and so do his other children. I'm an open secret—we French are so very mature about such things." His lips curved. "I believe his wife has a younger lover."

"Why did they ever marry?" She blurted out, unable to understand. Spencer was a bastard of a man, but at least his marriages and affairs had had some reason, be it wealth or lust.

"Money, sweet Charlotte. Money. It was understood that their families must merge to create an empire." His hand tangled in her hair.

"Does your mother…?" She stopped, aware that she might be going too far.

"I'm not offended, *chérie.* Your questions have honesty— that has never caused any harm. *Maman* was born poor. I can't fault her for choosing the life of a pampered mistress over that of working menial jobs until both her beauty and spirit died.

"We've never spoken of it, but I believe she enjoys her life. Not only does she have a lover who dotes on her, a son who respects and loves her, she has wealth and more importantly, she has freedom."

"I just—I'm afraid I have trouble understanding such lives."

"Ah, I've shocked you. I forget that you see the world through a lens I have lost."

She frowned. "Will you be as sophisticated in your marriage?" Why was she asking this when she knew that what they had would end as soon as Alexander's time at the vineyard was over? A woman like her couldn't capture a man like him, whatever feelings they'd both admitted to. Yes, she was special to Alexandre, but not special enough to hold him. How could she be, when none of those other far more experienced beauties, had ever succeeded?

Alexander rolled them both until he was braced over her, lips curved in a half smile. She couldn't read the look in those enigmatic eyes. His hand slid over her torso to enclose one breast.

"I'd never tolerate such a marriage. If my wife touched another man, I'm afraid I'd be most unsophisticated." A warning flickered in his eyes. "Some might say I'd react primitively."

She licked her lips at the wild air about him, extremely sure that a wife who strayed on Alexander Dupree would learn the very meaning of danger. "What about you?"

"Hmmm?"

"Does the same rule apply to you or are you free to keep a mistress?"

His thumb plucked at her nipple. "To ensure that his wife doesn't stray, a man must spend much time ensuring her pleasure. I intend to be very diligent in my husbandly duties. It would leave no time for distractions." Leaning down, he placed a wet kiss on her neck, nibbling his way up to her lips.

The hand on her breast continued to play with the exquisitely sensitive bud of her nipple. "*Maman* says I have a primitive nature—possessive and loyal. She doesn't know where I get it from, when neither of my parents know the meaning of possession."

Charlotte understood it absolutely. Right now, it was

blazing in his eyes. It would be a challenge being married to this man, for he'd demand complete surrender at times and complete loyalty always. But, she thought, he'd give so fully to his woman that those moments of submission would be gifts from his wife to him, a pleasure for both, a meeting of equals.

She ached to have him belong to her, this man who touched her with tender heat and looked at her with passion in his gaze. Yet, behind the passion was pain. Alexandre had been hurting his whole life and his charming facade couldn't hide that from her. Not when she looked at him with eyes full of a blossoming love.

Tonight, she'd hold him in her arms. Tomorrow, she'd think about how to go about healing his hurts until he began to believe in love and forever and commitment.

Alone in her greenhouse the following day, Charlotte mulled over what she'd learned about the man she was falling in love with, though she'd tried so very hard to keep her heart from jumping headfirst into pain.

He hadn't ever had a father who was proud to call him son. Instead, he'd been schooled from a young age to never expect the man who'd fathered him to acknowledge him in public. In effect, he'd been taught that he was shameful.

What had that done to a man of Alexandre's pride and heart? What had it done to the boy he'd been? Charlotte wanted to strangle his parents. Alexandre was loyal to his mother and she could understand why, but there was cynicism in his eyes when he spoke of her. He might be loyal to her, but he wasn't blind to her flaws.

Not only had his childhood been a mockery, the only other woman he'd trusted, Celeste, had betrayed him. Alexandre had never indicated that he didn't trust a woman's loyalty, but she could read between the lines. From what he'd seen of women, he didn't think that they could remain true to a man.

He'd said that his mother had been with his father for the longest time. So who else had she been with? Who else had a young and vulnerable Alexandre seen her with? Then there was his father's wife, with her younger lover.

Putting down the secateurs she'd been using to trim away dead leaves, she moved to the workbench. As she sorted through the heavily scented blooms she'd placed there, she knew she had to make Alexandre see that things could be different. But how could she, a woman who barely knew herself, reach the heart of this magnificent man she found herself entangled with?

"*Ma petite,* you have a most serious expression on your lovely face." Alexandre's body pressed against her back, his arms slipping around her waist. A kiss on the side of her neck sent goose bumps whispering along her arms.

"What are you doing here? I thought you were with Trace and James?" Her heartbeat accelerated at his nearness—as always, she was ultimately susceptible to him.

"We've finished our discussion and I've come to take you to lunch."

Disappointment weighed down her floating sense of euphoria. "I can't. I have to finish this." She gestured at the blood-red roses before them. "It's a special order from Mrs. Blackhill for her daughter's sixteenth birthday."

Personally, Charlotte had thought the requested flower arrangements too heavy and sophisticated for a sixteen-year-old's party, but after encountering Trina Blackhill, she'd realized that there was a big difference between the sixteen-year-old girl she'd been and the heavily made-up teenager she'd met.

"Can you not take a break with me for an hour?" His

fingers tangled with hers. "I find myself missing your company, kitten."

She bit her lip, undone by the husky reference to their night of loving. "I can squeeze out forty minutes."

"Then it's just as well that I brought a picnic basket, is it not?"

"Alexandre!" She turned in his arms, delighted. "How do you know me so well?"

Something that was almost guilt danced in his eyes. "Because I adore you."

Alexandre looked down into that lovely face and wanted to tell her about reading her journal, his nature protesting against continuing the lie of omission. But he had a feeling that if he admitted what he'd done, she'd retreat from him faster than he could think. Charlotte was an intensely private woman and he'd taken that privacy away from her.

And yet, he didn't regret it, not for a moment, not for an instant. If he hadn't found her journal, she'd still be backing away from him, refusing to let him inside that shell she'd grown to protect herself.

"Come, I've brought a wonderful wine for you to taste." He held out his hand.

"One of ours?" She let him lead her from the greenhouse to the golf cart he'd parked outside.

"Of course not. This is the best wine in the world." He gave her a smug smile as he picked up the basket from the passenger seat. "It's one of mine."

Her laugh was infectious. "Does Trace know you say that?"

"Why do you think he asked for my help in raising the profile of this winery among connoisseurs? You're commercially successful, especially with your Brute Cuvee Sparkling, but in this region, Louret is far ahead of you in terms of wines of distinctiveness."

Charlotte's lips twisted. "I hope they keep beating Spencer."

Alexandre's felt his brows rise. "You're not behind the Ashton Estate label?"

"I have nothing against it. I just like it that Louret is a big thorn in Spencer's side. After what he did to…" She paused. "You don't want to hear all this."

He led her to a sunny spot by her cottage, next to the tree where they'd previously picnicked. After spreading a picnic blanket on the ground, he set the basket on it and tugged her down to sit beside him. "Of course I do. Anything that concerns you is of great interest to me."

She let him hold her. "Oh, it's nothing new. Thanks to the recent scandal, most people know that Spencer married Caroline Lattimer and basically stole this place from her." She blew out a breath between her teeth. "I don't want to talk about him. He always makes me lose my appetite."

Alexandre chuckled. "Then we shall talk about other things."

They had a wonderful time. Charlotte was overjoyed by the pure happiness on Alexandre's face as he spoke to her without any hint of reserve. "You're not worrying over things?" he asked.

Trust him to remember the papers she'd posted to Nebraska today. "No. I've done what I can—I have to keep living life no matter what happens."

With pride in his eyes, he nodded.

All too soon, it was time to say goodbye. "I'll ride up when someone arrives to ferry over the flowers for the birthday party. Maybe you can sneak me a kiss?"

"When do you think you'll come up? I would certainly not want to miss a chance to kiss you."

"Aim for around six-thirty."

* * *

Just before six-thirty that evening, Alexandre drove a golf cart up to the estate house, intending to return to the winery after he'd claimed his kiss. There was something he wanted to finish looking at. His smile of anticipation died as he glimpsed Charlotte standing in the drive, talking to a young man.

Behind the boy, he could see a flashy red car. From the gift-wrapped package in his hand, he surmised that the boy was a party guest who'd arrived early. He caught the last of their conversation as he walked up from their blind side.

"Are you sure?" the boy asked, a smile on his face. "I could show you a good time."

"I'm afraid I'm involved with someone." Charlotte's tone was firm. "Thank you for the invitation."

"Well, when you get sick of the other guy, give me a call." He pressed a card into her hand.

Jealousy was not an emotion Alexandre was familiar with, but as he reached Charlotte and turned her in his arms, it gripped him by the throat. "She won't be needing that." Taking the card from Charlotte's hand, he slid it into the pocket of the boy's jacket. "I believe you have somewhere to be."

Without another word, the boy turned and left. Alexandre had a feeling that it had something to do with the look in his eyes.

Charlotte's soft chuckle had him glancing down. "Well, you're handy to have around. Thanks for the help. He was a tad persistent."

"An admirer, *chérie?*"

She rolled her eyes. "Just another playboy guest."

"You get such invitations often?" He was feeling very, very edgy but kept his tone amused through sheer effort of will. If he let her see the effect a little harmless flirting had

had on him, she might begin to guess at the depth of his feelings for her. And he wasn't even ready to admit those to himself.

She shrugged. "They don't matter. Now, kiss me."

His kiss was just this side of ravenous, his hunger held on the tightest of leashes. He wanted to possess, to brand, but he let her go with a caress that left her breathing deeply, eyes shiny with desire.

"Will you come to me tonight?" Her voice was soft.

He shouldn't go to her in his current mood. "I'll come."

Ten

Alexandre had seduced and coaxed and given Charlotte the kind of loving she'd fantasized about. But tonight, only a day after their first night together, he felt anything but gentle, anything but tender. He felt raw and hungry and his arousal was almost painful.

If he went to her as he'd promised, he knew that he'd scare her. She was a sensual woman, the most wonderfully responsive lover he'd ever had, but she wasn't ready for the wildness driving him. Neither was he. He'd never felt this raging need to brand a woman as his, to drive into her so deeply that he was embedded in her psyche, buried in the molten core of her.

He knew his jealous possessiveness was without foundation—Charlotte wasn't the kind of woman who'd encourage another man while involved with him. But the fact was, that guest had been hitting on *his* woman. Coldly discouraging the youth's advances hadn't been enough to calm the marauder he was at heart, turbulent and domineering.

He hungered to go to her. He wanted to strip her naked and rub his beard-roughened jaw across her sensitive skin. Not hard. Never painfully. Just enough to mark her a little, just enough to calm himself. Except he knew that even that wouldn't be enough.

This time, he needed absolute surrender.

Compliance.

Obedience to his every sensual desire.

Sometimes, I wonder what it would be like to give you such complete trust that I'd do anything you asked, without question…without hesitation.

Yes, she'd dreamed of playing an intimate game of control and submission, but if he went to her, it wouldn't be about fulfilling her fantasy. Tonight, he wanted to take for himself, to indulge his needs and not hers. He would of course ensure she found pleasure, that wasn't even a question, but it would be on *his* terms.

Pacing the guestroom, Alexandre gritted his teeth and accepted that he couldn't go to her in this state. Not for anything did he want to scare her. But neither could he remain in this room without going insane. A few seconds later, he was by the doors that led out to the second floor terrace. Before heading down the steps that led from the terrace to the ground, he set the latch to ensure the doors would lock behind him.

And then he started walking, his aim to exercise off the pounding, almost hurtful need in his belly. He didn't pay any attention to where he was heading, focusing only on the burn of muscle as his legs strode over the ground.

Some time later, he looked up and halted in shock. Charlotte's cottage lay barely a dozen feet away. Even after deciding not to inflict himself on her, he'd come to her, driven by impulses beyond his control.

He stared at the rectangle of light in the bedroom window. So, his lover was still awake. Waiting for him? Immediately, any good the long walk might've done was gone. He was rock hard, so aroused that he thought he might die if he didn't have her. Clenching his fists in the pockets of his dark slacks, he turned, intent on going back.

"Alexandre? Is that you?"

Startled, he spun around. She was standing in the doorway of the cottage, barely covered by a white shirt. Immediately, he scowled. "Why are you standing there dressed like that when you didn't know who it was?" He couldn't control the harsh rebuke in his tone. Charlotte aroused his most protective instincts and they had nothing of sophistication about them.

"I only opened the door fully when I realized it was you. Why are you prowling out there?" She took a step out the door.

"Stop right there."

"Why?" Hurt echoed in her voice.

"Don't sound like that—it kills me." He blew out a harsh breath. "I'm on edge tonight. I can't be sure what I'll do to you if you're silly enough to let me get my hands on you."

She started moving again. "That sounds very intriguing. What do you think you might do to me?"

He *growled* at her, losing his civilized veneer as she came dangerously close, close enough that he could tumble her to the ground and take her right now. The stark eroticism of the image ripped his already tenuous control to shreds.

"You must go back inside." He forced the words out. "Right now, I can't be the lover you need—I want you in a way that would shock you to your toes. I want you hot and wet and writhing under me. Definitely *under* me," he murmured, his proprietary instincts taking over as he glimpsed the sensual curiosity in her eyes.

"I want to drive into you so completely that you forget I'm not a part of your body. I want to touch your breasts and legs and anything else I please, any way I like, for so long as I choose. I want your reaction, your cries, your hunger, but I don't want you to be an equal party. I want you to surrender to me. Without compromise."

Charlotte swallowed at the description of just what her not-so-sophisticated Alexandre wanted from her. He looked like a wild wolf, undisciplined and ravenous. *For her.* Only she would do, she realized slowly, the femaleness in her exulting at having enticed such an intriguing male.

She refused to turn away from him tonight, not when he'd given her such tenderness the night before. The commitment implied by his starkly possessive words stunned her. This went beyond pleasure, beyond desire. Was she ready to accept the claim he wanted to make?

Mouth dry, she raised her fingers to the hem of her shirt and without giving herself time to think about it, tugged it over her head, leaving herself naked. "I'm all yours," she whispered, dropping the shirt to the ground.

He didn't ask for any more permission. Instead of ravaging her, he moved around her, stalking, prowling, as if he were inspecting every inch of her. The look in those sinful eyes was distinctly proprietary. It made her feel treasured, desired, wanted. There was no room for embarrassment or shame—his open need for her gave her the confidence she needed. As a woman. As a lover.

The throbbing between her legs increased, beating in time to the rapid thudding of her heart. She needed to touch him, but he'd asked for complete surrender and she'd acquiesced. So she remained silent and let her wild wolf move to her back.

His hands settled on her hips. She jumped.

"I'm going to take you out here, with the darkness and

the stars for company." It was a husky description. Moving her hair aside, he kissed her neck, nipping at her. "I so enjoy the way you taste, kitten."

After his words of raw hunger, she expected him to take her quickly. There was no fear in her. She trusted Alexandre to care for her, even in his passion. And she was ready for him. He brought the sensual, pleasure-seeking woman in her to the surface, turned fantasy to reality.

Strong hands roamed down her body. One slipped between her legs, shocking a gasp out of her. Seconds later, it slid down her thigh, urging her to part her legs. Feeling wild and untamed and uninhibited, she did as he asked, shifting her stance so that she was shamelessly open.

His fingers feathered through her curls and then they were gone. She felt his body heat and nothing more. A second later, his hands were on her hips and his shoulders were wedging her thighs apart and his mouth was on her like a brand. Her legs threatened to crumple as sensations bombarded her, hot and vicious and pleasurable enough to make her drunk. One big hand slid up to flatten against her belly and he began to knead her taut flesh, even as his tongue did things to her that had her shaking in reaction. Clutching at the hand on her abdomen, she widened her stance even more, unable to resist his silent request.

The hand on her hip clenched, the thumb rubbing across her sensitized skin. "*Tu es très belle.* You are so beautiful." His words stroked her senses, that voice of his like black velvet against the most hidden part of her. And then he began to flood her with pleasure, suckling and teasing and loving.

She wanted to plead with him to finish, but something kept her silent. Perhaps it was an awareness that tonight, Alexandre needed to claim her *his* way—a way that was untamed and utterly without boundaries. Maybe she should've been afraid of such a claiming, fearful that he'd take everything she had and leave her desolate—but she hungered for it, hungered to give him what he needed.

The first tumble into the maelstrom of erotic pleasure caught her unawares. One moment she was drowning in sensation and the next, wild shocks rocketed through her body, squeezing a scream from her throat and causing a volcano of heat in her core.

Opening her eyes, she fought to stay on her feet. Alexandre stood up behind her, his arms keeping her upright. Shifting her hair to one side, he nibbled at her neck, one big hand smoothing its way up her body to cradle a breast.

"Alexandre," she murmured, too sexually sated to be anything less than totally giving, totally his.

Instead of answering, one of his roving hands dropped lower, into her damp curls. The sudden shock of heat was a surprise—she hadn't believed her body could feel anymore. But as Alexandre kissed her neck, one hand teasing at her nipples while the other spread through her intimately, she found she'd been wrong. Desire tore at her, making her lose what breath she'd managed to catch.

She rubbed her face along his sleeve. His shirt was soft against her cheek, the scent of him locked in the fibers. "You're making me melt," she confessed, even as she felt another release approaching. It was an affectionate whisper.

He continued to nibble on the highly vulnerable skin above her pulse. "Again, kitten." It was barely a sound in the darkness, so husky the words were almost lost.

The impact of her second orgasm hit her as hard as the first. But instead of a shocking inferno, this one was a slumbering fire that continued to rage when she'd thought it would flare and burn her out. Alexandre's fingers kept working their magic and she kept tumbling over and over into the smoldering heat. Lights flickered inside her closed lids as she moved her body on his fingers, seeking more of the drug he'd addicted her to.

He gave her what she wanted. More and more and more, until her body was so limp that the aftershocks racing through her only made her moan, too weak to do anything else. Alexandre shifted and suddenly she was in his arms, heading toward the cottage.

Looking down into Charlotte's eyes, Alexandre was lost. He'd wanted to take her out there, under the night sky, but something primitive and possessive in him refused to subject her to the hard earth. Protecting Charlotte was already so much a part of him that he didn't even acknowledge it as an impulse. It just *was*. Pushing through the open door of the cottage, he kicked it shut behind him.

The beacon of light that was her bedroom drew him. Charlotte didn't say a word, rubbing her face against his chest, her arms around his neck. There was such complete acceptance in her that he was humbled, the tyrant in him soothed by her willingness to give him everything he needed. When he lay her down on the bed, she raised her arms. He went to her on a husky groan, covering her body with his.

Under his hands, her skin was smooth, honey-golden and warm. "I love the way you feel, *ma petite*," he murmured, licking the shell of her ear. "The way you move." Kissing his way across her jaw, he suckled her lower lip into his mouth. "The way you taste."

She shivered and whispered something he didn't catch. He just knew she wasn't saying no. Rubbing his face against her neck, he breathed in the scent of her, aware of her fingers threading through his hair. When he nuzzled his way down to her breasts, those graceful hands clenched in expectation. A smile on his lips, he brushed a soft kiss over the slope of one lush breast.

Under him, she squirmed. "Alexandre."

Chuckling, he moved his head and took her nipple into his mouth, having already learned what she ached for. The taste of her sent his senses spinning, drawing him into a vortex of desperate need that he couldn't fight, didn't even want to fight. Under him, her body arched, sensuous and compelling.

Hands on her rib cage, he held her still as he indulged in her. Her other breast tasted as beautiful as the first. A taste wasn't enough. Sucking hard, he held the taut morsel in his mouth while her fingers moved restlessly through his hair to grip his shoulders. He could feel her heart thudding in her chest, rapid and furious.

Then she whispered his name and his hunger became voracious. "I need to be in you." He rose over her.

Her eyes seemed to darken even further as her hands slipped from his hair and down to his belt. He let her get rid of the belt and unzip him. When she closed her hand over his length, he came close to shattering.

Somehow finding the strength, he pulled away only far enough to ensure her protection. Returning, he wrapped her legs around him and nudged at her with his pulsing arousal. Regret that he couldn't feel the silk of her skin through his trousers and shirt tempted him to stop and remove his clothes. Then the ravenous need he had for her grabbed him by the throat and retreat was no longer an option.

Proving her sensuous nature, Charlotte playfully slipped a finger into his mouth, permission for a dance he'd never take by force, no matter his urgency. Suckling at the offering, he pushed into her body in one heavy stroke. Tight, her muscles resisted at first and then pulled him into melting heat and sheer pleasure. Her finger slid out of his mouth, her hands going to clutch at his shoulders, her hands strong despite their apparent fragility.

With her body clenched around him, Alexandre had no ability to think. Glancing at her passion-drenched face to ensure that this was giving her as much pleasure as it was him, he let the final rein slip from his hand and surrendered to the firestorm. Around him, her body was sleek and giving, a perfect fit.

An absolutely perfect fit.

Charlotte Ashton had been made for Alexandre Dupree, was his last thought before his release hit him hard and low, powerful enough to have him seeing sparks. And then Charlotte moved under him and he realized that ecstasy could multiply until there was nothing but sensation sizzling over his skin and shooting through his bloodstream.

He surfaced to find his face buried against the curve of his lover's warm neck, his body cushioned by hers while they remained very intimately connected. Not wanting to leave, he licked at her skin. She shivered.

"Do you want me to move, *ma petite?*" He liked the feel of her silky soft body crushed under his.

She nuzzled him. "No. But could you take off your shirt? The buttons…"

She didn't have to say any more. He realized they had to be pressing into her skin. Barely rising off her, he said, "Undo them."

"You like giving orders too much," she grumbled, but her lips were trying not to smile. Her fingers undid every single button and he shrugged it off. "What about the rest of your clothes?" she said, when he settled back over her.

"To remove them I'd have to withdraw from you. I don't want to."

He felt her blush through the fine skin of the breasts pressed against him. "You were speaking to me in French while we…"

He allowed himself to luxuriate in her body, rolling the exotic scent of her in his mouth. "*Oui,* it's my native tongue. Did you not like it?"

"You know very well I liked it. I just want to know what it meant." Her arms were around his shoulders, lazily stroking.

Content, he lay there and let her pet him, the driving hunger in him calmed by her unconditional giving. "My words would make you blush."

Her lips parted softly at the roughness in his tone and the primitive in him punched to the surface. Leaning close, he began to whisper translations of his more intimate whispers.

"Alexandre!"

Looking down into her scandalized face, he broke out into a smile. "Is this the same woman who stood so proudly naked under the stars only minutes ago?"

Alexandre's sensual voice threatened to make Charlotte lose her train of thought. "Why?" she asked.

"Why?" He gave her a quizzical look.

"Why were you so edgy tonight?"

The skin of his face tightened. "I'm not ready to tell you that."

"You can't keep your secrets forever."

"*Non,*" he agreed. "But I'll keep them for tonight."

Alerted by something in his tone, she kissed him gently. "I know about commitment and loyalty."

He didn't respond with words but she knew he'd heard. For now, it was enough.

After that night, Alexandre's attitude toward her changed. He was no less tender, no less careful with her body, but there was a proprietary hunger in his eyes that stunned her each time he looked at her. And his touch… It made her shiver to think of the sheer possessiveness in it. Spending nights in his arms had become more than an indulgence—it was now a necessity.

But the nights were not all they had, she thought with a smile. Somehow, despite their schedules, they'd managed to sneak away for rides to San Pablo Bay and dinners in the nearby town of Sonoma. There'd also been a repeat of that magical moonlit picnic. It hardly seemed possible that she'd only known him for just under two weeks.

With every moment she spent with him, her sense of rightness grew. Nothing had ever felt as perfect as they did together. Nobody had ever made her dreams come true as he did. When she was with him, she even managed to forget about the envelope from the vital records office that she waited for every single day.

Part of her was glad it had been somehow delayed, giving her a few more precious days to pretend that her mother was alive. But another part of her wanted the truth so badly that sometimes, her whole body hurt. Hurt that only Alexandre's loving could diffuse.

Humming under her breath, she dethorned a long-stemmed rose in preparation for its use in an arrangement. How was it that a sophisticated way-out-of-her-league Frenchman knew her so well, so perfectly?

Perfectly.

Like a mental gunshot, that single word triggered an unexpected and awful train of thought. It was as if her subconscious had been waiting for the dam of her conscious mind to break, allowing the flood of information to roar through her like a river of betrayal.

Her hand stilled. Last night's loving under the starlight had been perfect. It hadn't been similar to what she'd fantasized about, it had been perfect. And before that—the picnics, the dancing, the romance—it had all been perfect, down to the last detail. Her mouth dried up as a horrible suspicion reared its head. The rose dropped from her hand. It couldn't be possible, she argued, how could Alexandre have read her journal?

Her thoughts raced back to the day he'd given her the bouquet, the day she'd found him standing outside the greenhouse. It was feasible that he'd gone searching for her and run across her journal. That day, she'd argued against her instincts, telling herself she was being paranoid. But what if she hadn't been wrong about the knowledge in his eyes? Her hand clasped the stem of another rose. Thorns stabbed into her palm. Wincing, she drew it away, blotted off the tiny pinpricks of blood and resumed dethorning.

It was useless. Her mind continued to circle around the almost certain knowledge that Alexandre had invaded her privacy. More than that, by never owning up to what he'd done, he'd cheated the faith she'd placed in him. Throwing down the flowers, she stalked out to her bike. The ride should've calmed her down but with every moment that passed, she became more and more convinced of the rightness of her suspicion.

Humiliation and anger burned in her cheeks, pain throbbed in her heart. She'd trusted him absolutely and all this time, it had just been a game to him. God, how he must've laughed to discover that in her fantasies, quiet Charlotte Ashton imagined herself a temptress. Tears threatened but she fought them off with fury.

She headed straight to the winery, ignoring the beauty of the spring-green vineyards lit by the late afternoon sun. Alexandre was standing by the steps leading down to the cellar, head bent and face set in thoughtful lines as he spoke to an assistant winemaker. As soon as she entered, his head came up, almost as if he'd scented her presence.

A smile dawned on his handsome face. For once, it didn't immediately soften her heart. She gathered up all her fury, all her anger and waited for him to come to her.

"Ma chérie," he began.

"I need to talk to you. Privately." Without another word, she left the winery and headed toward the vineyard, his prowling presence a dark shadow at her back. The second they were out of hearing range, she whirled.

His expression was wary. "You're angry."

"Yes." She could find no subtle way to ask this. "Did you read my journal?" It came out as a blunt demand.

The lines around his mouth went white. "Yes."

She'd expected anything but that, expected him to offer excuses before he admitted it. "You aren't even going to try and deny it?"

"Non. I did read your journal."

Frustrated, she cried, "How could you do that to me? Invade my privacy that way?"

"I didn't plan to do so. But when the opportunity presented itself, I wasn't strong enough to resist." He didn't attempt to touch her, as if aware how thin her control was.

"Well you should have." She clenched her fists. "They were private thoughts, private dreams. You had no right to read them." No right to see the side of herself that she'd never allowed anyone to see. Except him. She'd trusted him and it had been based on a lie. "How would you have liked it if I'd done the same to you?"

His shoulders tightened under the deep green shirt he wore. "Charlotte, you're so self-contained, so protective of your thoughts that I feared I'd never get to know you if I didn't take the chance when it came."

"That's your justification?"

He shook his head, remorse in his eyes. "No. That's simply the reason I told myself it was permissible."

His acceptance of guilt was driving her insane. "You think I'm protective of my thoughts? What about you? You've got a layer of charm that's more impenetrable than steel."

"I've told you things I've never shared with anyone," he said quietly.

She was too distraught to hear the depth of emotion in his tone, too angry to have paid heed to it even if she had heard. "Was this all just a game to you? Seduce the little Indian gardener in your free time?"

Those bitter chocolate eyes darkened to thunder. "I would stop before you go too far." His tone had turned silky, terrifyingly calm.

"Why the hell should I?" She fought the urge to cry— if she broke down in front of him, it would complete her humiliation. "You've had a good laugh at my expense. Well the laugh is over. We're over."

He touched her for the first time, capturing her chin between his forefinger and thumb. "Don't speak so in anger, *ma petite.*"

She jerked her chin away and began to move back. "I mean every word I say. I should be glad you've made it easy for me to break it off—I was beginning to worry that you thought there might be more between us than sex." The lie almost killed her.

For a second, she thought she saw Alexandre's body tremble as if he'd been hit with a hard blow. But when she looked into his eyes, his gaze was blank. It infuriated her that he could remain so calm while her heart was being torn to pieces.

"Now I don't have to worry about breaking your lying heart," she whispered. "Thanks for letting me practice on you—you went way beyond the call of duty. Next time a man seduces me, I'm sure he'll be happy with my skills."

She didn't wait for him to respond. Barely able to see through the haze of fury and pain blinding her, she ran to her bike. It was only as she was riding away that she realized Alexandre had made no effort to follow her.

Eleven

Alexandre lay awake late that night, Charlotte's words slicing through him like sharp knives. Her rejection was all the more terrible because he'd told her things he'd *never* shared with anyone, letting her glimpse the forces that had shaped his soul.

And yet she'd rejected him with such absolute force that he couldn't convince himself she hadn't meant every word. Had she truly been "practicing" on him, using him because he was available? The idea dealt a vicious blow to his inherent masculinity.

Turning, he punched the pillow into shape and tried to forget the incredible anger in her eyes as she'd walked away. He'd misjudged her badly when he'd thought her a woman of too much heart. If she'd been what he'd imagined, she'd never have hurt him so.

He knew he should forget her and move on but that was proving impossible. Adoring her had become as vital to him as breathing. How could he have been so wrong about her, so mistaken as to her nature?

Suddenly, he recalled one of the very first entries in her journal.

…for me, this act is more than bodies meeting, more than simple pleasure, more than just the physical…

She'd asked him how he would've felt if she'd invaded his privacy. In all honesty, he would've been furious—furious enough to do and say far worse things than she had in that flaring burst of anger and hurt—he'd wounded the woman he so desperately needed to protect and been so blinded by his own pain that he hadn't seen hers.

Cursing his stupidity, he got out of bed. The temptation to go to Charlotte and ask her forgiveness was hard to resist. Despite her anger, he knew she was too gentle to make him beg, knew that she'd forgive him the second she heard the sincerity in his tone and that was why he couldn't take that road. It would be too easy and her hurt deserved proper recompense.

He'd been arrogant in reading her private thoughts but he couldn't regret it, not when it had brought him Charlotte. Sweet Charlotte with her tenderness and her hope and her caring. Now she was feeling violated and betrayed by the man she'd trusted with her innocence.

He couldn't stand knowing that, couldn't bear to let the woman who'd given him flowers think that she was in any way lesser in their dance because he'd seen the sensual heart of her. To do that, he had to make her understand what he'd felt when he'd read her thoughts. And he knew only one way to do that.

Even as he began an apology that laid his soul bare, he shied away from the reason behind his driving need to lessen Charlotte's hurt. He wasn't yet ready to face that powerful feeling, not yet willing to accept how hard he'd fallen for a woman whose smile alone could destroy him.

* * *

Charlotte awoke later than usual, courtesy of a sleepless night. Guilt hadn't made a good bed-companion. Notwithstanding his own actions, she knew she'd hurt Alexandre and accepted that he deserved an apology. However, she hadn't been able to screw up the courage last night. Would he even listen? He was so proud under that charming sophistication, so conscious of his past that her horrible words would've wounded him terribly.

She'd tried to convince herself that of course he wouldn't believe what she'd said. Of course he'd know that for her, making love with a man meant something far more than physical pleasure. After all, he'd been privy to her innermost thoughts.

But she hadn't been able to rest easy, too conscious of the fact that in spite of his strength, Alexandre had deep vulnerabilities. Vulnerabilities such as those fostered by his father's implied rejection and his mother's lifestyle choice.

Deep inside, her beautiful, sensual Alexandre didn't believe he was good enough for love and loyalty. Her reckless words would've further cemented that impression. She'd said she'd been practicing on him! The recollection made her cringe. No, she couldn't let him think that he'd only been a convenience. Never could she let the man who'd shown her such tenderness think that.

Taking a deep, fortifying breath, she opened the cottage door. Her intention to go to him turned into panic when she saw the white envelope that lay on her doorstep, weighted down by a rock. What if he'd taken her words at face value and decided to break off all ties? Picking up the envelope with trembling hands, she retreated inside.

The envelope contained several sheets of paper covered

with words written in a strong, flowing hand. Hoping desperately that this wasn't what she thought, she forced herself to read.

Lover mine,…

Disbelieving, she collapsed in a nearby armchair. Surely, surely, Alexandre couldn't have done this, couldn't have given her this surrender after the way she'd hurt him? And yet he had.

Proud, elegant, intensely private Alexandre Dupree had given her access to his most secret thoughts, his most secret fantasies.

She lowered her eyes to the page.

Lover mine,
You ask me for my fantasies, for my dreams. Yet will you believe me when I say that you are my ultimate fantasy, a woman of fire and beauty, spirit and soul, breathtaking sensuality and heartbreaking tenderness?

Your smile can bring me to my knees. Your touch leaves me at your mercy. Ah, *ma chérie,* would that you'd be satisfied with that and ask for nothing more. But I know you have a right to demand the same openness from me that I forced onto you. For a man who's spent a lifetime keeping secrets, it's a difficult thing to do. Difficult, not impossible.

So what do I dream of my Charlotte doing to me? What makes me wake hard and aching for you? What makes me sweat even on the coldest night?

Let me tell you, kitten.

Inside her chest, Charlotte's heart was thumping at what felt like a thousand beats a second.

In my fantasies, it's always night and we're always behind closed doors. I'm not a man who likes to share you, though you know too well that sometimes I can't control the urge to possess you wherever you might be. And ever since that night outside your cottage (*merci, ma petite*), taking you under the starry sky has become one of my favorite erotic fantasies.

Charlotte licked her lips, a small smile edging her lips at the memory of the hunger in him that night. She should've realized right then and there that this was no game for either of them. Lifting her hair off her suddenly heated nape, she continued to read.

In my dreams, you're dressed in something that I'm sure would make you blush, but a man is allowed to take liberties in his fantasies and if they lead to strips of white lace and ribbon, well, I can only enjoy the sight.

White lace and ribbon?

Your clothing is so fine, so delicate, that it entices rather than hides, the silk curtain of your hair reflecting the flames in the fireplace by which you stand. Did I forget to tell you that we are in my chalet in Switzerland, snowed in?

The fire is to keep our bodies warm but I don't need its aid when you're standing there, looking at me like you'd like nothing better than to strip me naked and lick every inch of my skin.

Charlotte blinked and took a deep breath. Sometimes, that was exactly what she wanted to do to her charming lover with his too-sexy body and masculine beauty. She'd never admitted the scandalous desire.

> I confess that I'd enjoy being caressed so by you, being seduced by each slow flick of your tongue. But, I can wait until you're ready to give me such loving.
> In this fantasy, you undress me and then my dear, sweet, Charlotte, you touch me with hands that know I'm yours, utterly and completely. You tug me to face the fireplace and sink to your knees in front of me on the creamy sheepskin rug by the hearth. I ache for the touch of your lips, the temptation of your mouth, the heated torture of your slow loving.
> Smiling, you give me what I desire.

Charlotte stopped breathing. He was making her toes curl, making her want to give him everything he'd fantasized about. Her eyes widened. Was this what he'd felt when he'd read her journal? This need to fulfill his fantasies had nothing to do with power or being in control and everything to do with pleasing him—giving the man she loved exactly what he needed.

Her hand clenched on the page. *The man she loved.* She blinked and took a deep breath. Well, at least that explained why she'd acted so badly yesterday. In spite of her attempts to the contrary, she'd fallen soul-deep in love with the man. What was she going to do?

The decision was far easier than she'd thought it would be. He'd never lied to her about his intentions. Though he felt more for her than she'd ever believed he would, he was going to leave her one day soon. All she could do was love him for as long as she could.

Shoving aside the incipient pain, she focused instead on the depth of commitment implied by the words he'd written.

By the time she finished reading, her face was flushed and she knew a few things she hadn't before. Best of all, she knew that she was the only lover Alexandre thought capable of fulfilling his most scorching fantasies. Some of her earlier sorrow dissipated at the realization, and she let herself be drawn fully into his world.

The man had sensual eroticism in his blood. With nothing more than his words, he'd seduced her. And with his final confession, he'd conquered more than her body, he'd stolen the last pieces of her heart.

All this and more, I'd like you to do to me, *ma chérie,* but my deepest fantasy, the one I'd most like fulfilled, is to be allowed to fulfill every one of yours. Nothing pleases me more than your pleasure. Nothing.

Forgive me for any hurt I caused you, Charlotte and let me adore you as I ache to do.

Alexandre hadn't been able to concentrate on anything since the moment he'd left the letter on Charlotte's doorstep. It was just as well that the work that had originally brought him to the estate was almost complete.

"I've helped you as far as I can," he told Trace, as they stood outside the winery. "There is only so much that I can do in the short time I'm here, particularly given that you're not currently processing the harvest.

"I can point out areas of improvement and suggest strategies, but to build a reputation as a premier winemaker, you must devote long-term attention to every step of the process."

"Beginning with the grapes themselves," Trace said, a touch of humor in his tone. "Inferior, mass-produced grapes equal inferior mass-produced wine."

"Ah, I see I've beaten you over the head with that particular point too many times." Alexandre smiled but his heart wasn't in it. Where was Charlotte? Had he ripped open his soul and still been unable to win her back? What would he do if she didn't forgive him?

"James and his assistants are good at what they do," he continued, "but you need to hire someone whose goal is not mass production, but fostering distinctiveness—someone who isn't afraid to experiment and innovate. One team can't do both and produce great wines, not given the scale of this vineyard and your production levels."

"Are you happy to keep consulting for us?"

What if he'd lost Charlotte forever? Would he want to return to this place that held so many memories? "I will, of course, provide several reports arising from this visit, but beyond that, I can't promise anything. You're welcome to contact me and if the timing suits…" He shrugged.

"Can I try to make you an offer you can't refuse?"

Alexandre looked into the man's intelligent face. "You couldn't make me such an offer."

Trace gave a good natured nod. Before he left to walk back into the winery, he hesitated and then said, "I know you've been seeing Charlotte. I just want to say I've never seen her happier. Good luck sorting out whatever it is that's happened."

Alexandre knew he'd need more than luck. Charlotte had to be feeling betrayed and hurt, and more than anything else, that tore at him. Fists clenched in his pockets, he decided to walk off some of his excess energy. He wouldn't push Charlotte, even though he was dying every moment that she didn't give him an answer. Shoulders set, he'd taken no more than three steps when his cell phone rang.

Frowning, he pulled it out of his pocket. His frustration disappeared the second he saw the caller ID. "Charlotte."

A pause. "Are you free to come to the cottage?"

"*Oui*. I can be there in a few minutes."

"Well...I'll see you then."

Alexandre hung up and walked to the golf cart some-one had parked by the winery, his jaw clenched. Char-lotte's tone of voice had given nothing away. He wondered if she'd asked him over to tell him his letter meant noth-ing to her. His fingers tightened painfully on the wheel of the vehicle he'd commandeered.

Charlotte opened the door the second she heard Alexan-dre arrive. As she watched him cross the short distance be-tween them, she rubbed her palms on her wraparound skirt, her heart beating triple time. Could she really do this? Trust this man so much?

He reached her, those dark French eyes coolly emotion-less. Not so long ago, his calm elegance would've intimi-dated her. Now, she thought wonderingly, she could see beneath the surface and the man she saw had her heart tum-bling. There was a strange vulnerability about Alexandre, and suddenly, she knew that he thought she was going to mock his confession and reject him.

And yet he'd come.

"Good morning," she murmured.

"Is it?" His voice was rough, husky.

Tugging at his hands, she pulled him inside and shut the door. "Mine started out very nicely."

His lips curled faintly upward. "And why was that, *ma petite?*"

She hadn't been aware that she'd been waiting for the endearment. Putting her hands on his chest, she leaned in close. "I discovered that a gorgeous hunk of a man finds me irresistible." A flush streaked his cheeks. Her eyes wid-ened. "You're embarrassed!"

"Non," he refuted, scowling at her. "Alexandre Dupree doesn't get embarrassed."

It touched her that her compliment had done this to her urbane lover. More importantly, it gave her the courage to propose what she was about to. "Do you have to be back at the winery soon?"

"*Non*. All the practical work is done. I have to write a few reports but that can be done anytime within a month. There is no urgency."

Her heart slumped. So soon, he'd be gone. But, she decided, she wouldn't think about that, not now. If this was all she was ever going to have of the man she loved, then she'd take hold of it with both hands. "I'm so sorry about what I said. I didn't mean any of it."

"It is forgotten." There was no recrimination in his tone, nothing but tenderness.

Taking a deep breath, she asked, "Would you like to spend the day with me?"

His expression softened in a way that she knew was for her alone. "Of course. What would you like to do? We can go for a drive if you wish."

She shook her head. "I have another idea." A scandalous idea, especially since it was bright light outside.

His face was suddenly all male, as if she'd somehow given herself away. "Tell me this idea." Strong arms slipped around her waist, showing her that he was once more certain of his right to touch her, aware that she'd forgiven him.

Swallowing, she fingered a button on his white shirt and looked up into his eyes. "I'd like to make your deepest fantasy come true," she whispered.

Around her his arms firmed. "My deepest fantasy is to love you until you are drunk on your own pleasure." One hand flattened on her lower back, big and hot. His eyes were so intent, she felt devoured.

"I know."

He shuddered and leaned down to brush his lips across

hers. "How can you be so generous after I put tears in your eyes?" His tone was raw.

She heard the sincere regret in his voice. "Because you've also brought a thousand smiles to my heart."

He hugged her to him. "*Ma petite,* you destroy me with your honesty, with your capacity to forgive so much hurt. I promise to never again betray your trust in me."

Shaking her head, she cupped his face in her hands and said, "I understand the temptation you faced—I could no more have stopped reading your letter than I could've stopped breathing."

"*Oui?*"

She fought her blush. "I read every single word. And then I read them over. So, we're even."

The bright joy in his eyes rocked her. "Then, kitten, are you ready to play?"

"Yes."

"Do you know what I wish to do to you the most?"

"What?"

"I wish to love you as you wrote in your journal—a loving that demands submission and absolute trust."

She knew which fantasy he was referring to. "I trust you." Otherwise, she would've never gone into his arms. For her, there was no separating the physical from the emotional. She was his, body and soul.

Charlotte found herself facing Alexandre behind the locked doors of her bedroom. With the curtain pulled, daylight barely filtered through, creating an intimate darkness that caused desire to uncurl luxuriously within her body. It also lent a scandalous edge to this already wicked rendezvous.

In bare feet, Alexandre padded across the carpet to her. Without her own shoes, she felt even smaller against his compelling masculinity. But not in any way less of a woman. Alexandre liked her size, she thought, smiling inside. Every time he called her *ma petite* in that seducer's voice of his, he told her just how much he appreciated the woman she was.

"Are you sure?" Alexandre touched her cheek with a finger, his eyes lingering on her face.

Taking hold of his hand, she kissed the tip of that finger. *"Oui."*

At the teasing acquiescence, his face lit from within. That brilliance held something far more potent than lust, but she didn't want to question just what it was that she'd seen, didn't want to give herself false hope. Not now, not in this moment of utter truth between them.

He unclipped the single barrette she'd used to hold her hair back. Dropping it to the floor, he ran the strands through his fingers, letting them fall across her chest. The backs of his hands brushed her breasts as he played with her hair and she sucked in a breath at the sudden sensual heat.

Moving back, he raised dark eyes to her face. "Take off your clothes for me, Charlotte."

It was a gentle command, but a command nonetheless. Just as she'd asked for in her most shocking fantasy. Hands trembling with a combination of desire and nerves, she raised them to the bottom of her white top. It was simply fashioned, with a scoop neck and cap sleeves, but its magic lay in the way it shaped her body, following each curve with smooth perfection.

Without taking her eyes from his, she began to raise the material, arms crossed across her front. Heat sparked to life in the darkness of Alexandre's gaze as an inch of flesh was revealed, and suddenly she had all the confidence she needed.

She pulled the top off in a swift motion. It left her standing before him in a white lace bra and a knee-length skirt that wrapped around her like a sarong. When he continued to simply watch, she moved her hands to the side tie of the skirt and undid it. Her nerves returned and she held the two undone halves closed, unable to move her hands and drop the skirt.

As if he'd heard her unspoken plea, Alexandre whispered, "You are so lovely…take off your skirt for me. I hunger to see all that glorious golden skin of yours."

Swallowing at the molten heat in his gaze, she took the ends of the tie and unwrapped the skirt. Her hair swung in front of her as she dropped her head to watch the cool blue material puddle on the floor, a blatant exclamation mark of surrender.

When she raised her head, silken strands settled back over her lace-covered breasts. A little self-conscious, she didn't know what to do with her hands. Aware that her lacy underwear didn't hide much, she was tempted to cover herself but that would be cheating.

Walking to her, Alexandre took hold of her hands and gently placed them behind her back, playfully manacling them with one strong hand. With his other, he swept the concealing wings of her hair behind her back, so that her chest was shielded only by delicate white lace.

He looked at her for so long, her entire body flushed. "Tell me, Charlotte." He rubbed his thumb across one peaked nipple. She jerked. "Tell me why you're dressed so seductively." He lifted his head, that beautiful mahogany hair falling across his forehead.

No room to hide. Licking her lips, she said, "I wanted to be…luscious for you." Her voice was hoarse, her throat dry with anticipation.

One hand closed over her breast, molding and shaping. Something in his careful touch screamed possessiveness.

"*Merci, ma petite.* You are exquisite." Looking straight into her eyes, he asked, "How far?"

Her heart was beating in her throat. "As far as you wish," she said, giving him total control.

Twelve

Alexandre kissed her, his hand still on her breast. When she attempted to deepen the kiss, he pulled away. Frustrated, her body continued to press against his.

He released her. "Get on the bed for me, kitten."

Warmth coalescing in her stomach, she did as he asked, sitting on her knees with her back to him. Looking over her shoulder, she asked, "Is this okay?"

The maleness in his eyes sent shivers up her spine, the tiny hairs on her body standing up in attention. This fantasy was far more potent than she'd imagined, far more emotionally involved. As a woman, she was putting her body and her mind in his hands, to hurt or to pleasure.

That led to the inescapable conclusion that she would've only taken this step if she was certain of his nature, sure that he was a man who'd always choose to pleasure, never to harm.

"*Non*. Face me."

She turned, still on her knees.

"Brush your hair away for me."

Raising her hands, she moved her hair to her back, feeling the slide of it against her skin. It was suddenly erotic after a lifetime of being unnoticed. "Like this?"

"*Oui.* Put your hands flat on your thighs." The command held a rough edge, as if keeping his distance was torture.

She was suddenly aware that he'd placed her like a prize in the middle of the bed. "Now what?"

He smiled at her, slow and pleased. "Now you watch."

He undid the first button on his dusty-blue shirt. The heat in her stomach blazed into roiling flame. She'd never imagined that he'd pleasure her like this. So very masculine, control came easily to him, but this teasing show told her that he was comfortable enough in his skin to give her a little surrender. And that was the one thing she'd doubted about his ability to fulfill her fantasy.

Three buttons down, all she could focus on was the dark hair that lightly covered that glowing, healthy wedge of skin. Barely breathing, she watched him undo two more buttons before pulling out the tails of his shirt to complete the job. Leaving the shirt on, he undid his belt buckle and slid the belt out of the loops. Slowly.

Charlotte's body was leaning toward his. She wanted to touch him so badly, her hands began to drift up from her thighs. Alexandre dropped the belt to the floor and said, "*Non, ma chérie.* Place your hands as I asked."

Without a second thought, she obeyed, a thrill racing through her as she remembered her own words. She'd asked for *commands laced with rough tenderness* and Alexandre was delivering. His eyes held the open adoration that she'd dreamed of—confident and proud, he didn't mind letting her see the effect she had on him.

When she put her hands back on her thighs, he said,

"Very good, Charlotte." It was a husky whisper. "I should reward such perfect obedience."

A spark of rebellion appeared in her. "I think you're enjoying this too much."

He shrugged off his shirt, revealing an upper body as beautiful as any Greek god's. However, his grin could've done justice to the most wicked of devils. *"Oui,* of course. I have a beautiful woman half-naked and willing to do anything I ask. I would be an idiot not to take advantage."

His sheer delight in the situation had all her simmering outrage disappearing. Wonder took its place—her serious, sophisticated lover was playing with her. This was a game, a sensual, erotic game that could only be played between two lovers who were completely attuned to each other's needs.

He prowled over to her, so gracefully dangerous that her breath caught. When he reached the bed, he placed his hands on her shoulders and leaning over, pressed his lips against hers. Starving for a taste of him, she opened immediately, inviting him with the strokes of her tongue that she knew he liked. Moaning when he returned the caress, she had to clench her hands on her thighs to keep from thrusting them in his hair.

When he drew back from her, she wanted to whimper in disappointment. His eyes were dark ebony, glittering night. "The taste of you is like some forbidden drug."

In my fantasies, you are strong enough…to openly adore my body without seeing it as a weakness.

Charlotte wondered how fate could've sent her a lover so perfect. She knew him well enough to understand that this was no pretence, not merely an attempt to deliver her fantasy. To him, she was beautiful—a potent drug. What woman could resist such a lover?

Alexandre's attention suddenly shifted to something

over her shoulder. Unable to turn, she waited, nerves taut, as he walked around the double bed. After what seemed like an endless moment, the mattress depressed behind her.

His first touch made her shiver. Chuckling, he swept her hair over one shoulder, leaving her back bare to him. His lips brushed her nape.

"Alexandre," she couldn't help moaning.

Then he was gone and she felt the stroke of something unutterably soft against her skin, tantalizing and luxurious. After one melting stroke, warm breath whispered across the spot. Her entire body jolted into sensory overload. Alexandre repeated the action on her lower back and her whimper was of sheer pleasure.

One big hand slid around to lay flat against her belly, but before she could concentrate on that feeling, strong male teeth scraped lightly along her lower back, just above the swell of her bottom.

Alexandre felt Charlotte jerk, her stomach going taut under his hand. When he repeated the caress, a sheen of perspiration broke out over her skin. Her beauty continued to astound him. She was like a cool, clear lake, but one with unexpected depths, soul-deep loveliness hidden beneath the gentle outer layer.

Breathing in the intoxicating scent of her, he kissed his way up her spine until he knelt behind her once more. This time he put both arms around her waist. When she saw the feather he held in his hand, she laughed. "So that's what you were torturing me with."

"It was very accommodating of you to have a vase full of feathers for my use," he teased, dropping the feather so he could touch her skin more fully as he kissed the bared curve of her neck.

Sliding his hands up and down her arms, he gently massaged her, indulging himself with the feel of her skin. She sighed and leaned into his body, her bare back coming into contact with his chest. Both of them reacted to the skin to skin touch, but which one of them gasped, Alexandre couldn't tell.

"Will you move your hands to your sides?" he asked.

"Yes."

Unable to believe how much she trusted him, delightfully shocked by this strong woman who didn't always need to be in control with her man, he wanted to give her everything. Slipping his hands between her ribs and her arms, he spread his palms on her thighs where her hands had rested. Fine tremors shook her body as he moved his fingers along the sensitive inner faces.

Barely brushing the lace protecting her, he moved both hands up her body. Her moan had blood flooding to his already pounding erection. Breath labored, he moved his hands over her torso, warm and so soft, and cupped her lace-covered breasts.

He could tell she was fighting the urge to touch him. The fact that he tempted her just as much as she tempted him was an aphrodisiac greater than anything else on this earth. She fit perfectly in his hands, the high, taut fruit of her breasts shaped for him alone.

Closing his hands, he touched skin where the lace of her bra ended. Continuing to lave her neck with kisses, he began to massage her sensitive flesh. Her body arched toward his and the hands she held at her sides curled into fists and finally, clenched on his thighs, which he'd spread to cradle her body back into his.

He chuckled, riding the wave of desire threatening to swamp him. "You're cheating."

Under his hands, her breasts moved up and down as she gasped for breath. "Maybe you should just tie me up next time."

His breath caught. "I'll use silk scarves," he promised. "But, this time, I'll let you get away with it."

She laughed, the sound an intimate caress in the semi-light of the room. "You're making me...*melt*."

He wanted nothing more than to thrust into her melting heat, but this fantasy of theirs wasn't finished. Not by a long shot. He began to play with her breasts in earnest, feeling the cool slide of her hair against the back of one hand, a double sensory temptation.

Her body moved against his, sinuously rubbing his erection until his heartbeat was concentrated in that one spot, hot and hard. Feeling sweat break out on his back, he withdrew his hands, dropping them to lie on her hips.

"Alexandre," she moaned, turning her head to give him a reproachful look.

"Take off your bra, kitten." His voice was so rough, he wondered if she understood him.

But she did. Turning away, she reached behind her back, her knuckles sliding against his skin. Sucking in a breath, he said, "Behave."

He felt her smile in the way her body relaxed into his. Then she pulled away and unhooked the back catch of her bra. Moving her hands to her front, she peeled it off, holding the scrap of satin and lace for a second before throwing it to the floor.

He couldn't see her breasts yet, but the glorious honey-colored sweep of her back was open to his gaze. Murmuring his appreciation to her in his native tongue, he stroked that dusky-gold skin with both hands. Some of the words were spoken against her skin as he kissed his way across her shoulders, his hands stroking over her waist.

Her body relaxed into him. With a slight shift, he ensured that their bodies pressed together, temptation and torture for both of them. Hooking his left arm around her waist after ensuring her silky hair wasn't caught between, he whispered, "Lean over my arm."

Without pause, she obeyed the husky order. He cradled her slight weight easily as she arched, her lovely face looking up into his. All her hair slid off, baring her to him. As his free hand stroked up her stomach to close over a breast, he lowered his lips to sip from hers. A sip led to a deeper caress as he delved into her mouth.

Under his stroking hand, her flesh was taut and sheened with sweat, her heartbeat thudding against his fingertips. As he kissed her, he rolled a nipple between his fingertips. Her whole body jerked.

"Alexandre…I can't…" she moaned as he repeated the caress on her other breast.

"Shhh, kitten, take just a little more," he coaxed, sliding his hand from her breasts to the heat between her legs. Teasing them both, he ran his fingers along the top edges of her lacy underwear.

He was so aroused it was almost painful and yet he didn't want to end this delicious game of the senses. Carefully, watching her dark eyes go even darker, he slipped his hand under the elastic band to cup her. Her whole body went taut, her pupils dilated and then, fine tremors rocked her entire body.

Masculine satisfaction roared over him as he watched her shatter in his arms. Spreading his fingers, he stroked her softness, delighted when her body arched up and surrendered to another surge of pleasure.

When the last waves had broken within her, he lay her boneless body down on the bed. As she straightened her legs, the scent of heat and musk rose into the air. His nostrils flared, hunger punching to the surface. Moving to position himself between her thighs, he pushed both her legs up until her feet were flat on the bed, knees raised.

Long lashes lifted. "You look very pleased with yourself." Her voice held the tones of a woman who had been well-pleasured.

He dropped his head and pressed a kiss to the warm skin of her navel, breathing in the scent of her. "Are you pleased with me, Charlotte?"

"Oh, yes," she murmured.

Aching for relief, Alexandre knew he had to have a taste of her before he stormed her body. He kissed his way down her stomach, not stopping the caresses when he met the fine barrier of satin and lace. Surprised, she cried out, her sensitized flesh feeling too much, even through the fragile silky covering.

Cradling her bottom in his hands, he lifted her to his mouth, loving her through the damp material. Her cries urged him to lave pleasure upon pleasure as she lay spread out for his delectation. When she gave a tiny scream and started to shudder, he finally lifted his head, looking down at the lushness of her. He'd turned the satin and lace sheer, but even that silken shield was too much now.

His hunger was such that he almost tore them off, but at the last moment, he remembered that this was the fulfillment of a fantasy. "Take off your panties for me," he whispered in her ear.

Dazed eyes met his. "Alexandre?"

He kissed her, rubbing his body against the length of hers, feeling her softness and her melting welcome. "Will you take them off for me?"

She barely nodded. He lifted off her and she reached down and moved her body just enough to slip the scrap of lace to her thighs. It seemed beyond her to push them down her legs.

He reached out and helped her until she lay naked and golden below him. Shuddering, he stroked her thighs. "If you didn't look so satisfied lying there, I'd order you to finish undressing me," he whispered, well aware that he'd never last if she took on the job.

Her eyes widened. She licked her lips. "I think my strength is coming back to me."

"No touching this time." He decided to save that torture for another loving. Moving off the bed, he stripped his pants and underwear off with brutal efficiency, aware of her eyes eating him up. She didn't look away when he took care of protection, pure possession in her gaze.

When he settled back between her thighs, there was only welcome in every part of her, from her desire-blind eyes to her passion-warm body. "Shall I take you now?"

Her smile was slow. "You can do whatever you like."

Groaning at the way she'd played their game to the end, he entered her in one solid stroke. Her body held him tight, all creamy heat and feminine invitation. Hands holding on to her hips, he moved in and out once before her legs locked around him.

"Legs down," he managed to say hoarsely.

After a moment's rebellion, she put her feet flat on the sheets once more. Adoring her for being the woman she was, he kissed her. Then, using his tongue to mimic the way his body slid and out of hers, he set a slow but powerful rhythm that succeeded in driving his woman to one more peak before his own climax took hold of him, savage and hot, like white lightning in his bloodstream.

Sometime before four that afternoon, a knock on the door had Charlotte snapping her head up from the kitchen table. "Thank goodness I finally got dressed," she muttered. Taking off her apron, she closed the bedroom door, where Alexandre was dressing after their shower.

She'd escaped first, giggling from his unexpected playfulness under the streaming water. He'd only let her go after extracting a promise of hot coffee and food. Smiling at the memory, she opened the door.

It was Lara, one of the maids up at the estate house. She held out an envelope. "Came in special delivery, so I thought I should bring it down straight away."

Charlotte forced herself to reply through the buzzing in her head. "Thanks, Lara."

"You're welcome." The auburn-haired woman grinned and began to head back to her golf cart. "I better get back to help with dinner."

Charlotte closed the door with trembling hands. She was still standing there staring at the envelope when Alexandre walked out of the bedroom, shirt hanging open over his chest. "*Ma petite,* what is it?"

"It's from Nebraska's vital records office." Her voice sounded eerily calm, even to her own ears.

He nudged her toward the sofa and sat down beside her. Putting his arm around her, he held her as she gathered her thoughts and slit open the envelope. It was immediately clear that it contained only a single copied death certificate.

Heart pounding, she scanned the cover letter. "It apologizes for the delay—they had some trouble locating the certificates as I was unable to give them several required details. But, they're happy to inform me that they were partially successful.

"Enclosed is the death certificate for David Ashton," she read. "However, they're unable to provide one for Mary Little Dove Ashton…they're certain that no such record exists." A sob caught in her throat.

Alexandre pulled her into a gentle hug. "That's good news."

"I'm afraid to hope," she whispered. "What if they made a mistake?"

He didn't point out that the lateness of the response indicated that the records office had tried hard to locate the certificate. "That should be easy enough to check. Let's call the number they've given for further information." He reached behind himself to pick up the cordless phone from the end table.

Charlotte nodded and accepted the phone. Taking a deep breath, she punched in the numbers. An efficient-sounding voice answered. When she told the operator what she needed, she was transferred to the person who'd done the original search. The man double-checked his files.

"Thanks." A few minutes later she hung up the phone and looked at Alexandre. She couldn't seem to stop trembling. "They didn't make a mistake. There's no death certificate for Mary Little Dove Ashton. The clerk even checked under just Little and Dove and Ashton." The words were coming too fast. "If they died in the same accident and my father's certificate is in Nebraska, shouldn't my mother's be as well?"

He tightened his embrace, leaving her only enough freedom to look up at him. "It would make sense that they would both be filed at the same place. So, it says that your father passed away at the hospital in…Kendall?"

She looked at the copy of the certificate again, as if the information might've changed. "Yes. Kendall General Hospital." And suddenly, she knew what Alexandre was saying. "I need to go there. To be sure."

"They might not give you the information."

Her heart shattered at the tenderness in his expression. "We won't need anything more from them than to know if my mother was discharged. I can prove I'm her child with my birth certificate, and if we say she disappeared, they might help us."

Alexandre nodded. "With it being a small-town hospital, they might even know where she went."

Hope leapt in Charlotte's heart but she squelched it. "If she went anywhere at all."

Thirteen

After they'd made the decision to go to Kendall, things moved at breakneck speed. By the end of the day, Alexandre had organized to charter a plane from Napa County Airport to Broken Bow Airport. A rental car would be waiting for them when they arrived in the central Nebraska town. Kendall was around an hour and half drive from Broken Bow and had no suitable airstrip.

Charlotte accepted his help with the organization since she had to juggle her schedule in order to clear the next two days. Given the speed of the sleek twin-engine jet Alexandre had chartered, the round-trip could be done in a day. However, she knew that whatever they found, she'd need at least a day to calm herself.

"We'll leave at seven o'clock tomorrow morning," Alexandre told her as they lay in bed that night. "The jet can get us to Nebraska in under three hours. If all goes well, we should be back here for dinner."

"That plane—it's very expensive, isn't it?"

"Charlotte, I need to do this much for you." His arm tightened. "I can't change the past but I can help you find the truth. Don't reject my gift."

Her heart tumbled over. "How can I, after you said that? Thank you."

Nestling closer to his warm body, she wrapped an arm around his chest, feeling a sharp ache at the sudden thought that far too soon she'd be sleeping alone in this bed. Alone with a broken heart and shattered dreams. Yet, if she had to do it over, she'd take the same road. Loving didn't allow for easy choices.

"I guess we better get some sleep." She knew he'd ascribe her subdued tone to the oncoming trip, but right now, that seemed like a distant dream. Her reality was that soon she'd lose the man she loved. And there was nothing she could do. If all the beauties before her hadn't been able to, what hope did she have of holding a man so emotionally scarred, he didn't trust in love and loyalty?

"Are you sure you wish to rest, *ma petite?*" Alexandre's voice caressed her in the darkness.

She felt a bittersweet smile curve her lips, aware he couldn't see it in the unlit room. "Well, I could be persuaded into a little wakeful activity."

For Charlotte, the early-morning trip to Nebraska passed by in a blur. Alexandre sat with her but didn't attempt to draw her into conversation, as if aware that she needed the time to prepare herself.

When they arrived in Nebraska, she was struck by the dry heat, but her mind was too preoccupied to notice much else. Once they were on the road, her tension transmuted into a kind of nervous excitement that left her so jittery, she felt like she might shatter.

"Stop hurting so much, *ma petite,*" Alexandre ordered after half an hour.

"I can't help it."

He reached across and touched her cheek. Somehow, the simple contact made her feel better than a hundred words could have. For the rest of the drive, his small touches allowed her to gain a measure of peace.

And then they were in Kendall, the last known residence of Mary Little Dove Ashton. The hospital wasn't hard to find, the orange brick facade standing out from a distance. Despite her attempt at curing herself of hope, Charlotte couldn't help her thudding pulse and sweaty palms. Stepping out of the car, she closed her door just as Alexandre rounded the hood and took her hand in his.

"The moment of truth," she whispered, staring ahead at the building that might just change her life.

"Come, *ma chérie,* let's see what they have to tell us. Remember, I'm here with you." *Always.*

Her heart heard the word he couldn't say, haunted by his own demons. But as he was here for her now, she'd be there for him through the tough times. Sooner or later, Alexandre would begin to believe that not all women were fickle and manipulative.

Rebellion spouted inside her, deep and fierce.

Who said their relationship had to end the minute he left the estate? He seemed in no hurry to sever the threads binding them and she refused to let him walk out of her life without a fight. "I'm so glad you're here."

With those simple words, they walked the short distance to the hospital door and entered. The smell of antiseptic, the sound of a crying baby and the clean white walls hit Charlotte all at once.

Her father had died within these walls.

Somehow, she managed to keep herself together even as

that thought whispered through her mind. They went straight to the reception desk manned by a young woman in a crisp nurse's uniform. Her nametag read "Ann Johnson."

"Can I help you?" The nurse glanced up.

"My name is Charlotte Ashton," Charlotte began, taking strength from Alexandre's presence. He didn't try to take over this thing that she had to do, but she knew without a doubt that he'd never let her stumble. "My mother and father were admitted into this hospital almost twenty-two years ago. I was told that they both died."

"I see." Nurse Johnson's eyes had widened and she was giving them her full attention.

"However, when I applied for death certificates, I was told that there was no record of my mother's death."

"How extraordinary. Perhaps there was a mix-up?"

Charlotte couldn't quite pull off a smile. "That's what I'm trying to find out. I need to see my mother's record from all those years ago. Her name was Mary Little Dove Ashton."

"We don't really release that kind of thing." The woman's expression was sympathetic but firm.

"I have proof that she was my mother." Charlotte slid her birth certificate across the counter. "And this is my father's death certificate."

The young nurse appeared undecided.

"Look, you don't have to show us the file. Can you check and tell me if she died here? I just want to know if she…if she lived," she finished softly, unaware how haunted her eyes looked at that moment.

The nurse stood and carefully examined both documents. Finally, she pushed them back at Charlotte. "It's not really procedure but I can't see the harm. Records that far back were never put into the computer system so I'll have to go down to the basement."

Turning, she paged someone over the intercom. "As soon as Jack arrives to man the desk, I'll go down. Let me just copy down the date on your father's death certificate—it'll help me locate the files. I can't promise I'll find the information but I'll try my best."

"Thank you." Charlotte couldn't keep the feeling out of her voice. "Thank you so much."

Alexandre's arm slipped around her shoulders. "Where should we wait for you?" he asked Nurse Johnson.

The woman tucked a strand of blond hair behind her ear. "Just take a seat over there." She pointed to the waiting area. It already had four occupants—an elderly man, a woman with a crying baby and a teenager with a cast on one leg.

Just then, a male nurse arrived to relieve Johnson. Alexandre led Charlotte away from the desk and toward the free chairs in the back of the room. Because of its small size, they remained in close proximity to the woman with the crying baby.

"Oh, hush, honey," the mother coaxed. "The doctor will give you something to stop the hurt." She looked over her shoulder at them. "I'm sorry but he's—"

Alexandre interrupted her. "There's no need for an apology, is there, Charlotte?"

Charlotte blinked awake from the almost trancelike state she'd drifted into. "No, of course not. I hope it's nothing serious?"

"Allergies—nothing so bad, only he's got a rash and the itching's driving him crazy. But the doctor might've found something that'll help."

"I'm glad."

"What's his name?" Alexandre's deep murmur seemed to reach the child, for he stopped crying and hiccupping, blue eyes curious. "Hello, little one."

The mother was smiling in relief. "Oh, I should've

thought of that—his father's voice always calms him. Could you please just talk to him for a while?"

Instead of painfully waiting away the time it took for the nurse to find the files, Charlotte watched in delight as Alexandre revealed an aspect of himself that she never would've guessed. Not only was he willing to accommodate the mother's request, he spoke to the baby with tenderness that betrayed a genuine liking for children.

When her turn to see the doctor arrived, the woman thanked them both. "You should have a few of your own," she told Alexandre. "They'd be pretty as pictures what with her gorgeous skin and your eyes." Laughing at Charlotte's blush, she gathered up her things and left.

The feel of Alexandre's knuckles rubbing her cheek had Charlotte turning. He was smiling at her. "Would you like to have my *bébé, ma petite?*"

"I'd like to be married first." She teased him back despite her blush. "And we both know that's not a likely option between the two of us."

Until the stranger's laughing advice, Charlotte had never even allowed herself to imagine a lifetime with Alexandre. She'd fight for whatever he could give her, fight for more than this month, but she had no hope that he'd be hers forever. No one could keep a man who didn't want to commit, to entrust a woman with his heart. And she would never be happy with only half of him.

His eyes darkened. "Perhaps we should talk about—"

"Well, that didn't take as long as I expected," a cheerful voice announced.

Charlotte's head jerked up toward Nurse Johnson as the woman took a seat beside her.

"The filing system's very good down there."

She wanted to tell the nurse to hurry but instead threaded her fingers through Alexandre's and tried to stay calm.

"Let's see." Nurse Johnson opened the file. Her eyes widened almost immediately. "It says here that Mary Ashton was injured in a car accident which killed her husband, but that she made a full recovery. She was released from this hospital a week after her admittance."

Charlotte just heard the word "released." Her whole body threatened to shake. "Th—thank you."

"Do you have any contact details for her?" Alexandre asked.

"I'm sorry—we just have the address in Kendall. And I can tell you that she doesn't live there anymore." The nurse stood. "I hope you find her."

Shocked, Charlotte just sat there after Ann Johnson left. Alexandre wrapped an arm around her. "Come, *chérie.*" Grateful for his strength, she leaned on him as he walked her out of the hospital and to the car.

He didn't urge her to speak and it was only when they were driving out of the hospital that she said, "I never let myself think beyond finding out whether she'd lived or died. I never allowed myself to wonder why she gave us up when she loved us. I *know* she loved us. I remember!"

"Charlotte." Alexandre pulled the car off to the side of what appeared to be the main street, and reached out to cup her cheek.

She let him comfort her. "It hurts to know that all this time, she was in the world. All the times I needed a mother, she existed, but she didn't help me."

"*Couldn't* help you, *ma petite.* If what I've heard about Spencer is true, then he's a man capable of doing something as terrible as stealing an unwilling woman's children away from her."

She wanted to believe him, couldn't bear to think that her mother had walked away willingly. "Maybe. I only wish I knew where she was now."

"Doesn't look like things have changed much in this town over the years."

Nonplussed by what appeared to be an unrelated comment, she focused on the street. Kendall was flat, like so much of Nebraska. Spring had given the land a touch of green and the occasional tree bloomed pink and white, but the town itself was without character, the buildings coated with decades of dust. "No."

"Perhaps someone would remember your parents?"

Understanding his line of thought, she said, "It's a long shot but what can it hurt? We could ask them." She pointed to a threesome of elderly men sitting at a table outside a coffee shop. "They look like they've been there forever."

"It's worth a try. If they can't help, we could perhaps consult the town office."

Getting out, they crossed the empty street and made their way to the shop. It touched her that Alexandre accepted the hand she slipped into his without a word. In fact, his hand tightened firmly over hers.

When they'd almost reached the men, one of them squinted a pair of washed-out blue eyes and said, "Well, ain't that a sight? Haven't see anyone as pretty as you since Mary Little Dove moved away."

Charlotte froze. Disbelieving, she whispered, "You knew my mother?" Surely it couldn't be this easy?

He chuckled. "Little Charlotte Ashton, I'll be damned!" Slapping his thigh, he put his cards down on the table. "Didn't think we'd see you again after Mary sold up and headed out of town."

Obviously, the man thought she'd been living with her mother. She decided not to correct him. "That was…"

He scratched his head. "That would've been right after your father's death, now wouldn't it?"

One of the other men nodded. "Sad business, cut down in the prime of his life. Always liked David. Good man."

The father she'd never had a chance to know was suddenly a vivid picture in her mind. "Mama didn't keep in touch with anyone in this town, did she?" It felt strange to say Mama and know that somewhere out there, she did have someone whom she could call that.

"That's the God's truth. Heartbroken, she was. Just packed up and left and that's the last we heard of her." He smiled in memory. "Sure was a pretty little thing. All in all, though, I reckon it was a good thing she went back to her people—she needed some looking after."

The three elderly men started reminiscing about other things, already lost in their own world. Alexandre pulled her away. "You should eat something before we leave." It wasn't a suggestion, but an order.

"Do I look that bad?"

He led her into the shop. "You look lovely but you're neglecting yourself. I can't allow that."

The second they walked in, the waitress headed over. "You can pick your table—the lunch rush just finished," she said. "What can I get you?"

Charlotte let Alexandre order for her, her mind still abuzz with everything they'd learned. When the food arrived, she ate to placate Alexandre, but she couldn't have said what it was that she'd consumed.

An hour later, they left the town. "Heartbroken," Charlotte said softly. "Just over her husband or over losing her children, too?"

"You said she loved you," Alexandre's deep voice wrapped around her, making her feel safe and protected.

"I can remember her scent as she cuddled me, I can remember warmth. Yes, she loved us." Sighing, she laid her head against the backrest. "I hate Spencer. I hate him for whatever he did."

Her hands clenched into fists. "I know he gave us a good life and an expensive education, but if he stole my mother from me, then the price was too high."

Alexandre didn't attempt to pacify her, his hands capable as he drove the car. Somehow, she knew he not only understood her anger, he also supported her.

"I want to go see Spencer as soon as possible."

"Of course." Alexandre accelerated down the flat road, the land so empty that you could see for miles in every direction. "I'll inform the charter pilot of our change in plans. We can be in San Francisco by this evening."

Charlotte nodded, trusting him to get things done. The man had a presence that screamed capability. "No wonder people went crazy living here," she muttered. "I like land and space and sky, but this—it's magnificent and frightening at the same time."

"There's nothing to hide under," Alexandre added. "This is a place of truth."

Having found her own truth after so long, Charlotte couldn't disagree.

Alexandre waited until they were in the air before broaching a subject that had been preying on him for hours. "Charlotte, I want to talk to you about something very important."

"What?" Her eyes were clear and unhaunted when she turned to face him, her hair haloed by the light coming in through the window beside her.

He paused for a second to assess her condition. Though what they'd discovered was shocking, it was clear that the truth was erasing the pain she'd lived with for a lifetime. He decided that she was fully capable of hearing what he had to say.

"*Ma petite,* did you read the things I wrote to you?"

She blushed. "You know I did."

The memory of her response to his confessions heated his blood. "Do you think me a man who shares those thoughts with everyone?"

"No, of course not." Her puzzlement at his line of questioning was obvious.

"Then please explain to me why you've never considered marriage between us." Despite his attempt at calm, anger sparked off his every word.

"I—I…y-you…" She slapped her hands down on the seat. "I'm too emotionally distraught to talk about this right now."

"Chicken," he taunted, confident of her strength.

Her eyes narrowed. "I didn't consider it because I know your track record. You date gorgeous, elegant and sophisticated creatures and none of those relationships last longer than a few months.

"Not one of them succeeded in convincing you that a woman can be true to her man. I can't compete with them so how could I be expected to win commitment from you?"

He was amazed at her. "You are the loveliest woman I've ever known," he said. "Not only your face but your inner resources. The beauty you create with your hands, your loyalty and courage, your determination—*mon Dieu,* Charlotte, you don't have to compete with any other woman. You're in a category of your own."

"And what category is that?" she asked, her voice softer than the wind.

"The category occupied by my future wife, the mother of my children and my lover for life." He wasn't going to dance around this. The possessive tyrant in him had had enough subtlety. It was time to claim what was his.

The minute he'd written the first word of that letter to

her, he'd known that he'd fallen. And fallen hard. Whatever he'd tried to convince himself, that letter had been an invitation to much more than simple pleasure—it had been the key to his heart.

Only for his *petite* Charlotte could he have ripped himself open like that. And only this woman's reaction could've made the decision to bare his soul the most wonderful experience of his life.

He had every faith that she'd stick by him for life—Charlotte wasn't a woman who gave up on anything. Their visit to Kendall had only strengthened his belief. She was no more like his *Maman* and Celeste than he was like his father. Alexandre would never cheat his wife and children out of the love that was their right. And there was only one woman he could imagine in the position of his wife. Now, he just had to get her to agree to be his. Life without her was not something he even wanted to contemplate.

"Alexandre—are you proposing?" Big eyes became even bigger.

He glanced at the inside of the plane. "Forgive me, *chérie,* I'd intended to do this far more romantically, but this is the moment.

"I want you to be mine, Charlotte Ashton. I want you to take my name, sleep in my bed, spread your warmth into my home and love me for the rest of my life.

"I want you to give me daughters with your heart and sons with your spirit. But most of all, I want you to let me love you until the day I die."

Trembling, she reached out and touched his lips with her fingers. He kissed them gently, his heartbeat frozen as he waited for her response.

"Are you sure you want to marry me with everything that's going on in my life?"

"Ah, Charlotte, don't you know by now that I want you

to be mine, no matter what?" He spoke against those fingers, before reaching up to clasp that hand in his. "I'm dying here, *ma petite*."

"Even before I knew you, I loved you." Her heart blazed in her eyes. "I promise you that my loyalty will never change. You don't ever have to worry that I'll be fickle or unfaithful."

He adored her for understanding so much about the shadows that haunted him. "*Oui*, Charlotte. I know this."

Her smile was so bright, it shattered his heart. "I can't believe I'm going to marry you."

"You're not allowed to change your mind."

"Never."

Feeling emotion choke his throat, Alexandre raised the arm of her seat and pulled her across into his embrace. She came, wrapping her arms tight around him, her face buried against his neck.

"I want to go away somewhere private with you and just love you," she whispered.

"But you have to find out the truth from Spencer," he completed, dropping a kiss on the raw silk of her hair. "I understand. We have a lifetime to love." The primitive in him sighed in contentment.

She was his.

Fourteen

They reached San Francisco just after six-thirty. By the time they'd found a hotel and checked in, it was almost eight. Charlotte was beginning to feel exhaustion seep into her bones, but was determined to seek out Spencer.

"Will he be at his office?" Alexandre queried, as they sat side by side on the sofa in their suite.

She frowned. "He works late."

"Perhaps you should wait till tomorrow."

"I want to get this over and done with."

"I know." He enfolded her in his arms. "But right now, you're tired and shocked. Your uncle seems like the kind of man who'd take advantage of that—unless you've changed your mind and would like me to accompany you to his office?"

She could hear his desire to be there for her in his voice. "No, I have to face him by myself. I can't explain it, I just have to. But you're right about him taking advantage of any weakness."

"Good. I'll drive you to Ashton-Lattimer tomorrow morning and wait nearby while you speak with him."

"I want to catch him early," she said, "before his staff comes in—Walker once said that he's usually in his office by eight. It's going to be bad enough as it is. I don't want to create a spectacle."

"I understand. We'll aim to reach there by eight." His hand stroked over her hair. "You're very tired."

"But not sleepy," she murmured, raising her head.

Dark eyes gleamed. *"Non?"*

"Non." A smile bloomed in her heart at the way he looked at her, as if she were all he'd ever wanted. "I could do with a bath, though."

"Am I invited?" He spoke against her lips.

She kissed him. *"Oui,* of course…if you order room service." Her teasing got her thoroughly kissed.

And then, it got her thoroughly loved.

The next morning, Charlotte said goodbye to Alexandre at the ground floor of Ashton-Lattimer and headed to the elevator. He'd accepted her desire to face Spencer alone, but had refused to stay at the hotel. They'd compromised by having him wait at a nearby coffee shop, from where he could see her when she exited the building.

A short elevator ride later, she was standing in the outer part of Spencer's office. Stationed to the left of the door that led to his inner sanctum was a desk she assumed belonged to his secretary. It was an elegant curve against the wall, its surface pristine. However, on closer inspection, she saw that the back, hidden from the public, was buried in papers, cups, stationery and other miscellaneous items.

For some reason, it gave her courage that Spencer's

secretary wasn't a perfect robot. Squaring her shoulders, she took a deep breath and shoved open the closed door to his office. Surprise was her friend with the manipulative man who'd stolen her mother from her.

There was no one in the room.

Her heart plummeted. Wanting to throw something, she looked around for a chair where she could wait for him. That was when her eye fell on what looked like a jacket lying behind Spencer's executive chair. Except…there was something wrong with it, something that sent her nerves screaming with primitive terror.

Mouth dry, breath locked in her throat, she rounded the edge of the desk. All the air left her lungs in a harsh gasp, leaving her perilously close to fainting. But the thought of landing *there* snapped her back almost before the thought entered her head.

Spencer *was* in his office.

His body lay lifeless on the floor, appearing smaller and weaker than she remembered, his dominating personality extinguished. He'd fallen onto his back, his jacket parting to reveal a shirt stained dark with blood. More blood had congealed around him, turning the muted carpet almost black. Even to her untrained eye, it was chillingly clear how he'd met his end.

Spencer Ashton had been shot through the heart.

Shaking, she bent to touch his pulse, though she knew it was a futile effort.

"Mr. Ashton, I have…"

The feminine voice trailed off as Charlotte rose from behind the desk. She didn't have the energy to be startled, caught in a slow-moving river of emotion that was as thick as treacle. "He's dead."

Stunning violet eyes widened. "What?"

"Spencer is dead. Call the police."

The sharply dressed blonde walked over as if she didn't believe Charlotte, her legs long and slender beneath her severe navy suit. "Oh, my God." Her eyes fell on the body, then flashed up to Charlotte, suspicious.

"I'm Charlotte Ashton." She moved away from the body, taking the other woman with her. "Spencer is…was, my uncle."

"I'm Kerry, Mr. Ashton's administrative assistant."

"I just came to talk to him," Charlotte found herself saying. "Only a minute before you, I walked through that door and he was already dead."

"I guess it could just as well have been me." Kerry paused. "You really don't look much like a murderer anyway."

Charlotte didn't know why but both of them found that hilarious. Laughing, they hugged each other until they trembled. "I think we're hysterical," she said, when she was finally able to speak.

"Let's get out of this office." Kerry's voice quivered with more than a trace of shock. "We'll call the police from my desk."

Avoiding looking at the body, they walked out. Aware that they shouldn't disturb the scene any more than they already had, they left the door open.

Once they'd made the call, they sat together in silence. Charlotte fought the urge to contact Alexandre on his cell phone—the police had asked both her and Kerry to refrain from getting in touch with anyone else until they arrived. It didn't stop her wishing that he was by her side.

In under half an hour, the entire floor was swarming with police officers and crime-scene technicians. When they'd first entered, Charlotte and Kerry were asked their names and then told to wait by Kerry's secretly messy desk.

Ten minutes later, a striking man with dark hair stopped

in front of them. Accompanying him was a woman of average height, but with a suggestion of muscle about her. Neither was in uniform.

"I'm Detective Dan Ryland and this is my partner, Detective Nicole Holbrook." The man's eyes seemed to bore right through them. "Which one of you found the body?"

"Me," Charlotte said. "I came in to talk to him and he—he was just lying there." She'd never seen anything like that. The violence of it still had her shaking.

"If I could talk to you alone?" Detective Ryland's manner was efficient, but she knew he had to view her as a potential suspect.

She followed the two detectives after sharing a speaking look with Kerry, whose shock-bleached face told her what her own must look like. "Of course."

"Ms. Ashton, it's almost certain that the autopsy will confirm that Spencer Ashton died sometime last night. The blood…" Detective Ryland paused, his hazel eyes astute.

She could imagine hardened criminals confessing under the focus of that stare, but it barely penetrated her traumatized mind. "I've never seen anybody lose that much. I didn't know a person had that much in them."

Detective Holbrook touched her hand. "You've had a shock. Just hold on for a little while." Intelligent blue eyes watched her sympathetically from behind wire-frame spectacles.

Detective Ryland flipped open a notebook. "If I could eliminate you straight away, it would simplify matters. Where were you last night and early this morning?"

"I was in a hotel last night." She named the hotel. "I arrived here just before eight this morning. Security downstairs was trying to call up to tell Spencer I was coming, but I didn't wait for them."

"Were you alone in the hotel?"

Relief whispered through her. Because of one special man and the hope he'd brought into her life, she'd never be alone again. "I was with my fiancé. His name is Alexandre Dupree."

As his name left her lips, there was a commotion near the elevator. And suddenly, Alexandre was striding toward her, determination stamped on every line of his face. The cops trying to stop him didn't seem to know what to do against his strength of purpose.

All at once, she knew she'd been waiting for him, aware that nothing would keep him from her side once he realized that something had happened. Without hesitation, she flowed into his arms when he reached her.

"Are you all right?" His face was taut.

"I'm fine." And she was. A little shaky, still rocked by the violence she'd seen, but deep inside where it mattered, she was okay.

"What happened? I saw all these police officers when I decided to wait for you downstairs."

She smiled at his impatience, but before she could answer, Detective Ryland interrupted. "Where were you last night, Mr.…?"

"Dupree, Alexandre Dupree." Alexandre glanced at the open doorway to Spencer's office. "And I was with Charlotte last night. The hotel staff will verify that."

Something flared in Charlotte's brain. "We ordered room service and then there was that fax that got delivered to us by mistake after we'd gone to sleep."

"*Oui.* Several people can attest to our presence at the hotel for the entire night."

Detective Ryland closed his notebook and said, "You're free to go for now, but we may have further questions for you at a later date. In case you haven't guessed, Mr. Dupree, we're investigating a serious crime—the murder of Spencer Ashton. I'd appreciate your cooperation."

"You can reach us at the Ashton Estate, with the rest of the Ashton family," Alexandre answered.

The detective nodded. "Please don't contact anyone else about this—we'll take care of that."

Charlotte had been thinking about calling Walker. "When will you…?"

"Don't worry. It'll be very soon." With that, they moved onto Kerry, standing only a foot or so away.

"Who is that?" Alexandre asked, his tone low.

"Kerry, Spencer's admin. Let's wait and take her with us when we go—she might not want to be alone." She blinked as something Kerry was saying caught her attention.

"…they were arguing. It sounded ugly—I could hear them through the office walls."

Detective Ryland's whole posture changed. "That's Grant Ashton?"

"Yes." Kerry nodded, violet eyes looking bruised in her pale face. "According to my schedule, he was Spencer's last appointment for the day. But, he can't have done *that*." Her voice trembled at the end.

"Why?" Detective Holbrook asked, her tone softer than her more abrasive partner's.

Kerry looked at the woman. "Well, Spencer was still alive when Grant left."

Detective Ryland wrote that down but the look of intense interest on his face didn't fade. "Was Grant Ashton calm when he left?"

"N-no. He was pretty angry—furious…"

The noise of several technicians leaving Spencer's office drowned out the rest of the interview. Alexandre leaned down to whisper in Charlotte's ear. "Grant?"

"He's Spencer's eldest son from his first marriage." The implications of what Kerry had revealed made her heart race. "I don't know him but I can't imagine…"

Alexandre murmured soothingly and stroked her back. "The truth will come out. It always does."

Given what she'd discovered only hours ago, Charlotte agreed with him.

"Am I glad that's over." Kerry's relieved exclamation broke into her thoughts. "Thanks for waiting. I needed the support."

"You're welcome. We'd be happy to give you a ride home," Alexandre offered.

The other woman shook her head. "Thanks, but I think I'll take a walk."

"Are you sure?" Charlotte asked, worried.

Kerry nodded. "Some fresh air will do me good."

They parted on the ground floor, both of them deep in thought over what they'd witnessed.

By the time Charlotte and Alexandre arrived home, the estate was in an uproar, news of Spencer's death having beaten them to Napa. Lilah was a complete wreck.

Charlotte left Alexandre's side to help Megan and Paige calm the older woman. Lilah finally slept sometime in the small hours of the morning and instead of going to the cottage, Charlotte collapsed in Alexandre's room.

Nobody said anything about the arrangement and even if they had, it wouldn't have mattered. It wasn't a night to be alone, especially when the man she loved was more than willing to hold her through the dark hours.

The next morning, they drove a golf cart to her cottage so she could shower and change, before returning to the main house to join the others in the breakfast room.

Lilah appeared calm, but both Paige and Trace had dark circles under their eyes. Walker, who'd arrived late last night, seemed to be in shock. Megan looked marginally better—she'd spent the night in her own home and driven over with Simon early this morning. Charlotte had a feeling that Megan had only returned to the tense atmosphere of the house because it was obvious that Paige needed support.

After Lilah excused herself to go sit in the library, the rest of them stared at each other, not knowing what to say.

It was Walker who broke the silence. "I'm sorry you had to go through that, Charlotte."

"I wasn't alone," she said softly, glad that Walker and Alexandre were getting along. She'd introduced them last night and while Walker had been surprised by their engagement, he'd made no negative comments. It mattered to her that the two most important men in her life accept each other.

"What a mess," Trace muttered. "And it's only going to get worse. No one knows what he put in his will."

"Your father's not even buried and you're worried about the will?" Walker's tone could've cut glass.

Trace's eyes sparked with anger. "We have to worry. It's not only the vineyard that's at stake but Ashton-Lattimer, too. With Spencer dead, do you really think the others are going to sit back?"

At the mention of Spencer's two ex-families, silence descended on the table. The doorbell rang in the distance. A minute later, the housekeeper entered the breakfast room and leaned down to speak to Charlotte, who happened to be sitting nearest the door.

"Mercedes Ashton and Jillian Ashton-Bennedict are waiting in the front gallery." Irene kept her tone low.

"Thanks. Paige, Megan," Charlotte said, thankful for Irene's discretion. "We've got visitors."

When the men looked up, she attempted a smile. "Girls only." Kissing Alexandre on the cheek, she walked out with the others. "It's Mercedes and Jillian."

Megan brightened but Paige continued to look subdued.

When they reached the gallery just off the entrance, Jillian immediately headed over to meet them, graceful as always. "We heard what happened—we just came to say that if you need anything…"

"Thanks for coming," Megan said. "This is going to be a big mess, but at least the women are willing to talk."

Mercedes, always slightly reserved, nodded. "I'm worried—"

Before she could finish her sentence, a high voice screamed, "Get out!"

Whirling around, Charlotte found herself looking at Lilah. The redhead's usually cool, emotionless face was suffused with rage and she clutched a cut-glass tumbler as if she wanted to throw it. "Get the hell out of my house!"

"Mrs. Ashton," Jillian began, her tone gentle.

"He's not even buried and you've come to gloat?" Lilah cried. "Get out! Get out! Get the hell out!"

Paige went to her mother but Lilah shook off her hand. "Leave!" Striding to the entrance, she hauled open the door and pointed. "Get out."

Charlotte touched Jillian's arm. "I'm so sorry."

"It's okay," Jillian whispered. "I'll call you later."

The two women left without another word. Lilah slammed the door behind them and stalked back into the library, the tumbler still in her hand. It was only then that Charlotte realized the other woman had been drinking.

Late that night, she finally had a moment alone with the man she adored beyond reason. "Alexandre," she whispered, as they were getting into bed at the cottage, preferring the privacy it afforded over the estate house.

"Ma petite?" His masculine voice was a purr in the darkness.

"With everything that's happened the search for my

mother's been pushed into the background." She settled into the bed.

He slipped in beside her and cuddled her close. "But not forgotten. We know your mother left Kendall and returned to her people. It's not much but…"

"But if Spencer wasn't lying to me, my mother originally came from the Pine Ridge reservation."

"It makes sense to start your search there."

"Where else could she go—a woman who'd lost everything?" A lump lodged in her throat. "It can't be done from a distance. We'd have to go to Pine Ridge."

"Does it have to be you, Charlotte? Can you not hire an investigator?" Alexandre's voice was coaxing but not demanding. "You've endured much this past week—it hurts me to see you hurting," he admitted, shattering her completely. "I'd like to take you away from here for a while, show you my homeland, have you meet my *maman*."

The idea tugged at Charlotte's heart. "I'm tired of this place, too," she confided. "I want to meet your mother. But I don't want to give up on my own mother when I'm so close. I feel like I can almost touch her."

They were both silent for a while.

"If this is what you need to feel happy, then of course we'll stay in America and go to Pine Ridge," Alexandre began.

"I told Walker about our mother today." Charlotte couldn't forget the ravaged look that had dawned in her brother's eyes as she'd spoken.

"When?"

"After lunch, while you were talking with Trace. I had to tell him in private. And I wanted to do it before he spent too much of himself grieving for a man who didn't deserve his loyalty. You understand?"

"Of course. I realize what a shock it must've been. He, I believe, was very close to Spencer."

"Yes. He looked up to him, respected him, trusted him." She hated that Spencer was causing her beloved brother pain even from beyond the grave. "I was thinking…"

"Yes?" The single word was a stroke in the darkness.

"We can help with the research, but maybe Walker should be the one to go to Pine Ridge. He needs to do this, just like I needed to find out the truth."

"And how would that make you feel? You were the one who believed, but he'll probably see her first."

Charlotte smiled. Trust Alexandre to think of her welfare. "I want to meet her so desperately, but I love Walker. I can give him this because if the situations were reversed, I know he wouldn't hesitate."

Alexandre's hand spread on her stomach, warm and protective. "Then do you wish to remain here for Spencer's funeral?"

"I'm no hypocrite. I never liked him and if there were any choice, I wouldn't stay. But given the way Lilah's acting and the mess things are already in, I have to support the others at least through the funeral." She bit her lip. "Am I a terrible person for not being sorry he's dead?"

"No, you're simply honest. This man caused you only pain. Why should you mourn him?" He kissed her.

Her returning kiss held her heart. "Thank you."

"Then shall I book our tickets once we know the funeral arrangements? I'm sure we'll be given permission to leave after those detectives check out our alibi with the hotel staff."

"Yes." She frowned. "I just realized I'll have to find someone to take care of the greenhouse while we're in France."

He was quiet for a moment. "I want to ask you something about your greenhouse and this cottage."

"What?"

"If I had my way, I'd marry you right now. But, since we've decided to wait until things are calmer with the family, will you consider moving in with me when I establish a home in this country? It will be very soon—I want to get you away from the estate. From what I've seen, things are only going to get worse."

Smiling, she snuggled closer. "I'd love to move in with you but I can't abandon the greenhouse—it'd only put more stress on everyone."

"I understand, *chérie*. For the moment, we can find a house nearby so you can continue your work without being tied to the estate. Will that do?"

"It'll be perfect. And it won't be forever. I've always wanted my own business, independent of the Ashton name. Once things have settled down a little, I'll let the family know my decision to move on and we can decide where we want to live permanently."

"Maybe you can even do your work in France, *non?*" He turned to look down at her. This close, she could see his smile even in the darkness.

"Maybe." She smiled back. "Do you miss your home?"

"*Oui.* I worry about my vines."

"You're a winemaker to your toes." Her laugh bubbled out of her.

He chuckled. "You'll like my land in France. It's full of growing things." He dropped a kiss on the tip of her nose. "And I'm sure Paris will bespell you."

"Paris," she whispered. "I've always wanted to do something wild and romantic like run off to Paris."

"That wasn't in your journal. I would've noticed."

Joy whispered through her. No matter what happened in her life, so long as she had her wonderful Alexandre by her side, she'd flourish just like her flowers. "Don't you dare go near my journal again, Mr. Dupree."

"I won't need to."

"Why not?"

"Because, *ma petite,* I'm going to be such a wonderful lover, you won't be able to resist sharing your fantasies with me." It was a smug statement, but the tone was heart-breakingly tender.

Throwing her arms around him, she kissed him soundly on the lips. "I love you to bits, Alexandre Dupree."

"Then all my fantasies have come true."

* * * * *

ESTATE AFFAIR

BY
SARA ORWIG

Sara Orwig lives in Oklahoma. She has a patient husband who will take her on research trips anywhere from big cities to old forts. She is an avid collector of Western history books. With a master's degree in English, Sara has written historical romance, mainstream fiction and contemporary romance. Books are beloved treasures that take Sara to magical worlds and she loves both reading and writing them.

Look for Sara Orwig's exciting new novel,
***Dakota Daddy*, available this month from**
Mills & Boon® Desire™.

With thanks to Melissa Jeglinski

Prologue

June 1976

It was an unpleasant task but he needed to do it tonight. Standing in the library of his home in San Francisco, Spencer Ashton gazed out the night-darkened window. In his mind he was seeing the Ashton vineyard—in daylight—acre upon acre of lush, prime-producing vines bearing Pinot Noir and Chardonnay grapes.

His gaze roamed the library, with its shelves of leather-bound books; oil paintings in gilt frames on the walls; leather chairs; his immaculate, massive desk. Satisfaction shot through him because now his wealth would soar. What a long way he had come from Crawley, Nebraska!

At the sound of the door opening, his wife appeared. She rarely came to the library, and the children were forbidden to enter it. Spencer had proclaimed this room his domain, a haven from his family.

His gaze raked over Caroline. She wore a pink dress, typical for her. Ordinary and insipid. After tonight he would be rid of her for good. Distaste filled him. His only regret was that his split with her couldn't happen faster.

"You wanted to talk," Caroline said, her hazel-green eyes gazing at him.

"Yes, come in," he replied, thinking how mousy she was. Not the woman for him. Maybe at one time he'd been attracted to her and thought she might be exciting enough to hold his interest, but that feeling had soon been dispelled. Yet she'd been the means for acquiring what he'd wanted. and she'd served his purposes well.

Entering the room, she gazed up at him. "What is it, Spencer?"

"I'm leaving you, Caroline," he stated bluntly, glad to finally break their ties. "Our marriage is finished—but then it's been finished for quite some time."

She paled and flinched as if he had hit her, and his distaste deepened. Why was she acting surprised, he wondered. How could she have hoped to hold him?

"Leaving me!" she repeated as if she couldn't hear well. "Spencer, we have four small children—we took vows."

"I've filed for divorce. It's already done and will be in the paper tomorrow. I thought you would prefer to hear it from me first."

"You didn't discuss this—"

"There's nothing to discuss. I want out of this marriage. I'm taking the Lattimer Corporation stock with me, Caroline. Your father willed his shares of the investment banking business to me," Spencer declared, getting to the heart of the matter.

"You can't do that!" she cried, trembling badly. "My father left everything to you in good faith. As my husband and father of our children, his grandchildren, he bequeathed land and stock and money to you. He didn't give it to you to take everything away from his daughter and grandchildren! I won't let you do that!"

Her eyes flashed with a fire that surprised Spencer. He had expected her to burst into tears and plead and beg. Instead her fists were clenched, and she was shaking. Except for bright spots of color in her cheeks, she was deathly pale.

"Caroline, he bequeathed it all to me. Everything is mine. End of argument."

"I'll get my lawyer, and we'll see about ending this discussion. I'll contest the will. You can't take your children's heritage and my life support from us!"

"Think not?" He didn't like opposition and hadn't expected any argument from her. Spencer stepped closer to her, angrily grasping her shoulders and digging his fingers in until she flinched. "If you try to stop me, I'll take the children from you and you'll have nothing. I have people on our staff who will, if I want, testify that you're on drugs."

"That's a lie! I've never done anything like that!"

"These people will testify under oath that you have."

"You'll pay them to lie!" she cried, her voice rising. "It'll all be lies!"

"You can't keep me from getting everything your father passed down to me. Believe me, Caroline, I'm prepared. I can get the children and the estate and you'll have absolutely nothing."

"You're pure evil, Spencer!" she exclaimed in a low voice. "You can't take my children!" The tears did come now, spilling down her cheeks just as he had expected, while she trembled violently.

He dropped his hands.

"You do one thing to contest the will and you'll never see the children. Do you understand that, Caroline?" he snapped, furious that she was threatening him. He would ruin her if she interfered with him!

Caroline stared hard at Spencer through her tears. She'd been so wrong about this man, her husband. She'd known something between them was never right, that he was cold to their children, but she'd hung on for their sake. But now she saw him for what he truly was. A cold, heartless and calculating bastard. He'd never cared about her. Never cared about his own children. All he'd ever wanted was her inheritance. And she'd been fool enough to fall for his lies. He didn't deserve her tears.

"I can see you for what you truly are now, Spencer," she said, her voice shaking from fear and anger. "I can see that you don't deserve the children. They deserve so much more. I can't stop you from taking what my father left you, but I *can* raise *my* children to be honest and loving and have integrity. I can teach them to be nothing like you. And I still have the vineyard my mother left me. You can't touch that. So go, if you must. Perhaps you are doing us all a favor."

Stunned, Spencer stared at Caroline and saw something in her eyes he'd never seen before: strength.

Shrugging off the odd feeling this produced, he said, "You agree to accept my terms without a fight?"

Caroline squared her shoulders, even as fresh tears fell from her eyes. "Yes."

Spencer's pulse pounded with enthusiasm and victory. He was free of her and the children! He didn't ever want to see any of them again. He swept into the hall and almost collided with his oldest son.

Eight-year-old Eli Ashton gazed up at Spencer with round eyes, his skin as pale as his mother's. For a startled instant Spencer and his son stared at each other, and then Eli flew at him.

"I hate you!" he cried, his small fists doubled as he leaped at Spencer and pounded him.

Spencer swung his hand, his palm cracking against Eli's cheek, sending the child sprawling. Spencer headed to the door, where he'd left the bags he'd already packed. And then he left, turning his back on Caroline and the children forever.

One

Twenty-Nine Years Later

Who killed Spencer Ashton? Eli Ashton's gaze drifted over the remaining mourners who had come to the Ashton Estate to give condolences to the family at the funeral reception. The event was winding down, yet the family was still busy talking to friends and hadn't noticed Eli's presence. When and if they did, he was certain he would be asked to leave.

How many of these people had really liked Spencer? Eli thought his father's enemies were probably legion.

He was the only one of his family who had come to the funeral reception at the Ashton Estate and he knew why. Not one of them was welcome. The tension between the two families at the funeral had been palpable. But curiosity had overcome him and he had to see the house that should have been, and once was, his mother's. His grandfather's house and vineyards. All stolen by Spencer, Eli thought bitterly.

Jamming his clenched fist into the pants pocket of his charcoal suit, he strolled across the large reception hall and stepped outside onto the veranda. Beyond the manicured gardens were acres of lush green vineyards. As head winemaker for his family's vineyards, Eli knew the vines would be going into fruit set and already have tiny green grapes. It was the first of June in a season that, so far, had been good.

His gaze ran over the vineyards again and the knot of anger inside him tightened. All of this stolen from his mother! All of his family rejected by Spencer. And now, Grant Ashton, Spencer's first-born son, had turned up from Nebraska. The scandalous news had broken of Spencer's first marriage. A marriage that had never been dissolved. Spencer had committed bigamy, Eli thought. Legally Spencer shouldn't have been able to inherit this estate, mansion, vineyards, any of it.

"Sir, do you need anything?" a woman asked.

Eli barely glanced at her out of the corner of his eye. "I need a lot of things. Right now, solitude. I came out here hoping I would be left alone," he replied, clamping his jaw closed and knowing he needed to control his anger. He raked his fingers through his straight, brown hair. He had been too abrupt, but he didn't want to talk to a stranger.

"And I thought all the big egos were inside," came the soft reply.

Startled, Eli forgot his anger. He turned to look at the woman who was heading back into the house. Taking a quick inventory, he observed long shapely legs, high-heeled pumps, a sleeveless black dress that ended above her knees. Thick auburn curls were looped and pinned on her head. The tendrils that had managed to escape made him think about running his fingers through her hair.

"So, when you stir up the heat, you run?" he drawled.

She stopped and turned around slowly, as if she had all the time in the world to deal with him. The moment their gazes met, he could feel electricity snap between them. She strolled toward him, and her sensual, languorous movement made his pulse jump. When he looked into her light honey-brown eyes, with the thickest lashes he had ever seen, his breath quickened. Her eyes captivated him. As she slowly approached him, he saw sparks dancing in their depths. She had a sexy walk, a slight sway of her hips, but it was the provocation in her eyes that kept his pulse racing.

"Nothing you can do will make me run," she replied with conviction.

"Nothing?" he drawled, moving closer to her. "That's an interesting statement and conjures up all sorts of things I'd like to do."

"Like what?" she challenged, her eyes carrying their own defiance She was self-confident, intriguing.

"Like hold you in my arms and feel your softness against me. Like taste your lips in a slow, wet kiss," he confessed in a husky voice, a little surprised at his own admission. He didn't normally behave this way with women he didn't know. But she'd opened the door and invited him in. "For starters, I'd like to have a drink with you, and later, dinner," he replied.

"We're total strangers. I don't do that," she answered coolly, stopping only a few feet from him.

"We can remedy that quickly. I'm Eli," he said, extending his hand. "And you are—" he asked.

When she held out her hand, he grasped warm, slender fingers. The heat between them burned even hotter when they touched. It sent a current straight to his nether regions, while his gaze slipped down to her full, rosy lips.

"I'm Lara," she replied.

What would it be like to feel those lips against his, he wondered. "I didn't think I'd be around any firecrackers until next month, but now I see I was wrong," he said.

"Me? A firecracker!" She laughed with a dazzling smile and a flash of even, white teeth. "All I did was rock your quiet, climate-controlled world a tiny bit." He still held her hand while their gazes remained locked, feeling the same sizzling results.

"Let's get out of here and have a drink together," he said, and took her arm, touching her so lightly, feeling the contact to his toes. She smelled enticing, and then he recognized the perfume. For a second she hesitated. "Let's go, Lara," he repeated, liking the sound of her name. "You know you want to," he added.

"You're dangerous," she said softly.

"No, I'm not," he replied, touching her slender throat. "Your pulse is racing and you want to go."

She ran her index finger across his wrist, a slow, sensual stroke while pinpoints of fire danced in the depths of her gaze. "I think your pulse is racing, too."

"If we can do that to each other already, then we *have* to get to know each other," he said, linking her arm through his, knowing he wasn't ready to let her out of his sight.

"You're incredibly sure of yourself."

"Right now, I'm sure about both of us," he replied. He rarely acted impulsively, but he wanted to spend time with her, and they needed to get away from the Ashton Estate. He wanted her to himself. His gaze drifted down over her, over her slender throat and lush curves. He wanted to peel away that black dress and see what was beneath. "Let's go," he said, holding her arm as he took a step.

"All right, Eli, I'll throw caution to the wind and act on impulse. Don't make me regret it." She fell into step beside him. He was intently aware of her at his side, her head coming to just slightly above his shoulder.

"Midnight Desire," he said softly, and as she glanced up, her eyes widened.

"You know my perfume!" Lara exclaimed in surprise. "You must know a lot of women to identify a perfume quickly like that."

"No. It's not women in my life. I have a nose for scents. And I have sisters."

"Sisters—right," she said, obviously dubious of his declaration.

He directed her to a shiny, black sports car. When he opened the passenger door for her, Lara slid into the seat and watched him as he walked around the car. He was ruggedly handsome with riveting green eyes, but it wasn't just his appealing looks or his green eyes that had her seated in his car.

It was this breathtaking, hot attraction and her curiosity about him. He was mysterious and intriguing. He had been harsh on the veranda when he'd snapped at her, but she hadn't been any better with her smart-mouthed reply. She blamed the strain of the emotional day for her loss of control. She'd expected him to ignore her, but instead he had given her a challenge that she couldn't ignore. Now here she was in his elegant sports car, going to dinner with him.

She ran her hand over the soft, brown leather that covered the seat. She had never been in such a splendid car or with a man as exciting as Eli, yet she knew that she was out of her element with him. So far out of her element that she should get out of the car and go back where she belonged. She was an Ashton maid, domestic help, and when the fall semester started, a college student. Whatever he did, she guessed he was wealthy. But he was too enticing to pass up, and just this once she wanted to be with a dashing, stimulating man, riding in his fancy car, tossing aside cares and enjoying the moment.

When he slid onto the seat beside her and started the engine, she caught a whiff of his aftershave. She shifted, adjusting her seat belt so she could watch him. His profile was to her and she drank in the sight of him, looking at his brown hair, fantasizing about running her fingers through the thick strands.

They circled a glistening pond in the center of the drive and sped away from the mansion. When he had to stop to turn onto the highway, he glanced at her.

"You drive as if you have a destination in mind," she said.

"I always have a destination in mind," he replied. "There's a bar overlooking the Napa River where we can have a drink and talk. Later, we can have dinner together." He touched her hand. "You don't have a wedding ring, so you're single. Is there a particular man in your life right now?"

"No, there's not. And you don't have a ring, either."

"And there's no particular woman in my life. At least not until the past half hour."

She laughed. "I wouldn't say I'm 'in your life.'"

"Yes, you are," he insisted in his deep masculine voice. "And I intend to keep you there," he declared. She inhaled, knowing his words were ridiculous and yet unable to resist them. He was temptation, excitement, a sexy male.

"Do you always go after what you want with this much determination?"

One of his dark eyebrows arched. "You have no idea."

"So, Eli, let me guess what you do. You're too well-fixed to have a laborer's job. You have that look of money. At the same time you look as if you're accustomed to doing rough, physical activities."

"What's the look of money?"

"Your elegant sports car. Your fine suit."

"What makes you think I do physical work?"

She wondered if she was far off the mark, yet that was the way he appeared to her. He kept a barrier up and didn't reveal much of himself. She couldn't tell whether her analysis amused or annoyed him.

"I'll have to admit that when you linked my arm in yours, I felt your muscles. You didn't get them sitting behind a desk."

"I could sit behind a desk and work out at a gym and get muscles," he replied.

"No. You're deeply tanned. I'm betting that you do something physical," she said. He had revealed a rough edge on the veranda at the Ashton Estate that ruled out a myriad of professions. "Whatever you do, you're successful at it," she said.

"Where did you get that idea? My car and my suit?"

"Not at all. Your self-assurance."

He gave her a sardonic glance. "Enough about me. I'm a winemaker," he said. "Now, speaking of walking—" he reached over and drew his fingers along her arm, sending tingles spiraling in the wake of his touch "—you have a walk that is sexy enough to set a man ablaze."

"I don't set men on fire," she replied, feeling her cheeks flush.

"We can argue that one when I'm not driving."

Could she possibly send this man into flames? She couldn't imagine it. Her gaze roamed down his long legs and then back up to find him watching her, before he returned his attention to the road.

When they sped into Napa, anticipation fizzed in her veins. As they drove down Main Street, passing Victorian-style houses, she looked at the town she had known most of her life, yet now she saw it as if for the first time. They passed the Jarvis Conservatory that had been so pretty when the wisteria vines had been in bloom earlier. She looked at the plain Vintners' Collective Building, and in minutes they drove past the renovated opera house with its cheerful red awning. Crossing the winding Napa River, she saw a red and green Napa trolley as it rumbled along the street.

Because of the man beside her, the sky seemed bluer, the air fresher. Colors were more vivid, impressions carving into her memory in a day she would never forget. Gone was the emotional, depressing day with the funeral and all it involved. Now she felt full of life, anticipation bubbling in her.

In minutes they were seated on a terrace that overlooked a bend in the glistening Napa River. Tables were covered in white linen cloths, centered with vases of fresh daisies and roses. Orange and yellow nasturtiums filled pots along the terrace, while multicolored flowers spilled from hanging baskets and a musician played softly from somewhere inside the restaurant.

Eli ordered a bottle of Chardonnay and appetizers. Their white-coated waiter uncorked the wine and waited for Eli's approval. After pouring their glasses, the waiter left to return with the appetizers Eli had ordered.

Eli raised his glass. "Here's to us, Lara," he said quietly.

He leaned across the table and drew his fingers over her knuckles. "I want to take you to dinner Saturday night," he said. "We can go dancing."

"I need to know you better," she replied, a smile curving her full lips.

He touched the corner of her mouth.

"I like your smile, Lara. And we will know each other a lot better by Saturday. We can start right now. Tell me what you like to do and what you don't like."

"I like the usual things that everyone likes—dancing, swimming, reading. There's nothing unusual about me."

"That's not so," he said firmly. "Your brown eyes are unusually beautiful."

"Oh, please!" she exclaimed. Lara smiled at him, yet his compliment pleased her. He leaned closer while the fingers of his right hand lightly stroked back and forth across her knuckles. If anyone had unusually beautiful eyes, he did. Thickly lashed, filled with emerald fire, they were bedroom eyes, spellbinding eyes.

"Don't deny it. I've never seen eyes that shade of milk chocolate with golden flecks in their depths. Everything about you has been unusual, which is why I'm intrigued and intend to know you better."

She smiled at him, shaking her head. "I think you are having a reaction to the gloomy day we've had."

He traced his fingers along the corner of her mouth while he shook his head in denial. "Not at all. I will get to know you. I promise you that."

As his declarations sent her pulse racing, she wondered if anything in his adult life had ever stopped him or been unattainable for him.

"Try this dip," he said, spooning some on a cracker and holding it out. "Take a bite." She reached up to take the cracker from him, but he caught her hand with his free one. "Take a bite," he repeated in a low voice, still holding the tidbit.

She leaned forward to let him feed it to her. This brought her only inches from him, heightening her desire. His finger barely brushed her lip, and all the time, his gaze held hers. He was sexy, commanding.

"Maybe I'd better feed myself," she said in a breathless voice, looking at his sensual, well-sculpted mouth.

As the shadows lengthened, the sun became a fireball on the western horizon, splintering golden reflections across the swiftly running river. Tables around them filled and the noise level rose, although she barely noticed anyone else. Lara's world held only Eli and her.

"Lara," he said, turning her hand in his and leaning closer across the table. "Let's have dinner alone. Let me get a suite and we'll have dinner sent up and we can be together without all this," Eli said, waving his hand at those around them.

While the question, and all it implied, hung in the air, she looked into his green eyes and found them full of unspoken promises of passion.

Two

Lara inhaled deeply. She had to make a choice. Common sense told her to refuse, yet when she gazed into his seductive bedroom eyes, she knew she wanted the same thing he did. Why did it seem so right to be with him? She didn't want the evening to end, and the thought of getting a suite had her heart pounding.

He raised her hand and brushed a feathery kiss across her palm and then looked at her for an answer.

"Yes, Eli," she said softly. "A suite would be exciting."

He paid the bill, left a generous tip and then held her chair. She preceded him across the terrace until they reached the sidewalk. Eli took her hand and they walked a few doors down to a red brick five-story hotel that overlooked the river.

In the lobby he turned to her. "Wait here while I register us," he said.

She nodded, her pulse racing as she watched him walk away.

His features were rugged, yet softened by his thick eyelashes and emerald eyes. He had a purposeful walk, but then, he'd told her over drinks that he always had a destination. He was a man who knew where he was going and wasted no time getting there. And yet, for the past few hours he had given her his whole, undivided attention, hanging on every word she said as if she were rare and special. And she had done the same with him.

She shifted her weight and wondered about the attraction that had exploded between them the first time they looked at each other. Impossible. Only, it had happened and was still occurring. Right now her pulse was racing, and she didn't want to stop looking at him and she longed to run her fingers through his thick, brown hair. She wanted to kiss him.

Her heart thudded on that one. She wondered if she knew herself.

Then he was walking back to her and all thoughts fled as he took her arm.

Along with the bellman they rode the elevator to the top floor. The bellman opened the suite door and switched on lights for them.

While Eli tipped the man, she strolled into the sitting room of their spacious suite. A large bouquet of fresh flowers was centered on a fruitwood table in front of a grouping of chairs covered in off-white damask. One end of the room to her right held a small kitchen and between the kitchen and the sitting room was a dining area. To her left, she glimpsed a bedroom.

On thick, white carpet she crossed the room to the floor-to-ceiling windows to look at the view of the river and the mountains beyond it. The sun was sliding lower, and dark would soon descend.

Eli turned to her and she saw the white-hot desire in his eyes.

"Now, isn't this better?" he asked, shedding his coat and

dropping it on a chair. Before she could answer, there was a knock at the door and a male voice announced, "Room service."

The bellman set a tray on the table. It held an iced bottle of champagne, glasses and a fruit tray with bright red strawberries, yellow chunks of pineapple, slices of green kiwi and purple grapes. As pretty as the fruit looked, her appetite had vanished earlier in the day and had not yet returned.

When he was gone, Eli poured them both glasses of champagne.

Lara thought she might as well be in a dream, only this was real, but like nothing she had ever done before. She had fallen into a fairy-tale afternoon, taken out of her ordinary life like Cinderella by her prince. And for the next few hours, Lara decided she was going to continue to enjoy every minute *and* the sexy man who'd conjured it.

"I've never done anything so impulsive in my life," she said.

"Neither have I, Lara," he replied solemnly. "But this is different."

She wondered how it was different for him and if he were telling her the truth. She couldn't imagine a man like Eli hadn't had all kinds of experiences with women. Women far more sophisticated, beautiful and with the same lifestyle as his.

He raised the flute of champagne. "Here's to a fantastic evening," he said.

She touched her glass to his, hearing the faint clink and then she sipped the bubbling, golden liquid.

"Now, isn't this a lot better," he said, unfastening his conservative charcoal tie and tossing it on a nearby chair.

"Yes, it's better, but probably not the wisest thing I've done," she replied. As he unbuttoned the top two buttons of his white shirt, her throat went dry.

"I think it's one of the best things I've ever done," he said, his enigmatic eyes darkening. He reached out to pull a pin from her hair and let a lock tumble to her shoulder. With deliberation he removed another pin. His fingers tugging gently on pins fueled the fires building in her. "This is what I wanted to see," he whispered while his gaze roamed over her. "Your hair is magnificent."

She had never been told that before. In minutes her hair was free of pins, framing her face in a silky cascade that poured over her shoulders.

He took her glass from her hand and set it on the table next to his. Then, as he reached for her, she walked eagerly into his arms, wrapping her arms around his neck. Her heart drummed. Caution had gone out the window when she left the estate with him, and now she wanted to kiss him, wanted to explore and discover and be kissed.

Lean and hard, he was solid muscle. He smelled of a tantalizing aftershave that she could not recognize. His strong arms banded her waist as he looked down at her. "I've been wanting to hold you since I first looked into your eyes."

Before today, she would have thought a line like that would be pure fabrication, but with this man, she believed him. There was no mistaking the blatant need in his eyes. He gazed at her with a hunger that made her breathless.

She reached up with her forefinger and traced his lower lip. He inhaled deeply, and she was amazed at the effect she had on him. He reacted to her slightest touch.

"Lara," he said, his voice gravelly, "I want you."

She pulled him closer, and his eyelids became hooded. As his gaze lowered to her mouth, he leaned the last few inches to touch the corner of her mouth lightly with the tip of his tongue.

The contact sizzled. Her lips felt swollen, aching to discover his. She wound her fingers in his thick hair.

"I've wanted to do this all day," he whispered. He lowered his head and his mouth brushed hers. Seconds later, his tongue parted her lips, sliding into her mouth.

She returned his kiss, her tongue stroking his slowly. He was equally deliberate, launching a searing exploration of her mouth.

She'd never been kissed like this. She shook with fiery longing. Her fingers dug into his back and held on tightly.

One of his arms circled her waist while he shifted enough to be able to let one of his hands cruise across her breasts. Through the cotton dress and the wispy bra beneath, his caress was a lightning bolt streaking over her raw nerves. Her nipples were already tight, but his touch made them tingle, even through two layers of clothes—and made her ache to be free of the constriction.

Her fingers went to the buttons on his shirt to twist them loose until she could run her hand across his chest. She tangled her fingers in the thick brown hair on his chest, then brushed her hands across his flat nipples.

At her touch, he gasped and dipped his head to claim her mouth in another scalding kiss.

His free hand roamed over her bottom.

She tugged his shirt out of his pants, unbuttoned it and then pushed off his broad shoulders. She paused, opening her eyes with an effort to meet his hooded gaze.

She leaned back to let her eyes feast on him. He was thick through the shoulders and chest, his body tapering down to narrow hips. The mat of brown curls narrowed down to a fine line that disappeared below his belt.

His belt. She wanted to unfasten it and free him of the constraint of his trousers. She glanced up to meet his scorching gaze again. He took her shoulders and turned her, leaning forward to let his warm breath play over her nape. Then his tongue followed as he brushed kisses on her nape. His fingers tugged her zipper down, his tongue following the opening to her waist.

Turning her to face him again, Eli pushed her black dress off her shoulders.

It floated to the floor in a puddle around her ankles, but her attention was on him as his gaze lowered to her breasts.

"Oh, yes," he whispered. "You're perfection." He reached out to brush her nipples.

She gasped with pleasure and wrapped her arms around him, kissing him. He placed a light hand on her midriff, stopping her.

"I want to look at you, Lara." He ground out the words when she looked at him questioningly. "I want to savor you, to explore you, to kiss you. I want to know you as I know myself, to know your softness, your body, your reactions. I intend to learn what pleases you and what excites you," he drawled, his stated intentions heightening her fervor. "This night I want to drive you wild."

His words aroused her almost as much as his caresses inflamed her. This handsome, dashing man was sinfully tempting. She could barely think or talk, but she wanted the same thing he did. She wanted to discover all of him, to know him tonight as she had never known a man before. Then his kisses tracing her throat took her attention.

All she wore now was her pink bra and cotton panties that were cut low across her stomach. She wore thigh-high hose, and he reached out to roll them down. His fingers caressed her leg as he slid first one stocking and then the other off.

He stood and brushed her nipples with his fingers. The taut buds pushed against the fabric, and she shook with need.

Reaching out to touch his belt, she slid her hands to the

buckle to unfasten it and then unzipped his trousers to free him from constraints. She reached out to tug down his briefs, inhaling deeply at the sight of his manhood. Thick and hard, he was ready for her. "Eli," she whispered, stroking him.

With a groan he turned to her again, leaning down to trail warm kisses on her throat, nibbling on her earlobe while he unsnapped the clasp to her bra and pushed it away. As he cupped each full globe, she moaned.

Then his head went lower, seeking her pink, pouty nipples and letting his tongue circle first one and then the other. He pulled her partially against him, his tanned arm dark against her pale skin where he circled her waist. While he continued to kiss her breast, his hand drifted down over her stomach to push down her panties and reveal the thick auburn curls at the juncture of her thighs.

She trembled, nipping at his neck, kissing his shoulder, running her hands across his chest again.

He knelt in front of her, his fingers feathering along the inside of her thighs while he spread kisses across her stomach.

His tongue made burning paths on the inside of first one thigh and then the other. Closing her eyes, she clutched his shoulders tightly. Sensations rocked her. His fingers moved to her most intimate places, sliding through her thick auburn curls, to caress her.

She cried out when he increased the pressure of his fingers, finding the bud that was supremely sensitive. She moved her hips, lost now in mounting desire. While he kissed and rubbed her, his other hand glided down. His forefinger slid inside her, and her cry was muffled by his mouth. She hadn't known she could want a man to the extent she wanted him—or respond to one with the abandon he was driving her to.

When he stopped, she cried out, wanting more, consumed by

the need he had created. Hunger for him tore at her. She clutched his waist as he stood and looked at her, smoothing her hair away from her face with one hand and caressing her breast with the other. "What do you want, Lara?" he whispered. "Tell me."

"You are driving me wild and you know it. Oh, please," she said, all inhibitions gone, melted away by his hot loving. "Put your hand back on me," she whispered, caressing his throbbing rod.

He pulled her close to kiss her, a devastating kiss where his tongue thrust deeply and slowly, then withdrew, repeating the thrusts with deliberation, imitating the sex act. Clutching his shoulders, she dug her fingers into his back.

His leg pushed between hers, a roughness against her smooth folds, and she gasped. "Ride me, Lara," he whispered in her ear, his warm breath tickling her as his tongue followed the curve of her ear.

She clung to him, knowing she was wanton and not caring. He had driven her mad with his mouth and fingers, and now the exquisite pressure of his leg between hers was taking her to a brink. Her hips thrust wildly while he kissed her again hard. She closed her hand around his manhood, stroking him, but barely aware of what she was doing. All her being focused now on needs created by his leg between hers.

"You like that, Lara?" he whispered, and then kissed her again.

She couldn't answer, but gasped for breath as the need for a climax tore at her. She clutched at him and cried out.

"That's it! Ahh, Lara," he exclaimed. "I want to drive you wild."

She barely heard him. Her pulse roared and she was caught by a power that she couldn't control. While her hips gyrated on him, he increased the pressure of his leg between her thighs.

Release exploded in her, lights playing behind her closed eyelids.

"Sweet," he whispered against her mouth and put his fingers where his leg had been, building another storm. Urgency drove her as frantically as before until she burst over the brink.

"I want you, Eli!" she gasped, standing on tiptoe and pulling his head up to kiss him. His strong arms banded her tightly, holding her softness against his hard strength. She felt his hot erection pressing against her stomach. Framing his face with her hands, she tore her lips from his. "I want you inside me," she whispered, and his chest expanded as he inhaled deeply. His head dipped to kiss her again while his hands cupped her full breasts.

His thumbs circled her nipples slowly, tantalizing touches that fanned desire until it was white-hot. She knelt, looking up at him briefly, drinking in the sight of this ruggedly handsome man who went after what he wanted with all of his concentration. His thighs were hard, his stomach ridged with muscles.

She caressed his manhood, touching him with her tongue, circling the velvet tip and then finally taking him in her mouth.

He groaned and his fingers wound tightly in her hair while she sucked and kissed him and stroked him with her tongue. Her hand went between his legs to caress him, cupping him and touching sensitive skin.

Within seconds he yanked her up to kiss her passionately and then picked her up into his arms.

"It's never been like this," she whispered, astounded at the fireworks he set off in her.

Closing her eyes again, she wound her arms around his neck. He walked to the bedroom and placed her on the bed to roll her over on her stomach.

He moved to her feet, spreading her legs apart. She twisted around, wanting her hands and mouth on him. "Eli—"

"Shh, Lara. Let me kiss you," he said, running his hands along the inside of her legs. His tongue followed. She clutched the bed and closed her eyes, bombarded again by sensations that fanned raging fires.

He moved higher between her legs and his fingers slipped over her bottom, lingering while his tongue stroked the inside of her thigh until she spread her legs wide. Aching for him, she tried to turn over, but his hand in the small of her back held her gently.

"Wait, Lara. Let me learn what you like. Do you like this?" he said, his tongue dawdled along the inside of her thigh. "Do you?" he persisted while he continued to caress and kiss her.

"Yes!" she cried. He was nipping now, the faint stubble of his beard tickling her bottom. Then he shifted, letting her roll over. He moved between her legs and placed her hands high over her head. Then he drew his fingers down over her palms, her arms, down over her underarms to her breasts.

By this time she was straining toward him, and he circled one nipple with his fingers while he leaned down to take her other nipple into his mouth, biting slightly, just enough to make her gasp with pleasure.

Lara had never known desire as she did now. She wanted him with an overwhelming, consuming need that drove all else from her mind. All she could think about was Eli.

"I want you, Eli!" she cried. "I want you inside me!"

"I'll get protection," he promised, stepping off the bed and taking his billfold from his trousers to get out a packet. She put her hands behind her head to watch him, his male body creating sensual anticipation. As he approached the bed, she reached out to caress his hip.

He leaned forward to kiss her and then moved between her legs. He was virile and rugged, tanned to his waist from days in the sun. He lowered himself, and she wrapped her long legs around him, pulling him to her to kiss him while she ran her hand down his smooth back and over his hard buttocks.

He entered her slowly, withdrawing and then sliding into her again. She arched and tightened her legs. "Eli," she urged, "I want you."

"Lara," he murmured and filled her, hot and hard. He kissed her again as she thrust her hips and they moved together.

She knew he was exerting control, holding back to love her longer, but she thought she would come apart if she didn't reach a climax soon. She slid her hands down to his buttocks and pulled him more tightly to her. In minutes she could tell that his control was slipping away. Then it was gone, and he pumped hard and fast.

She burst with release. Clinging to him, she continued to move her hips while he still was thrusting, and in seconds urgency built in her again.

Moving with him, ecstasy once again exploded in her. Her cries were muffled by his kisses as he shuddered with satisfaction. While his thrusts slowed, they both gasped for breath. She could feel that his pounding heart was racing as fast as hers.

Kissing him, Lara held him tightly. Her legs were locked around him as she slid her hands up and down his back slowly, moving them lower over his bare buttocks, wanting to put her hands everywhere on his marvelous body.

This spellbinding, rugged man had whisked her away for one enchanted night that she would always remember. She knew she had to go back to her ordinary life, but right now, a Prince Charming—with some rough edges, but nonetheless, Prince

Charming—had loved her right out of her mind. And she suspected she had taken him along with her.

He turned to shower light kisses on her temple, stroking her hair from her face, and then he rolled onto his side, keeping her close so he could look at her.

"What you do to me is awesome," he said, studying her with such a solemn expression she wondered what was really running through his mind.

"It's mutual," she whispered, feathering her fingers along his jaw, delighting in touching him and loving the intimacy they were sharing.

"You melted my bones. I'm jelly now."

She poked his chest with her forefinger. "You don't feel like jelly," she said, and he grinned.

"Believe me, I am. If the hotel catches on fire, you may have to carry me out."

She laughed. "If the hotel catches on fire now, we're both in trouble. I'm not sure I can find all my clothes."

"They're here. I remember taking them off you," he said, his voice dropping a notch. He met her gaze and she wondered what he was thinking as she gazed into his unfathomable green eyes. He combed her hair away from her face and propped his head on his hand, leaning on his elbow to look down at her. Locks of his brown hair fell over his forehead, and the stubble of his beard faintly showed.

"You're beautiful, Lara," he said.

Her heart thudded with his compliment, and she ran her fingers along his strong shoulder. "Thank you. I'm glad you think so, but at this moment, it's the sex talking."

"No. At this moment I'm seeing more clearly than ever. Desire is temporarily banked and I can take an objective look. I'm also becoming aware that I have a stomach. We didn't drink the wine or eat the appetizers or drink our champagne. I'm ready for room service and I'd like to sink my teeth into—" he paused and looked down to draw his fingers over the rise of her breast.

"Into what?" she asked breathlessly.

He leaned down to nuzzle her neck, awakening new tingles in her. He shifted, tracing kisses lower on her stomach. Then he raised his head and slid off the bed. He bent over to pick her up in his arms.

When he did, Lara wrapped her arms around his neck. "We're going somewhere?" she asked, amused and curious.

"I think it's time for a shower, and then we can study the menu and decide what we want and order it up."

"Suppose what I want is a tall, dark, handsome man?" she asked.

He arched one dark eyebrow. "I don't know where I'll find him, and I can tell you now, I'm not interested in looking for another guy for you."

"You're handsome. All right then, a tall, dark, sexy man. How's that?"

He grinned. "Hopefully I can conjure up that man."

"We'll see what you can conjure *up*," she said in a suggestive drawl, and he smiled.

They entered a large black marble bathroom with a huge tub and gold fixtures. He carried Lara to the shower and stepped inside, setting her on her feet.

"We're doing this together?" she asked.

"Absolutely," he replied. "I'm ready. Are you?"

She felt his arousal against her stomach. Her gaze roamed down the length of him. "I'll say you're ready!"

His gaze glowed with pinpoints of steaming desire. "Why don't we do something about it?"

"I'd say I'm ready, too," she whispered, her voice fading. She scooted closer, slipped her arm around his neck and stood on tiptoe to kiss him. His arm banded her waist and he held her tightly.

Urgency tore at them as if desire hadn't been surfeited only a short time ago. Eli wanted her with a need that shocked him. He should be satisfied. Just minutes ago he didn't think he could move a muscle. Now desire enveloped him, stronger than ever. He framed her face with his hands. She was beautiful, with rosy skin, a smattering of freckles across her nose and that riotous mass of auburn hair shot through with brighter red strands.

He cupped her full breasts with both hands and stroked her nipples with his thumbs. Her intense responses to his lovemaking set him on fire, and he had never been so turned on by a woman's kisses.

When the water was on, he handed her soap, and they soaped each other slowly. His hands meandered over her while her every gasp heightened his need.

They rinsed, touching and rubbing together as he turned her. His manhood stroked her bare bottom, and his hands played over her breasts. Then he shut off the water and reached for a thick terry towel, drying her leisurely, rubbing the towel lightly between her legs while he watched her. He saw the searing longing in her brown eyes, and then she squeezed her eyes closed, her hands clutching his upper arms while she moaned with pleasure.

"Just a minute," he said, hurrying to get his billfold and get protection. He was back quickly and when he entered the bathroom, she was pulling on a white terry robe furnished by the hotel.

He put on the condom and then embraced her and pushed aside the robe.

As he kissed her, he picked her up. When she wrapped her long legs around him, he spread his feet to brace himself, lowering her body slowly on his swollen rod. He felt her surround him and knew he'd be unable to keep the control he had the first time. Her tongue flicked in his ear, driving him to thrust deeper.

"I want you to come again," he whispered. "I want to love you all night long and make you wild because of the way you respond to me," he added, and she turned her head to kiss him madly.

When he plunged again and again into her softness, she took him to paradise. He shook with satisfaction as he climaxed. She cried out with pleasure at the same time, reaching her own release.

He sagged back against the wall and in minutes let her slide to her feet.

"What you do to me is sinful," he whispered. "Deliciously sinful," he added. He stepped back into the shower, taking her with him, and they showered again, soaping each other.

"Do you think this is wise?" Lara asked. "We might not ever get out of this bathroom if we keep up this routine."

"There's nothing routine about it," he answered in a deep voice. He dropped a kiss on her shoulder before he gently soaped her. In minutes she stepped out to dry and put on her robe again and hurried to the sitting room.

He joined her in his robe, getting fresh glasses and pouring them chilled champagne to replace the almost untouched drinks he had poured earlier. He pulled out a chair, sat down and caught her wrist to draw her down on his lap.

"Now we can study the room service menu and decide what we want to order," he said, picking up a menu. She held one side while he held the other and they decided on steaks. Eli ordered, set down the phone and pushed open her robe.

"The cook said it'll be forty minutes before our dinner will be ready and delivered. I know how to make that time fly," Eli said, cupping her breast and caressing her nipple.

She inhaled, leaned forward as if she were going to kiss him, but then she halted only inches from his face. "You're insatiable."

"I think we both are," he replied. "And I love it." He wound his fingers in her hair and pulled her to him to kiss her while he felt her hands tugging at his robe to open it and explore him with her hands.

Eli thought he was hungry, but when their steak dinners came, after a few bites, all he wanted was to carry her back to bed. And he noticed her appetite was lagging, too. In minutes he gave up on food and stood to pull her into his arms.

It was a night of wild passion, but finally exhaustion was upon them. He pulled her close in his arms, relishing her softness, entangling his legs with hers. He dozed a moment and then stirred, stroking her silky hair that fell over his shoulder. "Lara," he murmured totally relaxed, barely able to put words together. "You've ruined me," he drawled.

"You loved it," she replied, and he chuckled, falling asleep.

Lara settled closer against him, tangling her fingers in his chest hair and smiling. She had loved every minute with him. What would tomorrow be like? She told herself not to expect him to pursue knowing her.

One-night stands weren't her style, yet from the way he had talked, they weren't his, either.

Soon enough she would know, she thought and snuggled close. His arm tightened around her and she twisted to look at him but saw he slept. Contented, she closed her eyes and drifted into dreams about Eli.

Lara awakened, momentarily disoriented as she stared at an unfamiliar ceiling. The bedroom was bathed in morning light.

Then she became aware of a warm body beside her. She turned to look at Eli. His arm was wrapped around her waist and he held her close against him. His leg was over hers. Locks of his brown hair tumbled over his forehead and his chest expanded with each deep breath.

Tantalizing, fantastic memories tumbled in on her. She wanted to lean down and brush a kiss across his mouth. She slipped out of bed and pulled on the white robe. As she did, she knocked Eli's billfold off the table. She bent to retrieve it. It had fallen open, and she realized that she had never learned Eli's full name. Last night passion had been paramount.

She glanced at his picture, looked at his name and froze.

Three

Lara leaned down to make certain she had read the name correctly. *Eli Ashton!* There it was in black-and-white and no doubt about it.

Aghast, she stared as the name *Ashton* leaped up at her.

When she looked back at the man sleeping in the bed, opposing emotions tore at her. He had been fantastic and appealing and sexy.

An Ashton! The last person on earth she would want to go out with, much less know on an intimate basis.

And now it all fell together so easily—why hadn't she seen it? She had been blinded by physical attraction that had overruled all else.

An Ashton! Tall, green eyes—but the world was filled with green-eyed people. She thought of Trace—brown hair, green eyes, but other than those two features, Eli and Trace hardly resembled each other.

Eli Ashton. She didn't know which Ashton family he belonged to—son, nephew, another family. It didn't matter which one of Spencer's offspring it was. Eli was an Ashton and she'd guess he was Spencer's son. He had the Ashton family traits—love of women, expecting to have his way, total confidence in himself.

Who was he? She knew Spencer had another wife before Lilah and he'd had children by her. A few months ago the news had broken that there had been a wife even before *that*, a first marriage to a woman in Nebraska that made the second marriage illegitimate. Which family did Eli belong to? The Nebraska Ashtons or the Ashtons who owned Louret Vineyards? Then she remembered that he was a winemaker.

Eli Ashton was from Louret Vineyards! Lara wanted to gnash her teeth, but she reassured herself that she wouldn't see him ever again. The two California Ashton families had nothing to do with each other.

Or they never had until recently. Her mother told her that two of Spencer's daughters from his earlier marriage had come to Ashton Estate to talk to Megan, Paige and Charlotte Ashton to make overtures of peace between the two families. Spencer's wife, Lilah, had thrown them out, so that probably had made the rift between the families even bigger.

Lara looked at him again, remembering the night and the passion, the intimacy between them. She was torn with conflicting emotions, hating that she had involved herself with an Ashton, yet at the same time unable to view the past hours with regret.

Panic gripped her. She had to get out of the hotel and away from him before he awakened.

Hastily, she gathered her things and rushed to the bathroom to dress. She fumbled with her clothes, yanking them on. How could she have gone off with a stranger the way she had? What had gotten into her to toss aside all common sense?

And the night of lust! She had been wanton and abandoned with a man who was a total stranger. She had never had a one-night stand with a man, much less one whose full name she didn't know.

Why had she thought it would be all right because she met him at the reception at the estate? It was only reasonable to expect the place to be crawling with Ashtons.

She held her breath and opened the door.

He was lying on his side, his arm thrown across the bed, and he didn't look as if he had moved since she had slipped out of his embrace. For one minute she was caught and held, her gaze roaming down the length of him while she remembered what it felt like to be in his arms. He was handsome in a rugged manner, far too appealing. Longing tugged at her, and she shook her head, shoving aside any yearning she might feel.

With her heart pounding, she crossed the suite and let herself out as quietly as possible.

She all but ran to the lobby to ask a bellman to get her a taxi. Within minutes she climbed into a cab and gave the driver directions. As the cab pulled away from the curb, she looked back at the hotel. Eli was in there asleep. She slammed shut that train of thought and turned her back on the hotel. She needed to put last night out of her mind. But she knew she would never forget Eli Ashton.

She would ask one of her friends, another of the housekeeping staff from Ashton Estate, to come pick her up. She didn't want to leave a trail behind that Eli could easily follow. If he even wanted to follow it. Once he knew her ties to his father's other family, he would lose all interest, she was certain. The Louret

Vineyard head winemaker would not pursue a maid from the Ashton Estate for more than one reason.

On the other hand, why wouldn't he want to see her? She had let him seduce her without the slightest protest. Far from it— she had been as eager and willing as he.

Why had she ever gotten involved with a man whose identity she didn't know?

If Eli searched for her—and she doubted he would—he couldn't find her without knowing her last name.

She had thought he was mourning Spencer's death. If he was a son Spencer had sired and abandoned, then his grim countenance had not been from sorrow but from fury. Lara realized that Eli had been hurting when he snapped at her on the veranda. She inhaled, trying to squelch the sympathy that stirred in her.

She sat back in the cab and closed her eyes. Eli Ashton. The appalling discovery of his identity still rocked her. She was shocked at her own behavior, astounded to learn who he was. The knowledge kept running through her mind over and over. And the knowledge that he may have been hurting badly yesterday nagged at her. Beneath all that rough exterior was a good man.

The cab dropped her in front of another hotel as she'd directed. She went inside and used the phone to call her closest friend, Franci Stanopolis, and asked her to come get her.

Once in Franci's ancient yellow car, Lara stared gloomily out the window while Franci's dark-brown eyes sparkled with curiosity.

"Well," Franci said, "are you going to tell me anything?"

"Yes, but you have to keep this one to yourself," Lara said and proceeded to tell brief highlights of how she had left the estate to go and have a drink with Eli.

"What's he look like? I'll bet he's handsome," Franci said eagerly.

"He's handsome and he took me to a restaurant in Napa and we talked. The time flew past. Franci, it was just an intense attraction—that's all I can say to explain it."

"Love at first sight."

"Hardly," Lara remarked dryly. "More like lust at first sight. He's handsome, wealthy, sexy."

"You're like Cinderella, except you don't have a glass slipper. Why do you look so glum? Did he walk out on you this morning?"

"I walked out on him."

Franci screeched, shooting a quick glance at her friend. "Why on earth would you do something like that? He sounds like Prince Charming!"

"Hardly. Franci, it sounds terrible now, but we didn't bother with last names. They just didn't come up. We talked about everything else under the sun."

"Ah, you hit it off in more ways than just physical. And I'll bet he's a great person."

"This morning I saw his open billfold. He's Eli Ashton."

"No! Which one of the other Ashtons is that? Spencer is beginning to turn up a harem of wives and children."

"Spencer liked women. So does Eli."

"You don't know that. All you know is that he liked one woman, a pretty redhead I know."

"He likes women. Believe me," Lara insisted.

"Which Ashton is he?"

"He's from Louret Vineyards. He said he is a winemaker so that rules out the Nebraska family that Spencer abandoned."

Franci glanced at her friend. "Why on earth did you walk out on him?"

"I can't believe you're asking that question. This is Spencer Ashton's son—you know how I loathed Spencer and his groping hands. Spencer made my life hell—yours, too, except he couldn't hold it over you that he would fire your mother if you didn't let him paw you," Lara said bitterly.

"That doesn't mean you hate his son or that his son is like him." Franci's black curls bobbed as she shook her head.

"To quote an old saying, 'The apple never falls far from the tree.'" She shivered. "I detested Spencer!"

"Don't let the police hear you say that one!" Franci exclaimed. "I still say you can't hold what Spencer did against his son. A son he didn't even raise. Trace isn't like that."

"No, he's not. Anyway, I'm out of Eli's league and, if he had learned I was an Ashton Estate domestic, he would have walked out on me."

"Only if he's a snob. Did you think he was a snob? And be honest."

"I don't care. For plenty of reasons the head winemaker of Louret Vineyards will not want to pursue getting to know a maid at the Ashton Estate. And you know how Lilah Ashton feels about that other family. She despises them and threw out those women from that family when they came on a peace mission recently. I just hope Lilah doesn't learn about this, because I wouldn't do anything to jeopardize Mom's job as head housekeeper."

"Lilah isn't going to fire your mother because you went out with one of those other Ashtons."

"You don't know that. Spencer threatened to fire people—and did—all the time."

"Lilah isn't Spencer. She might get in a huff, but she won't fire your mom for something you did. Besides, your mom is excellent at her job. Lilah isn't going to get rid of someone who does such a super job. Your mom or you."

"I hope you're right," Lara said.

"Tell me more about him. Is he a sexy kisser?"

"Franci! That's off-limits."

"I'm not asking intimate details, just is he a sexy kisser. On a scale of one to ten, where does he rate?"

"About one hundred," Lara answered dryly.

"Oh, my. Maybe you should rethink not seeing him again."

"Franci, he won't want to see me, a lowly maid. And I'll be back in law school again in the fall. Besides, I don't want to get involved with Spencer Ashton's son. And I've told you before, until I'm out of school, I definitely don't want a man complicating my life."

"Was Eli Ashton at all like Spencer last night?"

"Yes. He gets his way. He's very determined."

"That's not bad as long as he doesn't hurt anyone. Has he hurt people the way Spencer did?"

"I'm sure he hasn't," Lara admitted with a sigh. "When he mentioned his family, his voice was warm and his remarks were complimentary. Eli may not be like his father, but it doesn't matter. Our lives are not in the same world."

"You just like being in control. Maybe when you meet a man who also likes to be in control, it's dynamite."

Lara took a deep breath and stared out the car window. It had been dynamite, all right.

When she was finally home again, she hurried upstairs to her room. Each step she took, climbing to the second floor and then going higher to the third floor and the servants' quarters, took her farther from Eli's world of luxury.

She stepped into her small, yellow and white bedroom, closing the door and flinging down her purse. She went across the room, pulling off her black dress and balling it up, tossing it on the floor of the closet. In the bathroom she yanked off her plain cotton panties that should have given Eli a clue to her status. She tried to forget their loving yet she was unable to banish images of Eli—virile, naked, his hands creating ecstasy.

But despite what they had shared together, Eli was an Ashton and the Ashtons were not to be trifled with. In fairness, she had to admit that Trace, Megan and Paige were fine, likable people. Blood ties to Spencer hadn't turned them into monsters. It was Spencer who was the monster. Eli probably viewed Spencer as a monster, too.

But good or bad, Eli represented wealth and privilege and a world that she was not privy to.

She sighed and shook her head. "I simply refuse to think about you, Eli Ashton," she declared loudly in the shower.

She dressed in her black maid's uniform to begin her duties at the estate. As she wound her hair behind her head, she wondered what Eli would think if he could see her now.

Eli stirred and stretched and rolled over, running his arm over the cool sheets. He opened his eyes and then sat up to gaze around.

"Lara?" he called. When she didn't answer, the first inkling that something was amiss struck him and he swung his feet out of bed and stood.

Four

"Lara!" he called again, and still there was only silence.

"Dammit," he grumbled, going to the bathroom to grab a towel to wrap around his waist. He walked through the suite and then called the front desk, but a new clerk had come on, and no one knew anything about Lara.

Eli raked his fingers through his hair and searched the suite more carefully. With every passing minute his aggravation increased.

Lara had left without a trace. No note, no phone number—nothing. Lara who? He realized that he didn't know her last name. He hadn't particularly wanted to give his yesterday, but he should have gotten her full name.

He was disappointed, hurt and annoyed at himself. Today he had expected to exchange phone numbers, learn where she lived and tell her where he lived. He had expected to wake up and make love to her again. He would have had room service deliver breakfast and maybe he could have talked her into staying with him through the morning.

For a few minutes he was lost in remembering their moments of lovemaking and her wild responses to him. He became hot and aroused just thinking about her lush body and how her hands had played over him.

In frustration he raked his fingers through his thick hair again and swore quietly. Anger churned in him and made him want to forget her and go on home, but he couldn't. He wanted to see her.

Why had she just walked out on him? They had fallen asleep in each other's arms, and she had seemed warm and caring—not the type to just vanish without a word.

She was an acquaintance of Spencer's other family—she'd been at his funeral reception. But he couldn't expect any information about her from them. They wouldn't give him the time of day. Lara. That's all he knew about her name. But it wasn't all he knew about her. They'd had a firestorm of lovemaking last night.

From the very first few words they had exchanged, she had intrigued and attracted him. Everywhere he looked in the suite, he could see her in his imagination. He remembered everything about her, her kisses, how her hair sprang back into curls when he combed his fingers through it, her flirtatious brown eyes. Her fantastic long legs. Her kisses that set him on fire with a mere memory.

He swore softly. It wasn't going to help him any to stand around in the empty hotel suite and think about the night. He called room service, ordered breakfast and then headed for the bathroom to shower.

He drank a glass of orange juice, but his appetite had fled. Getting dressed in his rumpled shirt and trousers, he went to the lobby to check out. He made inquiries and tipped people and found a valet who had helped her into a cab.

No danger of anyone not noticing her or forgetting her, he knew. She was a beautiful woman, and it was easy to find someone who remembered her.

Eli checked out, got in his car and headed north. He called the vineyard and talked briefly to his brother Cole and said he was on his way home. All the time he talked, as he drove through Napa, he found himself looking for Lara, watching other cars, looking at people walking past on the street.

One minute he swore he would find her. Then the next minute he told himself to forget her. But forgetting her was impossible; he wanted to be with her right now.

He picked up his cell phone, called information for the number of the cab company and then tried to locate the driver who had driven her away from the hotel.

A dispatcher said he would find the driver and get back to Eli. After thanking the man, Eli broke the connection and tossed the phone on the car seat beside him in disgust. Let her go, he told himself. It was another disappointment like so many he'd had before.

His thoughts jumped to Spencer. Soon there would be a reading of the will. Would Spencer finally right some of the wrongs he had committed in his life?

Eli wondered if the police would ever catch the person who had murdered Spencer. If there were any clues, the police were keeping quiet about them. They had talked to him the day after the murder, but that didn't surprise Eli. It was well-known that he had no kind feelings for Spencer. But he and Spencer also hadn't crossed paths often, except for wine events—times when Louret labels had been given higher acclaim than wines from the Ashton vineyards.

How Eli had enjoyed every triumph that Louret wines had had over Ashton Estate wines. He guessed each award had infuriated Spencer. He hoped they had.

While Louret couldn't produce the quantity of Ashton Estate vineyards, Louret always topped Ashton in quality. Their boutique winery was small but superior, and Eli was proud of his part in the achievement of excellence, and he was proud of his mother for all she had done.

As he left town he thought about how his whole family had pulled together through the years and what a fine job they had done. His brother, Cole, was indispensable and his baby sister, Jillian, was becoming an expert. It amazed him how capable she had become and she was still learning. Of course, they were butting heads over some of her ideas. Little, stubborn "Shrimp" wouldn't give up on her vision for a *meritage*—softening the Cabernet Sauvignon with other varieties. Maybe he should listen to her.

His sister Mercedes surprised and pleased him, too, with her marketing skills. Mason, the youngest, was studying in France, and his knowledge should help them develop more superior wines. Together they were all building a premier boutique winery that rivaled some of the elite wineries of Europe.

As Eli sped north along the highway, unbidden, memories crowded out all thoughts of Louret wines. He could remember Lara's perfume, her laughter, her kisses. Why had she slipped away without letting him know?

He wasn't accustomed to being brushed off by women, much less one he had become intimate with. He knew nothing about her or where to start looking.

To hell with searching for her, he thought. If she wanted out of his life, fine. He could forget her. The world was filled with beautiful women. He'd get back to Louret and throw himself into work and forget her, he told himself. Yet even as he promised himself to stop thinking about her, he could envision her brown eyes and her smile.

He tried to remember his schedule for today. Yesterday he had cleared everything off his calendar because of the funeral.

He remembered that he was going to check on their oldest small oak barrels to see what needed to be replaced. Also, they were getting new white-oak barrels, which he preferred for maturing Syrah. Those were the best barrels to create a slow oxidation of the wine to give it the finest complexity of aroma.

He sped north through Napa up Highway 29 until he reached The Vines, the family estate. He turned onto the winding road and when the French country–style house came into view, he thought how much more charming it was, though not as large and elegant as the Ashton Estate mansion.

Sunshine splashed over the dark-gray slate roofs and bathed the gray and white rustic stone in warm light. Dark-green shutters flanked the downstairs mullioned windows. Bright green vines winding on trellises gave the home an old-world charm. Usually the sight of the house showered a glow of satisfaction on him, but today he couldn't shake his disappointment and annoyance over Lara's disappearance.

He strode inside through the pale-blue foyer, his heels scraping the bare wood floors.

His mother, Caroline, was just heading into the family room. Dressed in pale-yellow linen slacks and a matching blouse, she looked stylish and regal, and Eli crossed the hall to brush a kiss on her cheek.

Caroline held eighteen-month-old Jack Sheridan in her arms. Eli tried to banish thoughts of Spencer when he looked at Spencer's illegitimate offspring. Little Jack had been as tossed aside by Spencer as Eli and his family had.

The chubby-cheeked baby was cute and the whole family loved him. Jack held out a small stuffed bear to Eli. "Baya," he said.

"I see the bear," Eli answered, ruffling Jack's red hair. "He's a cutie," he said to Caroline. "Where's Anna?"

"I told her I'd watch Jack for a while and give her a little break. He's adorable, Eli. And he has a new word—he can say *light* now."

"Anna's an angel for taking in her nephew to raise. And you're an angel for giving them a home and security."

"You would have done the same thing. Imagine! Her sister dying and leaving a baby all alone. And now the press is hounding Anna, and she's getting threatening phone calls—Anna just needed shelter from the storm." Caroline looked at the little boy in her arms. "Anna's a strong woman—she'll get along and Jack is just precious. They can stay forever as far as I'm concerned."

"You'll get so attached to Jack, he'll be like one of your own. Watch out you don't get a broken heart. Someday Anna will leave."

"I know, but hopefully, she'll let us all continue to be part of their lives." Caroline eyed Eli and her eyebrows arched. "You look like you fell out of the car, Eli. I hate to say I told you so, but I knew going to the funeral reception would be rough."

"I'm all right, Mom," he said. "Seeing all of them just made me all the more proud of you and Dad and our family. We've done all right."

"That we have, thanks in large part to you."

He shook his head. "Dad taught us well," Eli said, referring to Lucas Shepherd, his stepfather. "We're all a competent team."

She smiled up at him. "You so rarely take a day off, then to spend it at *Spencer's* funeral…" Her voice faded away and she shook her head. "I don't want to see the house again."

"I like ours better," he said, walking away from her. "It's cozier. Mom, I still want you to give some thought to letting our attorney see if Ashton Estate is yours now. Spencer wasn't legally married to you, because he never divorced his first wife in Nebraska, so to my way of thinking, he couldn't inherit from Granddad."

"We've been over that, Eli. I don't want the bitter fight we'd have on our hands if we pursued it. It would only lead to unhappiness. You've got a satisfying life. You don't need that battle."

"Sorry to worry you. I just want you to think about it and talk to Dad about it."

"Lucas feels the same as I do, but I'll think about it a little more. You take care of yourself, Eli," she said, an uncustomary caution before she turned and disappeared into the family room while he wondered why she had said that to him. He could hear her talking to Jack and Jack babbling in return. Eli shook his head. That baby would have all their hearts before long.

Forgetting about Jack, Eli took the stairs two at a time to his suite, striding through the wide hall with a glance at the family photos adorning the walls, thankful that his mother had The Vines. At the back of the house he had his own suite, including a living room and kitchenette. He walked through the living room with its blue and green decor. The large oil painting over his mantel was an accurate picture of the Louret vineyards in summer.

He tossed his coat on a chair in his bedroom, where the colors were an extension of those in his living room. He got out a fresh shirt and trousers, pulling on a pale-gray sport shirt and

gray cotton slacks. He combed his hair and tried to keep from
thinking about Lara, hoping to immerse himself in work.

The cab company called him back a few moments later. They
had found the driver who had picked up Lara. The man would
return to the office in an hour. Eli thanked the dispatcher and replaced the receiver.

Stepping outside, he left for the office. Beneath peaked roofs,
the two-story winery had offices on the upper floor, the tasting
room on the ground floor. The warm, sunny June day should
have lifted his spirits, but he knew he was in a dark mood and
that he needed to snap out of it.

Eli glanced at the vineyards and saw his half brother Grant
looking at the vines and talking to Henry Lydell, Louret's new
foreman who had replaced Russ Gannon. Russ had fallen in love
and married Grant's niece Abigail from Nebraska a few months
ago. Eli liked Grant and experienced a connection with the Nebraska farmer. They both were men of the earth, Grant the farmer
and Eli the winemaker. It was a bond that was forged almost the
first day Grant was at their house.

Eli thought about the shock of Grant's revelation that Spencer had had a wife in Nebraska he had never divorced and Grant
and his sister were children of that marriage. Eli wondered who
had received the greatest shock—Grant at forty-three to discover
his father was still alive and had walked out on them, or all the
other Ashtons to learn of another marriage of Spencer's. When
he had been turned away by Lilah and Spencer, Caroline had invited Grant to stay at Louret.

The news had been a bomb when the press got hold of it. The
tabloids had carried bold, lurid headlines, especially after it was
revealed that Spencer had never divorced his first wife.

Eli entered the winery. For the next two hours he worked,

checking on the barrels, talking to Cole, walking blocks of the vineyards to look at the grapes and checking on the thinning of the canopy of green leaves so that the right amount of sunlight reached the clusters of grapes.

Shortly after three o'clock, Eli stopped work and left. Telling himself he was every kind of a fool, he got in his car and sped back to the cab company in Napa. It took only a few minutes to talk to the driver who had picked up Lara. He had deposited her at the Regency and the last he had seen of her, she had started into the hotel. Thanking the driver, Eli pulled out his wallet and gave the man payment for his information. At the Regency Eli ran into a dead end with no trace of her.

Eli drove home in a darker mood than before. She had gone to a hotel. Was she an Ashton relative who had flown in for the funeral and had stayed at a hotel in the city? A friend of the family? A call girl? The last he didn't want to consider, yet she was beautiful enough, kept things impersonal, and no telling who Spencer had known or been involved with.

Eli hit the steering wheel with the palm of his hand and swore, annoyed with himself for pursuing the matter. He clamped his jaw closed, and got his mind back on the vineyard.

It was early summer and the vines were doing well. Louret grew Pinot Noir, Merlot, Cabernet Sauvignon and Petite Verdot grapes. Their Caroline Chardonnay was gaining great reviews. At this stage of the summer, they had had inflorescence. The new shoots had blossomed and were about to transform into tiny green grapes that would ripen during lazy summer days until the fall harvest.

He could remember Lara sipping the glass of Caroline Chardonnay that he had ordered. He shook his head. "Get out of my thoughts," he said quietly.

* * *

Back at his office, Eli found a note lying on the desk. He picked it up to see that he'd had four calls: three from businessmen he knew and they involved the winery or the vineyard. The fourth was from a stranger: Stephen Cassidy, Attorney at Law.

Eli dialed the number and got voice mail. When he called the cell number, a man answered, identifying himself as Stephen Cassidy.

"Mr. Cassidy, I'm Eli Ashton and I'm returning your call," Eli said.

He listened to the deep voice. "Mr. Ashton, I was Spencer Ashton's attorney. He had his affairs in order, and we can get right to the reading of Spencer's will. I have to notify everyone mentioned in the will, and when I talked with your mother she said I should call you."

"That's fine," Eli replied. "I'll represent my family."

"Excellent. I've set a date for the reading next Monday morning, the thirteenth of June. For the family's benefit, we've made arrangements to meet at the Ashton Estate at ten o'clock. Will you be able to attend?"

"I'll be there," Eli promised and listened as the attorney told him goodbye. Eli replaced the receiver, wondering again if Spencer had made amends in his will.

Eli went to the vineyards to do some pruning and check for powdery or downy mildew. He snapped off suckers and inspected the tiny clusters of grapes that were forming. Even as he worked with the vines, his mind wandered back to Lara.

The rest of the week he failed to get her out of his mind. He made no effort to find her, but his family noticed his brooding. All of them chalked it up to tension over the reading of Spencer's will.

Monday finally came, and Eli dressed in a navy suit with a red tie. Driving up to the Ashton Estate for the second time in his life, he tried to keep out memories of meeting Lara at the funeral reception.

He rang the chimes, and a maid swung open the door to usher him through a large elegant foyer. They climbed four steps to a secondary foyer, and she motioned to an open door on the left.

"In the library, sir," she said politely, and was gone.

He entered the library, where people had already gathered. Folding chairs had been set up facing a massive desk. Eli noticed the sharp looks he received from the other Ashtons, none of whom came forward to greet him. He took a seat at the end of the row, leaving half a row of empty seats between him and Lilah Ashton.

Eli glanced around the library while bitterness welled up in him. The library was Spencer's domain. On the desk in a gold frame was a picture, turned slightly, and Eli could see the Ashton family, including Spencer. An oil portrait of Spencer hung on one wall. Bookshelves lined other walls, and even though it was a different library, the room brought back sharp memories of Eli's childhood and that stormy night when he had overheard Spencer tell Caroline he was leaving her and the children.

The tall attorney with his salt-and-pepper hair looked natty in a gray suit. He walked up to Eli and extended his hand. "I'm Stephen Cassidy," he announced.

"Eli Ashton," Eli said, standing and shaking the man's hand.

"Will others from your family be here?"

"No, I'm representing them."

"Fine." Stephen Cassidy turned as another man joined them. "Mr. Ashton, this is my assistant, Ty Koenig."

Eli shook hands with a stocky, black-haired man who smiled and gazed at him through thick glasses.

"We're all here and we'll start in just a few," Ty Koenig said. "Just have a seat."

"Thanks," Eli said, and sat as the two men walked away. Harsh looks were directed Eli's way, and he clamped his jaw closed while his anger mounted. Once again, viewing the house, the knowledge that Spencer had stolen all of this from his mother was a knife in Eli's heart. Eli hated being here as much as he hated the other Ashtons, but the attorney had called him, so he and his family were in Spencer's will. He remembered the argument he'd had with Cole when he told him about the call the next morning. Cole had stopped in Eli's office to give him a note from Mrs. McKillup, their bookkeeper.

Cole's green eyes had blazed with anger and he'd lowered the clipboard he held in his hands. Trotting after Cole was his dog, Tillie, a greyhound-Dalmatian mix. At the sight of Eli, Tillie wagged her tail and flopped down on the floor beside Cole.

"You're crazy to go," Cole snapped. "The attorney will have to give us a copy of the will whether or not we attend. It isn't like a contest where you have to be present to win."

"I'm going. I can represent the family, since no one else wants to set foot on the place."

"Damn straight, no one wants to," Cole said. "They don't want us there, either. I don't want to look at the Ashton Estate and think about what Spencer did to Mom. You'll regret going."

"Maybe I will, but I still intend to be there. Trace and Walker Ashton can't scare me away."

"They don't scare me. I just think I might take a swing at them. And if I might, you're going to."

"I'll control my temper."

"Yeah, right."

"I will. But I might not this morning if you keep it up," Eli grumbled, and Cole grinned, turning to hurry away. After he had widened the distance between them, at the door of Eli's office, he looked over his shoulder. "You can take Tillie for protection."

"Dixie's cat, Hulk, maybe, but never your wimp of a dog," Eli said, referring to Cole's wife's unusually brave pet. Cole's grin widened.

Now he was here at Ashton Estate and, so far, controlling himself just fine, but he'd be glad when this morning was over and done.

Seated in a cluster along the row of chairs were the other Ashtons. Eli glanced at Lilah Ashton and her children. Eli had occasionally seen Lilah Ashton. He had to admit that she was an attractive woman, one whose looks, he was certain, had been enhanced by Spencer's money. Black became her. Her chic, chin-length red hair was set off by her black dress. Next to her, in a flawless brown suit, sat Eli's cousin—Spencer's tall, black-haired nephew, Walker Ashton—who had been raised like Spencer's own son and now was the executive vice president of Ashton-Lattimer Corporation. The chair to Lilah Ashton's left was empty, but Trace Ashton stood a few feet away talking to his younger sister, Paige Ashton. Dressed in a gray suit, Trace was tall and lean and looked physically fit. His sister was shorter. Eli knew Paige Ashton was the event planner for the Ashton Estate. Her smiling picture had been on brochures and in wine magazines.

Beside Walker Ashton was his sister, Charlotte, Spencer's niece. Like her brother, her Native American heritage showed in her straight black hair. Eli wondered about Charlotte and Walker. Word was, that after all these years since Spencer had taken them in to raise after his brother's death, he had told them that their mother had also died. Now, according to rumors, Spencer's duplicity had been revealed when Charlotte had heard that their mother was alive. If that turned out to be the truth, Eli thought, it would be just one more evil perpetrated by Spencer. One more scandal to rock the family and feed the tabloids.

Taking a seat to the right of Charlotte was Megan Ashton, now married. Beside her was her new husband, Simon Pearce.

While Eli waited, he watched Stephen Cassidy take the empty seat beside Lilah Ashton, talking to her and patting her shoulder. For another five minutes the attorney conversed with her, this time putting his arm around her shoulders. Eli noticed the lawyer seemed unduly interested in her. Was more scandal going to rock the Ashtons? Eli wondered idly. Or was the attorney simply being attentive to the grieving widow?

Finally clearing his throat, Cassidy began the reading. He talked briefly about the gathering for the reading of Spencer's will and then he began: "I, Spencer Winston Ashton, being of sound mind…"

Eli listened, looking at the people nearby. He had cousins and half brothers and half sisters present, yet they didn't speak and they were almost total strangers. The world of wine was the only common ground that brought them into contact occasionally, but even there they gave each other a wide berth.

Jerking his attention back to the will, Eli listened attentively as Stephen Cassidy read: "I hereby bequeath my shares of Ashton-Lattimer stock to Walker Ashton."

Hot anger exploded in Eli, and he clenched his fists while he fought to keep his expression impassive and to sit still. Spencer left Walker, a nephew, his shares of Ashton-Lattimer Corporation, Eli's grandfather's company. Spencer was a bastard. Eli wondered why he had expected anything decent from Spencer. With an effort, Eli pulled his concentration back to Stephen Cassidy as he continued to read:

"To Charlotte Ashton, I bequeath the sum of twenty thousand dollars."

Eli glanced at her. She stared straight ahead and not a flicker of emotion showed in her expression, but she had to be disappointed or angry or hurt. Twenty thousand from Spencer was a paltry sum when all of his wealth and vast estate were taken into consideration. Compared to the stock shares that her brother received, the money was nothing.

Eli suspected that Spencer hadn't righted any wrongs he had done in the past, and Eli knew that would include his own family. Yet Cassidy had called him to hear the will, so there had to be some mention of Caroline and her family.

"To my beloved wife, Lilah Ashton and our three children, Trace, Paige and Megan Ashton, I leave my property which includes the Ashton Estate house and vineyards, the winery, all monies in my accounts, any savings and stocks aside from Ashton-Lattimer Corporation shares of stock. This property and holdings are to be divided equally in order that my family will share—"

Eli listened to the words, each bequest another punch to his gut. Caroline and her family had been cut out of the will just as Spencer had cut his family out of his life. Grant and little Jack hadn't been acknowledged, either. Nor had Spencer's two Nebraska grandchildren, Ford and Abigail, who had been taken in to be raised by Grant Ashton. Eli clenched his jaw, resolving to push his family to contest the will and to try to get back the Ashton holdings for his mother. Spencer hadn't deserved all that he'd ruthlessly taken. It would mean another Ashton scandal but one that Eli welcomed.

"To Caroline Ashton and each of her children—Eli Ashton, Cole Ashton, Mercedes Ashton and Jillian Ashton, I hereby bequeath the sum of one dollar each."

Eli's ears buzzed and his pulse drummed with fury. Cole had warned him that he was foolish to even go to the reading of the will, yet Caroline agreed with Eli that someone should represent the family. Cole had been right.

Hot and angry, Eli didn't hear the rest of the will. The walls of the room seemed to close in. He couldn't wait to get out and leave the estate and the Ashtons that Spencer had claimed as his family.

Finally Stephen Cassidy was finished and immediately back at Lilah Ashton's side. Eli started toward the door and almost collided with Walker Ashton.

"Did you actually expect him to bequeath anything to you?" Walker asked, blocking Eli's way. The animosity flowing between them was tangible. Eli fought to control his temper and his fists.

"Now you own the shares of my grandfather's business," Eli said bitterly, jamming his fists into his trouser pockets.

"They were my uncle's shares of stock," Walker snapped back, his brown eyes flashing with anger. "And he's left the shares to me. He wanted me to have them. If I recall the circumstances, your grandfather willed the Ashton-Lattimer shares to Spencer."

"He trusted Spencer and didn't realize what a deceitful snake the man was."

"Spencer was no snake," Walker snarled, visibly bristling as his face flushed. "You saw the hundreds of friends gathered for his funeral. Your grandfather left everything to Spencer because he wanted Spencer to have it all. Not your mother but Spencer," Walker reminded him.

Eli turned to stride away, knowing if he didn't get distance between them, he would resort to blows. He took two steps and faced Trace Ashton who had been talking to one of his sisters. Trace's green eyes were cold and his jaw set as he faced Eli.

"You need to get off this property," Trace said. "You weren't welcome here when Spencer was alive, and that hasn't changed now that he's gone. If he were here, he'd throw you off himself because your presence upsets my mother."

Eli clenched his fists again. "It's your property, but you know Spencer stole it from my mother. At one time this was all my grandfather's."

"My father didn't steal anything. It was given to him by your grandfather. Go back to your little vineyard."

"It's a damn fine vineyard whether it's small or not. We beat your wines in any competition."

"Get the hell out of here, Eli, before I throw you out."

"Don't worry. I was on my way. I can't get away from here fast enough." Eli ground out the words and brushed past Trace. Burning with rage, he fought the urge to take a swing at the younger Ashton.

Taking his hands from his pockets, Eli strode through the door, leaving the library and heading for the front entrance. At the top of the four steps into the lower foyer, he glanced back over his shoulder, half expecting Trace Ashton to follow him to see if he was leaving and half hoping Trace would. Eli would like to vent his pent-up anger and take a swing at Trace, but he wasn't going to be the one to throw the first punch.

When he looked back over his shoulder, he was immobilized. Was it his imagination playing tricks on him, or had he just seen Lara disappearing through an open door off the foyer?

Eli turned and strode back. The woman had been in a maid's uniform. Then he remembered the first time she had spoken to him on the veranda at the funeral reception. She had asked if she could get anything for him. He should have guessed, except she hadn't been in a maid's uniform then.

His pulse sped up as he stopped in the open door of a formal dining room. He barely saw the long, polished table and side chairs, the sparkling crystal chandelier, the breakfront with priceless antiques. The only thing he really saw was Lara.

She stood across the room from him, setting a silver tea service on a credenza. She wore a black uniform with a white apron tied around her waist. Her thick hair was fastened in a bun behind her head. Even with the plain uniform, hairdo and black oxfords, she made his pulse race and stirred erotic images.

He stepped inside the dining room and closed the door.

Five

When Lara heard the door close, she turned around. Her heart missed a beat as she met Eli Ashton's stormy gaze. "What are you doing here?"

"Finding you," he said. His eyes glinted with fire when he crossed the room, stalking her like a panther. "Although you made it clear you didn't want to see me again."

Trying to ignore her racing pulse, she raised her chin. He was as handsome and appealing as she had remembered. "I mean, why are you at this house?" she asked.

"They had the reading of the will," he said, his voice fierce with rage.

"Oh, of course!" she exclaimed, feeling ridiculous. Yet she had never thought about Eli being included in Spencer's will. While Eli closed the distance between them, her mouth went dry and heat coiled in her, memories of his lovemaking assailing her.

Even angry, he still set her heart pounding. A few more feet closer, and he would hear it for himself.

When he stopped inches away, she could detect his familiar aftershave. In a navy suit, he was devastating, and it was impossible to keep her gaze from skimming over his features.

"You ran out on me."

"I found out you were an Ashton," she snapped back. "That's enough reason to run." She hated her intense reaction to seeing him again, but she couldn't control herself. "You're Spencer's son."

"Don't ever lump me with him! I'm not anything like that bastard," Eli retorted, a muscle working in his jaw, and she realized he was furious with Lilah's family.

"You're his son. You look like him. You act—"

"Don't say it," he ordered. His hand closed on her shoulder, and the glacial chill in his eyes stopped her. "I'm not like him. I hope to heaven I don't look like him."

"It's your green eyes. Those green eyes are a dominant trait," she said. "All the Ashtons have green eyes. It doesn't matter. I'm glad he's gone. I don't want any part of the Ashtons," she said, momentarily remembering Spencer and his roaming hands.

"It looks like to me you already have a large part of this family daily since you work here and you live here. It's a free world. There are a lot of other jobs, but you chose this one."

"I grew up here because my mother is the head housekeeper. I've stayed because of her."

"I looked for you," Eli said, pushing open his coat and jamming his hand on his hip. His stance was almost intimidating, except he was too magnetic. She had no intention of allowing him to get emotionally close to her again. "I never would have thought to look here. You know I'm Eli Ashton. I want to know who you are. What's your last name?"

"Hunter," she replied, fighting to avoid letting her gaze drift down over him.

"Well, Lara Hunter, I plan to get to know you a whole lot better."

"Why would you want to? We're like fire and ice. One will destroy the other."

"A better comparison would be fire and dynamite," he said, lowering his voice to a cajoling tone. A muscle still worked in his jaw, and his color was heightened, but his voice had changed and the wrath had gone from the depths of his eyes. "The chemistry we had was spectacular," he added.

"You're talking about sex."

"Damn straight. Making love with you was fantastic."

"And so you want a repeat of that night? No, thanks," she replied in what she hoped was a haughty tone that would bring him down a notch. "And I've told you why. Besides, it's impossible for me to go anywhere with you," she said, raising her chin.

"Of course it's possible," he said, moving closer and studying her intently. "That night, there wasn't all this antagonism between us."

"That's because I didn't dream I was with an Ashton."

"Look, I'm not like Spencer," he repeated tightly with a tone of steel returning to his voice. "Lucas Sheppard is the man who raised me and the man I claim as my father. My whole family is not like this bunch of Ashtons."

"I find that difficult to believe," she said, her fury surging over his resolve to get her to do what he wanted. "You have Spencer's blood in your veins, and you're as strong willed as he was. This conversation is proof."

"You're strong willed yourself, but that doesn't mean you take after Spencer," he shot back at her. He reached out, smoothing her already flat collar. Tingles diffused from his warm fingers brushing against her collarbone and throat. Still torn between fury and attraction, she tried to ignore the reaction she was having to him.

"Spencer remembered you in his will," she remarked. "You wouldn't be here otherwise," she said, to steer the conversation away from her.

He dropped his hands to his sides and clenched his fists, clamping his jaw closed and gazing beyond her. "He gave me the same he gave my mother and my siblings—exactly one dollar to each of us."

"A dollar!" she exclaimed, momentarily forgetting her ire and seeing why Eli was so incensed. She realized that along with his anger, he had to be hurting.

"I want to see you again because I know what you were like before you connected me with Spencer. Go to dinner with me tonight."

She thought of Spencer's groping hands and his open threats to fire her mother if Lara rejected his advances. Loathing curled in her at the mere thought of Spencer, and as long as she thought about the father, she knew she would be able to deal with his son.

"I'm not getting to know you or any other Ashton better. And even if I wanted to go out with you—which I don't—I can't because of my job."

"Why on earth not?" he asked. "This family doesn't own your soul."

"What I do can jeopardize my mother's job as well as mine."

"That's a joke! Because of Spencer's infamous transgressions, Lilah Ashton's family is steeped in scandal and ours hasn't gone untouched, either. We thought we were Spencer's first family, but we aren't. There was a wife in Nebraska whom he didn't divorce, so he committed bigamy with my mother. How the media gloried in that scandal! Spencer's affairs were common knowledge. Now it's come out that he had an illegitimate child. In the next few days, maybe even tonight, the media will make public the will and that my family once again was snubbed by Spencer. Spencer's been murdered and they don't know who did it. The list goes on and on. Who knows what new scandal will break tomorrow! This family can't fault you for dating one of the outcast Ashtons," he said, and she realized his bitterness and hurt ran deep. She knew Eli had to have been just a little boy when Spencer walked out on him and his family. It had to have left permanent scars.

A straight lock of brown hair fell on his forehead, and Lara fought the temptation to push it back in place. Her reaction to him heightened her annoyance.

"I can't believe they would fire their head housekeeper because her daughter went out with one of the other Ashtons," he continued. "Besides, how will they even know? We can go farther afield than Napa. It's a short drive to San Francisco and we can eat dinner there tonight."

"Are you listening to me?" she said, her indignation rising. "This is how you're exactly like your father!" she exclaimed, the sympathy she had briefly felt evaporating.

"Just stop right there," he demanded with a flash of fire in his eyes. "I know what I want and I go after it, but I'll say it again and again until I don't have to—I'm not like Spencer Ashton."

"We're at an impasse!" she exclaimed. She had raised her voice and leaned toward him. She had spent a lifetime exerting emotional control, but from the start, Eli could provoke her into losing that reserve. He leaned closer to her. Both of them were breathing hard, with mere inches separating them. Their gazes were locked, and the proximity was volatile. In spite of all the wrath bound up inside her, she longed to be in his arms and she wanted to kiss him. Anger morphed into desire that was spontaneous combustion.

As Eli hauled her against him, his mouth came down on hers, demanding and possessive. Her insides clenched. She stood on tiptoe, wound her arms around his neck and let her fury and desire pour out in a passionate kiss.

As craving banished fury, she thrust her hips against him.

Memories of their night of lust assailed her. She had vowed never to kiss him again or go out with him or even talk to him, but here she was, doing as he ordered and kissing him blindly— and savoring every moment of it.

Dimly, in the back of her mind, she realized she should stop. If Trace Ashton walked in on them, he would probably fire her on the spot because of the bad feeling between the two families. The knowledge hovered in her thoughts like fog, but she continued to kiss Eli, winding her fingers in his hair.

She finally pushed against him. "No!" she said, stepping out of his arms. "We can't kiss here."

"I agree this isn't the best of spots," Eli said, and his voice was husky, all the rage in his gaze had transformed to such scalding hunger that her pulse drummed.

"Even if you aren't exactly like Spencer and even if Lilah doesn't object, it won't work for us to see each other for another reason," Lara stated, trying to keep her wits about her. "Your world is vastly different from mine," she reminded him. "People like you don't socialize with people like me."

"To hell with that. You make this sound feudal." He draped

his hand on her shoulder. "Lara, I want to see you again. I want to take you to dinner where we can talk. If Trace Ashton finds me in here, there may be a fistfight, but I'm not budging until you accept my invitation."

"No. It's just unthinkable," she said. "Eli, it won't work, and I'm not—"

"Shh. I'll pick you up here about seven." He leaned closer. "I can be persistent." He placed his hand on her throat. His fingers were warm, and she could see satisfaction light his eyes. "Your pulse is racing, so your hesitation isn't because you don't like me or find me obnoxious. That's not it, is it?"

"You know it's not!" she exclaimed in exasperation. "I've been giving you my reasons for avoiding you since you walked into this room."

"None of which are valid," he said with that maddening perseverance that indicated he was going to continue until he got his way.

She bristled, yet in fairness, she knew that beneath that rough exterior, the man she had spent a passionate night with had also been considerate. She knew he was hurting over Spencer's dealings, and she hadn't helped his feelings by accusing him of being like his father. He was too fine a person for that. She gave a shake of her head, knowing she had come around.

"If you insist, let me meet you somewhere," she said as she capitulated.

"Fine. How about seven o'clock tonight? Same restaurant as last week."

"This is against my better judgment," she stated darkly.

"Your heart gives me a different answer. Want to see if my pulse is racing, too?"

"No, I don't!" she snapped, and saw amusement light his eyes.

"I can promise you that it is." He was only inches away, and then he leaned closer and his mouth covered hers again.

One more time he had caught her off guard. Her hands flew to grasp his upper arms as he leaned over her. She intended to push against him, horrified that he would continue to risk kissing her here in the Ashton mansion. Instead, her only conscious thought was that she desperately wanted to return his passionate kiss.

As his tongue thrust deep, her pulse thundered. Slowly he explored her mouth, demanding a response, making her his in too many ways. This strong-willed male would be her undoing. With desire kindling low in her, she returned his kiss.

He released her, running his fingers along her throat in a feathery caress.

"Thank heaven I found you," he said in a raspy voice.

"It may be disastrous," she whispered, wanting to step right back into his arms.

"Until tonight, Lara," he said, and turned to leave the room. At the door he looked back at her, and she realized she hadn't moved. She clamped her lips closed, lips that still tingled from his kiss, aware that her racing pulse hadn't slowed.

As soon as he left the room, she inhaled deeply and followed him out. When the front door closed behind him, she hurried to a window. A tough man, Eli Ashton stormed through life getting what he wanted. Except for Spencer—he'd never gotten his father's love. Momentarily she wondered about the murderer. Eli had enough rage and was strong enough, but his basic goodness had shone through that first night. Today he had been hurting and he was steeped in resentment, yet she knew he was a worthy person. And now she had agreed to go out with him again.

Anticipation overrode her caution, and she wondered what she would wear. A few more hours with Eli, she thought, eager and wary at the same time.

Eli's long-legged stride covered the ground easily, and he slid into his black sports car. She watched as he spun the car around and sped down the drive.

Feeling dazed, she touched her lips. He was a forceful man. A small inner voice corrected her—he was sexy and irresistible. She turned around to face her mother, who was gazing at her with a quizzical look.

Instantly Lara became aware of her disheveled appearance. Strands of hair had tumbled loose around her face. Her uniform was wrinkled and she guessed that her mouth was red from Eli's kisses. Her cheeks flamed from embarrassment.

"Who was that man?" Irena's blue eyes were filled with curiosity.

"Eli Ashton."

"One of the other Ashtons?" Irena persisted.

"Yes," Lara replied, heading back toward the dining room.

"Lara, do you know him?"

"Yes, I do," she answered, tucking stray strands back into her bun. "I'm going to dinner with him tonight."

"Criminy! My daughter and one of the Ashtons! Imagine that one!" Irena exclaimed loudly, clapping her hands together to Lara's horror.

"Mom! Shhh! It's a one-time deal. It's nothing."

"Nothing my foot! Is he taking you to dinner?"

"Yes, but after tonight I won't see him again," she said, trying to smooth her uniform. "I need to get back to the dining room to pick up the silver."

Her mother laughed with glee, heading for the kitchen, and

Lara suspected her mother would share this tidbit with the entire staff at the estate.

Lara returned to the dining room to pick up a sterling samovar and take it to the kitchen, where she met the gaze of her friend Franci. Her brown eyes were filled with curiosity, and Lara could guess why.

Franci had a jar of silver polish and a sponge and was shining one of the large sterling trays. Lara set the samovar down to start polishing it. The gleeful look in Franci's eyes confirmed her suspicions.

"When are you going to dinner with Eli Ashton?" Franci asked.

"How do you know that I'm having dinner with him?"

"Your mother told all of us," Franci replied, waving her hand, and although Franci and Lara were the only two in the kitchen, Lara knew that her mother had informed all the servants she could find.

"Mom's irrepressible."

"Your mom is exuberant She's so quiet around the Ashtons. I doubt if any of them have any idea how full of life she is. Even after all these years of working here."

"I'd just as soon she hadn't mentioned Eli Ashton to anyone. If word of this gets back to Lilah, you know there'll be trouble."

"Not too much to my way of thinking. You and your mom are too capable for Lilah to rock your boat very much. Besides, I don't think she'll care if Eli Ashton wants to take one of the maids to dinner. What are you wearing?"

"I have no idea," Lara replied.

"At lunch let me come help you pick out something."

"Franci, tonight isn't special. Eli isn't special," she said, but her words had a hollow ring. "I can't afford to have him in my life, and I know that he doesn't want to be in my life for any lasting period of time."

"You don't know that. I think he's interested in you."

"Temporarily, he is. I shouldn't have agreed to go out with him. He takes charge too much to suit me."

"You just don't like losing control."

"I guess I don't," Lara admitted. "He surely doesn't want to lose it, either."

"Sounds to me as if he rings your bell," Franci said smugly, and Lara frowned.

"No. He's arrogant and controlling and strong willed—"

"Ms. Kettle, are you calling the pot black?" Franci interrupted. "Admit it. You gave in because you like the guy and fireworks go off when you're around him."

"Sort of. He's tough and determined. I think his abrasiveness and control go back to Spencer's treatment of him and his family."

"We all knew Spencer and what a jerk he was," Franci declared, picking up the silver tray to carry it to the sink to wash off the polish. As water poured over the tray, Lara's thoughts were still on Eli.

Why hadn't she been able to stick with her refusal to go out with him? She suspected there wasn't a simple reason. On a sexual level she responded totally to him. This morning, she had seen yet another facet of Eli—his hurt and his rage toward Spencer. Deep down, a part of her wanted to save him from his rancor and disillusionment. "Yeah, right," she said aloud to herself. As if Eli Ashton needed saving from anything—or would let anyone else do so.

When she and Franci were ready to return the polished silver pieces to the dining room, Franci headed toward the door.

"It's time for our lunch break. Let's go up and pick out something for you to wear tonight. I want you to be a knockout."

"You don't even know him."

"I know he's what you need. Don't tell me you didn't enjoy being with him."

Lara inhaled, remembering the magical night with Eli. He carried her out of her drab routine into excitement that was difficult to resist. Giving a slight shake to her head, she clamped her lips together and pushed open the kitchen door, waiting for Franci to follow.

"I don't want a man intruding in my life. I've been there and done that, and I don't want to go through it again. Not now, anyway."

"Go out and enjoy yourself."

"Oh, Franci, you're a hopeless romantic! Let me introduce you to him."

"He would not react the same to me. From what you've told me, I think there's something special between the two of you."

"No, there's not. Like I said, you're a hopeless romantic."

"Well, whatever I am, let's put up this silver and go look in your closet. I want to help you pick out something." Franci persisted.

Lara thought about Eli on the way upstairs to her room. She thought about his kisses and how his fingers had lightly caressed her throat. She had returned his passion equally with her own, something she hadn't intended to do.

She needed to be firm with him tonight. Tonight might not be the last time he wanted to see her. As quickly as that thought came, she rejected it. She couldn't imagine a man like Eli Ashton pursuing her. Not beyond tonight. She'd hurt his pride by walking out on him the other night and now he probably wanted to do his own walking. Whatever his reasons, she was going to spend another evening with Eli Ashton—her pulse raced at the thought.

Excitement over finding Lara and anticipation of spending the evening with her drummed through Eli's body. But as he approached The Vines, the reading of the will replayed in his mind. With every mile the car covered, Eli's fury increased until he was in a blistering rage by the time he turned into the drive at The Vines and headed straight for the offices. Following a lifetime habit, his first inclination was to talk to his brother.

Eli slammed the car door and stormed through the tasting room where Jillian was talking to a group of tourists, explaining points about wine to them. He shot her a glance and she blinked, momentarily faltering but then catching herself and continuing.

Boiling inside, Eli strode to the stairs and took them two at time. In long steps he reached Cole's office and barged inside.

In a gray knit shirt, Cole sat behind his tidy desk, the one messy spot in a ruthlessly neat room. He took one look at Eli and shut off his computer.

"So what did the bastard do—cut us off without a cent?"

"No. He managed to make it a helluva lot more insulting than that." Unable to sit down, Eli paced the office. As he walked he yanked off his coat to fling it on a chair. Then he tore off his tie, balling it up and giving it a toss.

"So tell me already."

"He left one dollar to Mom and a dollar to each of us."

Cole's face tightened. "I shouldn't be surprised, but…hell." He looked away. His fingers thrummed once, twice, on the arm of the chair, then clenched into a fist. "When have we ever been able to count on him for anything? That's a rhetorical question," he added, shoving his chair back and standing. "Don't strain your brain trying to come up with an answer. So did he leave everything to Lilah?"

"No. His shares of Ashton-Lattimer Corporation went to Walker Ashton."

"Damn," Cole said as he rubbed the back of his head. "At the moment the stock isn't worth all that much. That stock's been shaky ever since the story broke about Spencer's first marriage and baby Jack."

"The stock will come back," Eli said, raking his fingers through his hair. "Twenty-thousand went to Charlotte Ashton."

"Considering the size of the estate, that's not much. Guess he didn't care for Charlotte."

"She probably has too much Sioux blood for him," Eli said, grinding out the words.

"And the rest of the estate?"

"The land, vineyards, winery, house and money were split between Lilah and the three children."

"His 'keeper' family. Well, I'm not surprised by that. I'm surprised by the rest."

"Walker's his golden-haired boy. When it was over, Walker told me I shouldn't have come, and Trace Ashton threatened to throw me out of the place."

"Did you hit anyone?" Cole asked, interested.

"I was on my best behavior. One more remark out of Trace, though, and I would have punched him. And I have to tell you, I was hoping he'd make one more remark."

Cole snorted. "I'm glad he didn't. This isn't the time to go punching people, with the cops looking for a murderer."

"I have an ironclad alibi, remember? I was working all night, and Randy from the bottling room was with me. Trace better leave me alone."

Cole shrugged. "He won't come looking for you, and you don't have any reason to go back to the estate."

"Lilah Ashton ran Mercedes and Jillian out of there, just like she tossed Anna and the baby out when they went to meet the family. Spencer and Lilah wouldn't have anything to do with Grant. Those damn people—" Eli spun around to place his hands on his hips and face his brother. "Cole, I'm calling our lawyer. We're going to try to break the will."

"Why?"

Eli glared at him. "What the hell do you mean, why? Do you want to let that son of a bitch get away with this?"

"I don't want or need a damned thing of his," Cole said, his voice low and intense. "We've done fine without him and his money. We can go right on doing fine. Go stick your hot head under some cold water. You aren't thinking straight."

"Like hell I'm not," Eli snapped. "It's not like the press will leave us alone if we don't sue. We're involved in Spencer's scandalous life no matter what we do. I let the rest of you talk me out of trying to get back Mom's heritage when we found out that Spencer committed bigamy. His marriage to Mom wasn't legal, so to my way of thinking, Spencer couldn't inherit all of grandfather's estate."

Cole's lips twisted. "You know what that makes us. Mom doesn't want to stir up more scandal."

"We can weather it. Now this damn will—we're going to contest it because we're Spencer's family. As much as I hate it, we have his blood in our veins."

Cole studied him out of narrowed eyes. "We'd better discuss

this as a family. If you go through with this, Mom, Dad, our sisters, all of us will be affected."

"Why don't we ask Grant and Anna and our in-laws over to talk things out, too?" Eli snapped with dripping sarcasm, clenching his fists and facing Cole, his irritation radiating toward his stubborn brother. "Or maybe you'd like to put it all on a spreadsheet first. Examine the bottom line."

"Considering outcomes is the adult way to deal with things," Cole said coldly. "I'm going to call them. Dixie, too. And Seth. They've got a stake in this."

"All right, dammit, ask them to be here." Eli raked his fingers through his hair again and let out his breath, knowing Cole with his practical way of thinking was probably right. "Let's get the family together to discuss it."

Cole looked at his watch. "Jillian is educating a group of tourists about wine. Mercedes is probably in her office, and Mom and Dad are at the house. I'll get them together, but give me some time to let Jillian finish what she's doing."

"Shannon can take over for her."

"I'll see," Cole said, picking up the phone. Eli strode to the window and tuned out his brother while in his mind's eye he saw the Ashton Estate vineyards. "Damn Spencer," he said under his breath.

Cole made two more calls and then turned to Eli. "All right, we're meeting at the house in the library thirty minutes from now. Jillian will be through then and the whole family will be present except Seth. That ought to suit you."

"You don't agree with me, do you?"

Cole rubbed his neck again. "I just want to give it thought before we fly off the handle and do something we'll regret down the road. I agree with Mom—we don't need this fight. We have a great life with Louret Vineyards now."

"We'd let Spencer trample us again. His damned will sets my blood boiling. I don't see what we have to lose."

"I can't see what we'd gain. I don't think we can break the will."

"That's for our lawyer and the courts to decide. And we can tie things up for a damn long time."

"You don't want to do that," Cole said. "Trace and Walker may have infuriated you, but they couldn't help what Spencer did any more than we could. And Paige and Megan Ashton— they haven't done a thing to hurt us."

"Oh, hell. Then I guess it boils down to my wrath toward Spencer. All right, I'll be in the library in thirty minutes."

"Bring a cooler head with you," Cole called after him as Eli swept up his coat and tie and left.

Thirty minutes later Eli's rage hadn't abated. He couldn't stand still so he paced the library, looking around at his family. Lucas, in jeans and a navy knit shirt, was sitting protectively beside Caroline on the sofa. Jillian and Mercedes sat with their heads together while Mercedes talked about a marketing strategy for Louret. Both sisters had light-brown hair—Mercedes's was curly and Jillian's wavy. Eli could see family resemblances in them, but he suspected it was only because he knew them so well.

Cole strode into the room and closed the door behind him. Dixie sat in a wing chair, and her eyes sparkled when her husband entered the room. Eli saw the look that passed between the two and for a moment forgot the will while envy stabbed him. Since his marriage, Cole seemed happier, more relaxed, a lot less the uptight, all-business brother he had been before Dixie had come into the family.

Eli liked both of his new in-laws, and he was glad for the happiness his brother and sister had found, but it was difficult to keep from being resentful because of his own disappointments.

"Sorry, I had a phone call, but I'm only—" Cole glanced at his watch "—four minutes late. Jillian, any chance Seth could get away and be here?"

Jillian looked up. "No. He'd like to, but he had an appointment he had to keep. He said to go on without him."

"We can wait until tonight," Cole offered, but she shook her head.

"No, there are enough of us to make a decision. Eli told us about the will," she said.

Eli faced his family. "You know what's in Spencer's will. What I want now is an agreement from the family to call Ridley Pollard and get him to look into contesting the will. And when we know what our legal options are, we can meet again to decide if we want to proceed or not. I still think we should have him look into whether or not Spencer could inherit from our grandfather when Spencer had committed bigamy. Sorry, Mom, but that's the truth."

"I know it is, Eli. I just want all of you to remember I had no knowledge of Spencer having a wife."

"We all know that, Mom," Eli said as the others added their reassurances. Jillian frowned at him, and he knew she didn't want their mom upset.

"First things first," Eli said. "If our lawyer says it's feasible to contest Spencer's will and that legally we have just cause, I want him to pursue the matter."

"I think we should hold off," Cole remarked, leaning forward and placing his elbows on his knees. "Mom doesn't want to fight the will. We all have a great life here at Louret. Besides, I don't think it will benefit us to contest the will. When Spencer made his will, he had a perfectly sound mind. He cut himself off from us years ago. Why should he have left us anything?"

"Because it was ours to begin with," Eli said. "And because he was our blood father."

"None of that meant a thing to him," Cole stated. "What do the rest of you think? Mom, let's hear from you."

Caroline glanced at Lucas and then looked at each of her children, her gaze returning to Eli. "I willingly gave up my father's inheritance years ago for my children. Thanks to all of you, Louret is successful beyond anything I could have imagined. Why stir up more anguish and turmoil? It would be a bitter, hateful battle and I would dread it," she said, worry clouding her hazel-green eyes.

"Dad?" Cole asked.

Lucas rubbed his jaw and was silent a moment as if he were still thinking about what to do. He turned his blue-eyed gaze on Eli. "I personally don't think you'll get anywhere if you do contest it," Lucas said. "I also think we all should give a lot of consideration to what your mother wants."

"Jillie," Cole said. "What do you think?"

"I don't think we should try to break the will. It'll just create more ill will between the families—"

"So who's going to care if it does?" Eli snapped.

"When Mercedes and I called on Paige and Megan, they were friendly. It was only Lilah Ashton who wasn't. I don't see any point continuing a feud that was Spencer's doing," Jillian argued.

"Dixie?" Cole asked his wife, and she shrugged.

"I'm too new to the family."

"You can have an opinion," Cole said. "This affects you as much as it will me."

"Sorry, Eli, but if it were left up to me, I'd leave it alone,"

Dixie said and Eli nodded. He liked Cole's wife and respected her opinion whether it agreed with his or not.

"I see Eli's side, but I see the other side, too," Mercedes said.

"I'm definitely in the minority," Eli admitted and raked his fingers through his hair.

"Eli, let's all think about it," Caroline suggested. "For another couple of weeks we'll consider talking to Ridley Pollard and the possibilities if we contest the will. We can get together again. That way there won't be a hasty decision to go ahead or to drop it.

"Can Cole at least ask Ridley whether we legally would stand any chance if we contest it?"

"Let's wait a couple of weeks," Cole replied before Caroline could answer.

Eli glared at his brother. "Spencer committed bigamy. Our grandfather's will referred to Spencer as 'my son-in-law' and Spencer was not our grandfather's son-in-law. This could mean we could legally contest the will and possibly revert Ashton Estate and Spencer's Ashton-Lattimer Corporation shares of stock back to Mom. You can't just walk away from all of Grandfather's holdings without giving it a lot of serious thought."

"We can if that's what makes Mom happy!" Cole snapped.

"Cole, Eli," Caroline said in a calm voice. "We'll think about it, but I don't want to pursue a course based on revenge," she said, looking at Eli, and he knew she was directing her remarks to him now.

He clamped his jaw closed and nodded. "All right," he said. "Just think about it."

"And that concludes our discussion," Lucas said, standing and offering his hand to Caroline. "Mom and I need to adjourn. We're having a party tomorrow night, and your mother says there's a lot to do to get ready."

"I want to get back to the office. I have a phone appointment in twenty minutes," Cole said, taking Dixie's hand while Eli merely nodded. He sat with his long legs stretched out in front of him, his arms crossed over his middle while he thought about the will.

As they left the room, Jillian caught up with Caroline. "I can help you get ready for the party," she said.

"I've got just the job for you," Caroline said, and their voices faded as they left the room and walked down the hall.

"Stop brooding over Spencer's will," Mercedes told Eli. "Besides, I have special news."

"What's that?" he asked, looking up at her.

"Our sales of Caroline Chardonnay set a record last month. On top of that, our 2000 Merlot won a silver medal from the *California Wine and Food* magazine."

"That's excellent, Mercedes! You should have announced that to everyone."

"I've seen the others and already told them. You were the last to hear."

Eli stood. "You're doing a great job."

"We're all doing a first-rate job," she said. "Our family is a mutual admiration society, but there's reason for it."

"Do me a favor. You think about this will and grandfather's will. Spencer stole all that from Mom. She's happy, but that land is rightfully hers."

"I'll think about it, but none of us want to make Mom unhappy. It's not worth doing that."

"I know," Eli said, raking his fingers through his hair. His thoughts jumped to Lara and this evening.

At the thought of seeing Lara again, his pulse began to beat faster. The memories of their only lusty night escalated his eagerness to be with her. He remembered the moment at the funeral reception when he had turned and looked into her light-brown eyes and sparks had jumped between them. Together they shared a volatile chemistry that sent his temperature rocketing just thinking about her.

Thank heaven he'd found her! This time he wanted to learn more about her. He wanted to take her to his bed, but he knew in order to spend more time with her, he needed to slow down.

During the afternoon Lara went through the chores of the day as if she were a robot. The only thing on her mind was Eli. When it was finally time to dress, she rushed to her room.

She bathed and pulled on a deep-purple, sleeveless cotton sheath that she and Franci had selected. With care, she pinned a silver rose on her dress. She wound her hair up on either side of her head and let the back fall freely. As she put pins in her hair, she remembered Eli taking them out slowly, sensually, building the mounting tension in her.

Just the sight of him today had turned her insides to jelly. But she reminded herself that she was only going to spend the evening with him—nothing more.

When she headed downstairs to get her car, Franci and her mother were waiting at the servants' entrance. "You look great. Knock him dead," Franci said.

"Well, that would make for an interesting evening," Lara remarked dryly. "Franci, I don't have any place in my life for Eli. Even if I did, I'd only be risking a broken heart."

"Lara, don't be so cautious," her mother urged. "The man is obviously interested in you."

"Sure, Mom. I'll see you two later."

She left and as she went to her car she said softly to herself,

"If I let myself be with this man, it would just be a matter of time until my heart would be in a million, tiny pieces."

She left to drive into Napa. It was a cool June evening, but she barely noticed the weather. All the way to town, her anticipation grew. She knew she shouldn't be seeing Eli and she shouldn't be looking forward to it so eagerly, but she did. "This is the last time we'll go out, Eli Ashton," she said softly, promising herself to guard her heart against the onslaught of his attention.

A fine lot of shielding her heart she had done this morning, finally yielding to his persistence about seeing her again.

When she parked in front of the restaurant, she watched him get out of his sports car and come forward to greet her. Just the sight of him made her pulse leap. To her surprise, he was in a charcoal sport coat, a pale-blue shirt that was open at the throat and gray slacks. She was thankful she had picked the deep-purple dress and her high-heeled purple sandals.

Eli Ashton—forceful, sexy, her undoing. She had heard Trace and Spencer talk about Louret wines. Now she could understand why Louret produced such premier wines. She had been the target of Eli's dogged determination. Applied to wine making his care and attention gently encouraged the winery's success. But with her, his attention was seductive and hot.

His gaze wandered languidly over her. Approval glowed in his emerald eyes as he reached out to take her hand. When his strong fingers closed around hers, she inhaled. How was she going to resist him when his slightest touch set her quivering?

"Come on. I have a surprise," Eli said. "You can leave your car here, and we'll come back to get it."

Curious she tilted her head. "You're not going to tell me ahead of time?"

He shook his head. "No. Let me surprise you," he said.

Six

He held the door open on the passenger side of his car, and Lara slid inside, buckling up and watching him as he walked around the car, remembering too clearly the first time she was with him.

He backed out and turned to leave the parking lot, driving to a nearby airfield to a waiting plane.

"I chartered a plane. We're flying to San Francisco for dinner and dancing."

"It sounds grand," she admitted. At the thought of dancing in his arms, she suddenly realized withstanding his appeal might just become even more difficult.

They entered the sleek white plane and were seated in comfortable window seats with a small table between them. A pretty blond, female attendant, dressed in gray slacks and a white blouse, moved around the cabin for a few minutes and then buckled up as soon as she had closed the door. When the plane taxied down the runway, Lara gazed out the window, but she was more aware of the man only a few feet from her.

As they took off, she inhaled, almost pressing her nose against the glass. "It's beautiful!" she exclaimed, glancing back at him to find him watching her with a faint smile.

"I'm glad you like it."

"I've never flown before," she admitted, once again aware of the chasm between his lifestyle and hers.

"Then that makes it all the better that I can do this with you for the first time. Especially if you like it."

As they circled over Napa and then headed south, she gazed out the window with fascination. "It's gorgeous! And we're going so fast!" Embarrassed, she turned back to him. "I sound like a child."

"Nothing wrong with that."

As soon as the plane had reached cruising altitude, the attendant brought them glasses of Chardonnay.

"Lara, this time while we're together, I'm going to learn something about you," Eli said.

"I lead the most ordinary life," she said, turning back to him. "I'm a maid at the Ashton Estate and I'm going to law school again in the fall. There you've got it."

He leaned forward, tracing his fingers along her cheek. "You look gorgeous tonight," he said. "Is this an antique pin?"

"Thank you," she replied, conscious of his light caress. "Yes. This one was my grandmother's."

"How did you get to the Ashton Estate? You said your mother is head housekeeper."

"She's been with them fifteen years, now, so I was eleven when she got the job with them. My father died from a heart attack the year before she went to work for the Ashtons."

"Sorry about your loss. Other than what Spencer put you through, do you like working there?"

"It's fine. The rest of the family are pleasant, and I have friends on the staff."

"I'm glad I went for the reading of the will or I never would have remet you. I didn't expect to ever be back at the estate— at least not for a long time."

"I'm here tonight, but only—" His fingers on her lips stopped her in midsentence.

"Wait," he commanded. "And no more of that nonsense that we can't see each other because you're a maid and I'm a wine-maker. Or that I'm my father's son."

"You're forceful, Eli. You go after what you want. I told you that the first night we were together."

"I've had to be forceful. Spencer walked out on us when I was eight years old. The night he left, I overheard him tell my mother that he didn't want any part of us. He agreed to child support, but that's the only way he's ever acknowledged our existence. He called us brats."

"How dreadful!"

"That was Spencer," Eli said with a shrug. "When he came out of the library, I tried to hit him for leaving us, and he slapped me hard," Eli said, resentment creeping into his voice.

Lara's heart clenched and she reached out to squeeze his hand. When her fingers closed around his, Eli's dark eyebrows arched. "That was a long time ago and the hurt has diminished with the years. He left us with the vineyard that had belonged to my grandmother. My mother was alone with four little children and she didn't know how she was going to deal with any of it, but she did."

"What a frightening time for all of you!"

"Thank heavens for Dad—Lucas. To me he's Dad. He started teaching Mom the winery business. He gave me jobs, just simple things when I was eight, but I was tall for my age and before long, I got some muscles."

In spite of knowing that she shouldn't be finding reasons to like him, Lara couldn't help seeing the honorable side to Eli, who had done all he could for his family and helped build Louret Vineyards into a fine boutique winery. "I've heard Trace and Spencer talk about Louret on occasion—a few times I even heard Walker talking about it to them. It infuriated Spencer that the Louret Vineyards had better wine than Ashton Estate."

"I'm glad," Eli said harshly, gazing past her. "Maybe that's why I go after what I want. I've had to for so long, and it's gotten to be a habit. At first it was sheer survival—trying to help my mother any way I could. But later, when I was older, with Dad and my younger brother, Cole, our wine beat Spencer's. He never acknowledged our accomplishments."

"He was envious and seething. I know he was determined to develop better wines."

"So I heard. I know he hired Alexandre Dupree who is a noted winemaker. A premier winery takes a lot of work and attention to small details. Our whole family is involved in our business. My sister Mercedes has increased sales with her marketing. My baby sister, Jillian, has been a super worker. She's studied viticulture and enology at U.C. Davis. Just recently she revamped our tasting room, which has been her big project. When I was a kid, I wanted to make everything right for my mother. I guess I still do," he said, and a faraway look filled his eyes until Lara wondered if he had even forgotten her presence.

She held his hand and knew that beneath his capability and his sophistication, he still hurt, and she saw how wrong she had been to lump him with Spencer. Although far too bossy and harsh, Eli was an admirable person.

His attention returned to her and his anger vanished. "If it means anything to you, I've never told anyone outside the family that before. Our family is pretty close-knit. We have tiffs, but they're superficial. We've had to pull together for too many years."

"That's wonderful, Eli."

"Do you have any brothers or sisters?"

"No. I'm the only one so I feel a responsibility for my mother."

"She's got a good job and an elegant place to live. Is her health all right?"

"Yes. For years she's had to do Spencer and Lilah Ashton's bidding. She's earned a rest and time to do what she likes. I want to get her out of there. That's my goal and the reason why this isn't such a great idea tonight. I don't want to get entangled."

He leaned closer until he was inches away while he slid his fingers over her collar. "I wouldn't want to divert you from your goals. I just want to enjoy some time with you."

She smiled at him. "That's comforting to know."

The attendant appeared again with a snack tray, and Lara declined. Eli shook his head and declined having any also. Why did she always lose her appetite when she was with him? Lara wondered. Why couldn't she see Eli as an ordinary man?

"Penny for your thoughts," he said. Distracting her, he ran his fingers down her bare arm and then moved his hand to her knee. She inhaled and met his gaze.

He looked at her with an intensity that made her feel desirable and pretty. It also made her tingle. Her nipples tightened, pushing against her lacy bra and purple dress. Heat coiled low in her while memories of Eli's strong, naked body tormented her. Silently she once again vowed to avoid repeating their night of lust. She intended to resist him and hold fast to her resolution to shun complications. Especially six-foot, sexy complications.

"I was wondering about your daily life. Tell me about your winery," she said.

"You'll have to come see it. It's not big, but I think it's attractive. Jillian has done a bang-up job renovating the tasting room. We've had a lot of tourists for this early in summer."

"I think everyone is getting a large number of tourists," Lara said. "I've heard Trace and Paige talking about the numbers."

A few minutes later the attendant returned to take their glasses while the pilot announced that they were beginning their descent into San Francisco. The sun was setting in the west, but Lara could see the Bay.

"It's beautiful!" she gasped, wondering how many flights she would have to take to become as blasé about flying as Eli.

She watched until they touched down and sat back, smiling at him. "That was incredible!"

"You're easy to please, but then, the first flight is usually memorable and fascinating."

"How old were you when you had your first flight?"

He shook his head. "Probably about seven when some of us flew to Chicago. Spencer was giving a speech to a group of bankers on the future of investment banking and Cole and I got to go along, but the girls were too young and had to stay home."

"Do you remember the flight?"

"Not particularly. I remember wrestling with Cole until we both were in trouble. Here we are," he announced as the plane taxied to a stop.

They left the plane and hurried to a waiting black limo that whisked them downtown to one of the tallest buildings in the city. They took an elevator to a restaurant on the top floor. They followed the maître d' through an elegant room decorated with a thick red carpet, paneled walls and muted lighting. Across the room from their window table a piano player sang and couples were already dancing.

The white linen cloth held a flickering candle and a vase of deep red roses, and the window offered them a panoramic view of the city. It was dusk and lights were winking.

With Eli life was enchanting and seductive. As he discussed the wine with the waiter, she enjoyed watching Eli. His brown hair was short, combed in place. Candlelight highlighted his prominent cheekbones, throwing the planes of his cheeks in shadow. There was a craggy, rugged look to him that his personality matched, yet he was appealing and sexy.

They ordered wine and steaks, but just like their last dinner together, there was too much to talk about, and their wine and the juicy steaks were barely touched.

"Who do you think Spencer's murderer is?" she asked, and Eli shrugged.

"Who knows? I imagine there are a lot of people who hated him."

"The authorities questioned everyone at the estate. I suppose they questioned all of your family."

He nodded. "Briefly two detectives were out. I was working almost all night the night Spencer was shot and I have another worker with me so I had an alibi, if you're wondering and are too polite to ask."

"No!" She felt her cheeks flush and was sorry she had brought up the subject. "I don't think you killed him. You're not a murderer."

"You sound so sure," he said, giving her a quizzical look.

"I think you're a fine person, Eli," she said, taking his hand. The moment she touched him, she saw a flicker in his eyes and she knew she was taunting a tiger again. He turned his hand to hold hers. "I imagine all your efforts are directed at Louret Vineyards," she said, trying to get back on a less personal note.

"That's the truth," he said, while his thumb ran back and forth across her knuckles. "I hope we have a predictable summer this year. Two years ago we had a great crop in spite of the roller-coaster summer weather, cool and wet and then hot and dry. In spite of it, I think we'll have a terrific Cabernet that year. We had a superb one in 2000. It's been aged in American and French oak for almost two years. We've got a Chardonnay that's been aged on the yeast for six years and it's going to be great."

"In spite of living at the Estate, I don't know anything about the vineyards or wine."

"The vineyard is my life. My whole family's actually. I think in the future, we're going to have to get more into blended wines. It looks like they'll be the fad." Candlelight was reflected in his green eyes and he gave her a heated look as he continued to stroke her knuckles.

"Is that okay or something bad? You don't sound happy," she said, aware of the touch of his thumb. Her gaze lowered to his mouth. She drew a deep breath and tried to pay attention to what he was telling her when what she really wanted was to kiss him again.

"It's new and I'm not as fond of blends. Jillian has a great background, and we can let her take charge of blends now that she has the tasting room finished." He raised Lara's hand to his lips to brush a kiss on her knuckles. "I want you to see our winery."

"Maybe," she said cautiously. He smiled at her, a knowing, satisfied smile as if he were certain she would capitulate and do what he wanted.

"Enough about Louret Vineyards. How many hours will you take in law school in the fall?" he asked.

"Twelve probably," she answered, "since I'll continue to work."

"What kind of law are you interested in? Any specialty?"

"I like research. I don't intend to be a trial lawyer and I'm not interested in criminal law. I find it depressing to go to the courthouse. Oil and gas law interests me."

"Why is that?"

"I figure it'll be easier to get a job with a large company. There should be plenty of business in California, and I'd like to live in a large city."

"Good reasons. Too bad you don't have your degree in dealing with wills," he remarked dryly.

All the time they talked, he played with her hand or he reached out to caress her nape. Every stroke fueled her desire, but she was still determined to avoid getting too carried away. Finally he stood and offered his hand. "Let's dance."

Lara walked with him to the dance floor that was inside the dimly lit restaurant. When she stepped into Eli's embrace, she could feel his warmth, smell his aftershave. As they moved together, he pulled her closer.

"This is what I wanted. Better than the steak. You said your goal was to get your mother out of the Ashton job. How do you plan to do that?"

Lara looked up at him. "When I get established as a lawyer, I intend to move her in with me, maybe not into my house if she doesn't want to, but somewhere nearby. She deserves that and she's taken care of me my whole life. Now I want to take care of her."

"That's an excellent goal."

"That's why I don't want anything to interfere with school and getting my degree. Or passing the bar exam," Lara said, her thighs brushing Eli's. Too clearly, she remembered being held in his arms while they both were naked, remembered his warm breath on her ear as it was now. "There's no place for a man or a relationship in my life right now. I'm twenty-six. There will be time later."

"Baby," he teased. "I'm thirty-seven."

"Senior citizen," she flung back. "Or maybe you're heading for a midlife crisis. Thirty-seven and you've never been married?"

"Nope. I've had some disastrous relationships that I'd just as soon forget. Twenty-six and you've never been married?"

"No. I've had some disastrous relationships of my own that I'd just as soon forget. Some domineering men that I've known."

"So to add to my sins, I'm lumped in with the domineering men from your past?"

She looked away from his piercing gaze. "Maybe you are. You do fall in the masterful class."

"Hopefully I can make up for that in some manner with you," he answered solemnly.

"It's back to law school for me. That's why I don't want to get involved with anyone at the moment. I can deal with a man later."

"Did you ever think you could do both?"

"No. Law school is demanding, and I want to maintain my grades."

"You know that old saying about 'All work and no play makes Jane a dull girl—"

"Well, that's Jane's problem. I have an agenda and I intend to stick to it. Actually, I would guess you're focused when you want to be."

"I suppose. I'm thankful I met you in the summer when law school is out." He leaned down to trace her ear with his tongue and she closed her eyes. It was heaven on earth to dance in his arms and be held close, to move in unison with him. For a time tonight, she might as well enjoy herself. The witching hour would come soon enough when she'd have to return to her world and tell Eli goodbye.

She realized there was a lot more to him than she first thought. He wasn't a playboy and he wasn't like Spencer. Spencer thought only of himself. Eli put his family first in his life and she had to admire him for that. When he told her about his life, though, he sounded disillusioned and he was a fine man, too kind to go through life as dissatisfied as he sounded.

The next dance was a fast number, and Eli was adept and sexy as he moved, spinning her around and then pulling her back into his arms. One time he stopped, took her hand and hurried back to their table to shed his coat and then they returned to the dance floor. Too well she remembered his bare, muscled chest. As they danced his eyes were hooded, hot with desire.

Fast and slow, they went from one dance to another and sat down only when the piano player took a break. As soon as the pianist returned they were back on the dance floor.

"You like to dance, don't you?" she remarked.

"What I like is touching you, holding you and looking at you," he said in a husky, sensual tone that quickened her pulse. "Dancing allows me to do that.

"I want you, Lara," he whispered in her ear, turning her insides to jelly.

"Stop trying to seduce me," she said, leaning back and putting a degree of distance between them.

"I merely answered your question. And when you move—that's seduction!"

"It's getting hot here on the dance floor."

"I can think of some remedies. Come here," he said, taking her hand. They walked off the dance floor and out of the dining room to the elevators. She looked at him quizzically while her pulse drummed. She was not going to another hotel room with him.

"What are we doing, Eli?"

"You said you were hot. There's a terrace on the roof and it'll be cool."

When the elevator opened, they stepped inside. He pushed the button and then turned to put one hand on the wall beside her while he leaned close. "I know I'm on fire," he said in a husky voice. He was too close, his mouth too tempting and memories too vivid.

She put her hand against his chest, "Eli—"

"At last," he whispered and leaned down to cover her mouth with his. Her heart thudded as his lips pressed hers and his tongue touched hers. She opened her lips to him, melting when his arms closed around her. She slid her arms around his neck while her drumming heartbeat drowned out all other noises. She was only aware of Eli's strong body against hers, his mouth on hers, fiery and magic all at once.

She slid her hands over his chest and desire swept her with the force of a forest fire. She was hot, aching for him, holding him and stroking his back, all her resolutions about resistance going up in smoke.

He wound his fingers in her hair, tumbling her locks and

spilling her pins. A cold draft of air hit her and she pushed against his chest. She twisted and saw the elevator doors were open. "Eli!"

He raised his head, and the blatant need in his eyes heightened her own desire.

"The doors—" she whispered, stunned by the consuming look he was giving her.

"Eli—" she said again.

He pushed a button and the doors closed and they started down. When he reached for her, she went into his arms, wanting him with all the pent-up need that he had built within her all evening.

The doors opened to the restaurant and two laughing couples entered the elevator. Lara blushed as she stepped out. They gathered their things and then left.

When they were in the limo, he pulled her into his arms to kiss her again.

But knowing they weren't alone, she quickly cut him off. He made her lose all restraint. He brought out the dangerous, impulsive side of her. She had so much to lose—but she couldn't deny she wanted him, too. At the airport they boarded the plane. As they taxied to the end of the runway, many of the interior lights switched off. Eli pulled her onto his lap and wrapped his arms around her waist after buckling them both into the seat.

"Now if you want to see a pretty sight, look at San Francisco when we take off."

She wound her arm around his neck while she turned her attention to the window. In minutes they had clearance and the plane gained speed, finally lifting into the air and climbing.

She looked at the sparkling array of lights below, far more than she had seen from the tall building. "It's beautiful!" she gasped. She turned to look at him. "I sound like a country bumpkin, don't I? But it is dazzling! Thank you for this—for the whole evening."

"I'm glad you're enjoying yourself. You have a passion for life, Lara."

"I have a passion for you," she said in a soft, sultry voice. Inhaling, he tightened his arms and kissed her, taking up where they'd left off in the elevator.

When he reached for the zipper of her dress, she caught his hands. "We're not alone."

"The flight attendant is gone. She stayed over in San Francisco. The pilot is busy and I'm just kissing and touching you a little and you like it, don't you?"

"Far too well," she whispered before his mouth covered hers again. His hands played over her breasts and she ached to get rid of the barriers of clothes, but knew she needed to guard her heart against the onslaught of this charismatic, strong-willed man.

They flew back to Napa and Eli drove her to the restaurant where he parked near her car. He cut the engine and turned to her. "My family is having a party to welcome some new neighbors tomorrow night. A couple has started a vineyard north of us and my mother wants to get to know them and introduce them to the neighborhood.

"That's friendly, Eli, even if they are competition. Although Louret Vineyards doesn't have to worry about competition from a new vineyard."

"No. They really are new at this and they're doing it on a shoestring, which also gets my mom's sympathy."

"Your mother sounds like a great person."

"She's a blue-ribbon mom," he said, and Lara could hear

the warmth in his voice when he talked about his mother. "Right now, residing with us, we have both my half brother, Grant Ashton, and Jack, Spencer's illegitimate baby, and Jack's aunt Anna. Grant's niece, Abigail, was with us. My mother would take in just about anyone if she thought he needed a place." Eli drew circles on Lara's knee with his forefinger while he talked. His casual touch was fiery. She hoped she didn't indicate the depth of the reaction she was having to his slight touch. "I want you to go the party with me, Lara. It's casual. No big deal."

Startled she stared at him. "I can't meet your family—"

"It's informal," he repeated. "C'mon. It'll be a far more interesting party if you're there, and of course you can meet my family. Half of Napa already knows them."

"Eli, we shouldn't get so involved with each other," she said. Her arguments seemed to run off him like water off glass.

"Lara, I know you're going to law school in the fall. But we can be friends and go out together this summer. The party is at seven. I'll pick you up at half past six."

"Are you listening to me?" she asked.

"I want you with me and it'll just be a bunch of people from this area. My family will be friendly."

"I'm not worried about your family being unfriendly."

"Good. I'll be there to pick you up." He leaned close to kiss the corner of her mouth, touching her lips with his tongue. Before she could turn her head to kiss him, he leaned away. "I promise you'll like my family."

"Do you understand the word *no*?"

"All too well. I don't want to hear it now."

She closed her eyes and gave up. As his arms wrapped around her, he kissed her soundly. One more night out with him. A family gathering with neighbors. Where could the harm be in that, and how risky would a few hours with his family be to her heart?

She pushed against his chest, determined to keep his hot kisses from escalating. "All right, Eli. Tomorrow night for the family party. I'll drive to your house."

"Nope. We did that tonight. I want to pick you up."

She sighed in exasperation. "You'll have to come around to the servants' entrance. I'll see to it that someone will let you in the gate."

"That works for me. I'm not overly welcome at the Ashton Estate anyway. Having you at the party will make it a whole lot better."

"I need to get names straight. Your brother is Cole."

"And he has a new wife, Dixie."

"Mercedes and Jillian are your sisters."

"Right. Jillian is married now to Seth Benedict. Seth has a little girl, Rachel. They're all friendly people," he repeated.

"I'm not worried about them," she said, leaning closer to him and pronouncing her words slowly as if he were deaf or couldn't get through his head what was bothering her.

"There's no need to worry about 'us' because there is no 'us,'" he said.

"You say that, but then you turn right around and ask me out again. There will be an 'us' if we keep seeing each other."

"No, we'll agree to keep this casual. In the fall you'll go back to college and I'll be working night and day at harvest."

"Eli, to put it bluntly, you're a complication I don't need in my life now."

"You're pragmatic, practical. You have solid, admirable goals for your future. I think you'll stick to them whether we spend time together or not."

"You can't always predict whether you will or won't fall in love."

"Neither of us has time for love," he said. "We both control our lives, and we're not going to let someone else step in and interfere."

"Maybe that's why we clash even though there's an attraction—we're constantly fighting for control."

He arched one dark eyebrow and nodded. "I suppose. The attraction is bigger than the clash."

"Do you think so?" she asked sweetly, and he narrowed his eyes.

"See what you think," he growled, and pulled her to him to kiss her passionately. His kiss possessed her, made her his woman, spoke volumes about wanting her that he never put into words. His tongue stroked her mouth sensually, stunning her because she had never felt this way before.

With her heart drumming, she wound her arms around his neck and returned his kiss, trying to have as devastating an effect on him as he did on her. Her toes curled and heat scorched her. Desire was compelling, making her want him just as she had that first night, but she fought her feelings and pushed away.

"I need to go," she said, and climbed out of his car. He got out and walked around. He pulled her close beside him as they strolled to her car. She turned to him. "It was a wonderful, magical night that I will never forget. When I'm with you, I'm Cinderella."

"I hardly qualify for Prince Charming," he said. "I can't go that route."

She didn't tell him that he did qualify for Prince Charming in too many ways.

"And as for Cinderella," he continued, "She never gave Prince

Charming this much trouble. She was never as feisty as you. She was dazzled and simply fell at his feet."

"Don't hold your breath on that one," Lara remarked dryly, and he wrapped his arms around her and leaned down to continue where he had left off with his kisses, creating a storm of need in her.

She trembled as she kissed him. She wanted him with all her being, wanted another night of wild passion.

Her arms went beneath his coat, and she ran her hands over his back, remembering every muscular inch of him, mentally envisioning him naked and loving her. She was on dangerous ground and she knew it. With all the willpower she could muster, she broke off their kiss and leaned away. "I have to go now. It was a fabulous evening."

"Yes," he said in a husky voice. "Until tomorrow night." He opened her car door and closed it behind her, waved and then strode away to his car.

She started her engine and backed out, heading toward the highway. He followed her, staying close until she turned into the Ashton Estate. Then he turned around and drove north to his home.

She sighed and shook her head. She was on fire with wanting him. Eli was bitter and sounded jaded about love, as if he had given up on it. Yet she could see the heart of gold that he hid.

She thought back to the spectacular night they'd had and the exciting man that Eli was. She was charmed by the references to Cinderella. Even though Eli denied it—and he was far more lordly and earthy than Prince Charming—he was a prince to her. For five more minutes, she decided, she would believe in the fairy tale and then she would return to her practical world where fairy tales didn't happen.

She went to her tiny room in the servants' quarters and slipped into a nightgown. She ached with frustration and unrequited desire.

Tomorrow night she would meet his family. Trepidation filled her. He swore he wouldn't get serious, yet why was he taking her home to a family party? And what on earth would she wear!

The following night she took a deep breath and went downstairs and outside to wait at the servants' entrance. The back door opened and Irena and Franci stepped outside.

"Mom!" Lara smiled at her mother and friend. "I take it you both want to meet Eli."

"Yes and since you're standing out here, I guessed that you weren't planning on bringing him inside where we can meet him."

"No, I'm not. I prevailed on one of the gatekeepers to let him in, but Eli isn't welcome here. At least not with Trace, Lilah or even Walker." She heard a car and turned to see Eli circling the house. "Here he comes." Right on time, she watched as he drove up and climbed out of the car, coming to meet her.

Convinced that Lilah Ashton would be furious to find one of her staff associating with Eli, Lara had intended to get right into his car the minute he arrived. She was anxious to get into the haven of the car and drive away from Ashton Estate. Then she forgot all about Lilah Ashton as Eli stepped out of his car and came toward her. He wore chinos, a tan knit shirt and brown loafers and her mouth went dry.

Fighting the urge, she smiled at him. Solemnly he let his gaze drift over her and then met her gaze.

"You look gorgeous," he said in a husky voice and she was aware of her silky blouse and black slacks, her high-heeled sandals. He glanced beyond her. "Is this your mother?" he asked, walking up and offering his hand to Irena.

"Mom, Franci. This is Eli Ashton. Eli, I'd like you to meet my mother, Irena Hunter and my friend Franci."

"I've heard about you and now I'm glad to meet you," Franci said, shaking hands with Eli.

"Yes, Lara talks about you all the time," Irena said.

"Mom! I do no such thing!"

Irena, Franci and Eli all laughed. Irena's eyes sparkled with delight. "You two have a fine evening."

"We will, Mrs. Hunter. It was nice to meet you both." Eli linked Lara's arm in his and they walked to his car.

"Your mother is good-natured."

"She enjoys herself and everyone around her."

He took Lara's hand. Her back prickled with sudden apprehension. She wanted to get Eli off the estate as fast as possible. She would never understand why he'd insisted on picking her up. If any of the Ashtons saw her with Eli, she was as good as fired. At the car, when Eli opened the door on the passenger side, she glanced back at the house. Her heart leaped to her throat at what she saw behind them.

Seven

A woman walked along the drive. Lara's heart missed a beat. Then, to her relief, she recognized Charlotte, who waved and smiled. Lara returned the wave, and Eli followed her gaze. "That's Charlotte Ashton, isn't it?"

"Yes," Lara answered when she slid into his car. She watched Eli go around the car. As he did, he waved to Charlotte, and as soon as he started driving, Lara turned to him.

"You don't know Charlotte, do you?" Lara said.

"No, I don't, but I'd like to. I don't think she was close with Spencer, and he only gave her a token bequest in his will."

"Charlotte is friendly and has always been kind to me. Actually, I feel rather close to her. She doesn't treat me like a servant. Sometimes I feel like woodwork to some of them, mainly Lilah. I don't think they even see me, but not Megan or Charlotte. Both of them seem like friends."

Eli glanced at Lara. He wished he could take care of her, but he knew with her independent nature, she would have none of it. He wanted to sweep her off her feet, but it was obvious from all her arguments about going out with him that he had to back off or else he would lose her.

Last night he had wanted to get a hotel room and take her there, to make passionate love to her again, but she would have been gone like a flash if he had made any such overtures. He'd overcome her arguments so far about spending time together, but he was treading as lightly as if he were in a minefield. He didn't expect this relationship to end any less disastrously than others had for him. Yet Lara was different from all other women he had known—more exciting, more independent, sexier.

Lara was quiet when he drove under the iron arch of curving vines that protected the entrance to Louret Winery and swept up to the house. "Here we are," he said.

"Your home is beautiful."

"That's my mom's doing," he explained proudly. "It's comfortable, a real plus in my book. I'll show you my suite when we get a chance."

"I'm surprised you live at home."

"I often work until three or four in the morning, so it's handy to fall in bed here."

"I don't think you trust a lot of people," she said, "but you trust your family."

Annoyed, he shot her a stormy glance and then shrugged. "I suppose that describes my life. I hadn't ever thought about it. People have a way of disappointing me, but my family doesn't." He drove around to the back where people were congregated.

"That's sort of bleak, Eli."

"So, do I have your sympathy?" he asked softly, cutting the motor and leaning close to her.

"You don't need sympathy or want it," she said, drawing herself up. "You're strong and self-sufficient and—"

"Don't tell me arrogant again," he said. For a moment he thought he might have elicited her sympathy, but it had vanished with his question. There was fire in her eyes and she had put that wall up that kept her heart shielded. He knew he had his own protective barriers, too.

"Come meet everyone," he said, climbing out of the car and walking around to hold her door. He took her hand, but, to his amusement, she shook free of him. "I may be arrogant, but you're as independent as a person can be," he said.

Even though she smiled sweetly, he knew that demure countenance hid a will of iron. He wondered if there was a time she would ever let someone take care of her even in little ways.

A small combo played: a bass, a fiddle, a clarinet and a drum. Brisket was being smoked in a cooker by the caterers and tempting smells wafted in the air. Round tables, each with a yellow tablecloth, were scattered across the patio. Centered on the tables were pots of pink geraniums with clusters of balloons anchored to the pots.

"How pretty this is, Eli!" Lara exclaimed.

"My mother has a knack for decorating. There's an artistic streak in the family. It bypassed me, but my mother and my sister Jillian have it. Come meet all of them."

While uniformed caterers served drinks, Eli took Lara's arm to lead her through the crowd toward an attractive woman in a lavender blouse and gray slacks.

"Mom," he said, and the woman with dark-blond hair that was stylishly short, turned to smile at him. When she looked at Lara and extended her hand, her hazel-green eyes were friendly. "This is Lara Hunter," Eli said. "Lara, meet my mom, Caroline Sheppard."

Lara smiled as she shook hands briefly with his mother.

"Welcome to The Vines. I'm glad you could join us tonight." Caroline turned to catch the arm of a slender, gray-haired man. Twinkling blue eyes met Lara's gaze as he held out his hand.

"Lara, this is my dad, Lucas Sheppard," Eli said. Lucas enveloped Lara's hand in a warm handshake that made her feel welcome.

"You'll have to get Eli to give you a tour," Lucas said. "Just don't let him talk about grapes all night."

"Maybe I'll learn something about vineyards," Lara replied pleasantly, aware of Caroline's curious gaze still on her.

"I'm going to introduce her around," Eli said, taking her arm to steer her to another group of people.

Lara met a dizzying array of friends and relatives and tried to get his immediate family members firmly fixed in her mind.

When he introduced her to the new neighbors for whom the party was being held, she was surprised at how young they both looked.

"Lara, this is Kent and Rita Farrar," Eli said. "They have Farrar Vineyards just to the northwest of us."

Lara shook hands with a tall, blond man and a slender blond woman dressed in a denim skirt and white cotton blouse.

"This is so nice of you and your family to welcome us to the area like this," Kent Farrar said.

"Glad to have you as neighbors."

"If we can get half as tasty wine as Louret Vineyards, we'll be thrilled," Rita Farrar added with a smile.

"We've worked at developing these wines for a long time now," Eli replied. "It takes time and weather and luck."

"And ability," Kent Farrar said. He held up his glass. "This Cabernet Sauvignon is delicious."

"It's a 2001 release. An excellent year," Eli answered. They discussed wine briefly and then Eli took Lara's arm to introduce her to other guests.

"The Farrars look young to be starting a vineyard," Lara said as they walked away from the couple.

"Kent told me they got out of college last year. His grandfather put up the money for their winery."

"I'd think they'd want experience working for someone else for a few years first. I hope they succeed," she said.

"We've had some economically hard times. That's why the Farrars got their acres at a bargain price. Competition is getting fierce, too."

"Your family is nice to welcome them. After all, they'll be your competition."

He shrugged. "That's my mom and dad—Mr. And Mrs. Friendly. We're established and we've weathered the downturns. We can afford to be friendly."

"I'm glad," she said, squeezing Eli's arm. The moment she touched him, Eli looked down at her and covered her hand. A look passed between them and for a moment the world disappeared. Only Eli existed and she wanted him with all the hunger she had felt that first night when they had abandoned logic for passion.

A newly arrived guest called a greeting to Eli and shattered the moment. Eli's fingers tightened slightly on her arm. "Come meet my brother Cole and his wife, Dixie. He's Mr. Dollars-and-Cents. He does an excellent job on the business end of things even if he is a bit stubborn and doesn't always understand some of the expenses I have."

"I suspect your brother thinks you're a bit stubborn, too," she said with amusement. "You're fortunate to have such a wonderful, big family," she said.

Before they could reach Cole and Dixie, a man came up to Eli and shook his hand. He had broad shoulders, fine lines in his face and looked to be in his early forties. His green eyes hinted that he might have Ashton blood in him, but she knew it wasn't Eli's brother. The man smiled broadly and Eli flashed a rare smile in return. "Lara, this is Grant Ashton, my half brother from Nebraska. Grant, this is my friend, Lara Hunter."

Grant's large hand enfolded Lara's as he shook her hand and smiled at her. There was an earthiness and strength to both men that had been evident the moment she first met them.

"I'm glad to meet you," she said.

"Glad to meet you. Are you getting introduced to too many Ashtons?"

She laughed. "No. I'm delighted to meet them, and everyone has made me feel welcome."

"This family excels at that. They've made me feel welcome, too." Grant turned to Eli. "The Farrars are overjoyed with this party. They're like two friendly pups."

"It's Mom and Dad's deal. The Farrars can direct their thanks to them."

"I haven't had a chance to talk to you, but I heard about what happened yesterday at the reading of the will. Spencer stayed a bastard to the very end."

"I should've known not to expect anything," Eli said grimly.

"I can't believe that you did. He tossed people out of his life like unwanted trash." Grant shook his head. "But this isn't a night to discuss Spencer. I don't want to think about him. I'd better give my regards to Lucas and Caroline. I just got here and haven't talked to them yet. It was great to meet you, Lara." Grant walked away, and Eli took Lara's arm again.

"Grant didn't even know Spencer was his father until this past year. He saw a picture of Spencer on TV and recognized him from a picture his mother had."

"What a shock!" Lara exclaimed, looking over her shoulder at Grant. "I've heard talk floating around the estate about the news. And, of course, the press picked up the lurid details and scandalous rumors."

"They weren't just rumors. It was the truth. One more scandal that Spencer brought down on everyone he ever touched. Grant is Spencer's first son. Spencer walked out on his family in Nebraska more than forty years ago. Grant is a salt-of-the-earth man," Eli continued to explain.

"I don't know how Spencer had such fine sons when he was so selfish," she remarked.

"Other people have raised us, not Spencer," Eli replied, and bitterness laced his voice.

Lara wrapped her arm more tightly in his. "Let go of your bitterness, Eli. Spencer is gone forever."

"His legacies and scandals and hurtful actions aren't," Eli ground out the words. Taking a deep breath, he tried to shake off the bad feelings. He smiled at her. "Come see our vines." Eli led her away from the party, and she saw row upon row of vines ahead of her. When they got close, she saw that the vines already bore clusters of tiny green grapes.

"There are lots of grapes."

"We'll thin the clusters. Then when they ripen, I walk, sample and taste the grapes in every vineyard block daily. That's the only way to tell when the grapes reach the necessary sugar levels. Then we'll know it's time to harvest."

"Is that difficult?"

"Just busy. In harvest, we work around the clock. We use the cordon method for the vines," he said, pointing to the wire trellises stretched along each row that supported the vines. "With this method, pruning and tying the vines are simple." Eli snapped off a sucker he spotted and brushed his fingers over the tiny grapes. "These are Pinot Noir grapes, a thin-skinned grape and one of the oldest varieties. Are you familiar with the grapes at the estate?"

"No, not really."

"I know they grow Pinot Noir." Eli knelt to pull a weed away from the vine, and he picked up a handful of dirt. "This is the lifeblood of Louret—this soil, the vines and the grapes," he said solemnly.

"You like your job, don't you?"

"I can't imagine doing anything else." He stood and brushed off his hand as his gaze roamed over the acres. "Sixty-five acres to produce some excellent wines. We have our Cab, Pinot Noir, Merlot and Petite Verdot grapes. We buy Chardonnay grapes. Beyond these rows are the Cab grapes next. As far as the wine is concerned, my taste runs to our Merlot. I don't know your favorite. What is it?"

"I don't know wines like you do, but I mostly prefer Cabernet Sauvignon."

"Great. That's what we're serving tonight. That and our Caroline Chardonnay." He looked around. "When I have a problem or my temper boils over, I come out here and work."

She gazed up at him. It was obvious Eli had inherited Spencer's hot temper, yet she knew he could hold that temper in check—as he had done after the reading of the will.

He took her hand. "Come with me and I'll show you our horses and the lake. Over there," he said, pointing east, "we have a carriage house and a guest cottage. Right now, Grant is living in the carriage house, and Anna and Jack are in the guest cottage." Eli took Lara's hand. "First of all, let me show you our tasting room. I told you that Jillie did it over this spring. She did a great job."

They walked toward a building set amid the vineyards to the west. Like Eli's family home, the winery was an inviting structure. It was two stories with peaked roofs and a large front porch.

After they crossed the porch and stepped inside, Eli switched on lights to reveal exposed ceiling beams. Lara admired the floor-to-ceiling Paladian windows and the wall color—a French blue. The tasting bar was marble.

"This is beautiful, Eli! Your sister is very artistic."

"I'll have to admit, she surprised me on this project."

"You still see her as your baby sister," Lara said with amusement.

He gave her a crooked smile. "I suppose I do. It's difficult to see Jillie any other way, but I guess I'm going to have to."

Lara touched the corner of his mouth. "I like it when you smile. Which you do only on rare occasions."

"I've been told I take life too seriously, but I guess it's the way I've been programmed."

"You're too bitter," she said softly, and ran her finger along his cheek. His eyes darkened and he inhaled, reaching for her.

"Give me a reason to be otherwise," he said in a husky voice.

She slipped out of his embrace. "One excellent reason is the delightful party your family is giving. Let's go back to it."

Amusement showed in his expression as he switched off the lights and took her hand again. "First let me show you our horses. Then we'll rejoin everyone."

She walked with him and listened to him talk about wine. They visited the stable and she looked at the lake, the still water shimmering in the late evening. Finally they returned to the party.

They joined Lucas and Caroline again, along with a couple of neighbors. In minutes Caroline recognized a young woman who approached them with a smiling baby in her arms.

"Lara, this is Anna Sheridan," Lucas said. "And this is little Jack. Anna, meet Lara Hunter."

As Lucas made introductions, Jack held his chubby arms out to Lara. She laughed and reached for him.

"You don't have to take him," Anna said, but Lara lifted him into her arms.

"He's adorable," she said, looking into big green eyes as he smiled at her.

"He'll steal your heart," Lucas said. "He's a lovable baby."

"And everyone is spoiling him," Anna stated, but Lucas shook his head.

"You can't spoil that baby. He loves the world and the world loves him," Lucas said. "Watch out, Lara. He likes earrings, too," Lucas said, catching Jack's tiny hand as he played with her thin, gold hoop earring. Jack laughed and held his arms out to Lucas. "Up," he said.

Lucas took him from Lara. "Here's my boy and my ears are safe."

As they stood talking, Lara realized that the man who raised Eli and his siblings must have been a great father to them. Lucas was easygoing and pleasant and she suspected he had none of Spencer's narcissistic ways or high temper. Baby Jack got passed around and finally set on his feet when he wriggled to get down. Anna excused herself and left to follow him through the crowd.

The dinner bell rang and Eli took Lara's arm. "Let's get in the buffet line. I've already spotted our place cards and I know which table we have."

"It's wonderful that your family took in Anna and the baby. I saw her when Lilah turned her away."

"No one in our family would think of turning her away, least of all my mom or dad. And they'd never, ever turn a baby away," Eli said. "I think Anna was desperate when she came here. I hope this is a haven for her and we can protect her and Jack."

"I'm sure you can protect her from the press."

"That's not all. She had some threatening phone calls and she was worried about Jack's safety."

"I'm glad she's here," Lara replied as they got into line at the buffet. They picked up plates and filled them with steaming brisket, thick barbecue sauce, potato salad and buttery, golden ears of corn. Lara found herself seated between Eli and his sister Jillian, whose husband, Seth, and three-year old daughter, Rachel, were on the other side of Jillian. Beside Rachel was a Napa family, the Trents, who had two children. While Eli talked about grapes to Don Trent, Jillian turned to her.

"I'm glad you're here."

"Thanks. It's great to be here," she said to the wavy-haired brunette. Jillian had the family's green eyes.

"You're good for Eli. He's more cheerful tonight." Jillian looked around Lara and saw that her brother was engaged in conversation with Don. She shifted her attention back to Lara. "He's never brought a woman home before."

Lara laughed. "Maybe not, but in this case, it doesn't mean anything. We're just having fun together. Both of us are too busy for anything serious. I'll go to law school in the fall."

"Eli's too busy making wine," Jillian said with a smile.

"I've noticed, but he must be very good at what he does."

"He is," Jillian agreed. "Especially if everyone does things his way," she added, and Lara smiled.

"I heard my name," Eli said, returning his attention to Lara and looking around her at his sister.

"It was complimentary," Lara said, smiling at him.

"I doubt that, if Jillie's involved," he teased, and Jillian wrinkled her nose at him.

While they ate, the sun went down and lights came on across the patio. Lara enjoyed the group at their table and the easy banter among Eli, his sister and brother-in-law.

Later, after dinner, Eli took Lara's hand. "Come upstairs. I want you to see where I live."

She walked at his side, aware of his hand holding hers and their arms brushing. The intimacy of seeing where he lived worried her. It would make saying goodbye even harder. She thought of starting law school in the fall, reminding herself that she needed to keep from getting more entangled with Eli. Once she started school, there would be no place for him in her life. Every moment spent with him now would make that goodbye more difficult. Yet how wonderful the night had been! His family was delightful and friendly. He had been relaxed and attentive, another side to him revealed.

The sounds of music, laughter, people talking and the clink of glasses faded as they entered the empty house, going through the family room decorated in shades of green with comfy sofas and lots of family photos.

"This room looks cozy," Lara said.

"It is, and the family spends a lot of time in here. We used to spend more time here when we were kids. Now everyone is getting scattered. Jillian and Cole are married and have moved out.

Mercedes has her own place. Mason is studying in France. I'm upstairs at one end of the house, and Mom and Dad are downstairs at the other end."

They passed through the covered lanai before entering the formal living room. It was cheerfully decorated and held many antiques.

"Your mother is a wonderful decorator," Lara said.

"It's her magic touch," Eli said, sounding pleased as he held Lara's hand.

Passing through the gallery, they took curving stairs to the second floor where Eli showed her the sitting room and theater with a huge projection screen. More family photos adorned the main hall on the second floor, and she paused to look at them, looking at pictures of Eli when he was a child.

"You have a great family," she said.

"I agree with you," he answered. "Now come see where I live." Eli led her to his suite that was decorated in bright blues and greens, giving it a cheerful air that didn't fit the man who resided there.

"This is great, Eli! It's attractive and masculine. Did your mother do this room?"

"Actually, I picked out some of this, but I took Jillian with me," he said, closing the door behind them. "Here's the kitchenette," he said. Lara stepped into a small room decorated in more festive blues and greens with antique ash cabinets.

"Come see my bedroom," he said, and she glanced at him sharply, but he merely took her hand and led her into a spacious bedroom with a four-poster king-size bed, an ornately carved writing desk and an entertainment center. One wall was lined with shelves, and when she strolled over to look at his books, she saw most of them were on growing grapes or wine production. There were novels, a sizable section of books about France and a few children's books. She touched the spine of a familiar book.

"That was mine when I was a boy," he said from behind her, his breath fanning her ear. He turned her to face him, and the look in his eyes set her heart fluttering.

When he drew her to him, Lara put her hands against his chest to stop him. "Eli, you'll wrinkle my blouse and I'm not returning to your family's party all rumpled."

As she talked, he leaned down to kiss her throat and she felt his fingers deftly unfastening her buttons. "We can take care of that," he whispered.

She pushed again, yet closed her eyes with the onslaught of seductive sensations caused by his feathery kisses. "Eli, we're at a family party. Anyone could come in—"

"Not to my suite. No one will come in, and besides, they're all outside partying. We could be on the moon," he whispered, showering kisses along her throat. He slipped her blouse off and tossed it onto a chair. Pulling her into his arms, he covered her mouth with his and closed his strong arms around her. His tongue explored, tasting, stirring a storm in her. His kiss was deeply possessive, demanding her response. It seduced her, driving all logic and will away. Her heart pounded while she clung to him and responded in kind.

He kissed her as if she were the only woman he had ever known. Moaning softly, ablaze, she thrust her hips against his. She was lost in the storm his kisses created. Passion burned away her logic.

Trembling with longing, she ran her hands down his back and then up over his thick shoulders.

His hand cupped her breast, and through her lacy bra she felt his thumb circle her nipple. Felt it tauten, tingle. She gasped with pleasure, closing her eyes and tightening her arm around his neck. Then his fingers slid to the clasp of her bra. With a flick he unfastened it and shoved away the filmy lace.

Both of his large hands cupped her breasts. His fingers were rough and callused, and the contact was erotic. He stroked her nipples before leaning to use his mouth. His tongue traced one nipple and then he bit it lightly. She cried out with pleasure and wound her fingers through his hair.

"Eli," she whispered, clinging to him, on fire now from his kisses and caresses. She was caught in a flood of longing.

A storm of need shook her. She no longer cared what his family might think they were doing. All she knew was Eli was loving her, and she wanted him intensely.

"You're gorgeous, Lara," he whispered as he laved kisses on first one breast and then another. Her pulse roared and, dimly, she knew his hands were on the zipper of her slacks. Desire was a driving force and all the protective barriers she had wrapped around her were ripped away by the onslaught of his caresses and kisses.

"Eli," she whispered. He nipped at her shoulder and then trailed his tongue to her breast again.

Her slacks fell around her ankles and then his hand was in her panties, caressing her intimately, finding her soft folds and secret places.

Her hands slid over his chest and she discovered he was bare-chested. She didn't know when he had tossed away his shirt. She tangled her fingers in his chest hair. His fingers built her need. Her caution blew away like leaves in a storm as she clutched his upper arms. Her hips thrust frantically while she sought release. Pressure built, and then she crashed over a brink, hot waves of desire rocking her.

"Eli!" she gasped. She held him tightly while her heartbeat slowed. "We have to stop."

"All right, Lara," he whispered, showering kisses on her face. "I want to love you for hours," he whispered, his tongue tracing the curve of her ear.

She pushed away, bending down to yank up her slacks. With shaking fingers she fastened her slacks and then looked up to find him watching her while he pulled on his shirt and buttoned it. His thick rod pushed against his slacks, his arousal obvious.

"Stop looking at me," she exclaimed, his hungry gaze making her want to walk right back into his embrace.

"You're gorgeous," he said in a raspy voice, "and I could look at you forever."

Aware of his gaze on her that kept her pulse drumming, Lara yanked up her bra to put it on. When he reached out to caress her breast, she drew a sharp breath. "Eli, you have to stop. I can't get emotionally involved with anyone. You don't want to, either."

"It's physical, Lara, and I like being with you."

She shot him a look, wondering if all he wanted was sex. She dressed swiftly. She crossed the bedroom to a cheval mirror and tried to comb her hair with her fingers. He walked up to stand behind her and handed her a comb. "Here's a comb. This may be easier than using your hand."

Wordlessly, she took the comb to fix her hair, thankful she hadn't pinned it up tonight because she would never have gotten it back in place without her hairbrush. He brushed a kiss across her nape.

"Eli," she said solemnly. "We have to get some distance between us."

His hooded eyes regarded her, and she wondered if he knew that her pulse was pounding. He merely nodded as if he had no intention of pursuing her or seducing her.

"Stop worrying. You look just like you did when we left the party. They expect me to show you my suite and the house." He took her hand. "Come sit down and let's just talk. I've had enough socializing with my family and the neighbors.

Before they left the bedroom, he tugged on her hand. "Lara, hold on. I have something I want to get," he said, and crossed the room to open a drawer. He returned and held out a box wrapped in rose paper and tied with a silk rose ribbon.

Startled, she looked up at him when he held it out to her.

"Go ahead. I want you to have it."

She took the box and carefully opened it.

He chuckled. "You can tear the paper. This is going to take all night."

She pushed away the shiny rose paper and lifted a lid on a small box. Nestled inside against blue velvet was a gold filigree necklace.

"Eli, it's gorgeous," she said.

He lifted it out and looked at her. "Can I put it on you?"

"Of course. It's so beautiful! Thank you, but you shouldn't have."

"None of that," he said. "Turn around." As he fastened the necklace, he brushed kisses across her nape, creating tingles. She looked down at the necklace and turned to slide her arms around his neck.

"It's so pretty. It's an antique, isn't it?"

"Yes. I asked Mom if—"

"Eli! I can't take your mother's necklace," she exclaimed, aghast.

"Shh. I asked her if she had one that she didn't wear and I told her you collect antique jewelry. She was happy to let me have it. Believe me, Lara. She doesn't wear it and she was glad to pass it on. It was my grandmother's."

"Eli, you can't do this. Someday you'll get married and your wife should have it."

"She might hate antique jewelry. I want you to have it. End of conversation."

She stared at him a moment and then put her arms around his neck again to kiss him.

He held her tightly, returning her kiss, until she pushed against him. "Eli, if we don't stop, we'll be back where we were just minutes ago."

"And that would be bad?" he asked with an arch in one dark eyebrow. Before she could answer him he took her hand in his again. "Let's get something to drink and talk awhile."

He took her hand to go to his kitchenette. "I have pop, grape juice, wine, iced tea," he said, dropping her hand and looking in his refrigerator.

"Iced tea, please," she said.

In minutes they were seated close together on the sofa in his living room, their drinks on a coffee table in front of them. Eli faced her and played with her hair with one hand while he had his other hand on her knee. "I'm glad you came to the party to-night."

"And I'm glad to meet your friendly family. They've been wonderful."

"I'm proud of them. We've come a long way since Spencer left us. I wish I didn't have one drop of his blood in my veins," Eli said, and a muscle worked in his jaw.

"You shouldn't let old animosities destroy your happiness," Lara said, touching his cheek with her hand and then sliding her fingers to his nape. She wound her fingers in the short strands of his hair above the back of his neck.

Eli ran his hand across his forehead and looked as if he was gazing off in the distance. "I guess all my life I wanted Spencer to acknowledge us and what we accomplished. I saw him twice at wine tastings. He just looked through me like he didn't see me and went on his way."

"I'm so sorry," she said, hurting for Eli. She ran her fingers over his hand that rested on her knee.

"I guess there's that eight-year-old-kid still in me that wanted some kind of recognition from him," Eli said. "Damn him, anyway."

"Let it go, Eli. Spencer isn't worth agonizing over. I don't know who the killer was, but I'm glad Spencer is gone."

Eli's gaze swung to her and his eyes narrowed. "What did he do to you? I can just imagine—you're beautiful, Lara. That bastard tried to seduce you, didn't he?"

Eight

"**I** think he tried to seduce every female under forty who looked even remotely appealing. He threatened to fire my mother if I didn't cooperate with him," Lara said with distaste.

"Damn! You—"

"I didn't give in to him. But he threatened often enough, and it was just another reason to hate the man." She shivered. "He was a beast."

"The killer probably had a lot of reasons for pulling the trigger," Eli said.

"The first suspect was Charlotte because she found his body, but thank goodness she has an alibi—she was with Alexandre Dupree. Even so, Alexandre was going to take her to France, and now they can't go. The police won't let her leave the country."

"It's a good thing a lot of us have alibis," Eli said, brushing his fingers back and forth on Lara's nape. She inhaled deeply, tingling from his caresses, wondering if he was even aware of what he was doing or if he noticed her fingers tangled in his hair. "I'm known for my temper—which I inherited from him, I'll have to admit. I told you that I was with one of our workers and I'm glad I have an alibi because people know the animosity I felt for Spencer."

"The detectives questioned everyone at the estate. Several of us on the staff were playing cards," Lara said. "I'm thankful I have an alibi because I don't think it would be wise to have it come out how much I disliked Spencer," she said.

"I want to see if we can break Spencer's will," Eli revealed bluntly. "My family disagrees with me."

"I've heard rumors since the reading of the will. Rumors about all the Ashtons constantly fly through the staff. Of course, you may have a legitimate cause," she said. Lara thought about the Ashtons and how shocked they would be if Eli and his family did contest the will.

"You look worried," he said, one dark eyebrow climbing, and she heard the bitterness creep back into his voice.

"People continually disappoint you, don't they, Eli?" she asked, knowing he was hurting and indignant over Spencer's will.

"I suppose your sympathies lie with the other Ashtons."

"I was just thinking how it will rock their world if the will is contested. And it'll come in a year when they have had one scandal after another hit them."

"Thanks to Spencer," Eli snapped.

"That's true, but Megan and Paige and the others were as innocent as your family."

He inhaled and looked away, and his fingers stilled in her hair. "Walker Ashton shouldn't inherit my grandfather's stock," Eli insisted, his voice laced with anger.

Lara hurt for Eli and placed her hand against his cheek. His gaze returned to hers and he turned his head to kiss her palm. His hand covered hers and held her palm to his lips while his tongue traced a circle in the center of her hand. As tingles radiated from his kiss, she forgot families and wills. All Lara wanted was to be in his arms again. And she saw the same desire in the depths of his eyes.

"Lara," he sighed, pulling her onto his lap to cradle her against his shoulder and kiss her deeply. Lara wound an arm around his neck to return his kisses. Once again she was caught in the dizzying spiral of his kisses. Desire escalated, threatening to shatter the control she had fought to keep.

Finally she pushed away from him and stood. "Oh, Eli. I'm wrinkled."

"Your blouse has a few wrinkles. It's night. No one will notice."

"Of course they'll notice. Your patio has lights. We should join the others."

Standing, he framed her face with his hands. "I want you, Lara. I want you in my arms. I want you in my life."

"We both got carried away that one night. It mustn't happen again."

His eyelids drooped and fires danced in the depths of his eyes. His arm tightened around her waist and he leaned forward, pulling her against his chest. His mouth came down on hers hard and his tongue went into her mouth, kissing her possessively, melting her opposition. He kissed her until she wound her arms around his neck and returned his kisses.

He swung her up. Bemused, she opened her eyes to look up at him, and she knew how thoroughly he had proved his point that he would get his way.

She shook her head. "Doesn't matter what you do tonight. I'm not going to be seduced. And I should go. It's late and I don't want to go down and find everyone except your family has gone. Worse, I don't want to come out of your suite as your family is coming inside to go to bed."

"Mom and Dad have rooms at the other end of the house on the ground floor. No one else is around. Mason's room is the closest and he's in France."

"Let's go, Eli," she insisted, and he draped his arm across her shoulders.

"Whatever you want," he said.

The party was still going when they went downstairs, but a few guests were beginning to leave. After another half hour, Lara told Eli that she should go, so they said goodbye to everyone and she thanked his mother and father for the evening.

As they left the lights and the party, Eli drew her to his side.

He gave her a crooked smile. "My family liked you," Eli said as they walked to his car.

"Of course they did. You finally brought home a woman. And it sounds as if they like everybody."

"Oh, no. They would let me know if they didn't like you. No one is fond of Craig Bradford, Mercedes's on-again, off-again boyfriend. But then, I don't think Mercedes is that fond of him, either. No, you'd know. They like you."

"It was a great party," she said, wanting to get away from the discussion of his family liking her. She was returning to her plain life, and she didn't want to dwell too much on the evening.

Eli held the car door for her and in minutes they were on the highway, heading south to the Ashton Estate. When Eli parked near her door, he cut the motor and turned to her. "I'm glad you came tonight. Let me take you to dinner tomorrow night."

"I had a wonderful time at the party and I enjoyed meeting your family," she said carefully, her heart beating fast. "Eli, we might as well say goodbye right now. I've told you, I have plans, and our going out together is no part of them."

"If I thought you didn't like me, I'd say fine and leave you alone," he said in a low voice. "But I know differently. When we're together your heartbeat is as out of control as mine. There's a chemistry between us that is as combustible as a flash fire. You have plans, but you told me they're for the fall. What's it going to hurt to go out tomorrow night?"

"Every hour we're together makes saying goodbye more complicated, and you know I'm right. We're not going out again," she said forcefully and stepped out of the car swiftly. She ran and almost made it to the door before he caught her. He spun her around and they looked at each other.

"No," she whispered.

"You say no. Your heart says yes."

"This time you're not going to change my mind. Until you came into my life I've always had control over my emotions and I'm not going to lose that control."

"You're fighting yourself right now," he remarked.

"You act as if you can't hear a word I'm saying to you. Eli, this is goodbye. And if you say one word, then you're more like Spencer than you want to admit. He had—"

"Dammit. Maybe I'm not worthy of your love, but stop accusing me of being like Spencer!" Eli snapped.

His words stopped her cold. "Love?" Lara looked at him searchingly. "Eli, what—"

Eli was angry now. "Never mind. It was a stupid slip of the tongue. It didn't mean a thing—nothing at all."

Lara knew what he really meant: he was reminding her that

although their time together had been magical, it was still insignificant to him. She turned and pushed buttons to unlock the door. The moment she did, she stepped inside and slammed it behind her. She was gasping for breath and she hurt.

She clenched her fists and wished she had been able to control her emotions. All her life she had been able to keep a cool head, but with Eli she couldn't. She suspected she was testing his restraint, too, but if it had taken that to get him to listen to her, so be it. Yet his words broke her heart. Even though she knew what they'd shared was temporary, hearing Eli's angry words tonight had hurt. And he wasn't like Spencer—not in the ways that really counted.

She headed for the stairs in the silent house, climbing them and thinking about the party that had been so wonderful. The night had been enchanted, and she reflected on the moments in Eli's arms, his kisses that she knew she could never forget. In her small room she closed the door and let the tears come, because in her heart she didn't want to tell him goodbye.

A light tap on the door made her wipe frantically at her tears. She glanced at her clock. It was past midnight. She swung open the door, thankful she no longer had to worry about Spencer. Franci stood there in striped orange-and-black pajamas and an orange cotton robe. She waved a tray of cheese and crackers and two bottles of pop.

"I can't sleep and I wanted to hear about your evening."

"Franci, do you know how late it is?"

"Are you going to sleep now?"

"No," Lara admitted and swung open the door. Franci sailed inside and plopped on the bed, placing the food on the small bedside table. "I'll fix the cheese and crackers while you get ready for bed and tell me. Did you have an exciting evening?"

"I had a wonderful time," Lara said solemnly, and Franci looked up, her eyes narrowing.

"You've been crying. Did you fight with him?"

Lara sighed, knowing Franci was her best friend and that sooner or later, Franci would learn what had happened. "I told him I won't go out with him again."

"Why?" Franci shrieked and then clamped her hands over her mouth.

"Shh! You'll wake up the house. And I don't want Mom asking me a million questions and discussing this with the entire staff."

"You like him. Why on earth would you tell him you won't go out? Franci asked, kicking off fluffy orange slippers and sitting cross-legged on the bed while Lara changed to yellow cotton pajamas. She emerged to hang up her blouse and slacks. "I have to stop before things get out of hand," she said woodenly. She crossed the room to the bed to find Franci staring at her.

"You're in love with him!" Franci exclaimed, wriggling with excitement and making her thick mop of black curls bounce.

"No, I'm not!"

"Yes, you are," Franci argued. "You're in love! Why won't you go out with him if you're in love?"

Lara thought about Franci's accusation. Was she in love with Eli? "I may have fallen in love with him, Franci, but he just seems to want a physical relationship. And he seems to be so single-minded."

"Give it up a little. Give him a chance," Franci said, slicing cheese and putting it on a cracker. Lara shook her head.

"I can't eat a bite."

"Oh, my. You're definitely in love. You always have a little snack with me when I bring one to your room. No appetite, tears. Go out with the man and follow your heart."

Lara shook her head, hating her churning emotions and the threat of more tears. She took off the necklace Eli had given her and turned it in her hands. "He gave me this because he knows I like antique jewelry. It was his grandmother's."

"He loves you, too!"

"No, he doesn't. It's a bauble to him. I'm going to mail it back to him tomorrow."

"You can't, Lara! Stop tossing away happiness with both hands, for heavens sake!"

"I have to do what I have to do," Lara said, placing the necklace on her dresser.

"Okay. Tell me about his family. Are any of them overbearing like Spencer?"

"Eli is probably the one who is most like Spencer, but he'd hate to hear me say that. No, they're not. They're wonderful people and I had a marvelous time. Franci, I hurt him tonight. I told him that he was like Spencer and he got so angry. I just need to take care of Mom and go to law school, and I don't have a place for a man in my life right now."

"You're in love and you have to go out with him again."

"No, I don't," Lara said woodenly, and in minutes she claimed a headache and shooed Franci out of her room, sagging against the door with relief when she was alone. She switched off the light and climbed into bed, but memories of that first night with Eli plagued her. He didn't belong in her life, and the more she saw him, the bigger the heartbreak would be. And heartbreak would come. Eli didn't want any commitment. She had a plan for her life to follow and there was no place for Eli in her plan.

Yet his words haunted her. *Maybe I'm not worthy of your love, but stop accusing me of being like Spencer!* Lara wondered if it had really been a slip of the tongue. Could Eli have fallen in love with her? Did he really think he was unworthy of love because Spencer had abandoned him as a boy? Her heart broke anew.

She balled her fists against her eyes and hated that she couldn't govern her feelings. "Eli," she whispered. "Eli, I love you."

Eli drove home and took the stairs two at a time to go to his suite. He closed the door and walked to the bedroom, tossing off his clothes, throwing them over a chair. He paced the room and felt on fire. He wanted Lara and she didn't want to go out again—and it wasn't because she didn't like him. Her reasons frustrated him and he tried not to be angry. Worst of all, he'd said the *L* word—which he didn't understand at all. Where had *that* come from? She'd just got him so riled.

"Damnation," he said, raking his fingers through his hair. He spun around and went to his closet. In minutes he was dressed to swim. Leaving the house, he crossed the yard and headed to the lake. He switched a light on, on one tall pole along the dock at the lake. It threw a shimmering silver beam across the inky water. He dropped his towel and kicked off his loafers, making a running dive into the cold water.

He swam until he was nearly exhausted and finally climbed out, toweling off and slipping back into his shoes. He turned off the light and walked through the vineyard to go back to the house.

Picking a grape leaf, Eli rubbed his fingers over it, feeling the texture. His thoughts jumped right back to Lara and her kisses. She'd had a good time tonight. "Forget her," he told himself, striding back to his suite where he uncorked a bottle of Merlot and poured a drink. He sat in his living room, thinking about being there with her hours ago. He wanted her in his arms. He wanted her in his bed. He glanced at his bedroom and, for the first time in years, thought about getting an apartment in Napa. He wanted his own place.

He raked his fingers through his hair. "Dammit," he mumbled. Even if he had his own place, she wouldn't stay with him. She was a woman with a plan that didn't include him. He had to forget her, but she wouldn't stay out of his thoughts.

He had to respect her plans to take care of her mother. From the time he was eight until Louret became a success, Eli's whole purpose in life was to take care of his mom and his siblings. He and Lara were alike in that, and he admired Lara for it. And he admired her independence—so long as she didn't direct it toward him.

She wasn't like any woman he had ever known. Independent, poised, driven—and sexy beyond measure.

He took a long drink and lowered the glass, staring into space and seeing Lara, thinking about her light-brown eyes and her thick auburn lashes. remembering holding her in his arms, dancing with her. Another disappointment in a lifetime of disappointments and rejection. And Lara wondered why he didn't trust people.

He rubbed his forehead. *Was* he in love? Had he ever been in knots before, even when he had been in serious relationships? He'd been hurt, but not as though his heart had been ripped out.

He groaned and, like an animal in a cage, got up to pace the room. His tall clock chimed three. He strode through his suite and dressed in chinos and a knit shirt and left again, heading to his office. He knew he wasn't going to sleep, so, hopefully, if he threw himself into work, he would forget her for a while.

Over a week later, on the twenty-second of June, Eli stood,

brushed dirt off his work pants and climbed back on a tractor. He had been plowing under their winter cover crop of barley and legumes that had been planted between the rows of vines. He glanced at his watch and saw that it was four-thirty in the afternoon. As he reached toward the ignition, his cell phone rang. Eli pulled it out of his pocket and answered, "Eli, here."

"It's Grant."

Eli frowned because Grant's voice had an unfamiliar rasp to it. Instantly he suspected a problem. "What's wrong?" Eli asked.

"Two detectives from the SFPD are here," Grant replied in a tight voice, and Eli's stomach clenched. "They're taking me in for questioning," Grant added.

"Damn!" Eli swore. Concern for Grant's welfare mushroomed because Grant didn't have an alibi and, worse, he had a motive. Yet Eli didn't think Grant could have committed the murder any more than he himself could have. "I'm in the vineyards right now and I'm hot and dirty, but I can be ready soon. Will they let me ride into the city with you?"

"I'll ask," Grant said, and Eli could hear muted voices before Grant returned to the phone. "No. I have to go alone with them. At least there are no handcuffs so far."

"Have you told Mom or Dad?"

"No. You're the only person I've called. I'm still here at Louret," Grant said. "I asked them if I could clean up and change clothes. They said I could."

"I'll clean up and get there as soon as possible," Eli said. "You need a lawyer. The family will take care of it."

"Thank God for your family! Tell your folks thanks until I can tell them myself. I'm glad you're coming. It'll be reassuring to have someone with me."

"You wait for an attorney to get there before you answer any questions. I'm on my way." Eli jammed his phone in his pocket, started the tractor and headed home. He dreaded breaking the news to Lucas and Caroline because he knew they were fond of Grant and would be upset. His mother answered the phone in a friendly voice.

"Mom, I've got bad news." Eli tried to cushion what he had to say, pausing a moment. "Grant just called and the detectives are taking him in for questioning."

"Eli, that's horrible! You know Grant wouldn't have shot Spencer," Caroline exclaimed.

"I know, but as far as the police are concerned, he had a motive."

"A lot of people had motives. We'll hire a lawyer for Grant. I'll see if I can get Ridley Pollard to recommend an experienced criminal attorney," Caroline said. "You call Grant and tell him we'll have a lawyer meet him in the city."

"Thanks, Mom."

Minutes later he raced up the stairs to his suite. As soon as he closed his door, he yanked off his clothes and tossed them down as he rushed to shower. He was toweling dry when his cell phone rang again.

It was Lucas. "Eli, the attorney for Grant is Edgar Kent, and Ridley will go along with him for moral support. Are you going into town?"

"Yes. I'm dressing as fast as I can."

"Keep in touch. Someone's at the door so I have to go."

Eli yanked on a burnt-orange knit shirt and dark-brown slacks. As he was jamming his feet into his loafers his phone rang again. Expecting another call from Grant, Eli answered. Instead of Grant, he heard his dad.

"Eli, Detective Holbrook is here at the house," Lucas announced, and Eli closed his eyes. He knew from Lucas's tone that bad news was coming. "The detective is taking your mother in for questioning, too."

Eli turned to ice and clenched his fist. "What? Where are you?"

"We're still at the house. She's getting her things."

"Dammit to hell!" Eli swore. "Will they let you ride with Mom?"

"Yes," Lucas answered. "We're leaving now. I've already called Ridley Pollard back to get another criminal lawyer for Mom. We don't want to take the one away from Grant."

"Will you be in an unmarked car?"

"Yes. It's a black four-door sedan with antennae all over it," Lucas remarked dryly. "We won't be hard to spot, and I'll be with her. There are two detectives and they're in plain clothes."

"How's Mom?"

"She's fine. She didn't shoot Spencer, and she said she had no reason to. Maybe when all of you were babies, but not now. She's calm about the whole thing because she's certain of her innocence. Besides, she was home with me that night, but that didn't satisfy them because I left for a brief time. We have to go in," Lucas said in such a soft voice that Eli could barely hear him.

"Sure," Eli said. "I'll call the others. Everyone has gone home for the day. I wondered if the detectives waited for that to happen."

"I don't know. Let's just pray the press doesn't get wind of this. Goodbye, Eli," Lucas said.

Eli broke the connection. He hadn't thought about the press. The tabloids would feed on this latest development.

He swore as he pulled on his belt and combed his hair. He jogged to the garage, flinging himself into the car. His mother.

How could they haul his mother in for questioning? And just as she said, if she'd ever harbored murderous intentions toward Spencer, why wait thirty years to do it—when she was happily married and Louret Winery was a huge success.

"Dammit!" Eli swore again as he jammed his foot on the accelerator and took off down the drive with a squeal of tires.

He yanked out his phone, breaking his own rule about not using the phone while the car was moving. He called his siblings to inform them, getting Cole and Jillian but unable to locate Mercedes. He called Jillian back to tell her, and she said she would continue trying to get Mercedes.

Louret Vineyards to San Francisco was an hour-and-a-half drive, but within twenty-five minutes Eli spotted the police car ahead of him on the highway. He eased up on the accelerator and gradually passed the unmarked sedan. When Eli saw his mother and Lucas in the back, he hurt all over at the thought of his gentle mother being questioned by the police.

He thought about Anna and how she had fled from the press. Would the press already know about Caroline and Grant?

Eli clamped his jaw closed until it hurt. If there were reporters waiting, he would smash every camera he could get his hands on. "Right, Eli," he told himself, knowing if he tore into the press, his actions would ensure front-page coverage. He hit the steering wheel with his fist. His mother hauled in like a criminal—suspected of murder. His gentle mother who was kind to everyone and had given shelter to Grant, Anna and Jack and constantly did things for others.

When his cell phone rang, Eli answered to hear Anna's voice.

"Eli, I heard about Caroline and Grant. Jillian said the police want to question them both," Anna said, sounding alarmed.

"That's right. I'm on my way to San Francisco now. I passed

Mom and Dad so I'll get there before they do and I think Grant and the other detectives are behind Mom and Dad. I should get there before any of them."

"Thank goodness! Please let me know about them. I can't imagine—"

"I'll call you, Anna, as soon as I know something," Eli promised.

"Thanks, Eli." She hung up and Eli tossed down his phone. His stomach was in knots.

While the sun moved lower in the western sky, Eli raced down the highway, finally tearing across the Golden Gate Bridge and heading to the police station, still in shock and disbelief at the latest turn of events. Another scandal to rock the Ashtons! More lurid notoriety that essentially had been caused by Spencer!

When Eli turned into the parking lot of the San Francisco Police Department, he swore again. Two television vans were parked by the door. A man stood leaning against the building, and Eli suspected he was a member of the press. A woman in a white blouse sat in a car. Nearby two men stood talking beside two cars, and Eli guessed they all were reporters waiting for Caroline and Grant to appear.

Eli clamped his jaw closed tightly, knowing the best he could do when his family arrived was get on one side of his mother and let Lucas stay on the other and try to get her into the building without too much hassle from the reporters. But he hated that the story would be in the papers and on television. He watched two men get out of a television van and lift out cameras and equipment. Another cameraman was already set up near the door. Hopefully, the detectives would help and not add to the problem.

A car like the one Lara drove turned into the lot. Eli stared at it grimly. A woman in a floppy hat and dark sunglasses was behind the wheel, and he shifted his attention back to the street to watch for the arrival of the car with his mother.

Since he hadn't spotted Grant on the way to the city, he guessed Grant was farther behind and would come after Caroline and Lucas arrived.

The car like Lara's pulled alongside Eli, and he frowned. He didn't want anyone to get in his way. When he looked at the woman, she motioned to him. Startled, he frowned and took a harder look. His stomach clenched.

Nine

Lara got out of her car and slid into his, closing the door.

"What are you doing here?" he asked sharply, stunned to see her. He ached to pull her into his arms.

Her bright red, Look-at-me! suit had a matching red silk blouse. She wore high-heeled red pumps on her feet. The hat that framed her face was a perfect background for her peaches-and-cream skin. While his mouth went dry and his pulse pounded, he wanted to reach for her and pull her into his arms. Instead, he kept his hands to himself and tried to listen to what she was telling him.

"I was in town and heard on the news that the police intend to question your mother about Spencer's murder. I figured you'd be here and thought I'd see if I could help in any way," she said.

"I didn't recognize you at first," he replied, looking at her floppy hat and the dark sunglasses. He couldn't see her eyes, and the hat hid her hair and part of her face.

"If the press gets my picture, I don't want to be recognizable."

"Your red suit practically screams for attention, and everyone will notice you," he said roughly. The urge to pull her hat off and run his fingers through her hair grew by the minute, but he controlled his impulse.

"I came to the city three hours ago. I can't do anything now about my suit. This is an old hat I had tossed into the back of the car."

"I think the reporters will focus on my family, but if you get out of the car, you'll be on the news with us," he said, his mind only half on their conversation, the rest of his thoughts swirling over Lara. Why was she here?

"That's what I figured. Lilah Ashton would be less than happy to find I'm here to support your family at this moment. Where is your mother?"

"I passed them on the way here. They should arrive any minute now. The police intend to question Grant, too."

Lara nodded. "That's on the news."

"Damn, I hate this," Eli grumbled. "I hate it for both of them. Our lives have been one crisis after another, and this last year has been pure hell. It's not the first time, but I think we've had more than our share of trouble. Always the turmoil goes back to Spencer. He couldn't even die without tormenting us."

Lara squeezed Eli's hand, and he focused on her. "If you don't want Lilah Ashton to know you're here with us, you better leave," he said, still surprised that Lara had come. She seemed cool and remote, and he suspected her presence didn't mean her feelings toward him had changed, but at the moment he couldn't sort it out. Right now he was in knots about his mother and Grant.

"There are already two television crews here, and I'm sure

there are three reporters. Here comes another damned reporter," he said when a woman drove into the parking lot. "Lara, don't jeopardize yourself. Dad and I are here, and the others are on their way."

"I'm not too recognizable. My face is almost covered and I don't wear this hat at the estate. I want to be here, Eli."

Her words strummed across his heart. She *wanted* to be with him and his family. Was it pity? Sympathy? Or something deeper? How much did she care?

It was tempting to tell her to get in her car and go because now there were two women he wanted to shield from the media instead of concentrating on one. Yet deep down, in spite of her aloofness, he was glad to see her and he couldn't send her away.

Her perfume stirred vivid memories of Lara in his arms, Lara pressed close against him. He wiped his brow while he watched a long, dark-green car whip into the lot and park. Three men climbed out, all dressed in dark suits and all of them carrying briefcases. They hurried toward the building to disappear inside.

"Thank God, there go our lawyers!" Eli exclaimed.

"Do you want to let them know you're here?"

"No, they knew I was on my way. That tall, black-haired one is Ridley Pollard, our family attorney, and he's here for moral support. The other two are criminal lawyers he recommended. I haven't met them yet. Mom hired Edgar Kent for Grant."

"Your mother has the proverbial heart of gold."

"Yes, she does. I want to wait for Mom and Dad so I can help Dad shield her from the press as she goes into the building."

"When you mother arrives, I'll go with you. I'll just be an-other person to keep reporters away from her."

"Here they come," he said, watching the unmarked sedan pull into the lot. The television crews jumped into action, running toward the car with their cameras already going. As the reporters gathered, Eli stepped out of the car. When Lara joined him, he took her arm, and they rushed to the official car. Eli merely nodded at Detective Holbrook whose blue eyes were impassive behind her glasses. Eli didn't know the other tall, thin detective.

Keeping Lara at his side, Eli shouldered his way past a reporter. He knew a television cameraman was filming every second. Caroline emerged from the car. She looked stylish in a black suit and a black silk shirt, but she was pale and visibly trembling, which sent Eli's anger soaring. Only a few feet in front of her a flash went off and then another one while other cameras whirred.

As Eli moved close to her right side, the detectives stepped in front. Lucas had his arm around her waist on her left and they all walked together. Eli glanced over his shoulder to see Lara directly behind Caroline as she said she would be.

There was no way to totally shield Caroline, Eli thought as reporters crowded in, taking pictures and shouting questions. A microphone was jammed in front of Eli, and he heard questions that were aimed at him, but he had no intention of answering. Furious, he reached out to grab the camera, but Lara caught his arm, and he held back. Simmering with anger, he knew he should control his temper.

Suddenly a television cameraman got through, shoving the camera in Caroline's face as he shouted questions at her.

Eli's temper exploded, and he grabbed the camera. For an instant there was a tug-of-war between the two men, but Eli yanked, and the camera slipped out of the newsman's hands. Eli tossed the camera to the ground and it smashed against the asphalt, pieces splattering.

Several of the newsmen shouted at Eli, but he ignored them.

He could hear one of them yelling at the detectives to arrest Eli. Instead, the detectives walked faster, and Eli and Lucas hurried Caroline along.

"You'll have to pay for my camera!" came a shout behind Eli.

The thirty yards to the door seemed a mile, but then the detectives were there. The man held open the door, and Detective Holbrook stepped back to block the reporters.

Caroline and her entourage swept inside, and Detective Holbrook closed the door. Eli looked down at Caroline. They strode down a hall into a room that held a desk with a sergeant on duty and another desk with a dispatcher. Detective Holbrook led them through a closed door into a large waiting room.

"No reporters will be allowed in here," she said.

Chairs lined one side of the plain room, with a drinking fountain on the other side. A low rail divided the area from another room filled with desks. Eli barely noticed his surroundings as he looked down at his mother.

"You okay?" he asked, and she patted his arm, but she was paler than before, and he knew the past few seconds from the car to the station had been upsetting to her.

"Thanks for being here." She turned around. "Lara, thank you, too."

"I'm glad to help in any little way," Lara replied, and Caroline squeezed Lara's hand.

The three attorneys joined them, and Ridley Pollard introduced Edgar Kent and Amos Detmer to all of the Ashtons and Lara.

"Ridley, you may have to bail Eli out now," Caroline said, giving a worried glance to her oldest son. The attorney nodded his head and turned to Eli. "I'll talk to the cameraman. He may have already contacted his attorney."

"Thanks," Eli said, all his worries focused on Caroline. At the moment he wasn't concerned with the reporter.

Detective Holbrook had stepped to the desk, but she returned. "Mrs. Sheppard, if you'll please come with me."

It was a nightmare for Eli—a moment he never expected to see. He wanted to fling himself between his mother and the detectives, but he knew he'd only make things worse. He let out a long breath. Also, he wanted to hug his mother, but there wasn't a chance. Lucas gave her a quick hug and stepped back as Amos Detmer moved to her side.

Lucas looked over his shoulder. "Eli, thanks for all your help. You're sticking around, aren't you?"

"Yes. Grant isn't here yet."

"Watch for him. The reporters will swamp him." Lucas glanced at Lara, and his eyebrows arched. "Lara," he greeted her. "It was good of you to come be with us."

"Hello, Mr. Sheppard," she said, removing her sunglasses. "I'm sorry this happened."

"Thanks. We'll get it sorted out, and the truth will prevail," Lucas said calmly. "We might as well sit down, because I'm guessing this is going to take some time." He walked away, leaving Eli and Lara alone.

"I'll wait outside for Grant," Eli told her, unable to resist touching her as he brushed a tendril of auburn hair away from her cheek.

"You won't want the reporters questioning you," she reminded him. "They watched you walk in with your mother, so now they'll have a hundred questions for you," Lara said. "They're unhappy with you at the moment, anyway."

"You're right. I don't want to tangle with them. I probably didn't help Mom or my family. I guess I'll stay inside."

"I can't go out without questions, either, because they don't know who I am. As we came in here, several reporters asked my name and how I know the family. One asked me if my name was Anna Sheridan."

"Well, hell. I guess we just sit tight and let Grant fend for himself." Eli studied her and thought she looked thinner. "You shouldn't have gotten involved."

She shrugged. "It's dreadful that the police suspect your mother."

"It's ridiculous. If she intended to shoot Spencer, she would have done it when he left us. Not now." Eli pulled out his cell phone. "I'm going to call Cole, Jillian and Mercedes and tell them to park somewhere else, that the back lot is filled with media. I'll be with you in a minute."

"Take your time," Lara replied, and waited quietly while he made his calls. When he finished, Eli looked over her head. "Ridley Pollard is back. Excuse me a minute while I see what he learned."

Eli walked away, talking briefly with their stocky, blue-eyed attorney and then returning to Lara while Ridley Pollard sat down with Lucas and Edgar Kent.

"Ridley's going to contact the television station and tell them I'll buy a new camera and see if he can head off charges being filed against me," Eli told Lara.

"I'm sorry all of you are going through this," Lara said.

His gaze went past her. "Here's Grant. Just a minute and I'll be back." He left Lara to greet his half brother, shaking hands with Grant and clasping him on the shoulder. "Mom is already here." Eli said as he shook Grant's hand. Eli merely nodded at Detective Dan Ryland and the other detective who accompanied Grant. The detectives stepped away to go to the desk and talk briefly with the officer on duty. Looking grim, Grant turned his attention to Eli.

"Thanks, Eli, for coming. It means a lot," he said. "Hi, Lara," he added, calling and waving to her.

"Cole is coming, too," Eli said. "I think they all may be here except Mercedes. As far as I know no one has been able to get in touch with her."

Grant said, "I really appreciate everything all of you are doing."

"Anna wanted to know about you and Mom. She called me." Edgar Kent came forward and Eli introduced him, walking away so the two men could confer.

In another minute Detective Ryland joined Grant and the attorney. "Will you come with us," he said, and Grant and Edgar Kent turned to follow the detective.

Eli held Lara's arm. "We might as well sit down unless you want me to try to get you back to your car without too much hassle."

"No. I'll wait with you."

"Here comes my brother," Eli announced, seeing Cole come through a door on the opposite side of the room. Eli waved to Cole and Dixie, who strode toward them. "My practical businessman brother," Eli said, looking at Cole. "He'll be as lost in this situation as I am. There's nothing either of us can do for Mom or Grant now except give moral support."

Dressed in brown slacks and a tan shirt, Cole came forward. While he greeted Lucas and Ridley Pollard first, Eli waited and then greeted his brother and sister-in-law. Eli thought again that Cole had married a beautiful woman. Dixie wore a brightly patterned shirt and green slacks. Her straight, dark-blond hair had a silky sheen and she smiled at Lara and Eli.

"It's nice to see you, Lara. Thanks for lending your support," Cole said.

"Mom and Grant have already been taken somewhere for questioning," Eli said. "An attorney named Amos Detmer is with Mom. Edgar Kent is with Grant."

"Great," Cole remarked. "I guess we just wait. We've been listening to the news. You attacked a cameraman."

"That didn't take long to become news. I smashed his camera. I didn't attack him. He jammed a camera in Mom's face and yelled questions at her," Eli said, and Cole nodded.

"Under those circumstances I might have done the same thing. Have you talked to Ridley Pollard about it?"

"Yes. He's already been on the phone with the television station trying to keep them from pressing assault charges against me."

"That's all we need," Cole said grimly, rubbing the back of his head. "I can't believe this is happening."

"I feel the same way," Eli said. "Mom looked pale and I know she has to be upset."

"We might as well sit down," Cole suggested, turning toward the chairs and taking Dixie's arm.

As soon as they were all seated in the hard, brown wooden chairs that were worn and scarred from use, Lara turned to Eli. "Your family is here now. I'm going to leave."

"Reporters will be all over you," Eli said. "They saw you come in with us." He turned to his brother. "Where are you parked, Cole?"

"Like you told me. Down the street. No one paid any attention to us."

"Lara, give Dixie your car keys. They won't know Dixie, and she can drive your car out of the parking lot to the street. We'll go out the front," Eli said. "Cole, do you want to stay here in case Grant or Mom need us?"

"Sure," Cole replied. "Unless you want me to come with you," he said to Dixie, but she shook her head.

Eli held Lara's arm and looked over her head at Cole. "I'll be back."

Lara told Cole, Lucas and Ridley Pollard goodbye and walked out with Eli. At the door she turned to him and pulled her hat lower. Eli put his arm across her shoulders and they left the building.

"There's no one out here," she exclaimed in surprise, and Eli let out his breath in relief.

"Thank God!" Eli exclaimed. "Cole said there wasn't any press here when he and Dixie arrived."

Eli and Lara went down steps and walked to the drive from the parking lot. "Here comes Dixie with your car." Eli turned to face Lara, dropping his arm from her shoulders. She tilted her head, looking up at him from beneath the wide hat brim. She had the dark glasses on again and he couldn't see her eyes.

"Thanks for coming," he said. "The whole family appreciates it. It'll mean a lot to Mom and Grant."

"I don't know about that," Lara replied. "I was glad to be here and give any support I could. I'm just sorry they're being questioned. I'm sure it'll be in the news how things turn out."

"I'll let you know. Actually, Grant is the one I'm worried about. He had a big motive and no alibi. Dad was with Mom and they ought to get that straightened out quickly. We've got excellent lawyers."

"Here's Dixie. Goodbye, Eli," Lara said.

He wanted to see her again, but he knew she would refuse. It was a situation that was only headed for disappointment. He watched her walk around and get in her car and heard her thank Dixie.

While he stood watching, she drove away, and he wondered if she were driving out of his life forever. Dixie joined him to go back inside. "That was supportive of her, Eli."

"Yeah," he said. "Even so, there weren't enough of us to help get Mom inside without a reporter getting in her face. The reporters and the cameramen mobbed us."

"I'm surprised one isn't stationed around here at this door."

"They probably think everyone goes in the other way," he replied, his thoughts still on Lara. He held the door for Dixie, and as he started inside he glanced around to see Jillian and Seth approaching. "Go on," he told Dixie. "Here comes Jillian and Seth, and I'll wait for them."

He stood at the top of the steps, his thoughts in turmoil over Lara's appearance and Caroline and Grant being questioned. Once again, as he watched his sister and brother-in-law approach holding hands, he was reminded of the void in his own life. He missed Lara every second of every day.

As soon as Jillian and Seth joined him, his sister looked at him with curiosity in her green eyes. "Didn't I see Lara drive away?"

"Yes, you did," he said, holding the door for them and following them inside. "She heard about Mom and Grant."

"I wasn't certain whether it was her or not. She had on a big hat. I thought you said you weren't going to see each other again."

"She wasn't here long," he said, and Jillian turned away to talk to Cole and Dixie. "Mercedes will be here soon," Jillian said.

Eli joined the others as they sat down, but in minutes he got up to pace the floor. He couldn't keep his mind on their conversation. As he stood gazing out a window, Lucas joined him. "Stop worrying, Eli. The police don't have any hard evidence, and they sure won't have anything to tie your mother to it. Or Grant."

"Except motive for Grant. Although, if it were based solely on motive, there would be a hundred other suspects. Spencer had enemies everywhere," Eli said.

"Stop worrying, son," Lucas said, and walked back to join the others.

Eli raked his fingers through his hair. In minutes he heard everyone greet Mercedes, and he turned to say hello to his sister. Her light-brown hair was fastened on top of her head and she wore chic yellow slacks and a striped yellow-and-white cotton blouse. She crossed the room to Eli.

"How's Mom?"

"She's fine, I guess. She was when she left with the detectives."

"They can't hold her. They don't have any evidence to tie her to Spencer's murder," Mercedes said.

"There isn't anything that we know about."

"You know there's nothing to tie Mom to Spencer's murder. I spoke to Ridley. Cole told me he's making phone calls to get you out of hot water. He said you smashed a camera."

"The guy was right in Mom's face."

"I'm glad you did it, but I hope you don't have to go to court over it. Or jail," she added.

"Ridley will take care of the situation, and I'll pay. I don't think I'll have to go to court, although at the rate the Ashtons have been making headlines, I may have to."

"Thanks for getting here as quickly as you did," Mercedes said. "I know Mom and Dad were glad to have you here. Grant, too. I'm sorry you couldn't get hold of me. I left my phone in the car instead of my purse when I was running errands in Napa."

"That's okay." He looked over her head. "That didn't take long. Here's Mom."

"Eli, she looks as if she's going to faint," Mercedes said with a frown.

"Dammit," Eli swore. Lucas was already past them as he strode forward to meet Caroline, who smiled. Her face was white, but she appeared fine, and Amos Detmer smiled at Lucas. "She's been released," he said as the family gathered around her and she hugged first one and then another of her children.

"Thank God," Eli said, while Lucas turned to Caroline. Ridley Pollard patted her shoulder.

"You're cleared now." Riley turned to shake hands with the other attorney. "Amos, thank you." As the two lawyers talked, Lucas took Caroline's arm.

"Let's get you out of here," Lucas said.

"Seth and I can drive you home," Jillian volunteered.

"You take them home," Eli said. "I'll stay to see about Grant."

"We can stay with Eli," Cole added while Mercedes said she would follow Jillian and Seth to go home with Lucas and Caroline.

One by one, the entire family thanked the lawyers before the men turned to go. Ridley shook hands with Eli. "I'll get back to you. It may be tomorrow before I know whether there will be charges pressed against you or not."

"Thanks, Ridley. I appreciate what you're doing."

"Try to get out of here without taking a swing at anyone," he said, and turned to leave with Amos.

As soon as the family parted, Cole motioned toward the chairs. "This may take hours. We haven't eaten. What about you, Eli?"

"Nope, but I'm not hungry. I'll stay here. You and Dixie go get something. If anything changes, I can call you on your cell."

Cole and Dixie left, and Eli paced the room slowly, finally standing by a window. It was dark outside and streetlights had come on. He was thankful his mother had been released, but he had a growing dread over the lengthening time it was taking for Grant to be questioned. Grant had struck a chord with Eli, who liked him enormously. Grant had that same streak of kindness and generosity that Caroline did. Grant had raised his niece and nephew when their mother had run out on them and his grandparents died. Grant couldn't be the murderer, yet he was a likely suspect.

Eli raked his fingers through his hair and thought about Lara. He was still surprised that she had come to help today. She must care about him to do that. He had to admit that he had fallen in love with her, but a lot of good it would do him. Still, Lara's showing up this afternoon gave him pause about the future.

Cole and Dixie returned with sandwiches, but Eli's appetite had diminished the day he'd met Lara and only grown less since then. He knew from taking his belt in that he was losing weight. Idly, he wondered whether he was losing more sleep or more weight over her. He hardly slept anymore, catching an hour or two and then waking and wanting her.

An hour later Eli paced the floor again. Cole stretched out his long legs and looked at his brother. "Eli, sit down. You'll wear out the floor."

"They're taking too long."

"Yes, they are," Cole answered solemnly. "Ridley thinks Edgar Kent is the best possible lawyer we could get, so at least Grant is in excellent hands."

Eli raked his fingers through his hair and sat down in a chair facing Cole and Dixie. "You two can go if you want, and I'll stay."

"We're fine," Cole said, glancing at Dixie, who nodded. He leaned closer to her, draping his arm around her shoulders. "Tell me if you want to go."

A look passed between them, and Eli was reminded again of Lara. Every time they were together Cole and Dixie's love for each other made Eli feel all the more cold and empty.

It was after nine before Grant and Edgar Kent reappeared. Eli, Dixie and Cole all went forward to him. As soon as Eli introduced Edgar Kent to Dixie and Cole, he turned to Grant. "How'd it go?" Eli asked, knowing from Grant's scowling expression that the answer wouldn't be what he wanted to hear.

Grant's face flushed, and his eyes snapped with anger. "They're not going to hold me here, but I can't leave the area," he announced gruffly. "I'm definitely their prime suspect."

"They don't have any solid evidence to tie you to the crime," Edgar Kent reminded him. "If they want to question you again, just call me first. You know how to get me at any hour, day or night."

Grant turned to the lawyer and extended his hand. "Thanks for being here tonight."

"Glad to do it. I'll see you in my office tomorrow morning," Edgar Kent said and turned to tell the others goodbye.

"I'll take you back with me, and Cole and Dixie can go home," Eli said.

"You didn't do it, Grant. The truth will come out."

"Not if they stop searching for the real killer because they think they've found the murderer in me," Grant said. He held his hand out to Cole. "Thank you and Dixie for coming tonight. It makes me feel better to know that this family supports me. I can't tell all three of you how much that means to me."

"You're part of our family," Eli said. "We'll all stick together. And we know you're innocent."

"The reporters are probably still hanging around in back. Let's get you out the front," Cole said.

"I have to get my car," Eli replied. "I'll make a run for it and meet you—how about in front of St. Mary's Cathedral? You take Grant that far with you, and I'll pick him up there. I can lose any reporters between here and the church."

Cole nodded and the three of them went out the front. Eli strode to the back door, took a deep breath and stepped outside. When he dashed for his car, reporters closed in. Ignoring their questions, he pushed one aside at his car and slid in, locking his doors instantly.

With two cars speeding behind him, Eli raced out of the parking lot and down the street, accelerating up and down hills as he wound through San Francisco. When he decided he had lost everyone on his tail, he headed for Geary Street to pick up Grant.

Keeping an eye on the rearview mirror, Eli's thoughts returned to Lara. He wanted to see her again. The realization that he was in love shocked him, but he had always known what he wanted and now he wanted Lara. It went beyond physical desire. He wanted her in his life, and maybe she was having second thoughts about not seeing him again, too.

He came to a decision about his future.

With clouds of fog hovering over the ground the next morning, Eli drove through the Ashton Estate gate and watched it close behind him. Thanks to Charlotte Ashton, he could get in the private entrance. He thought about his phone conversation with her, setting up a visit to Ashton Estate. He wanted to see Lara and he suspected if he called her, she would refuse.

Eli followed Charlotte's directions and drove around the house to park near the winery. Alexandre said he would be there to pick him up with one of the estate carts and take him to the greenhouse on the east.

Eli stepped out of the car and strode toward the front of the winery where he was to meet Alexandre. Eli knew he would have to do something to show his gratitude to Charlotte and Alexandre for setting up this rendezvous.

Eli remembered meeting Alexandre at a wine tasting event in Yountville, and he had liked the winemaker immediately. They shared a love of wine making, and Eli was impressed with Alexandre's reputation and expertise. Alexandre was obviously deeply in love with Charlotte Ashton, and Eli was glad because he suspected Spencer may have given her a hard time.

As Eli walked, he lifted his face and inhaled. The air smelled damp, but he loved the fog because he knew how great it was for the grapevines. It would also keep him from being seen by anyone in the house. Charlotte had told him that Lilah would be ensconced in the mansion, talking on the telephone to her friends. Trace would be in his office. Walker would not even be at the estate so Eli should be able to safely come and go without interference from the family. Charlotte also promised to get Lara to the greenhouse. Then Eli was on his own.

A twig snapped under his feet. He inhaled again, enjoying the damp air that lifted his spirits in spite of the grayness. The late-morning sun soon would burn off the fog, yet it kept the ground cool and moist in the early part of the day.

Eli's gaze ran over the buildings. He glanced over his shoulder at the magnificent mansion shrouded in fog. Bitterness knotted his stomach. He intended to talk to Mom and Dad again about the will. Spencer shouldn't have inherited it, and Ashton Estate was too much to toss aside with a shrug. Eli knew that part of his motive was revenge against Spencer even though he would never know anyway.

Eli's nerves were raw. He missed Lara more with each passing day, and he prayed that her appearance last night meant she still cared about him.

As he turned a corner, he almost collided with Lilah Ashton.

"You!" she gasped. "What are you doing on our land?" Her eyes widened. To his horror she screamed, a loud, terrified cry that shattered the quiet morning.

Ten

"**T**race, help! Trace!"

"Mrs. Ashton," Eli began, intending to explain that he was there to see Alexandre—a story they had decided on earlier if Eli ran into any of the other Ashtons.

Trace burst out of the winery and sprinted toward them. His face was flushed and his fists clenched. "You damn bastard!" he yelled. "Leave my mother alone! I told you to stay away from here."

"You're here to spy on us," Lilah accused. Barely listening to her, Eli braced his feet apart.

"Trace, I'm here—" Eli began, wondering if either mother or son would listen to an explanation.

Trace never slowed. He swung his fist, connecting with Eli's jaw. Eli staggered, and lights danced before his eyes.

His temper snapped and he waded in. His fist shot out in a

right to the jaw. With a crack of bone on bone, Eli sent Trace sprawling.

"Call the police! Call the police!" Lilah Ashton screamed as Trace sprang up to lunge at Eli, tackling him. Both men toppled and rolled across the ground.

"Mrs. Ashton!" Lara cried, running up to join them. Eli heard her voice and wanted to shake Trace off him. He didn't want Lara to take any blame for his being at the estate.

He rolled over on top of Trace, broke away and stood.

"Call the police!" Lilah Ashton still screamed while Lara stood in front of her.

"Ms. Ashton, don't call the police," Lara commanded forcefully enough to startle Lilah Ashton into silence.

"Eli Ashton is here because—" Lara started, but was interrupted by a deep male voice.

Alexandre approached them, stepping between Trace and Eli as Trace got to his feet. Trace's lip was cut while Eli's cheek was bleeding. Both men had smaller cuts. Eli's sleeve was torn, and Trace's shirt was ripped with blood oozing from a scratch on his shoulder.

"Eli Ashton is here to see me," Alexandre announced. "We share a passion for France, and I have maps and pictures for him. Sorry if this caused an upset."

"Next time, Alexandre, tell someone." Trace clamped his jaw closed and turned to stride away.

Frowning, Lilah Ashton blinked and rubbed her forehead. "Very well," she said, turning to hurry after her son. "Trace, wait," she called.

Eli turned to Alexandre. "Thanks for stepping in and saving the situation," he said quietly and offered his hand to Alexandre.

"Glad to. I can take both of you to the greenhouse where you can talk in private."

"That won't be necessary," Lara said. "But thank you, anyway, Alexandre."

He smiled at her, nodded and left them alone.

Taking out his handkerchief to wipe his bleeding cheek, Eli turned to her. "I wanted to see you. Charlotte and Alexandre helped me set up a meeting. Charlotte was going to call you to come to the greenhouse."

"She just did. That's where I was headed when I heard Lilah scream. Then I saw you and Trace. Why didn't you tell me you wanted to see me?"

"I figured you'd refuse."

She frowned at him. "Come with me and we'll wash your cuts."

"I'm all right."

Her fingers closed around his arm. "You come with me," she said, and he fell into step beside her. She led him upstairs to her tiny quarters on the third floor where she closed the door behind them.

Eli glanced around the room that was yellow and white with bright, primary colored pillows and a rocker. Circus prints were hung on one wall and plants were scattered around the room. She had a twin bed that she motioned to.

"Sit there," she said and disappeared back into the hall. He looked around the bedroom/sitting room and thought it was cheerful and cozy and looked like Lara.

She returned to hand him gauze and bandages, antiseptic and a towel. She had a wet washcloth that she dabbed against his cut cheek.

"This is where I live. This floor is for the staff. We have a bathroom down the hall."

"This room looks like you. It's cozy. I like it."

She frowned at him. "It's tiny, Eli," she protested. "You live in that wonderful suite. This is a shoe box."

"It's livable, while the rest of this house looks like a museum—the parlor, the library, the dining room all create a feeling of look, don't touch. Besides, this room is yours, so that makes it special," he said and she shifted her attention to his cut. He noticed that her cheeks were flushed.

Since she was not on duty, she was dressed in a bright-blue cotton shirt and blue cotton slacks and her hair was tied behind her head with a matching blue ribbon. She had sandals on her feet. His mouth went dry as he mentally stripped away the clothes and remembered how she had looked naked in his arms.

In seconds she stood between his legs so she could treat his injured face. When he rested his hands on her hips, she frowned, but then went back to dabbing at the cut on his cheek.

"I think you gave worse than you got," she remarked.

"I grew up wrestling with Cole. Trace only has sisters. He doesn't have my experience," Eli replied dryly. "Walker's enough older than Trace that Trace probably didn't tangle with him much." Eli took a deep breath. "Lara, I want to see you again."

"Eli, you know I can't. I—"

"Charlotte said you're off duty this morning. Is that right?"

She glared at him. "Yes, it is, but that doesn't matter."

"It matters to me," he said, standing and taking her hand. "You're not in uniform, so you must be off duty. Come on. We're going where we can talk."

"I'm not—"

He turned to her. "Lara, please. I want to talk to you," he said in a tone that made Lara's heart melt. As she inhaled deeply, he took her hand and turned to go.

They hurried through the house, and he was glad they didn't encounter any of the Ashtons. At his car he held open the door for her.

"How did you even get through the gate this morning?" Lara asked as she slid into the seat.

"Charlotte and Alexandre," he replied.

Eli strode around the car to sit behind the wheel. "Charlotte saw you leave with me for our family party. You said she was friendly to you and I've met and talked to Alexandre before, so I called Charlotte and told her I wanted to see you. I told her that for the past week, when I've called you, you've simply hung up the phone."

"That's because I've said everything there is to say."

"Charlotte said she would arrange it so I could get in and talk to you at her greenhouse."

"Oh, my word! Charlotte's in love and she sees the whole world in a rosy glow. So what happened?"

"I looked for Alexandre, who agreed to be here this morning to take me to the greenhouse. He said he's finished his work here and they're waiting until Charlotte can go to France with him. Anyway, I ran into Lilah Ashton who, according to Charlotte, would be in the house on the phone."

"She usually is in the mornings. She likes to talk to her friends, she reads the paper and she gives my mom any additional instructions about the staff."

"The minute she saw me, Lilah started screaming for Trace, and he came on the run. As soon as he appeared, we got into it. All the time we fought, Lilah screamed for someone to call the police."

"That's what I heard. I ran out because I thought Lilah was in trouble."

"Even though Trace threw the first punch, I know I shouldn't have hit him. It felt damn satisfying to slug him, though."

"I'm sorry you and Trace fought."

"I'm thankful Alexandre appeared," Eli said. "I wouldn't want you in any trouble because I came to see you."

"This is foolish, Eli," Lara said quietly, and his insides clenched.

He prayed his instincts were right and seeing her wasn't going to be another rejection.

"I want to go where we can be alone and talk. I have things I need to tell you," he said as he sped toward Napa. "I've missed seeing you. It meant a lot to my family that you were there for Mom and Grant last night."

"I was glad to be present. What happened with Grant?"

"At this point it looks as if he is a prime suspect."

"Oh, no!" she gasped. "That's terrible!"

"They didn't arrest him, because they don't have enough hard evidence, but they told him he can't leave the area."

"That's awful and I know it upsets your family!" Lara exclaimed.

"We're worried that the police will stop searching for the murderer. They've been under pressure to solve the crime. The press is wild to get news about the scandalous Ashtons and the murder. Meanwhile, our whole family believes in Grant's innocence. That man could no more have done such a deed than Dad could have."

"You said Grant doesn't have an alibi and he has a motive."

"There has to be more than that to take him to court. In the meantime, he's on edge about the situation. The family, including Anna and little Jack, try to cheer him."

"He's fortunate to have all of you."

"We're glad to have him in the family. For such a rotten man, Spencer fathered some likable people."

"I saw you on the news last night, and your picture is in the paper this morning."

He groaned. "I figured. I didn't look at the paper today and I didn't watch the news last night, but I'm not surprised. I haven't talked to our lawyer yet about it, but he's trying to keep me out of jail."

"Don't even say that!" she exclaimed.

Eli glanced at her, longing to touch her and wishing he could pull her close against his side. "I'm going to look at apartments in Napa."

"Why?" she asked.

He shrugged. "I thought I might want to be off on my own this coming year. I can stay at the house whenever I want. That's what Mercedes does all the time."

As they talked, he drove into Napa and headed to the restaurant and hotel where he and Lara spent their first night together. When he parked and got out to open her door, she looked up at him.

"What are we doing here?"

"I told you. I want to talk to you alone. Come on. We'll just talk and then I'll take you to lunch."

He took her hand to enter the hotel, and Lara's pulse raced. She should say no firmly and insist they talk somewhere less private, but Eli had a determined look in his eye and a steely note in his voice. And she had missed him beyond belief.

She watched him cross the hotel lobby to the desk. Looking sexy and adorable, he wore navy slacks and a navy knit shirt that now had a rip in the sleeve. In spite of the cuts and bruises and the rip in his clothes, he was incredibly appealing.

She had hurt terribly for him and for his family yesterday when she'd heard the news on the radio. She'd felt compelled to go see if she could help them in San Francisco.

Memories of their first night assailed her, and she grew hot just thinking about that night. Then he was striding back to her, his scalding gaze consuming her and making her heart pound.

"Let's go," he said, taking her hand. Upstairs, they had the same suite, and she wondered if he had made arrangements ahead of time but then decided he hadn't. She suspected her appearance last night had triggered his visit today.

He unlocked the door of the suite and held it open for her. She entered and turned to face him, trying to summon the strength and resistance she knew she was going to desperately need.

"All right, Eli. We're alone and we can talk, but it won't change anything."

"I hope it will change everything," he said in a husky voice, closing and locking the door and then turning to face her. He stepped to her to catch both of her hands in his.

"Lara, I know I'm hot-tempered and I know I like to be in control. Maybe way too much of both of those. I know I'm not worthy of your love because of—"

"Eli," she said, interrupting him, hurting for him and wanting him. "That isn't why I don't want to see you. You're worthy of my love, of any woman's love!"

He dropped her hands to frame her face with his hands. When he stepped closer and gazed down into her eyes, her heart thudded so loudly she was certain he could hear it. Standing this close, she couldn't keep from looking at his mouth, his full underlip, and remembering his kisses. She wanted to kiss him, but she fought the temptation.

"Lara, I've missed you and don't want to be without you," he said in a husky voice.

Lara's pounding heart missed a beat as she gazed up at him. "Eli, I have plans—"

"Shh," he said without letting her finish. "Listen to me. I want you in my life. Adjust your goals and make room for me. If we're married, you can still go to law school."

"Married!" she exclaimed, her eyes widening, shocked by his statement. "We haven't even talked about being in love."

"I guess it took our separation to make me realize the depth of my feelings. I've been miserable. I've missed you every second. I see you everywhere. I can't eat or sleep or even work efficiently. My vineyards that I used to love so much no longer hold my interest. I love you. I know what I want, Lara. I want to marry you."

Stunned at the depth of his feelings for her, she gazed up at him while her heart thudded. Everything in her cried out, yes! She'd known she loved him. Yet she knew the responsibilities she had in her future. Trembling, she ached to reach for him, to kiss him and toss aside all other considerations. This tall, strong man was the love of her life, and she knew there would never be another like him for her. Hurt and sadness and hot desire warred in her while she tingled all over.

"Eli," she said woodenly, "I want to take care—"

"You want to take care of your mother. Lara, don't you think that I, of all people, can understand your need to care for her?" His eyes blazed. "From the time I was eight years old until I was twenty-one and Louret was successfully established I wanted to do all I could to make my mother's life easier. Even when Mom married Lucas, I still wanted that. My goal of making Louret successful was for her sake. That's all I ever wanted. If you marry me, we can both take care of your mother."

Stunned, Lara stared at him. Never had she imagined that he would make her such an offer. "Eli, I don't know what to say…"

"Just say yes that you'll marry me, and I'll take care of the rest," he said, his gaze searching hers. "Lara, will you marry me?"

The words hung in the air like golden baubles dangled before her, promising undreamed-of delights. Marry him! All her reservations fell away. He had promised law school and that together they would take care of her mother. The moment those concerns were resolved, Lara let out a long breath and threw her arms around his neck.

"I love you, Eli!" she exclaimed, and then kissed him before he could reply.

Her mouth covered his, her tongue seeking his to stroke and taste while he kissed her in return. Her insides clenched, and heat started low in her belly. She wanted him with all the pent-up desire that she had battled since that first night. They were so close she could feel his hard erection.

Eli shifted away a few inches to allow him access to her clothing. His fingers twisted free the buttons on her blue blouse to pull it off her shoulders. In minutes he whisked away her blue slacks. "I love you, Lara, and I want you. Heart and soul and body—I want you. I want to kiss and lick every inch of your body," he whispered in her ear, his warm breath tickling her. "I've waited and dreamed of this moment." His husky voice was a mere rasp.

As he pushed her away, she tugged his shirt free, seeing the bulge in his slacks that proclaimed his readiness for her. The moment his strong, muscled chest was bare, she ran her fingers over him, touching his flat nipples and brushing her fingers over his chest hair, then letting her hand drift down to unbuckle his belt.

While she removed his slacks, he kicked off his loafers and peeled away his socks.

"You're so handsome," she declared, running her hands over his bare hips and relishing the male perfection of him. He loved her! It was magic to know. They would marry! Her heart pounded with joy and desire. She slid her hands down to his strong thighs.

"How I love you!" she exclaimed.

While she caressed his legs and teased her fingers up and over his flat stomach, he cupped her breasts, flicking loose the fastener and pushing away her lacy bra.

"Ahh, perfect," he said, palming each soft breast in his big hands. His rough, callused fingers were a sexy abrasion to her tender skin. As his thumbs circled her nipples with deliberation, she gasped and closed her eyes. Clinging to his strong arms, she wallowed in sensations that set her ablaze.

"Eli," she whispered.

"Do you like this?" he asked as he caressed her nipples. He leaned down to take one in his mouth and slowly circle the taut bud with his tongue. Warm and wet, each stroke of his tongue heightened her need until she shook. She slid her hands down, closing her fingers around his smooth, thick shaft. Then she let her tongue circle one of his nipples before she knelt in front of him.

Her tongue lazed down across his flat belly while she let her warm breath sigh over him, her tongue flicking around his shaft, tormenting him until he groaned. Then when she licked his long, throbbing rod, he wound his fingers in her hair.

"Lara!" he rasped, while she slipped one hand down between

his legs to cup him and stroke him. She curled her tongue around the velvet tip of his thick shaft. He shook, and the fingers of his left hand bit into her shoulder.

With a groan he bent down to pull her to her feet. He stopped and removed a packet from his trousers and then he scooped her into his arms to place her on the bed. He tossed the packet on the bedside table. Eli caught her ankles to pull her to the edge of the bed, kneeling between her legs to gently bite and tease along the inside of her thigh.

Lara's heart pounded and she combed her fingers through his hair. She wanted him inside her. She ached, all the longing she had lived with through lonely nights compounding the desire she had now.

"I want to make you come again and again," he whispered while his lips and tongue brushed her inner thigh. She raised her head to find him watching her. He spread her legs, moving between them, parting her soft folds to stroke her with his tongue.

"Eli!" she gasped, closing her eyes while she clung to his strong shoulders. He pushed her back on the bed, lifting her legs over his shoulders and then his tongue licked her intimately. She moved her hips, spreading her legs wider. She was open, utterly his.

"Eli, I want you."

"I'm going to love you until you come apart in my arms," he whispered, holding her legs wider and exploring her with his tongue. Hot and wet, each touch increased the urgency that was coiling in her.

She moved, lost now to his loving. He lifted her hips, giving him more access and then she felt his finger enter her, another torment that pushed her closer to a brink. She spasmed over the edge, her hips shifting in a pounding rhythm while she held him.

"Eli!" she cried in ecstasy. The world vanished except for the sexy man loving her. "Come here. I want you in me."

"Later," he said. "I want to make love to you for hours, Lara," he whispered. He lay down beside her, his hand going where his mouth had been while he propped himself up and leaned down to kiss her breast.

Now his fingers stroked her, an erotic friction that created a stronger need than before. She sat up to nuzzle his neck, teasing him, taking his shaft in her hand to stroke him, but then as his fingers rubbed between her soft folds, she gasped and squeezed her eyes shut, her hips moving again, seeking release and lost to his touch.

"I want you!" she cried.

"I need you to want me," he whispered. "I want to do everything I can for you, to make you climax again and again. When you're excited, it excites me," he said against her throat.

She barely heard him for her pounding pulse. Urgency drove her as she spiraled out of control.

"Eli!" she cried, winding her arm around his neck and pressing him into the bed. She stretched on his naked body, feeling his erection pulse between them while she kissed him hard on the mouth. His hands played over her bottom and slid down between her legs.

Consumed by desire, Lara straddled him and grasped his thick rod.

He shifted and picked her up in his arms, his body warm and naked against hers. "Not yet, babe. Later when I've loved you senseless."

He sat on the edge of the bed and turned her, settling her on his lap. His legs wrapped around hers. He spread their legs wide while his hand played with her nipple and his other hand went between her thighs. "Look, Lara. I love to look at your body, and I've dreamed about you every night since that first night," he said. "Look at us," he commanded.

She opened her eyes and gazed across the room at the mirrored wall. She saw their reflections, her skin pale against Eli's dark body, his strong, tanned arm around her and his hand cupping her breast while his thumb played over her nipple. Their legs were entwined and his fingers moved on her intimately, stirring tension again. She blushed and then gasped and closed her eyes as he drove her to move her hips faster.

"I want you!" she exclaimed. "I can't keep on. I want you now!"

He kissed her ear, his tongue tracing the delicate curve while his fingers continued the sensual magic that was taking her into a raging fire.

When she was on another brink, he released her, turning her to cradle her against his chest and kiss her. Wanting him, loving him with all her being, Lara knew her heart was already his. Ablaze with carnal need, she pushed him down, sprinkling kisses over him and then sliding to the floor to kneel between his legs while her tongue traced along his inner thigh on first one leg and then the other. She pushed him back on the bed with her hand and flicked her tongue over him, taking his shaft in her mouth to lick and suck.

Eli groaned, sliding off the bed to the floor where he pulled her into his arms to kiss her. She clung to him, kissing him passionately in return, rubbing against him and wanting him desperately. He reached out to grab the packet from the bedside table.

Standing, he picked her up, placing her on the bed and moving between her legs. He watched her, his green-eyed gaze as stormy as a windswept sea while he put on the condom.

She drank in the sight of him, ready to love, aroused and hot, the man she would love forever. He came down between her legs, sliding an arm beneath her to hold her while he pushed into her slightly and then withdrew.

She cried out, clutching his bottom and pulling him to her, locking her long legs around him. "Love me!" she demanded hoarsely.

"We're taking our time. Slow, hot loving to drive you wild," he said and kissed her ear while his shaft entered her again before he withdrew. She arched beneath him, her hands raking over his firm buttocks again to pull him close.

"You want it, don't you?" he whispered in her ear. "I want to drive you wild."

She held him tightly with her legs wrapped around him while the exquisite torment created a heart-pounding craving.

"Love me, Eli! Love me now," she cried, raking her fingers down his smooth back and squeezing his buttocks.

He bit her throat lightly while he moved slowly, thrusting and withdrawing. His forehead was beaded with sweat. She thrashed beneath him, urging him to give her more until he lost his iron control. His hips thrust in a primeval rhythm that set off fireworks in her. Lights exploded behind her closed lids and sensations racked her as her urgency grew.

While release sent tremors coursing through her body, she held him tightly. She knew he'd climaxed when his strong body shuddered. His weight settled on her. This was Eli in her arms, Eli loving her, Eli one with her, Eli wanting to marry her!

"I love you, Lara," he said solemnly, and raised his head to rain feathery kisses from her temple to her mouth where he lingered with a thorough kiss.

Sated, Eli rolled to his side and propped his head on his hand to look at her while he drew his fingers languorously down from her throat to her breast, then across her stomach and lower to her thigh. His heart pounded with happiness and he wanted to trail kisses all over her.

"You're beautiful. And perfect. Creamy and pink and auburn hair. I've dreamed about you and wanted you. And I wanted to drive you wild with loving, to make you want me.

She raked locks of his short hair off his forehead. "I couldn't possibly want you more than I do. You do drive me wild. I'm exhausted. I can't stand on my own two feet," she remarked as her fingers traced his jaw. "You're getting a black eye."

"It was worth getting to slug Trace."

She sighed. "I've fallen in love with a fiery, strong-willed, incredibly sexy man who has my heart completely. I'm mush with you."

"Delicious mush," he murmured as he nuzzled her throat. Happiness filled him to the point he couldn't stop smiling at her. "You're as necessary to my life now as those vineyards I love. I love you with all my being, and I want to spend a lifetime making you happy and taking care of you."

She sighed and curled her arm around his neck to kiss him. When he raised his head, he showered light kisses on her temple.

"I worried about my temper," he said, trying to put worries into words. "My family thinks I'm hotheaded and I guess I am. I hate to admit it, but I know where I get my hot temper."

"You'd never vent it against someone you love. I'll bet you've never lost your temper with your mother," she said.

He shook his head. "No, I haven't. And not with Dad or Jillian, either. Mercedes and I have had some hot arguments. Cole and I have our moments."

"That's sibling rivalry, I'd imagine, although I don't know much about brother-sister relationships. I don't think you'd ever really hurt anyone you love."

He grinned. "In the past, Cole and I have gotten plenty physical."

"I love it when you smile, Eli," she said. "You don't smile very often. You're so earnest about life."

"I've had a lot of reasons to be. I've had hell in my life and I've been to the point of giving up on everyone."

"Not anymore," she said, rolling over to smile at him. "You're a good man."

Eli inhaled deeply. "I'm the luckiest man on earth now," he said. "I have you and that's the best."

"You're ridiculous," she exclaimed, laughing with a sparkle in her eyes.

"When can we marry? Make it as soon as possible, Lara."

She rubbed her forehead and gazed into space. "My mother has cousins who live back east. I'll be in law school, too, which means I'll need more time to plan. With Spencer's murder unsolved and everyone in a turmoil, I think we should have a small, quiet wedding. And if we'll wait a bit, maybe they'll have Spencer's murder solved and that won't be in everyone's thoughts constantly."

"Whatever you want, love," Eli murmured, running his tongue in circles on her breast.

"Eli!" she gasped and caught his head to frame his face with her hands. "I can't think about anything when you do that."

"Is that so?" he asked, amused. "All right. You need some time to plan our wedding, so what month are we talking about? October?"

"I was thinking more like January."

He groaned. "That's incredibly long. How about November?" he asked as if he were bidding at auction. He played with silky locks of her hair.

"I'd like December. Then we can have a Christmas wedding," she exclaimed with enthusiasm. "I'd like that. Now, are you going to give me a hard time about this?"

"December it is. Let's find an apartment right away and move into it." He gazed into her light-brown eyes and wanted her as if they hadn't just made love for a couple of hours. "Will you?" he asked and when she nodded, he smiled. "I'm the happiest winemaker in the whole wide world."

She laughed and nuzzled his neck. He tightened his arm around her tiny waist and relished her softness and naked body against him. "We need to tell the family and your mother. The other Ashtons can go to hell."

Lara sat up and shook her head. "No, they can't," she said solemnly. "I've grown up with them. You may not like them, and I know there's bitterness between you and Trace—"

"And Walker and Lilah Ashton," he interjected, running his hands across Lara's breasts and watching her nipples tighten. She inhaled and caught up the sheet to hold it in front of her.

"Listen to me, Eli. I've known them forever. Paige and Megan are fine people. So is Simon Pearce, Megan's husband. Charlotte has been wonderful, and I like Alexandre."

"I wasn't talking about Charlotte and Alexandre."

"I know. You were thinking about Trace and Walker. I want all of them at our wedding. Trace and Walker are fine people, too. They're not like Spencer. Trace isn't at all."

He stared at her, seeing a stubborn tilt to her chin. "Are we having our first fight?"

"I don't know. Are we?"

Suddenly he gave her a crooked smile. "Ask the whole rotten family if you want to. Even Trace. He won't attend my wedding, you know."

She hugged Eli and laughed. "He'll attend mine. They're not rotten. Stop letting Spencer influence your feelings," she said suddenly, sitting up to gaze at him solemnly.

Eli played with her hair and shook his head. "I don't think I can. But for you, I'll give it a try."

"I'm going to make you so happy you won't think about Spencer or your anger at Trace. Or always being in control," she exclaimed, leaning down to tease his nipple with her tongue.

He laughed, treasuring her softness, loving her kisses and knowing his life was changing for the better forever. He rolled her over to lie on top of her and gaze into her warm brown eyes. "From this day forward, my life will be better than ever before," he admitted to her. "Happier, sexier, more fulfilled. How I love you! Let's go tell our families. Maybe we'll all go to dinner tonight and celebrate. We can ask Charlotte and Alexandre to join us."

"That would be wonderful!" Lara exclaimed, her eyes shining.

"I want to ask the Nebraska Ashtons. We can call Russ and Abigail now."

"I don't know them," Lara said.

"Russ was foreman for our vineyards. Russ's dad was Lucas's best friend and when he and Russ's mother were killed—"

"Let me guess. Lucas and Caroline took Russ in."

"Of course. Russ was my right-hand man—he was fantastic with the vineyards and I miss him like hell. Abigail was raised by Grant, who's her uncle. I want Russ and Abigail to know about our engagement. And we have to call my younger brother, Mason, who is a winemaker and studying in France."

"Doesn't Grant have a nephew, too?"

"Yes and we'll invite him to the wedding. I think he and Grant are close. I think Grant's sister, Grace, is the one who is like Spencer. She abandoned her two kids, and eventually Grant ended up raising them."

"Where is Grace?"

"No one knows. At least not as far as I know. Grant sure as hell doesn't and neither does Abigail. That's Spencer all over again. I don't want to think about Spencer today." He brushed a kiss across Lara's lips. "I'll reserve this suite for the rest of the week. For now, let's drive into San Francisco and get you an engagement ring."

"Just like that?"

"Just like that," he answered. "We'll find something you like."

Her laugh was smothered by his kiss.

Epilogue

The last night of June, music and laughter wafted from the terrace of The Vines. Lanterns shed soft light on an engagement party that Lucas and Caroline were holding for Eli and Lara.

Eli moved out of a circle of friends and searched for Lara. He'd gotten separated from her earlier. He saw Grant talking to Charlotte and Alexandre. Eli worried about Grant, wanting the police to find the real murderer, because the press was hounding Grant and printing stories about his life in Nebraska, focusing on him as if he were Spencer's killer.

He found Lara in a group with Franci, Anna, Jillian and Seth and two of Jillian's friends. The women were admiring the three-carat emerald-cut engagement ring he'd bought her the very day he'd asked her to marry him. Jack had already been tucked into bed and a sitter was with him so Anna could attend the party. For a moment Eli feasted on the sight of his fiancée who looked ravishing in a sleeveless yellow dress. She wore the necklace he had given her and no other jewelry except his ring. With his pulse racing, Eli took Lara's arm.

"Excuse us," he said. As soon as he pulled her aside, he placed his hands on her shoulders. "I've partied long enough. I want to get you to myself and make wild, passionate love with you."

She smiled at him and stroked his arm. "Sounds super to me except we're the guests of honor so I think we're supposed to stay until the last of the company leaves."

Eli groaned. "I was afraid you'd say that."

"I'm not going to have your family think I don't know what's proper. Just hang on to your coattails and wait a little longer. Jillian said she and Seth are leaving soon. Mercedes and Craig Bradford have already gone. I think the party will break up in the next hour. Anna is leaving any minute now to relieve the sitter. It'll be over soon."

"Can I show you my etchings in my suite?" he asked, and she laughed.

"No, you can't! Not now. Just be polite and enjoy the evening. I'm having a wonderful time, and I love your family."

"Good. I love them, too. And your mom is a character. I'm getting to know her better."

"Charlotte and Alexandre asked her to ride over with them. Speaking of them, did Alexandre tell you that he and Charlotte get to leave the country?"

"Alexandre told me. I'm glad, except I think it's at Grant's expense because all suspicion has been turned on him."

"You're right. The police have told Charlotte that she can go, so she and Alexandre leave in three days. The police suspected her at first because she's the one who found Spencer's body."

"I'm glad she's cleared, but I worry about Grant. I hope he's cleared soon. I think Anna worries about him as much as our family does. Of course, she and Jack are part of our family now, anyway."

Cole and Dixie approached. "We're leaving," Cole said. "Congratulations again, we're happy for both of you. Lara, you're going to have to be patient to put up with my brother."

She laughed. "I think I can manage," she said, as Eli slipped his arm around her waist.

"He's joking," Dixie said, giving Cole a gentle poke with her forefinger. "It's been a great party."

"We've got to find Mom and Dad," Cole said.

Eli pointed. "There's Dad, talking to Grant."

Within the hour the party broke up. The only ones left were Caroline and Lucas.

"Thank you so much for the delightful party," Lara said.

"We're glad to have you as part of the family now," Caroline said.

"It's been great," Eli said, brushing a kiss on his mother's cheek. "Thanks, both of you." Lucas clasped Eli on the shoulder.

"I'm happy for you and Lara," Lucas said. He looked at Lara. "You're a great influence on him."

"I hope so," she said, smiling at his parents.

"We'll see you tomorrow," Eli said, putting his arm around Lara's shoulders to lead her away.

He drove to Napa and pulled into the garage of a tall, Victorian that Lara loved.

"Eli, I still can't believe you bought this house. You were going to get an apartment."

"Don't you like our house?"

"I adore it. I feel like Cinderella with you."

He laughed. "I can't quite see myself as Prince Charming. And you as Cinderella—no."

"I had an ordinary, routine, rather drab life until you swept me out of it."

"That describes me and my life," he said.

"Hardly! And this house is fantastic. More than I ever dreamed I would live in."

"It's great because you're here with me," he replied. "We can stay in my suite when we want to be at Louret. In the meantime, we have this house, and it's close enough. We'll find a house here in town for your mom. Lara, I meant it. Your mom can quit her job right now if she wants to."

"I've talked to her about it," Lara said as they walked beneath a trellis covered by yellow roses. They crossed the wraparound porch, and Eli unlocked the back door, holding it for Lara to enter.

"She wants to work until the wedding in December. By then we'll have a house here for her and she can quit."

Eli pulled Lara into his arms. A soft light burned over the counter across the kitchen from them, and she wrapped her arms around Eli's waist, looking up at her adorable fiancé. "I love you with all my heart, Eli."

"It's so great. You've made me the happiest man on this earth," he replied, and then his mouth covered hers, taking her answer. He leaned over her, tightening his arms around her while he kissed her.

Lara stood on tiptoe, pressing against her strong hero while her heart pounded with excitement and joy. She knew she was the happiest bride-to-be on earth. She loved Eli with all her being and knew she would all her life.

* * * * *

DYNASTIES: THE ASHTONS
continues in May 2010 in Mills & Boon Spotlight™.

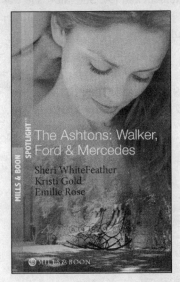

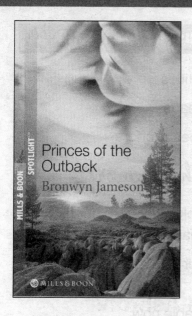

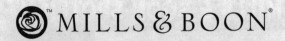